# Darwin's Pause

By J. Gregory Smith

Published by RedAcre Press

Cover design by Malcolm McClinton

Printed in the United States of America

First Printing, 2015

ISBN 9780692528105

For Julie

# Chapter 1

"Will he die?" Philippe Gagnon looked up at the rangy medic he relied on for his most discrete emergencies. Jean-Paul may not have been formally trained as a doctor but Gagnon saw him, and his burn-scarred hands, save a score of soldiers across several continents. Plus, he was well paid to keep his mouth shut.

The medic's expression told Gagnon it was more a question of time. "How long do you need?" The medic asked.

Jean-Paul had missed the first act of the drama where the wild-eyed old man pounded on the doors of Assemblyman Thibaux's office. At least that fool had already left for the day. If Gagnon hadn't ventured out personally to teach the derelict a lesson he might've missed the opportunity the old man now presented.

Despite the ancient man's crazed appearance, he'd spoken flawless French for the first couple hours. Since then, the old fellow's fluency seemed to falter along with the rest of him. Now he'd shifted to another tongue altogether.

Gagnon sat on the edge of the single wooden bed with the thin-mattress in the safe house where he'd brought this character with the white cotton hair and wrinkled cocoa-skin. Gagnon knew just enough of this other language to get the gist. "I need him long enough to reach Hoku. He said he must go home."

Jean-Paul looked surprised. "The island? So he was speaking Hokutian? Nothing goes there unless you can get a private plane on short notice, and permission…"

Gagnon glared.

"Of course. But Monsieur, even if the engines were turning at the airport as we speak I doubt he'd last that long. Any idea of his age?"

"Old as dirt. Where's that damned translator?" He spoke as much to himself as Jean-Paul.

The old man began singing to himself in a cracked and breaking voice. Gagnon didn't recognize these words but the soft pronunciations sounded Hokutian.

Gagnon heard the screech of brakes and footsteps tromp to the door. He rushed over and opened it without looking through the peephole. Stephon, a huge, athletic commando on his payroll hulked alongside a middle-aged dark-skinned man with close cropped jet-black hair.

*Too dark to be local. He better know his stuff.*

"Wait here." He pointed to the hall just inside the apartment and didn't bother introducing himself to the translator Stephon brought. He took Jean-Paul aside into the small kitchen.

"Keep him alive. Whatever it takes. Awake and alert."

The medic caught his gaze. "I have my kit. But at his age, the strain…"

"You already told me he'd never make it to the island." Gagnon got an idea. "Any chance you could convince him that we already brought him there?"

"We don't have time for that sort of work, sir." He shrugged. "You may have to settle for alert or what passes for it with this fossil. He may not be lucid at his best."

Gagnon fingered the heavy bar in his pocket that the old man brought. "He's from Hoku and he knows something." He gestured to Jean-Paul to follow.

The translator joined them at the man's bedside. Jean-Paul prepared an injection.

"My name's Marc, sir. Thanks for thinking of me on such short notice."

As the Chief of Staff for one of the prominent assemblymen in the French Polynesian government, Gagnon was used to tolerating the diplomatic niceties of his position most times. This wasn't one of them. "Stuff that. How's your Hokutian?"

"I can get by. This man is singing about a rare jewel in the sea and a land of green. Who is he?"

Gagnon didn't care for the vacant gaze in the old man's eyes. He nodded at Jean-Paul who administered the shot. "He said his name is Hunapo, and that he's royalty on Hoku and he needs to get home."

"Interesting. That's a name in the line of chiefs, but they, and the colonists who live on the island, seem to recycle names. It can get confusing."

Hunapo looked like he'd been given liquid electricity. His wrinkled hands trembled but that thousand yard stare was gone. He stopped singing and settled his gaze on Gagnon.

"I'll get right to the point. He said in French that he knew a secret and he gave me this." Gagnon pulled the bar from his pocket and let the men stare at the mass of gold. Crudely formed, it had to be ten ounces, easy.

Hunapo smiled at the sight of the yellow metal. He spoke in a whisper and pointed at the bar. Gagnon looked at the translator.

"He said: 'You people love this above all. I know real treasure, but take me home and more of this is yours.'"

Stephon and Jean-Paul frowned when the gold bar came out, but Gagnon gave them a tiny shake of his head that told them to hold their tongues.

Marc whistled softly. "That's real? He looks homeless. Where'd he find it?"

"Ask him. Ask him *exactly* where and say we'll take him home tonight if he tells us."

Marc translated in a halting manner that had Gagnon hoping the fool got it right. Hunapo, while alert, reminded Gagnon of a light bulb burning extra bright right before it went dark forever.

The old man's skin around his forehead looked tight and waxy. He reached out and gripped Gagnon's forearm with surprising strength. He whispered urgently.

"He says he will show you. When he is home." Mark paused. "Now he's repeating 'They keep it. It is their past, their present, and their future."

"Where, damn it? More bars like this. No riddles…" Gagnon fought to check his temper.

"More than you can count," Marc translated. Hunapo laughed and lapsed into a coughing fit Gagnon thought would shake that skinny body to pieces.

The effort drained the old man's strength and Gagnon saw him begin to fade. "No! Where?" He looked around the room. "Do we have a map handy?"

Jean-Paul shook his head. "No time."

Gagnon pointed to the syringe. "Again." He looked at Stephon, "Then see if pain will help him focus."

Jean-Paul readied the syringe and Gagnon ignored the stunned look Marc gave him. The others knew how to get results and that their window was closing.

Hunapo jolted from the second stimulant. His forehead became slick with sweat that reeked like low tide. Stephon held one of the old man's hands as if to give comfort, then pressed hard against a pressure point between the thumb and index finger.

Hunapo gasped and looked at the group as if seeing them for the first time.

Marc lunged and Gagnon hauled him back. "We have our reasons. Do your job. Ask again. Exactly where and he can be comfortable."

Marc translated. Gagnon saw fear mingle with the pain on Hunapo's face. Also anger. Good. Gagnon knew how to work with these.

"He says he lives forever among the trees. He cannot die." Marc looked between Gagnon and Stephon who'd let up the pressure but still kept a tight grip on Hunapo's hand.

"Brave words." Stephon said.

Jean-Paul lifted the other wrist. "Pulse too rapid to count. Work fast."

Gagnon felt the pressure in his head climb to the point where it would soon became difficult to hear. After that, he wouldn't be able to restrain himself. "Stephon."

Stephon wrenched Hunapo's hand around and Gagnon heard the tendons creak over the whooshing in his ears. Hunapo screamed.

But the fog had vanished from the ancient eyes.

Marc again tried to interfere. Gagnon wasn't gentle this time. He punched the translator in the kidney and yanked his arm behind his back. "Last chance. Where do they keep the gold?"

Gagnon had to trust that Marc passed the message along correctly.

Hunapo saw what was happening and when Stephon eased the pressure on the man's wrist he spoke in a clear voice taut with fury.

Marc, a typical, soft civilian, fought to get the words out through his own pain. Gagnon listened intently. "He said, 'If you find the real treasure, then you can never leave.'"

More riddles. Gagnon was about to release Marc so he could squeeze a sensible answer out of the old man when Hunapo went rigid and his final breath rattled out of his body.

"Merde!" Stephon tried CPR, to no avail, and after a frantic minute left the bedside in disgust.

Gagnon released Marc who shrank away from him in fear. "You killed him."

Jean-Paul gave Gagnon a dispassionate look while he spoke. "No. He was going fast. His body was shutting down before we asked the first question."

The rage slowly subsided inside Gagnon. He needed to think clearly. "Bon. Marc, you did well and I'm sorry for my…impatience. You don't understand how critical this information was."

Marc had regained his footing. He still looked like a lamb cornered by wolves. "You didn't have to hit me. I thought the man wanted to speak."

Gagnon held up his hands as if to agree. "I apologize. I overreacted and sometimes don't know my own strength." He dug into his pocket and pulled out a fat wad of French Tahitian Franc bills with their vibrant reds and greens and flower-wearing girls. "You work well under pressure. I like that. There's much more where this came from. We may have need of your services on the island. I assure you, without further rough handling."

Marc took the bills with a shaking hand and nodded his head. "Yes, thank you. I'd be happy to help."

Gagnon saw the lie in the way the man looked for the door. He stepped aside. "Excellent. Stephon, please take Marc home or wherever he likes."

Marc spoke too quickly. "No need, thank you. I have a friend nearby. I can walk."

Gagnon nodded. "Ca va. See him to the door, then." He caught Stephon's gaze. Marc scurried out the bedroom door and Stephon followed.

He and Jean-Paul waited until they heard the thump. A moment later Stephon returned to the room. His tanned face was flushed. Gagnon pointed to Hunapo's body. "See to it he is found by the right people, in a day or so. I have some arrangements to make."

Stephon followed Gagnon into the hallway. "And this one?"

Gagnon stepped over the dead body and admired the cant of the neck indicating a clean break. He bent over to retrieve the wad of cash. "See to it he's found by the sharks.

# Chapter 2

*Papeete, one week later.*

Fin Campbell resisted the urge to ask the "Le Truck" driver to step on it. He'd lived in this slice of paradise long enough to know that hurrying was for tourists fresh off the plane. Besides, he could have hired a car if he was that worried. He checked his watch, an old Timex that had belonged to his father.

He'd just make it. Fa'a'a airport was coming up and he knew the place like it was a second home. He traveled light and often and felt the familiar weight of his Canon Digital SLR. Once state of the art, the camera had been eclipsed by newer models, but it still got the job done and he took pride that it was the shooter, not the equipment that defined a professional.

He ran his fingers through his shoulder length blonde hair. Just a few grays sneaking in but he cared about those as much as the fact that he'd been thirty almost a full year now.

A pasty, heavy-set woman who looked like her hobby was sweating pointed at his bronzed skin and then his suitcase. "You going home now, love?" He could tell from her voice she hailed from the UK.

He shook his head. "Nope, I get to live here. Don't tell anyone, they might change their mind and kick me out."

She gave a wheezy laugh. "Lucky you. Where you headed?"

He hoisted the camera. "Last minute assignment. They buy, I fly." He saw the entrance for the airport approaching and noted he was the only one on the garishly painted green and blue bus with luggage, so he rung the stop bell.

"Have a good trip." She waved to Fin and her flabby bingo arms waggled in counterpoint.

Fin snatched up his case and hopped off the bus. The whiff of diesel from its exhaust overpowered the light perfume of gardenia flowers.

He checked his watch again. Fifteen minutes to go. And they'd wait, wouldn't they? That was supposed to be one of the perks of a private plane, but then again, he wasn't the guest of honor. His buddy Hua, no last name, thanks, was the VIP. Anyone next in line to head a tribe of natives for a whole island qualified.

In all the years he'd known Hua, his secretive friend had rarely shared details about the mysterious island and certainly never suggested Fin visit. He'd given up trying to wrest information about why the island of Hoku was so special to be designated a United Nations World Heritage site, cordoned off by elements of the French Navy, no less.

No amount of beer could get his friend off the official lines about a unique culture living side by side with the descendants of a failed mining colony. Colorful, sure, but was that worthy all that effort and expense? Fin had heard plenty of cover stories and this one flunked his crap meter. Yet, the rest of the world went along with the act, or so it appeared. Outsiders were barred from visiting without special permission.

Now, out of the blue, Hua sprung an invitation not only to visit, but to come as a paid photographer to record a ceremony never before seen by outsiders. He wasn't about to turn that down. Even so, he was worried about his friend despite assurances Hua was ready to return to Hoku for good.

Something was up.

* * *

"You're late." The slender light brown-skinned guy in the yellow cotton shirt paced the short dock area at the north end of the airport. Dressed as he was, he looked like one of the locals. The long sleeves covered most of the intricate designs scarred on his arms marking him as Hua, son of Maru, Chief of the natives of the island of Hoku.

"Two hours' notice for a trip to the mystery kingdom?" Fin stopped when he caught his friend's expression. "You okay? I don't think I ever saw you nervous before."

"I lost my … grandfather. We're accompanying the delegation who insists on attending the funeral on the island."

"Hua, why didn't you say something? I'm sorry."

Hua looked past Fin and shook his head in annoyance. "He was old. Foolish and old."

Fin knew better than to pry. It was clear there was plenty of history between the two. "I'm honored you asked me to join you."

"We aren't flying alone. I want to go over the rules."

"Dude, I won't embarrass you. I can be polite when I want. I came back alive from Africa, didn't I?" After barely surviving close scrapes in several regional wars, a photography coffee table book on the continent's dictators wasn't his smartest move, but he'd managed to sweet talk his way out of jail or execution. "We'll have hours on the plane."

Hua's usual easygoing nature had deserted him. He shook his head again.

"Not around the others. They'll be here soon."

"The French? The nice folks who you said are letting me tag along on their plane so we don't need a week to get there by boat?"

Hua's jaw clenched and Fin felt a spasm of concern.

"They aren't our friends. Remember that."

"I know outsiders rarely come to Hoku, but you must get visits by officials sometimes, right?"

"These are not just any visitors," Hua pointed at Fin, "and unlike you, they are not invited." He craned his neck. "I see their car."

A sleek black Mercedes sedan pulled up near the end of the dock. The doors opened and four men emerged. Two of them hustled to the trunk and removed luggage. All wore khaki pants, button down shirts and sport coats.

Hua stared and spoke in a low voice while the men were still out of earshot. "Say nothing about what you know of my people around the French. They never stop prying into our affairs."

"I hardly know anything about the Hokutians to share."

"As far as they are concerned, keep it that way." Hua strode toward the group and flashed a smile Fin would have taken as real if he hadn't known better.

Fin watched the group approach. It was easy to spot the leader, a short man with a blocky build walked in front of the rest. He appeared a few years older. If not for the piercing dark eyes, Fin might have mistaken him for an ex-boxer with small scars on his face and forehead that looked white compared to the man's tanned skin.

The man's gaze took everything in, nothing punchy about this guy. He wore his hair in a crew cut with a sprinkling of gray that made Fin think of a retired or senior military type. The men behind him were tall and heavily muscled. No tag-along tourists, these dudes could have been active duty soldiers pulling body guard duty. They looked surreal in this tropical setting.

The men looked at Hua like he was a potential threat until the boss took Hua's outstretched hand. They'd barely said hello when the group moved to Fin.

The leader turned to one of the men next to him who consulted a smartphone and replied something in French that Fin didn't catch.

"You must be Monsieur Campbell."

*That was fast. When did Hua give them my name?*

14

"That's right, and you are?" Fin extended his hand to shake. The shorter man's grip felt like a vice inside a catcher's mitt.

*Ah. One of those kinds of people.*

Fin squeezed back enough to protect his hand and let the guy win the stupid contest. Most of these alpha types would lay off if he showed he wasn't looking to be top dog but also wasn't a pushover.

"Philippe Gagnon, on behalf of Administrator Thibaux," Gagnon stared into Fin's eyes.

Fin gestured to the three bodyguard types. "And they are?"

"With me." Gagnon strode past and the burly trio followed him to the edge of the dock. An open topped motorboat was tying up at the dock and now Fin saw a seaplane coming in for a landing several hundred yards away. He knew the boat would take them out to the plane.

Fin caught Hua's gaze and was about to make a goofy face to lighten the mood when he saw the undisguised fury in Hua's expression. Then he flashed that grin again and clapped Fin on the shoulder. "We are all here, my friends. Let's bring everything to the dock."

Fin did as he was told and he also turned on his camera and one-handed it to document the departure.

"Non!" One of the goons saw him and held out his hand like a traffic cop and rushed toward Hua and Fin.

*Crap.*

One of the things he liked best about working for himself was that he did his job as he pleased and as long as his actions didn't get him arrested or killed, anything was fair game.

Fin let the camera drop back to his chest and raised his own hand to show he heard.

"No pictures." It came out "peek-churs" to Fin's ear. The guy blocked the way and pointed at the camera. "Ici."

"Ici, bullshit. You're not getting my camera." Fin swung the camera to rest on his back and kept his hands up, wary of a sucker punch.

The guy looked amused and stepped closer.

"Stephon!" Gagnon's voice cut through the air and his goon froze at once.

Gagnon's heels thumped on the boards and he soon stood next to Stephon. At a nod from Gagnon the big man stepped aside.

"I am sorry, Monsieur. While we permit you to join us, I must be clear we are on official business for my government and require some, how do you say, discretion?"

"You knew enough about me to know my name but didn't know my job or reason for joining the trip?" Fin rode the "fight or flight" adrenaline that still coursed in his veins. He didn't wait for an answer. "You understand maybe one photographer in five or ten years is allowed to travel to Hoku and take pictures? I'll leave you and your…friends out of the shots. That's fine, but if I can't take my camera there's little point in making the trip."

Gagnon appeared to consider this.

Hua stepped forward and spoke rapidly in French. Gagnon appeared surprised then smiled. "I am reminded by Hua that you are his personal guest and that you understand the limits you must work under."

"Of course." Fin said to get rid of him. His French wasn't good enough to catch all of the exchange but he got enough to sense that Hua had tried to pull rank.

"Ca va. All right." Gagnon started back to his people who now loaded their gear onto the transport boat. He turned back. "You will allow Stephon to inspect your photos prior to our return."

\* \* \*

Fin sat fuming in the front row of seats on the seaplane, a Cessna Caravan large enough to hold ten people. Hua had made clear he needed to drop the incident for now, and the two sat in silence with headphones over their ears. As pissed as he was, it was nothing compared to the slow burn he saw in his friend, normally one of the most cheerful, laid-back people he knew.

He couldn't wait for a chance to speak with Hua in private after they landed.

He noticed Gagnon and his people huddle in the back and spoke in low tones over the thrum of the engines.

The plane flew northeast toward a chain of islands called the Marquesas. Hoku was nearby and over the years since he first met Hua he'd even found maps that excluded the small island that the world seemed to forget.

After an hour the speakers in the headphones crackled and Fin heard Gagnon's voice. The din of the small plane's engines made the headphones a must for anything other than face to face conversation.

"Monsieur Campbell. We got off on the wrong foot, non?" Gagnon and his group stared at him.

"It's cool, sir. I just want to be able to do my job."

"Of course. How do you know Hua?"

Fin suspected even on short notice this guy had pulled some sort of file on him so he decided it best to play it straight even though he didn't trust these meat heads. "We went to the University together and shared an apartment for a while."

"So you know each other well?"

Fin wasn't sure what Gagnon was implying but he did know Hua was married with a little boy on Hoku. If Gagnon didn't, then it was none of his damn business. "I dunno. After I graduated I crashed there but my job takes me all over the world so I'm not home much."

"I see. Do you know about where you are going?"

What was this? Fin wasn't as young as he looked and knew better than to take small talk from an arrogant bureaucrat at face value. Hua's icy stare confirmed his instincts. "No, sir. Hua's a pretty private guy. I only know what I read online about the place. Not that there is much. He just told me about a sudden opportunity to see the island first hand."

"Bon. You know about the other residents? The Dwazen?"

Fin searched his memory figuring anything he'd read in public was fair to discuss. "Dwazen? The descendants of the colonists, you mean?"

"Oui. Dwazen is Dutch for 'Fools,' they call themselves this in memory of the original settlers who came from South Africa looking for gold."

Fin thought for a moment. "Fools, like Fool's Gold. I get it."

"Exactly so."

A bunch of questions in Fin's mind popped up. Maybe this guy would drop a few crumbs. "If they didn't find gold why did the colonists stay there? And why did generations remain on the island? I mean, I'm sure it's an amazing place…" He winked at Hua who sat like a sphinx.

"Monsieur Hua will not say? I suppose you can ask them yourself. I am new to this job and look forward to learning how they get along. We are merely administrators charged with this as part of

18

the territory we manage." Gagnon raised his voice and slowed his speech in what Fin could swear was a patronizing tone toward Hua. "We are very proud to manage you as a living example of our cultural diversity."

Hua's back stiffened and he keyed the microphone in his headset. "I speak Dutch, Afrikaans, English, and French as well as Hokutian, Monsieur Gagnon. If Fin requires a translator I can pass along any questions. I extend the same courtesy to you and your party."

Gagnon pressed his lips together and seemed to pause to gather his thoughts. "We thank your highness for his generous offer but as you well know we aren't here to intrude on your lives. However, protocol demands we attend your grandfather's funeral." He looked at Fin. "You see, my government, as well as the United Nations representative," Gagnon gestured to one of the other thugs in back, "traditionally deal with the colonists and leave the natives to do whatever it is they do."

Fin was surprised so much bullshit didn't overload the small plane. If that goon was UN, then Fin was an investment banker.

# Chapter 3

*Island of Hoku*

The plane swept in low and the island grew in the windows. It appeared to be a small round piece of land, about thirty-five square miles according to Fin's research. The land was dominated by a long sloping volcanic mountain and raised edges with deep green valleys. Fin imagined giant invisible fingers lifting a pinch of wrinkled green cloth.

He snapped pictures and nobody grabbed him or shouted at him.

The French spoke in hurried whispers while the plane touched down and Hua remained silent and stared out the window. If his friend could hear the Frenchmen, he gave no sign.

Fin saw rocky shores and one concrete docking pad amid an untouched green hill on the near side of the island. A narrow road snaked away from the crumbling concrete. Large, rusting posts anchored the dock and a huge old freighter was berthed along the dock wall. Fin guessed the ship was probably around 150 feet long.

He'd seen it once before after he got to know Hua and he'd moved to the apartment they'd shared. Though Hua spoke little about the ship, the vessel was a gift from the UN that allowed the South African descendants to bring needed supplies, and it made the trip once or twice a year. Otherwise, the two groups were allowed to remain in isolation and the UN support amounted to a safety net.

An old fishing skiff with an outboard motor putted up to the plane when it had concluded taxiing. Fin noticed right away it wouldn't hold everyone and he was curious what the protocol was for visitors.

Gagnon looked at the boat and one of his people laughed. "After you, your highness. If you trust this boat then we will know it is safe."

"Come on." Hua gave the men his back.

Fin wondered if he'd hit a nerve by mistake when he sometimes called Hua "Prince," but the happy-go-lucky friend he'd hung out with in Tahiti was AWOL right now.

The man at the controls was a burly white guy who looked to be in his early fifties and sported a full beard and weather-beaten face. He gave a brief nod toward Hua who returned the gesture. He glanced at Fin who stood holding his small suitcase next to Hua. Then, the man stared at the faces looking out the windows of the plane.

They managed to make it onto the rocking small craft without taking a dip in the turquoise water. Fin noticed two things, one was that the guy could handle the boat like he was born to it and second, that they didn't often ferry passengers to shore.

When the boat motored toward the dock Hua looked slightly more relaxed. "Gert, this is my friend, Fin. Fin, Gert is the captain of the *Verdragen*."

"Is that Dutch?"

"Ya, it means 'endure.'"

Fin felt encouraged by the response. "Can you tell me why you call yourselves 'fools'?"

"The first settlers came looking for gold and found pyrite. We like to remember where we came from." Gert's voice had a rough, deep quality. His English was clear but he had a strong accent that Fin thought was either Dutch or Afrikaner. Gert appeared respectful but not in any way deferential toward Hua. Fin didn't think Hua's status held sway over the colony folk.

The explanation matched what Gagnon had said, at least as far as it went.

Fin held his tongue for the remainder of the ride since he still wasn't sure about what was appropriate to say or do. The last thing he wanted was to piss off his ride home. He was scheduled to stay after the French returned home in a couple days. Hua had been vague about return plans and now Fin wondered if it would be aboard the *Verdragen.*

"Fin, the French and the UN people work with the Dwazen mostly. We don't deal with outsiders unless we must." Hua looked toward Gert who appeared to focus on his approach to the mooring on the opposite side of the pier to the ship.

"Lucky you." Fin shouted and he thought he saw a slight reaction from Gert but the beard made it hard to tell.

\* \* \*

Gagnon waited in the bobbing seaplane for the mangy sea captain to return and carry him and his men to shore. He saw the pilot appeared anxious about the incoming tide. The tiny anchor the pilot threw out must be mostly for show as the plane drifted toward the rocky shore.

"Make sure you aren't late. I will call you on the satellite phone. If I have to sleep on this backward time capsule one extra night I'll have your wings, n'est pas?"

The pilot gave a vigorous nod, and Gagnon turned to his men and whispered. "When the savage delivers us, Stephon will remain with me. Henri et Julien, you will… explore."

The two gathered their cases. Gagnon wasn't worried about them. They'd been together since their time in the Legion and he'd hired them both right after they completed their service. Good men who didn't question orders. He looked at Stephon. "They will not be happy to see us arrive. They will be less happy by the time we leave. En garde, oui?"

"I understand." Stephon said, and Gagnon saw a smirk. He took in a deep breath.

"Monsieur, this is not an operation. You represent the United Nations and are here to observe. As such, you will observe my back, but you aren't here to frighten them." Gagnon paused, then added, "That will be my privilege."

\* \* \*

The instant their bags were on the concrete pier Gert spun the boat around and sped toward the waiting seaplane.

Fin saw narrow paths cut into the dense rain forest not far from the edge of the pier. In the distance he could see clearings with some corrugated tin roofs in what looked like primitive fishing villages. Right near the pier stood some structures that appeared if not modern, more civilized and he recognized a storage tank and pumping station as well as a small building with an exhaust pipe. Probably a diesel generator. Some power and water lines came off the *Verdragen*.

"We live on the other side."

Fin saw paths on the crests of ridges that appeared the only way to cross the valleys. He took scenery shots and noticed a small group approach the start of the pier. He made a point not to aim the camera at them. They were white and dressed in plain work clothes. Including one lady.

"I guess I could keep my case on my head. Carried a surfboard that way a couple miles one time when our jeep crapped out. This is the welcome wagon?"

"Please wait here." Hua strode to the group and they met on the pier far enough away so Fin couldn't make out what they said, but their body language spoke volumes. The whites were grilling Hua and he appeared frustrated. All of them looked worried but by the time they approached everyone wore a careful smile.

Fin glanced over his shoulder and noticed the French now were boarding the boat. He could hear the seaplane start its engines when they pulled off.

"Fin."

Hua's voice startled him and he turned to see several burly men, including one man who looked to be in his fifties. The lady he now saw was younger than he'd guessed at a distance. Mid-twenties at the most and stunning. She wore cargo shorts ending just above the knee of her tan athletic legs. She wore a simple blue cotton work shirt with rolled up sleeves and hiking boots on her feet. Her brown hair was in a ponytail and she had intense, deep blue eyes and light freckles sprinkled across her nose.

"Sorry." Fin held out his hand to whoever wanted to take it. "Fin Campbell."

The older man shook his hand. Right away Fin saw he had the same eyes as the young lady. "Willem DeBruin. And this is my daughter, Saskia."

Her hand was warm and strong. Enough callouses to tell Fin she must work hard. "Fin. An interesting name."

Dutch accent, and a voice as strong as her grip. If he'd been on the phone he'd have guessed an older woman. "My parents were hard-core surfers and my mother named me Fin, like on a surfboard. She said I brought her stability."

*Jeez, Fin! Babble much?*

She smiled and looked past him at the incoming boat. Her mouth set in a hard line. She glanced back to him. "We can talk more later. You must excuse me now." She strode forward to assist with the lines.

"You know these men? Did you hear any of their talk?" Willem spoke to him.

"No, sir. I just met them." Confusion washed over Fin. He remembered his job. "And I want to assure you, sir, that I won't take any photos without...." Willem moved past Fin like he hadn't even noticed the camera.

Hua tugged on Fin's sleeve. "We should go. You'll meet the rest of the colonists later. The chief is expecting us."

They were alone for the moment. "Hua, what's with the French? What's going on?"

Hua's expression turned to stone. "They are uninvited outsiders. We have to tolerate them from time to time. Lucky for us the Dwazen usually keep them away."

Fin knew Hua was holding back but this was a land of secrets, what was one more? No sense starting an argument on the pier. "Okay." *For now.* "Lead the way."

# Chapter 4

*Hoku, Dwazen's town*

Gagnon and Stephon followed DeBruin and his people through the "village" that was little more than an expanded compound. Henri and Julien waited with the gear at the outskirts of the buildings. It was strange that nobody approached them out of curiosity. Rather, they shied away from the strangers and gave the whole place a deserted feel.

But unlike the war-shattered towns he and his men had rolled through all over Africa, this place seemed more like a living museum. Every doorway was tidy as if it had just been swept. Laundry flapped along a clothes line and planters with herbs grew lush and green.

Window curtains twitched and he saw the shine of an eye peeking out. He could see smoke coming from a chimney and caught a whiff of fresh baking bread that made his stomach growl, though he'd be damned if he asked for any.

Gagnon knew the Neanderthals on the other side of the island lived in shacks and huts with few amenities. Here, in what they called New Cape, the South African rejects had built up a quaint collection of rough brick and mortar constructions along with ugly but sturdy concrete buildings, mostly one story. Other places looked more flimsy and one large barnlike concrete building appeared to serve as a meeting house and likely storm shelter.

Gagnon doubted the corrugated roof structures would survive a serious tropical pounding. He'd been briefed by the outgoing sycophant to Monsieur Thibaux that there were around fifty whites and a couple hundred or so of the natives. He wasn't worried about them. They lived up to their public facade that they just wanted a pristine, simple existence.

*Let them.*

As for the colony time forgot, they'd hidden from the real world long enough. Gagnon looked forward to bringing them their first economics lesson: Inflation.

\* \* \*

"Sit, please." DeBruin pointed to five chairs around a wood table inside the large concrete building. "Saskia, some drinks?"

The daughter, for all her beauty, gave the French a hard look. Gagnon could see her intelligence and realized he'd need to keep an eye out for her.

Her father looked nervous, which pleased Gagnon. Actually, he'd been surprised by the building's interior. The craftsmanship of the wood flooring and polished beams warmed the interior and the furniture was antique carved mahogany with seashells on the chair legs that ended in clawed feet.

"Everything came in on that ship?" Gagnon took a seat and DeBruin sat across from him with the sweaty sea captain he'd learned was called Gert.

Gert nodded. "Over time. You know we come to Tahiti twice a year for supplies."

"Some in our colony have become master craftsmen." De Bruin added.

"I'm surprised they had the time." Gagnon said. From their clumsy demeanor it was obvious to Gagnon that these weren't going to be the hard-nosed Dutch business negotiations he'd expected.

Gert looked impatient. Made sense. The sea captain dealt more with the outside world. DeBruin lived a life of seemingly self-imposed exile.

"Mr. Gagnon, this is not how we usually do business."

"It's long overdue."

DeBruin showed some life. His face reddened. "It's been a simple arrangement that has worked out well for the past several administrators."

"It can still be simple." Gagnon looked around when Saskia entered with a silver pitcher and a set of cut-crystal glasses. He stared at Saskia, waiting for her to leave so they could resume the meeting.

She frowned and took a seat next to her father.

DeBruin motioned for her to be quiet. "Saskia has grown up here. She's been on Hoku nearly her whole life and as her mother, rest her soul, didn't come with us she has been my confidant. She knows all of our operations."

Gagnon shrugged "Ca va. You ask for simple and I give you simple. We are content to continue our existing arrangement, including the protection by the United Nations with the help of the French navy."

"That's it?" Gert asked.

"Oui. That is it, but…" Gagnon wanted to savor the moment. "Times change. Costs have risen for everyone and so, my friends, for you."

"How much?" Saskia snapped.

"Considering how long you have taken advantage of Monsieur Thibaux's indulgent nature over the years I think double the payment."

All three looked like he'd just doused them with cold water.

"Do you require a translation?" Gagnon asked.

DeBruin spoke first. "Outrageous. Blackmail. That's what I hear."

"Blackmail? Such an ugly word. I prefer 'Tribute.'"

"Thief." Gert scowled.

"You wish to make this personal. I am but the messenger."

Saskia shook her head. "Thibaux didn't tell you this. Double? We are not stupid. The price of gold rises as well. Based on the current price, that's nearly five million dollars in pure gold every year. All you have to do is leave us be. How is that not enough?"

"First of all, I am not stupid either." Gagnon pointed at Gert. "When you insult me with your pathetic complaints that your mine is running low after all this time how can you be surprised when I want to see for myself?" Stephon shifted in his chair. He was a man of action and didn't appreciate the fun in making someone in an untenable position squirm.

DeBruin pounded on the table. "My people have kept their part of the bargain for longer than you've been alive."

"You are the ones being unreasonable. The times have changed and technology moves on. Your island and people are more interesting than ever to a growing world with access to information. Keeping the planet at bay is more expensive. We handle the United Nations," Stephon nodded on cue. "We provide the cover story and we also make sure you get the material subsistence you need. All based on the faith that you are working to do your share and able to keep some for yourself."

DeBruin shook his head. "We are a small group. We work hard as it is. You see we live plainly and it isn't right to ask us to struggle just to please some bureaucrat."

Gagnon let a smile slip out. "Monsieur, I *thought* we were having a miscommunication. Why didn't you say so? I have ready access to manpower. They'd be happy to help."

Gagnon wished he could record a video of their faces draining of color.

Saskia looked at her father. "Impossible."

"I know what you are thinking." Gagnon said.

She fixed him with an icy stare. "I doubt that."

"You're worried the people I bring in will not keep quiet about your big secret, that you sit on one of the richest accessible gold mines in history and the legend of the fool's gold was always a cover to prevent a mad rush flocking to the island."

DeBruin gritted his teeth. "Mines play out. You know that."

"If I can report to Monsieur Thibaux that your circumstances have changed perhaps you no longer need our assistance? Let the whole world see for itself?"

Gert spoke. "We don't like that you even brought these people here."

"If we have a deal, you have nothing to fear. Not from them or anyone else. I personally guarantee it." Gagnon struggled not to laugh at what his guarantee must mean to them.

DeBruin hissed to the other two, who held their tongues. "This decision involves the lives of everyone here. We must discuss it." He paused. "As for your offer of labor, that is out of the question. We can find help on our own."

"Where?" Then Gagnon realized DeBruin meant the natives. "Those monkeys? Ca va. That is your concern."

"Step outside and we will tell you what's next." DeBruin sounded more assertive.

Gagnon nodded to his people. He didn't care if the man wanted to feel in charge.

\* \* \*

Outside the room Gagnon could hear heated discussion but the words were too muffled to discern.

"So easy?" Stephon whispered.

"Non. These lunatics love gold more than their lives, almost. But they fear the outside and exposure more. They will try to get rid of us, but if they simply give in, it will tell us much."

"Like what?"

"That Henri and Julien have work to do."

* * *

Back inside the room Gagnon thought that the three looked like they'd just chased each other around the table. High crimson color flooded their cheeks and Gert wiped perspiration from his forehead.

Saskia tried to stare a hole through his chest and Gagnon found himself thinking she must be a handful in bed. He sat and waited for them to make the first move.

DeBruin spoke, his voice shaking with fury. "You ask too much. But you already know that. Let us be clear. You want what you call tribute to increase from five thousand troy ounces a year to ten thousand. We can't and won't do that."

"I see." Gagnon said nothing else.

DeBruin took a deep breath. "We agree to seven thousand, five hundred ounces a year. No more and we will show the expert you brought our operation so he can see for himself."

Gagnon paused long enough for the Dwazen to think he considered their offer. He leaned forward with his elbows on the table and clasped his hands together like he was about to say Grace, something he hadn't done since he was a boy. "Perhaps. If I can assure Monsieur Thibaux about your situation we might be able to work this out."

"Well?" Saskia glared.

"How long will it take you to raise half the gold?"

"Half?" DeBruin spoke through gritted teeth.

"I need to have something to show your good faith to Monsieur Thibaux…"

"To hell with him. Two months and then you piss off until we bring you the rest on the *Verdragen*," Gert interrupted.

Gagnon leaned back and motioned Stephon in close and whispered gibberish into his ear. Stephon nodded. "I do not wish to attract attention. We can return in one week for your grand feast with the Hokutians. A perfect time to retrieve that man-child photographer with Hua and you will bring me twenty-five hundred ounces. You can get the rest later."

"Impossible." DeBruin said.

Gagnon lowered his voice. "Because of a rough upbringing my appearance sometimes leads others to assume I am unsophisticated. Do not make that mistake. You have reserves. Tap them or enslave the entire other half the island for all I care, but when you celebrate in a week it will mark a new era of prosperity. For all of us."

Apparently the men and woman in front of him weren't as foolish as their nickname. They'd read the threat and each one appeared to wilt inside.

Gagnon buried the urge to laugh.

"You'll have it and that will be the last time I ever see you again." DeBruin growled.

"As you wish, but I shall think of you often." Gagnon let his gaze linger on Saskia. Yes, a tiger in bed for certain. "Mademoiselle, you too. And if you ever need a travel guide outside the island…"

"Pig." Saskia spat the word.

"We will leave Henri and Julien here and you will show them the mine and your so-called played out vein and they will contact me to confirm you are ready."

"We have no phones here, just the ship's radio."

"No cell towers, only limited power…" Gert added.

Gagnon held up a hand. "Yes, yes. We brought a satellite phone. Just let them know when you have the gold ready."

# Chapter 5

*Hoku, the Hokutian Village*

Fin thanked the gods of nausea that he didn't suffer from seasickness. That natural talent had come in handy on countless remote photo shoots where gorgeous models spent hours with heads dangling over the side on the way to location while nervous assistants held their hair out of the way.

He almost got fired when he dubbed one skiff the SS Bulimia and the model he thought spoke no English turned out to have a most colorful vocabulary, indeed.

But those trips paled in comparison to the outrigger amusement park ride he and Hua found themselves on during their trip to the other side of the island. The canoe, while large compared to the ones he'd played in as a kid, seemed a toy alongside a real ship or even the tender Gert had used to ferry them ashore when they'd arrived.

Like a tour guide, Hua pointed out parts of the lush jungle, clusters of palms, ferns, breadfruit and others. Then he showed him a spot on the central volcano where an ancient eruption had blown out one side. Once they'd passed the easternmost tip of the island the currents grew powerful and the winds picked up to create a violent chop.

Now Fin and Hua accepted the paddles handed over by the two strong Hokutian men. Loto and Kai had greeted Hua like a brother and eyed Fin with polite suspicion.

"Time to sing for my supper, eh?" Fin didn't know if the men spoke his language since they hadn't said a word to him.

Hua turned and gave him a puzzled look. Fin's sayings often landed with a thud around his friend despite his college experience. "I'll try to earn my place, Hua."

Hua nodded and spoke to the other two who grinned before putting their backs into the paddling. The outrigger surged ahead and

Fin struggled to keep pace with their rhythm. He marveled that the ride smoothed out as they matched the current.

"Must be getting old." Fin gasped about ten minutes later. His arms and shoulders burned with the effort. Other than a sheen of sweat running down the intricate diamond tattoo and scar patterns on the two native men's bare backs, Fin saw no sign that they were fazed by the exercise.

"And soft." Hua yelled. Aside from a perspiration soaked shirt, Hua matched the locals' pace with ease. "Save some strength for the end. Kai says the tide is joining us. The waves should be rowdy."

*And me without my board.* Fin wished he could make a proper entrance, taming some monster, but he'd yet to see a board with a luggage rack.

"Will my gear be okay coming in?" Fin wasn't scared for himself, but the cameras weren't surf proof and he didn't want to put the plastic zip bags to the test.

"If you do your job, my friend." Hua shouted into the wind.

* * *

Whatever was going to happen would be in front of a live audience. Fin saw the sandy shore where the sharp rocks at last had given way to a wide black volcanic beach.

Native Hokutians stood along the sand watching. A hundred people or more, mostly dressed in loincloths for the men and bright cloth sarongs for the women. There were a few children playing together in a small group.

The guides, Kai and Loto, dipped the paddles into the water and back-paddled just enough to keep the canoe outside of the surf line. They were waiting for the perfect time to make their move, much as a surfer will wait for the right set of waves.

Loto peered back. The raised bumps of scars made Fin wonder how much it must have hurt. He had a couple tattoos of his own, one of a wave and the other of a beach at sunset with two surfboards planted in the sand like gravestones with his parents' initials on them.

"Go!" Hua shouted the instant Loto turned to face the shore.

Adrenaline surged and Fin dug in with the rest and the canoe rocketed toward the beach. They raced the incoming swell and he saw the bow of the canoe rise when the wave caught and lifted the wooden craft. Loto was out front and pulled in his paddle first. The rest of them followed his lead and Fin heard the crash of water as the canoe tobogganed down the white, foamy surf.

Water splashed all around and the canoe rushed forward until it felt like someone had slammed on the brakes. The audience on the beach cheered and several men waded into the surf to take hold of the sides and pull the canoe the rest of the way ashore.

"Nice landing." Fin said and hoped at least the sentiment was clear.

"Better than a LeTruck, hey?" Hua laughed and stepped out of the canoe. He picked up both pieces of luggage and another man grabbed Fin's bag and carried it up the beach.

Hua had barely hit dry sand when he was mobbed first by kids and followed by several women while the men smiled from nearby.

Fin stood alone and watched. He wished he could capture the moment on camera, but his gear was still packed. He also felt completely dependent on Hua for social cues.

The beach gave way to a tree line that looked impenetrable from the water but up close he could see clearings in the distance and the outline of huts. Smoke rose in several places behind the first line of trees. The scent of some kind of gardenia filled the air, punctuated by a tantalizing whiff of roasting meat. Fin wondered if Papeete had once looked like this.

The people were all shouting and laughing as they swarmed their prodigal son. Up close Fin noticed only some of the men wore the loincloths. Others had cloths wrapped around their waist like he might wear a towel out of the shower. Still others wore simple shorts and shirts with what looked to be bone buttons.

All the men had tattoos and scars to one degree or another. One serious looking fellow had full sleeves and his entire chest covered with primitive patterns.

Many, but not all of the women he saw had some markings as well. They hung back while the kids and men mobbed Hua, then Fin saw one striking lady in a bright red sarong step forward and the group parted for her. Hua, with a tiny loin-clothed version of himself dangling off his neck, went to her and the three of them embraced.

Fin assumed this was Amira, Hua's wife and his son. He knew the boy was around nine or ten but in the decade he'd known Hua, the man would only go home once or twice a year, usually on that big ship.

Like everything else about his real life, the one here, Hua had said little. From the joy in their eyes Fin was beginning to see why Hua seemed anxious to return.

Hua looked like he belonged here and more and more the last few months he seemed "done with civilization" as he once put it.

"Fin! Come and meet everyone." Fin saw the broad smile of his friend, the real deal this time, not the fake stuff he'd given the French. With the greeting it was like a dam broke. The crowd closed in, and he saw smiles and curiosity from the group, but no hostility.

*I guess it pays to have friends in high places.*

Fin extended his hand and Hua's wife Amira took it. Her grip was firm and her skin was slightly rough. She had dark brown eyes and long black hair and teeth so white Fin would have sworn there must be a cosmetic dentist in one of those huts.

"Nice to meet you, Fin. I have heard much about you." She released his hand and gently nudged the boy forward. "This is our son, Ruru"

Fin knew it was wrong but he couldn't help but think of Mowgli from *The Jungle Book*. Then the boy seized his hand by the fingers and thrashed his arm up and down in a frenetic handshake.

Amira said something to Ruru and nudged him.

"Hullo. Meester. Feen"

Kid must've practiced. Fin knelt in front of the boy. He was glad to see no signs of ink or scars on a little dude but knew he shouldn't cop an attitude about another culture. "What's up, Ruru?"

Hua rubbed the boy's head affectionately. "It means 'little owl.' He's smart as a whip."

"Gets it from his mother," Fin said, and Amira hid a smile with her hand.

"Come on, my friend, we will get settled." Hua and Amira walked together and Ruru dashed around their legs like a puppy. The crowd followed at a respectful distance.

* * *

After Fin dug out his camera and changed clothes in the small hut they gave him to use he stepped to the center of the village where the food was being prepared. He wanted to make sure he thanked whoever he'd displaced for his visit. The simple hut sat elevated on a bamboo frame. Woven mats would serve as a bed and cloth blankets sat folded in one corner. The air was warm enough that he thought he might only need them to deter insects.

Torches lit the way and a gentle, steady breeze kept mosquitos away. Fin hated the pests and was glad he'd brought repellant. He hoped the immunizations he'd already received would be enough. He'd left too suddenly to even ask a doctor if there were shots for coming here.

In the clearing he saw villagers wandering about and several pits dug to roast pigs. The fragrance set his stomach growling. Low, rough-hewn tables held wood platters piled with pineapples, mangoes and cooked breadfruit.

"I thought you must have fallen asleep," Hua called out and Fin wandered in his direction. Hua wore shorts and a shirt that looked homemade, which he supposed they were. The shorts lacked pockets and closed with a bone button.

Amira waved at Fin as she stayed huddled with the rest of the women. In the dark it was hard to count how many people were here but one thing that struck Fin was that there were few children and no elderly.

*Maybe the primitive conditions limited lifespan.*

"When do we eat?" Fin stepped to Hua and the men near him, one he recognized as Loto from the canoe, stepped back.

Fin lowered his voice. "Hua, do I stink or something?"

"Probably. But we aren't used to visitors. You'll get to know them." Hua said.

"So, when do I get to meet your dad?" Fin saw Hua flinch before he answered.

"The chief will speak to us after the food. He insists that our guest must enjoy hospitality before we talk business."

"Is he going to cover rules about how I can take pictures?" Fin had held off out of respect. He still couldn't believe he'd been invited. In so many ways it felt like he'd paddled through a wormhole and jumped back in time.

Hua looked confused for an instant. "No. About the funeral arrangements."

"Aren't they set?" An awful thought occurred to Fin. "He's not just learning about the death?" Fin knew communication was severely limited with the outside world though they'd known Hua was coming.

"Of course not. But we rely on radio calls to the Dwazen who have to relay the message. Long explanations aren't possible."

"I'll follow your lead. Try not to let me say anything stupid in front of him."

"Then you might never speak." Hua looked like he was suppressing a grin, then he turned serious. "He is a proud man and very respected here. He's kept us safe as long as I can remember and we trust him. If he has a rule it's for a good reason. And there aren't many. We're a big family."

Someone blew on a conch shell and the crowd lined up like a great outdoor luau.

Before anyone ate they all turned to see Chief Maru enter. He was tall like Hua but more muscular and he wore a feathered top and headdress. The feathers were a mixture of a layer of mottled brown over iridescent greens and blues.

He waved to everyone and glanced toward Hua and Fin. Fin guessed he must be in his early fifties though it was hard to tell. He radiated health and strength.

Maru gave a small nod then shouted something in Hokutian Fin took to mean "Let's eat!"

\* \* \*

"Hua please, tell her no more." One of the ladies named Hahana kept bringing plate after plate heaped with food. She was shy but persistent. Every time he accepted her offering she giggled and ran off only to return soon after with more.

Fin noticed that many, including the chief, watched him and all seemed pleased when he continued to pack away the fruits and pork.

"We don't often get to entertain, but it's always been our custom to welcome guests and ensure they aren't hungry." Hua said.

"I won't be hungry for a week, bro." Fin took a final bite of breadfruit and waved his hands in what he hoped would be accepted as defeat.

The crowd whooped like he'd just scored a goal and everyone seemed satisfied that they'd accomplished their mission.

The fires burned low and now Fin saw while the women cleared the tables groups of men and boys gathered around the fires and the men took turns telling stories. Hua and Fin sat out the edge of one group and while he couldn't understand the words it was fun to try to guess the topics based on the gestures of the story tellers.

Fin could see different personalities emerge. Some were flamboyant speakers with wild articulation and animal sound effects Fin took to be part of a hunting tale. Another seemed to describe a fishing trip and judging by the groans of the audience, telling whoppers about fishing was high art.

Others seemed shy and spoke in halting tones while the audience cajoled them. All the while, Chief Maru sat atop a large rock and smoked a long pipe. He said nothing but watched over the party with a peaceful expression.

When Maru tapped out the ash from his pipe the wood made a sharp sound on the rock. Hua looked up and nodded. "Come, it's time to talk to the chief."

"Are we supposed to climb up that rock?" Fin had been feeling at ease with all the strangers around him but now he felt the awkwardness return. Hua's grim expression didn't help at all.

"No, we will meet him at his hut. This way." They stood and when Fin looked back the chief had vanished.

# Chapter 6

*Hoku, outside the chief's hut.*

Fin followed Hua to the larger hut. They'd stopped by Hua's place where he'd retrieved a rectangular box. Fin didn't know what it was and wondered if local custom called for some sort of gift.

Fin could smell that there was a small fire burning inside the big hut. Hua spoke and they heard Maru respond. Hua motioned for Fin to follow.

Inside Fin saw woven grass walls and assorted shells and objects decorating the simple dwelling. Maru sat shirtless next to the small fire burning fire inside a huge stone bowl. Fin noticed the headdress and top in the corner on a crude mannequin, like some sort of native scarecrow.

Fin thought for a moment that the chief wore a shirt until he saw in the dim light that below the neck he was covered in tattoos and scars.

"Come. Sit." Maru said and the two sat next to the chief. He spoke with an accent Fin assumed was Hokutian as it sounded Polynesian but unlike anything he'd heard before. Hua's English was flawless.

"Thank you." Fin saw Hua in those dark eyes but they seemed sharper and stared right through him in a way Hua hadn't learned.

"You eat enough?"

Fin patted his stomach. "Plenty, yes, sir."

Maru nodded. No cheering, more like a task that needed doing before he could move on. "You came with the French man?"

Fin wasn't sure how to take that but the expression on Maru's face left no doubt how he felt about them. "We were on the plane together, sir"

Fin had gone through a month of "sirs" for him, he usually saved them for when he thought he'd landed in serious trouble.

"What did…" Maru's face scrunched in concentration and he turned to Hua and spoke in rapid Hokutian.

Hua nodded. "He wants to know what sort of man you thought he was. Can he be trusted?"

"He didn't ask you?" Fin wondered.

"He did, but I am from here, and despite exposure to the outside world the nuance is considerable, as are the stakes. He wants to get your thoughts as one who was born and raised off island."

"Right. I wouldn't trust him as far as I can throw him. Do you have an expression that is close?" Fin said.

"I believe so. We say someone's words are as precious as pig farts."

"I like it." Fin smiled.

Maru didn't. When Hua was done, his face clouded. He resumed speaking in Hokutian.

Fin couldn't follow but thought he heard the name Hunapo. He figured they were discussing the funeral.

Hua pulled out an envelope and unfolded a piece of paper. It had the official seals of the UN and the French Polynesian government. He spoke softly to Fin. "This may get ugly. Perhaps you want to step outside."

Fin started to get up but Maru pointed at the floor. "Stay here."

Fin watched Maru scan the document and felt a moment of disconnect. All through dinner he realized the village was real and not just a show for the tourists like a "genuine" Hawaiian luau. Now seeing an authentic "primitive" reading a letter seemed out of place, but of course he shouldn't be surprised the man was literate.

Maru's jaw muscles clenched and he spoke two words in Hokutian. It sounded like a question.

Hua shook his head and reached for the box he'd brought. He looked like he expected to be beaten. He handed it over and said simply, "Hunapo."

One peek inside the box told Fin what they'd brought along with them on the plane. It was a cremation urn.

Maru clearly understood as well. In an instant the man's light brown skin looked like cocoa mixed with blood. His dark eyes blazed and he crumpled the paper in his fist.

There was nothing hospitable sounding about Maru's next words. He didn't raise his voice but Fin thought the tone could cut through the grass walls. Maru tossed the wadded paper into the low fire where it flared briefly before turning to ash.

Maru rushed outside and now he shouted at the top of his lungs.

Hua looked ashamed. "My…grandfather was cremated. It was done before they ever told me he'd died. We wanted the body transferred here. Intact."

"What was in that letter?"

Hua scowled. "It was the official word that Gagnon would attend the ceremony and it passed along his regrets."

"How did they get the body in the first place?"

"Gagnon told me the police contacted him when they identified the corpse. But I should have received the call. Certainly in time to make a decision. Not that they care."

More shouting outside.

"What's he saying?" Fin asked.

"He's furious."

"That already translated."

"He said no outsider would see the ceremony, especially after desecrating the body. This Gagnon treats us like animals. The chief has declared that in the morning we will take what is left," Hua pointed at the urn, "and honor Hunapo properly."

"What can I do to help?"

Hua smiled. "The chief knows you're not involved with any disrespect, but our ceremony is for Hokutians only. You will have to remain here. We will be away most of the day. The funeral party will leave at dawn. You can keep Ruru company."

"You want me to babysit?" Half the time Fin didn't think he could take care of himself.

Hua laughed. "I'll be surprised if you can keep up with him."

\* \* \*

The next morning Fin awoke to the sound of female villagers calling out in wailing voices. It was too regular to be real crying and he remembered where he was and what happened the night before. He stepped out of the hut and saw a long line of natives filing out of the village.

He popped back into his hut and grabbed his camera. He tried to be as discrete as possible while shooting his pictures. He doubted there were any existing shots of a Hokutian funeral procession.

*No sense interrupting them. I'll let Hua have a look before I go home. Better to have them and not use them than miss such a rare opportunity.*

He wasn't crazy enough to try to follow them. The last thing he wanted was that furious expression of Chief Maru directed at him.

If questioned he'd keep the camera hidden under his shirt and explain he was going to use the primitive "bathrooms." They were a clever bit of work where the user held a bamboo trapeze rig and dangled his rump over the lower part of a stream and the waste would wash out to sea.

When he was done he headed back to his hut and almost had a heart attack when he stuck his head inside.

"Meester Feen!"

"Ruru? You sure you aren't called Ninja Owl?"

Ruru, dressed in a simple loincloth, laughed as if he understood and grabbed Fin by the hand. He led him to the now empty clearing and grabbed a mango and gave it to Fin who peeled and ate it.

Breakfast complete, Ruru led Fin all over the village showing him the places he played, and when they ran into other kids they followed for a while at a distance. The women also seemed to send the signal that he was welcome but at arm's length. Fin did catch Hahana peeking out a window at him before another woman scolded her.

She was cute, but he had to be careful. Sometimes surfer girls were younger than they looked and he never aimed to hook up when he went surfing, but sometimes things happened. Not as often as they used to, but he still attracted attention every now and then.

Out here he was content to take his pictures and support his friend.

* * *

The day wore on and Fin decided this little kid was on a mission to kill him. The boy, who acted like he could survive being dropped into the deepest jungle, was showing Fin how to catch small fish with a little spear and homemade net. Fin missed the silvery things that weren't much bigger than sardines. He showed Fin boar tracks and did a decent imitation of the animal's grunt.

Fin got plenty of pictures of the village and surrounding jungle along with some residents, mostly women. Ruru loved having his picture taken and hammed it up at every opportunity.

Ruru stopped at a coconut tree near the beach that angled high into the sky. This one had to be over fifty feet. The fronds waved in the steady breeze and Fin could see a cluster of coconuts near the top.

Without any warning, Ruru scampered up the trunk like a gymnast.

"Wait! Don't!" Fin realized he hadn't even learned basic words yet in Hokutian but he figured the tone must be clear.

Ruru laughed but never broke stride until he reached the top where the nuts and leaves bunched. It looked like a little green hut in the sky from Fin's vantage.

Ruru just sat there.

He was stuck. Fin felt panic pluck inside his chest. No fire department waiting for 911 calls. He reached his arms around the trunk and tried to duplicate Ruru's move and found himself sliding down the scaly trunk before he'd gotten ten feet up.

"Can you get down?" He yelled up, feeling foolish.

Ruru answered but the wind took his works, not that Fin would be able to understand him.

Now Ruru took his hands off the trunk and pantomimed taking a picture. Fin's heart jumped into his throat when all the kid held on with was his feet. He'd never been a big fan of heights and only pride and a drive to do his best allowed him to set his fear aside and get some shots from a cliff one time.

"Okay, okay."

Fin snapped away with his camera but that knot of fear wouldn't leave until the kid was back on the ground. He wanted to find a way to ask Ruru if his parents would allow such daredevil stunts.

Ruru started pointing toward the water and yelling. At first Fin thought he was mugging for the camera but no, he definitely saw something. Fin looked but couldn't see anything beyond the surf which was much calmer than yesterday when he'd arrived.

He shrugged his shoulders and racked his brain trying to get the kid to come down. He waved his arm in a "come here" gesture Ruru.

Ruru seemed to get that one and nodded, but instead of climbing back the way he came, he reached way up and gripped one of the coconuts.

Then his legs slipped.

No, it was a deliberate move. The little guy dangled from the round ball. Fin looked down and saw a large rock on the beach right under the tree.

"Climb up!" Fin yelled and tried to think. Could he catch him? At least maybe break the fall…

Luckily the tough stem seemed like it had no problem bearing the kid's weight.

Then Ruru kicked out his legs in the air and turned his body so the coconut began to twist.

"No!"

Ruru spun once, twice, and halfway through the third revolution Fin heard a tearing sound. The coconut broke free and Ruru dropped like a stone.

Fin was out of position and lunged to try to absorb some of the impact.

Too late.

"Eeeeeeee!"

The coconut landed at Fin's feet, and the boy not much further away.

Fin heard the impact and looked up expecting to see the kid crushed on the rock. Instead the boy had landed on the soft sand and made no more than a large divot. Ruru leapt to his feet and shrieked with laughter.

Fin hadn't realized he'd been holding his breath until he exhaled. He jumped up and in relief felt parental rage that the kid could be so reckless. He was about to scream some words of wisdom when he heard the sound of an engine and looked up to see the motorboat powering through the surf.

Gagnon had arrived.

# Chapter 7

*Hokutian Village*

Gagnon and Stephon leaned against the bow of the motorboat while the hirsute barbarian Gert drove the boat toward the shore of the native village. Gagnon looked for a spot for the boat to tie up and saw only breakers and a beach beyond. The mountains climbed sharply on the sides and the valley before them appeared like a fertile wedge-shape, much as did other sections of this forsaken spit of land.

He turned to Gert. "Where do we dock?"

Gagnon thought he saw a smirk under that beard. "No dock. Hang on, both of you, we go in on the waves."

*That bastard never told him that.*

While Gagnon and Stephon may not have been in designer suits for the ceremony, they weren't dressed to get drenched, either. Gagnon sat down and pulled off his brown loafers and removed his socks. Stephon did the same, rolling up the cuffs on his khaki pants.

"Hang on." Gert said and powered the boat alongside a breaker. They rode the wave in and Gagnon was surprised how little water splashed into the open craft. Gert may have resembled a caveman but he handled a small craft like a professional. The bow knifed into the soft sand and Gagnon felt like he had stepped into an alien world.

"Where is everyone?" Stephon said as he hopped over the bow and planted his feet in the wet sand.

Gert shrugged. "They can be shy." He held Gagnon's shoes and socks in one hand and waited while Gagnon climbed down.

Gagnon made sure the single shot flare tube remained dry. "They better not be too shy or I will signal you at once."

Gert pointed at his watch. "I'll be back in two hours. If there's no signal, then an hour before sunset. After that, I will see you in the morning."

Gagnon made sure the big South African saw him shake his head. "No overnight. Pas ici." The last thing he needed.

He could already hear a rare steak and vintage bottle of Bordeaux calling to him from Papeete, not to mention a tasty mademoiselle for dessert. He'd make sure she was no older than the wine.

Gert powered the boat back and pivoted the craft toward the breaking surf. He rammed the throttles forward and Gagnon had a vision of the craft swamping, trapping them there. Gert's boat pierced the oncoming wave and the boat cruised out onto the water where Gagnon saw the big man stop to bail before leaving.

He'd get wet after all.

When he looked up and down the beach he finally saw someone. That long haired photographer and a small feral child following him like an adoring puppy.

"See if any of the natives wear gold or other valuables," Gagnon whispered to Stephon.

"They're primitives. You think they care about things like that?" Stephon said, as the pair approached.

"Maybe not, but then this'd make a good hiding place without concern about theft, non?"

Stephon nodded, then Fin shouted a greeting to them. Gagnon waited until they were a few paces away before responding.

"Where is everyone?" Gagnon angled his head so he'd be able to look down his nose at Fin despite the aging surfer being a head taller.

"They all left this morning." Fin looked at the boy. "Most of them. Some women and kids stuck here."

"Which one are you?" Stephon blurted out and Gagnon felt irritation whip though his body.

"Ignore him please. The boat ride made him seasick." Gagnon smiled at the little boy who shrank back and flashed teeth at him like a startled monkey. Just like every other child he met. "And who do we have here?"

Fin looked at Stephon. "This is Ruru, Hua's son. I guess he's keeping me company while the others are gone. They said the ceremony wasn't for strangers."

"Do you mean the funeral?"

"Didn't mean the wedding."

"But, that is the reason we came all this way."

"I'm another outsider, like you two. I don't make the rules." Fin said.

Gagnon thought the man was halfway to a beating for the undisguised contempt, but now wasn't the time. Besides, his mind reeled at what amounted to a diplomatic snub. Did these savages not realize the importance of good relations with the only people who protected the island from tourists and worse, treasure hunters?

"When will the funeral party return?"

"No idea. You can wait with me if you want." Fin said.

"Ask the boy. When? We don't have forever. We came here on good faith..."

Fin held up his hand. "He's only ten. Not sure he knows but even if he did, I don't speak Hokutian. Do you?"

Gagnon felt his jaw muscles bunch. Even feigning diplomatic patience felt excruciating. "Never mind. Stephon, we will leave the official letter for Chief Maru. That and the personal note already given to Hua will have to suffice."

Stephon pulled an envelope out from his jacket pocket and held it up for Fin to see.

"I can see that gets where it needs to go for you." Fin said.

"I'm sure. We have a ride back to the colony, but before that we'll tour the city and deliver the message ourselves. Please tell them we came as soon as possible." Gagnon seethed. He wasn't sure which was worse; Fin's smug attitude or that he thought he could get away with it.

*Ca va.* He had a long memory for slights.

\* \* \*

"Like the others?" Gagnon caught up with Stephon. They stood amid the thatch roofed huts.

"Oui. You know the American expression 'Ghost town?'" Stephon said.

Gagnon nodded, they both enjoyed old western movies. "Only this one comes with real ghosts." Fin had spoken the truth. The entire time they were in this flyspeck of a village they heard and glimpsed natives who he could feel watching them. Women and children scurried into the dense jungle when they approached.

It was irritating and it set his warrior instincts on edge. Part of him reflexively wished for a weapon in response to an impending ambush.

On the other hand, it enabled them both to bumble about as if they were just looking for a warm body and enter all the huts for a peek.

"Did you see anything inside that we need to worry about?" Gagnon spoke in French with a low voice. He wanted to be careful because someone listening might know enough to be dangerous.

"Nothing to pay the rent," Stephon understood the need to be circumspect. "But some antique items like a ship's compass and quill pens. I thought that was unusual."

"Yes. I saw the same. Antique souvenirs but only valuable for their age, otherwise it is like a culture frozen in time." Gagnon shook his head.

*Who would choose to live like this?*

"Ready for the chief's hut?" Stephon waved the official letter. They'd spotted the larger more prominent dwelling and for a moment Gagnon had worried it might be guarded.

One side of the chief's hut faced the jungle and the other faced toward the beach. The place was roughly double the size of the other huts and this one sat atop a flat rocky outcropping. The entrance was supported by bamboo scaffolding. A thin blanket served as a door, most likely to discourage insects and for a modicum of privacy, Gagnon imagined.

"Watch the outside." Gagnon climbed up. He made the pretense of knocking on the bamboo door frame. "Allo?"

No response.

Gagnon stepped inside, letting the blanket fall behind him. Right away he could tell the hut was empty as he no longer felt watched. While his eyes adjusted, he smelled an odd mélange of odors ranging from minty/menthol to a spice that made him think of some sort of exotic curry. The stink of old sweat seemed to cling to the walls along with a sweet tobacco reek, strongest from a gourd-based pipe Gagnon saw in a corner.

And he saw books. A whole wall was filled with books, some in Dutch, English and even French. Histories and geography as well as classic literature. Camus, Shakespeare and Aristotle.

Almost as out of place, he saw a steamer trunk with an old style lock. At once he wanted to pick the lock but something about it made his hair rise and he recalled a time in Angola when he ignored that sense and nearly died from a booby-trapped box inside a leader's shack. Only a poorly connected switch had prevented his face from being blown off.

He nudged the trunk with his foot and while it was full of something, it couldn't have been packed with gold bars, judging by the weight.

He looked forward to meeting the chief when he returned.

Gagnon took the letter Stephon had given him and placed it on the bed, a rough cot of bamboo and thatched leaves covered with a dark blue cloth blanket. On a whim, Gagnon took out a small tin of mints and left them on the conventional pillow at the top of the bed.

Gagnon slipped out and saw by the way Stephon jumped that he felt the same tension. "Eyes in the jungle, no?"

"Remember the Congo?" Stephon said, never taking his eyes off the wall of trees fifty yards away.

"Sometimes women and children are just that," Gagnon tried to keep his tone light but he did remember. What should have been a quick snatch and grab in the eighties turned into a three-day escape and evasion with a young recruit in tow. He almost killed the lad himself just to shake the pursuers. Not one of their enemy had been over sixteen. It was like being hunted by wild dogs. With rifles.

Gagnon stepped to the side of the hut opposite the jungle where he could see he had a moment of privacy. He unzipped his fly relieved himself, making sure he splashed as much as possible on the side of Maru's hut.

* * *

"He took one." Stephon paced like a caged panther.

"You are sure?" Gagnon scanned the sea beyond the breakers. The village continued to be a tomb and the distant jungle foliage danced with unseen snoops scurrying about like rodents.

"No. It could have been a dozen but I know that camera was pointed in our direction. It was a mistake to let him keep it."

He'd already fired his lone flare and Gagnon didn't have the patience for this argument again. "Let it go. We will deal with it when we return. He isn't going anywhere and you and he can have a nice chat about it on the trip home."

"I can catch him and be back in time for the boat."

Gagnon could see his old friend was blustering to save face. "That would be most undiplomatic, Monsieur United Nations, don't you think?"

"Ca va. But when we return…"

Now Gagnon saw Gert and the boat that looked so tiny against the shallow, turquoise water. "Oui. It will be different."

# Chapter 8

*New Cape, Hoku*

All the way back to the colonist's town of New Cape Gagnon's mind swirled with the incongruous images he'd seen in the chief's hut. It did make sense that there'd be signs of modernity. Nowhere was completely isolated, not even Hoku, despite their best efforts.

Still, that collection of books jarred him. Maybe because it hadn't fit his expectations and he never liked being caught off guard.

Gert piloted his boat with skill especially considering it would be dark soon, yet earlier Gagnon couldn't help but wonder if he'd timed the wave breach to ensure he and Stephon were soaked.

*Let him have his petty victories.*

His clothes would dry and what he'd receive in a couple weeks' time would enable him to buy an entire store filled with the finest garments.

Stephon matched his silence. Gagnon knew the man fumed over the pictures they were certain the photographer Fin had taken of them. Sometimes the big man's emotions could cloud his appreciation of the larger view. As long as Stephon hadn't acted on his impulse it wouldn't matter later.

Julien waited for them at the dock. He wore the sat-phone backpack and was sitting so he could watch both the ocean and the dock.

Gagnon didn't need to see the man's head swiveling back and forth to know he was nervous. Julien was one of his most resourceful men and the fact that he was keeping the vital comms on his person told Gagnon he wasn't comfortable.

Near Julien, Gagnon saw several men he hadn't met yet along with Saskia and Willem.

The locals crowded them while they got off the boat. Julien wanted to talk, Gagnon could see, but not in this group.

"Welcome back. How was your visit?" Willem said. His piercing blue eyes scanned Gagnon.

"It was interesting, however they left without us to conduct their ceremony."

"A shame," Willem shook his head slowly. "I'd hoped to learn more. In all our time here we've never been included in one of their funerals."

"If you knew we'd be excluded why didn't you tell me?" Gagnon knew he should drop it but couldn't.

Saskia answered. "We thought, considering your important status and all, they might make an exception."

This time Gagnon swallowed the insult. They just wanted to get his goat.

Now Gagnon noticed that one of the strangers never went far from Julien's side. It reminded him of North Korean "minders" who shadowed visitors to make sure they only went where they were supposed to go. And saw what they were supposed to see.

"Sadly, no. However, we passed along our message that we look forward to meeting Chief Maru in a little over a week when we return to join you in your feast."

He noted with satisfaction that stung them back as a reminder that they needed to part with more of their precious gold. It wasn't just business with this backward lot.

"You spoil us with so much personal attention." Willem said.

The stiff formality made Gagnon wonder how much Willem shared with the rest of his people. It was a tiny community. Word of their contentious deal could spread in an hour.

Apparently Willem didn't want everyone to know.

*Interesting.*

"Not at all, the feast sounds like a wonderful opportunity to meet everyone at once. Is it always held here in New Cape?" Gagnon saw torches being lit in the distance along what amounted to the main street of the colony.

Saskia spoke. "We rotate every year. Last year we were all at the islanders' village. It was quite a spectacle. You should have been there."

Gagnon smiled at her and noted the grimace forming under Willem's close-cropped beard. "Now that I've met you all I would have dropped everything to do so."

Gert finished securing his boat and stepped onto the dock.

"It's a tradition that goes back decades between our peoples. As you saw, we are very different but we both share a passion for Hoku.

Gagnon chuckled. "If for different reasons."

"You might be surprised." Saskia's voice carried an icy edge.

Gagnon saw the tiny shake of Willem's head.

"I might at that," Gagnon decided to let it go. He glanced at the boat. "Tell me, when it is your turn to join the natives, or even when they come here how do they arrive? Is there an overland route?"

Gert jumped into the conversation. "We use the *Verdragen*."

Gagnon looked at the big ship and nodded. "Of course." He noticed they ignored the second part of his question.

Julien stood and shifted on his feet like a boy who needed to pee.

"Will you excuse me? I need to speak to my man." Gagnon waved Julien over and sure enough, the minder began to follow.

Gagnon walked to the end of the dock and left Saskia and Willem with Gert.

"Stephon, keep that one busy." Julien walked with Gagnon while Stephon intercepted the handler, a lean, fit-looking young man in black pants and a cotton homespun shirt.

He heard Stephon speak in a friendly tone but knew he'd block the kid's path before he let him get any closer.

"Where is Henri?" Gagnon whispered to Julien.

"He is back at our shack. He wasn't feeling well."

"How so?" Gagnon's instincts perked up.

"The shits. Came on sudden but I gave him something for it."

Now Gagnon wished he'd brought Jean-Paul along. All of them were trained for the field and shits came with operating in unsanitary hell holes the world over. And yet the timing made him wonder…

"That's all?" Of course it wasn't.

"I tried to explore, like you wanted, and I saw some things but this boy, Johannes, never left my side. He stuck to me worse than a cheap whore's perfume."

"What about Henri?"

"He has his own shadow. He said they showed him one of the stream beds where they found gold and also a played-out mine."

"And?" Gagnon fought to keep his voice low.

"He pan-tested samples and said there was plenty of gold there though it was getting finer and if he were running the operation he'd conduct extensive digging and pumping to run the dirt."

"Expand the operation to follow the gold vein." Gagnon didn't care for the sound of that. It was like work, at least the kind of time consuming labor he'd no interest in himself.

"Exactly. But he said the equipment he saw there and at the rough tunnel into the mountain looked wrong."

"How?"

"He said it looked almost staged from long ago as if they wanted it to look like a mine. There weren't any signs of recent digging except for one spot he thought was for show. Also, he sneaked a soil sample from the mine."

"And?"

"Pyrite."

"In Dutch, 'dwazen goud." Gagnon thought about the history and the cover story the island clung to for ages. "I'll wager that was the original ruse mineshaft."

"Yes sir." Julien hoisted the pack. "Then there's this."

"What?"

"I'd left the sat-phone while I toured the town. When I took a break, I checked it."

"It still works?"

Julien nodded. "It's fine, but someone had been through our gear."

"You're sure?"

"Positive. They found the metal detector."

"We can explain it." Gagnon didn't like Julien's expression. He whispered, "Come on, out with it, man."

"It is ruined."

"Can you fix it?"

"No. It shorted out when I switched it on. When I opened up the unit, it was wet inside, with a layer of fine gold dust applied to the circuit board. The electronics are fried."

"And they want to send a message." Gagnon's mind raced. "Bon, they have told us there is something to be found if they know our machine could detect it."

"But not where." Julien didn't sound so confident.

"There are many ways to learn things, Monsieur."

Julien's eyes glinted in the fading light. "I thought I was to be a civil servant."

Gagnon nodded. "For now. While I am gone be careful and only if absolutely necessary become an un-civil servant. You still have your weapon?"

Julien brushed his hand by his waistband where Gagnon know he carried a compact 9mm pistol. "I sleep with it."

"Good."

"Sir, how aggressive should we be with our minders? I may not be able to discover what you wish with that dog turd on my shoe. I could lose him, but they know the terrain. Of course, accidents happen…"

"If these mongrels are already suspicious and playing games let's see how far they wish to take it. Use your judgment but we need that information. Blame orders from me and proceed. Test their resolve but make sure you're able to get word to me. Guard that radio."

"With my life, sir. Or at least theirs." Julien smiled.

"Make sure the barrel is not plugged with gold dust, n'est pas?"

# Chapter 9

*Hokutian Village*

Fin had watched from the beach until the boat disappeared around the side of the island. Ruru was with him and the boy's rambunctious mood remained damped until the craft was gone.

The sun hung low in the sky, readying for its spectacular exit.

Ruru led Fin back to the village where the rest of the kids came out and they all played a version of tag where Fin was home base. The dozen kids were safe as long as they stayed near him or that big rock he'd thought was going to be the end of Ruru.

The person who was "it" waited in the middle and called out, then the kids scattered and raced to the rock. The "it" kid caught one and the rest waited. Now two were "it" and they raced around to catch runners.

Fin remembered a game he'd played called sharks and minnows that was similar. He'd never played with a person as base before and wondered if he was supposed to do anything besides watch. He took some shots of the kids racing towards him and then without warning he took off running.

All the children erupted in laughter as if they had never seen anything so ridiculous. Fin guessed the rules said stay put and he got some great candids of these boys doubled over and grinning.

He was laughing too and saw some ladies watching from the huts and hiding in the lengthening shadows.

All of a sudden, the kids clammed up and scurried away. Fin turned toward the jungle and saw why.

Hua, along with Chief Maru and the rest of the village funeral party in tow, stepped into the clearing. Fin brushed sand off himself and stepped aside to let the throng pass. But the ceremony was over and the group dispersed to the various huts without any formal signal. Hua and the chief stopped and whispered to each other and Fin shivered when the chief skewered him with a look before turning toward his hut.

Fin let Hua approach him. "My friend. I am so sorry."

*Huh?*

"Hua, no worries. That was important. And I had a great time. At least until Gagnon and his buddy showed."

"Are they still here?" Hua's gaze panned the dim beach.

"Relax. They got all huffy and went back to the other side. I think they left a note or a proclamation or something and then they couldn't go fast enough. Fine by me. I trust everything went well? Or as well as can be expected?" He thought he should shut up before he said anything too stupid.

"We all did our duty. But I'm afraid we won't be relaxing anytime soon. Come and walk with me." Hua headed down to the beach where the calm surf provided background noise.

"What's up?"

Hua put a hand on Fin's shoulder. "When I invited you here I thought it would be a good chance for you to see my home, and by the time you left you would understand a bit about how we live and why we shun the outside."

"Right, so what's the problem?"

Hua took his hand off Fin and folded his arms. "You must believe me, I never realized how serious our situation was or I never would have brought you."

Hua's stress flowed into Fin. "Serious?"

"We are in great trouble."

"From what?"

"Gagnon."

"He's an asshole, but that's not what you mean." Fin saw anguish on his friend's face.

"Fin. After the Feast, promise me you will not fly back with them."

"I can't *swim* home. I won't talk about anything I see. I already promised."

"It's not that. You're a threat to him and I don't think you'd survive the flight."

Fin felt like he'd plunged into an icy pool. "That's not funny."

"Who's laughing? My friend, we'll find another way to get you home. Gagnon is dangerous."

Fin shook his head. "Back up, partner. What are you saying? Gagnon has no reason to want me dead."

"You have it backwards. After the Feast he has no reason for you to live."

"Explain."

"The less you know, the better." Hua's protest sounded feeble.

Fin's chill thawed to anger. "Look. I'm trying to respect your 'ways' and your culture, and all that. But I know bullshit when I hear it. I get that Gagnon is some sort of hard-ass and his UN staffers are thugs of one kind or another, but you're leaving out a big-ass elephant in the room."

"Elephant?"

"Just an expression." Fin waved it off. "You do not get to tell me in one breath some goon might kill me, then pull this 'but it's better you don't know why,' crap."

"Maybe." Hua looked like he wanted to dive into the surf or bury himself in the sand.

"Maybe, my ass! Why won't you tell me? Or are you all going to kill me too? I had no idea I was so popular."

Hua's shocked expression scared Fin more than anything so far.

*Jesus, did he think I was serious? Or worse, had that been considered?*

"Wait until the morning. I must get permission from…"

"With all due respect, prince, I wait for waves, not death threats. I'll ask the chief myself." Fin bolted up the beach.

\* \* \*

Fin ignored Hua's protests behind him and beat him to Chief Maru's hut.

*Now what?*

Was he ready to burst in uninvited on a powerful man who'd just buried his father?

*Yup.*

Fin scrambled up the short bamboo ladder to the narrow platform in front of the door. The hut trembled with the vibration and Fin noticed the cloth "door" was closed. He'd almost tried to knock on it and instead rapped his knuckles on the bamboo frame.

"Yes?" Maru's voice came from inside and a beat later Fin realized he'd spoken in English so he must have anticipated his arrival.

"May we talk? In private?" Fin's voice sounded loud in the settling evening.

"It is not locked."

Did Maru just make a joke? Fin's anger dipped with the confusion, but he moved the blanket door aside and saw the man sitting at the back of the hut near his bed. Rich tobacco smoke mixed with something spicy perfumed the inside.

Even without his headdress, Maru looked powerful and compact. He sat straight up with a yellowed photograph of a man he guessed was Hunapo in one hand and a pipe with a long stem in the other while he puffed.

The dim yellow lamplight danced on a crude table and Fin could see more detail in the scars and tattoo designs along his body. Some looked like intertwined plants inked among patterns of raised flesh.

Fin also saw the shelves with books, some he recognized and others in a number of languages he couldn't read.

"Sit." Maru placed the photo gently on the table and nudged a chair out for him.

"Thank you, sir. I'm sorry to interrupt..."

"Smoke." Maru held the stem out to him before he could say anything else.

All Fin could think of were images of American Indians and peace pipes but decided to keep that to himself.

Fin took a shallow drag and the smoke tasted sweet. He held it in his mouth like a cigar.

Maru took another puff and Hua burst into the room.

Hua began to speak in rapid Hokutian between panting to catch his breath.

Maru remained seated but Fin saw a flash of anger in the man's eyes and a coiled strength in his muscles, like he could leap across the hut to reach his son if he wanted. He replied in English. "Leave us. Can you not see we are smoking?"

"I..."

Maru handed the pipe back to Fin who took another puff and noticed his own anger was receding. His head felt clear and calm but nothing like when he and his friends would sneak joints before surfing.

"I will call you if I need you. Until then, do not break our circle."

Though he spoke in a calm voice the words seemed to hit Hua like a lash and he backed out of the hut and closed the blanket door.

Fin returned the pipe and Maru set it down in a hand-crafted polished bamboo holder that allowed the bowl to remain upright.

"Now we can talk." The anger was gone from Maru's eyes and he regarded Fin with unwavering focus.

Fin tried to order his thoughts and the best way to ask complex questions in simple English. As if his brain decided on its own that he was overthinking things, he opened his mouth and blurted, "Who wants to kill me and why?"

Again, Maru's attitude appeared unsurprised that Fin would ask such a thing.

"Always our struggle here is to be left alone. For as long as I can remember."

Fin looked around. "You seem to be succeeding." He rephrased, "Doing well. And waved his hand in what he hoped was an all-encompassing gesture.

Maru gave a little smile and Fin began to feel foolish. He glanced again at all the books in different languages...

"You understood me the first time. Your English is better than you let on, isn't it?"

Maru traced his fingertips around the photograph of Hunapo. "Often is it wise to be only as smart as needed."

Now Fin's mind raced. "But why play dumb? Wouldn't that just make people want to barge in to 'help' you?"

"Our situation here is not so simple. We are protected from the outside only as long as the governments in charge desire it."

Fin was about to say something about the United Nations designation as a World Heritage site but then he'd always thought that sounded suspicious. "Wait. You're doing something for these guys."

"The stars are not the only things bright this evening." Maru refilled the pipe and lit the bowl off the flickering lamp flame. "But we prefer to let the Dwazen deal with the outside."

Fin took the pipe but hesitated for fear of chasing away the thoughts marching across his brain. "But what can either of you offer powerful governments?"

"Governments are made of men. Men are weak. Find what the right ones love and you can make them do what you wish, even if all you wish is isolation." Maru pointed at the pipe and Fin took a drag before it extinguished.

"How do you do that if you stay here?" Fin's thinking remained clear. "Hua? Is he the connection?"

Maru shook his head. "Hua was allowed to learn about the outside world and understands we islanders have all we need here." He returned the pipe to its resting place. "The Dwazen find the men who control the power and give them what they want. It is hard for them, but necessary."

"What do they have that is so valuable?" Fin wondered why the colonists persisted here on the island for so long.

"What do men from your world want?"

Fin felt like he was back in a classroom with the most peculiar professor on Earth. He started with the most basic motivations. "Money, power, sex…" Now the thought snapped into place so firmly Fin could swear it made an audible click. "Holy shit. That's why they stayed! Gold. Or something super-valuable. Am I right?"

Maru grinned and his teeth, while crooked, blazed white in the dim light. "You already know you are. Long ago the Dwazen wanted to protect what they found, so they pretended to fail."

"And in order to keep anyone curious from poking around…"

"Yes. They went and found the right men who were as weak as they were about that metal and they struck a bargain."

"But what about your people?"

"We were always here. We don't care about money and all of the wars it creates for you people. We let the Dwazen have it and in return for using some of the gold to keep the island safe, we live in peace and help them with fishing and other things."

"Makes sense. So what's the deal with Gagnon? He must know about the arrangement." Fin said.

"Of course. But he is new to this role and he wants more. I am surprised it took this long. In the end, no amount of gold ever satisfies. It is like a sickness."

Fin's thoughts returned to the immediate threat. "But what would that have to do with me? I'm not rich and I sure don't have any gold."

Maru shook his head. "It is what you know."

"I don't know anything."

"You know about us now."

"Only because *you* just told me."

71

"It is only fair. You need bright sunlight on an un-fogged beach to decide what you should do next." Maru leaned forward in the chair.

"Why does Gagnon think I know?"

"For men like him it is enough to suspect. Why should he take any chances?"

"I don't understand, what chances? Why would I expose all of you?"

"Gagnon is re-writing the rules. The leaders of the Dwazen will be here in the morning and we will discuss what we should do next."

"About me?"

"About everything."

# Chapter 10

*Dawn, Hokutian Village*

Fin wasn't sure he'd slept, but a chunk of time seemed to have passed and now it was getting light out. He'd spent the rest of the evening alone, trying to process what Maru had said. Hua walked him to his hut but Fin saw that one hard look from Maru put the padlock back on his friend's mouth. All Hua said was "In the morning…"

Now it was morning, barely, and Fin felt his nerves jumping. Everything Maru told him made perfect sense, as far as it went. The shelter the island enjoyed came on the back of some sort of large-scale bribery.

But Maru's explanation raised questions as well. Even if the islanders wanted to maintain a simple existence why would that be true of the descendants of the original Dwazen? If they were so gung-ho for gold, why didn't they find a way to own the place outright and skip the secrecy? As far as he could see, they lived scarcely better than the native Hokutians.

Gagnon's interests seemed to make more sense. As the new face on the government scene, why not shake things up and increase the ongoing extortion?

That thought jumped right to him. Would Gagnon really hurt him to protect his secret? Only the wishful thinking part of his brain pretended Gagnon would bat an eye at getting rid of some drifter photographer.

Maru hadn't had to share all this with Fin. What would it matter to the Hokutians? Fin was nobody to them (except Hua.) Now that he really knew the island was a treasure trove, Fin represented a potential threat to the islanders.

Yet Maru *had* included Fin and while the knowledge brought danger, it was far better than not knowing, and walking right into a trap.

"You are awake?" Hua's voice cut through the thin bamboo walls.

Fin jumped. "Uh, yeah. Is it okay to come out?"

"You aren't a prisoner." Hua looked stung by Fin's question.

"I'm not sure where I stand. I don't think your people are holding me but I do feel like somehow I'm worth more dead than alive around here."

Hua hung his head. "No one who matters thinks that."

"I wish that made me feel better."

"Me too." Hua raised a bowl with fruit pieces. "Let's eat. I'll try to explain what will happen today."

Under a palm tree Hua and Fin ate the light breakfast. Around them Fin saw the village return to an appearance of what must be normalcy. Except nobody walked past them or even looked their way. He was a rare stranger here, yet this morning not even the small group of kids paid any attention to him.

Fin jumped in. "I guess you know what your father told me?"

Hua nodded. "The chief thinks it is important you know what is at risk."

"I got the part about Gagnon. Tell me, do you think people here," Fin gestured to the clusters of huts, "want to give me over to those Frenchmen?"

"No. Not yet, but some would do about anything to keep outsiders away."

"And you? Or the chief? Don't I bring you danger?" Fin needed to know where he stood.

Hua shrugged. "We aren't so different from you on the outside. We want to be left alone. When that is threatened from outside or inside we want to fight. But in some cases that means lashing out without thinking."

Fin nodded. "Plenty of that in the world. But forgive me for worrying most about Fin-land," Fin tapped his chest.

Hua smiled with his eyes the way he would when he was proud of himself for getting a joke back in Papeete. "The chief and I always worry most about our people. But you aren't the source of our danger."

For the first time this morning Fin felt a spark of optimism. "And the Dwazen?"

"They have their own mind."

Fin heard the sound of an engine and he and Hua turned around. At first Fin thought it was going to be the motorboat, but the sound came from the sky.

He saw the seaplane circling overhead and when it was over the beach several hundred feet in the air the wings waggled. Then it passed the village and banked away over the sea.

"What was that all about?" Fin said.

"I was going to ask you the same thing."

* * *

An hour later Fin heard another motor and this time he saw the powerboat with several people aboard chugging toward the beach. This morning the waters seemed calm and the craft glided smoothly ashore. Hua and several men approached the beach. No sign of Chief Maru.

Kids hovered on the edge of the tree line. Fin could tell they wanted to come close but the stiff body language of the adult islanders implied a formality that must have warned them to keep their distance. Fin wasn't sure if that message was also for him, so he stood alone on the sand and waited.

J. GREGORY SMITH

Willem DeBruin jumped out of the boat and helped Saskia onto the beach. Gert worked with two strong-looking islanders Fin recognized but hadn't met. The three hauled the boat past the waterline.

Fin saw Hua approach and the younger men left the group and returned to the village. Fin stayed put. The three whites formed a tight circle around Hua and, judging from the hand gestures and snatches of raised voices, were having a heated conversation. Fin grew uncomfortable and felt like an out-in-the-open eavesdropper.

Then they started to point at him and the agitation became more pronounced. Gert glared at him and Willem clenched his fists. For a moment, Fin wondered if one of them was going to take a swing at Hua, who appeared to alternate between apology and defiance. Now Hua shook his head and Willem folded his arms across his chest.

Saskia looked at him and broke away from the group, heading toward him. Fin felt odd just standing there but he didn't know how they would take him walking forward, either.

"Hey."

"Hello, Fin." Sakia's expression was impossible to read. She looked sad, angry, and was there a trace of a smile on her lips?

"I'm sorry if my being here is causing so much trouble…"

"We're awash in trouble. You're just playing your part in the storm by getting wet." She wore a work shirt and had her hair pulled back in a ponytail.

"That's deep. Never thought of it that way," Fin wanted to keep things light.

"We aren't comfortable with outsiders knowing our secrets."

*So much for that.*

Now she looked just like her father with her arms folded across her chest. He noticed her figure again and decided not *just* like her dad.

"I thought that had something to do with the shouting. I was *told*. It isn't like I spied on you." He didn't think this was helping. "Your secrets are safe with me. Like I told Hua, I'm on your side. I mean both of your sides. I don't want to screw up your life here and I sure don't want anything from you."

"A shame." Saskia wore a predatory expression Fin would swear belonged on an older woman. It reminded him of the cougars who'd drop off their daughters at the beach to go surfing back when he was a teen. Sometimes the single moms would look at Fin and his surfing buds like they were meat. Most times that was just fine by them.

"I mean you don't need to worry about me…"

"We need to worry about everything but if it helps, you're not the biggest concern. Maru should have waited to talk with us before he decided to tell you."

Fin felt an urge to protect the chief. The last thing he wanted was to be a flashpoint for friction between the two groups. "You don't think I would have put it together on my own?"

She looked at him again like she was appraising him. "Maybe." She took his hand and traced a finger along his palm. "No sense dwelling on what is done. If you're so smart, perhaps you can help us find a solution."

Fin didn't think that was a request so he let her take him to the waterline. Besides, her hand was warm.

\* \* \*

Willem and Gert barely acknowledged Fin when he and Saskia joined them. Hua glanced at him. The group seemed to have reached an uneasy agreement and they all followed Hua in silence.

In the village, Fin noted how most of the islanders kept their distance. One of the men, Fin remembered, Loto, joined them.

"Follow please. Maru is waiting."

The Dwazen seemed to have expected that but Fin was surprised when they marched past the chief's hut and headed into the jungle. Fin saw the narrow path through the dense foliage and they proceeded single file.

Loto led the way and Hua dropped back to walk behind Fin. Saskia moved up the path and they had relative privacy.

"Good news."

"You guys aren't going to kill me?" Fin thought it would come out as a joke when he opened his mouth. Instead, the question hung in the air.

Hua grabbed Fin by the shoulders and spun him around so they faced each other. "Never say that again. You insult us all."

"I didn't mean…"

"We are pledged to defend you. The chief trusts you and that means we protect you with our lives if necessary. The Dwazen have to respect that. Whether they agree or not."

Hua stared into Fin's eyes with a blazing intensity that was a world away from the gentle roommate back in Tahiti.

"Thank you. Seriously." Fin turned back and picked up the pace to catch up and burn off some of the nervous energy.

When he came to a small clearing he noticed several paths branched off. The others remained out of sight. He saw a groove worn in in the tangled roots and dead leaves on the ground. Must be the way.

"Stop!" Hua hissed. "Over here."

Hua took a final look at the path that appeared to climb up into the volcanic mountain. He followed Hua along another. It was hard not to get disoriented and at times the wide leaves brushed his face as the path dwindled to little more than a rut in the jungle floor.

*Did everyone else sprint?* "Hua, did we lose them?"

"They know the way."

Judging by the sun filtering through the canopy they were climbing the mountain in a wide loop around the base.

Fin nearly ran into Hua's back when he stopped short. A pair of tall coconut palms leaned at sharp opposing angles forming a giant, living X.

"Lookout Cross, I think is what you would call this," Hua said.

Fin could see the bark at the intersection of the trees only nine feet up appeared worn from use. Hua sprung up and scampered up the trunk until he was sitting on the intersection.

"Hua, buddy. I shredded my arms when Ruru tried to teach me this trick. You should have told me the meeting was in a tree house."

It occurred to Fin that Hua must have been putting him on all these years when he'd pretend to let Fin teach him various sports and he never came across as particularly athletic. Now he looked like a big version of his son and Fin felt closer to fifty than twenty.

"Wait here. I'll call the elevator." Hua scrambled up the trunk and vanished into a tangle of foliage where one of the trees appeared to lean against the side of the mountain.

Fin felt worse when he realized if there was a space up there that the rest of the group had not only gotten up there but had smoked him and Fin to the spot. Fin thought he was in shape.

*Time to rethink.*

Fin noticed the other trunk pointed directly away from the mountain and it appeared to give a great view of the lower part of the island and the sea below. The scaly bark had a worn appearance here as well so he presumed it was the lookout the name advertised.

After a few minutes of listening to the sounds of the jungle, including bird calls and frogs communicating, Fin wondered if they'd forgotten about him or if he was meant only to join in the march up the hill.

Then a heavy snake slammed onto his shoulders and knocked him to the ground, face first.

In the tangle of thoughts he concluded it must be a constrictor. He cried out and fought to wrestle it off his back all the while thinking that if he could avoid a gripping bite and wriggle clear he'd survive.

Fin scampered from under it and rolled to his feet, wishing for a knife…and saw he'd been flattened by a coil of rope.

Loto didn't even try to spare his feelings and laughed loud enough to drown out the wildlife.

Hua stood next to Loto, looking relieved. "Loto says you look like a yellow-haired sand crab. Are you all right?"

Fin could have a cracked shoulder and he wouldn't feel it with all the adrenaline in his body but the soft ground had broken his fall. He waved that he was okay.

At Hua's direction Fin made a crude harness, glad of his seamanship skills. A lifetime on sailboats and the water and he'd just turned a simple rope coil into a python.

# DARWIN'S PAUSE

*Get a grip, Fin. It's just a meeting with a strange commute.*

# Chapter 11

*Lookout Cross*

Once in the harness, the rope tugged tight and Fin shot up into the trees. When he reached the trunk he saw a bamboo platform concealed in the foliage that led to a cave opening invisible from the ground.

Fin loosened the rope and shrugged off the harness. He stepped across the platform. Inside the cave, he noticed the interior was lit by sunlight filtering down large cracks in the ceiling. They looked like fissures all the way to the top of the mountain.

One side was a well-kept area where everyone waited. On the other he could see and smell traces of pungent, ammonia-rich bat guano and he figured it must get busy at the entrance come dusk. Toward the back of the cave he saw shadows that might have been passages leading deeper into the mountain.

"Welcome." Chief Maru sat at one end of the cave on a bamboo stool.

Loto sat on the floor and Hua stood. Saskia leaned against a stone outcrop and Gert and Willem occupied a crude bench.

"Thanks, I guess."

Maru turned to the Dwazen. "We will speak plainly and in English for Fin. Our choices are simple, if difficult."

Willem leaned forward and rested his elbows on his leg like he was going to lunge forward at any moment. "We were supposed to keep our business private." He glanced in Fin's direction.

"Gagnon has forced himself on our lives in many ways, including Fin's. What does the Frenchman want from you?" Maru asked.

"From *us*." Saskia interjected.

Maru just nodded as if to concede her point.

Willem continued. "He wanted double the payment."

Maru listened. "And what did 'we' say to that?"

"We told him to go to the devil." Gert spat the words. All of the Dwazen, Saskia included looked like they'd sipped bitter tea.

"I thought 'we' would."

Willem fumed. "Even if we thought such extortion fair, it is too much to ask."

"Is it?"

"We haven't the manpower to extract that much gold."

"How much is it?" Fin whispered to Hua who waved off his question.

"I leave that to you to decide, but what did Gagnon say to your answer?" Maru asked.

There was a small pause but Fin detected a discomfort ripple through the Dwazen. Willem cleared his throat and cast his gaze to the floor. "We told him we'd increase to seventy five hundred ounces."

"Of gold? Holy shit!" Fin mouth let out his reaction before he could stifle it.

Hua shot him a look and Saskia nodded.

Maru held his hand up. "So you made the decision on your own as well. I know this pains you, but can you deliver?"

Willem grimaced. "We had to tell him something. We aren't used to these visits. We needed to buy time."

"So he will be satisfied until next year?" Maru said.

"That demon will never be satisfied," Hua said. "How will you meet such an increase?"

"Tell the rest, Papa," Saskia said.

"Gagnon expects twenty five hundred when he returns next week. We can bring the rest to him later."

"Will he get it?" Maru asked.

Fin could see that despite Maru's stake in the outcome he'd gone to great lengths to stay out of the mining operations.

Gert spoke. "That is the next part of the problem. We can't mine that much in a mere week."

"Not even if we skipped preparations for the Feast," Saskia added.

Now the Dwazen let the pause grow from uncomfortable to awkward.

Maru looked unfazed but under all the scars and tattoos he noticed beads of sweat in the relatively cool cave. "And how did Gagnon expect you to deliver?"

Willem spoke. "He offered to supply men..."

Now Maru sat forward. For the first time he looked like he didn't know what was coming next. "And?"

"I told him we had all the extra help we needed here." Willem let the words hang in the air.

Maru's jaw clenched and Hua paced the cave like he was about to attack someone.

Gert pointed to Maru. "Now you see how our problems walk arm in arm."

Saskia walked to the middle of the cave. "We had to say something. Gagnon wants to see the entire operation for himself. No doubt to adjust the extortion even higher."

Willem spoke next. "He's left men behind to review our mines."

"What will you show them?" Maru said.

"Only what we want them to see." Gert said.

Fin couldn't help himself. "Excuse me but while you're here the rest of them are still on your side of the island? You really think you can trust them to wait for the guided tour?"

The entire group looked at Fin but he could see they heard him at least.

"The French are in good hands. We have people with them at all times and they know where to take the one to see an old mine."

Questions burst out of Fin's head. "If you want them to think the mine is played out, then how do they expect you to increase production? I mean, how did you get the last guy to agree to the old terms?"

"We dealt with the representative and struck the bargain. Away from the island."

Saskia interrupted. "We only agreed to the change to buy time. The old arrangement worked well and we think it can again."

"Why would Gagnon give his raise back?" Fin thought it was an obvious question.

Gert looked at Fin. "You should wait under the tree while we make our decisions."

Fin's face heated with embarrassment. He felt like a kid watching his friend's parents in an argument.

Maru shook his head. "He stays."

Gert and Willem exchanged a look. "All right he stays. But mark my words, Maru, if he threatens our plans, he answers to our colony as well."

"We're wasting time." Saskia said. "Don't we have enough enemies?"

Fin didn't like where this was going. "Maybe you're right. I should wait outside. I know too much already. I just came to take pictures and…"

"You stay." Maru snapped.

Loto hopped to his feet and blocked the entrance. No more laughing. Hua didn't even look at Fin.

*Damn.*

Willem spoke. "We know you'd never agree to mine work. We will give Gagnon his blood money next week from our reserve."

The words seemed to squeeze out of Willem's throat.

Gert nodded and took over after glancing at Fin. "Yah. He will leave and we will begin the real work. When we're ready we will steam to Tahiti. Maybe we say we're taking our friend here home in a month. When we reach Papeete I will find my contacts and we see about fixing Mr. Gagnon's luck. Thibaux's too."

Willem's body swiveled around and he looked at Gert. "We never said Thibaux…"

Saskia shifted on her feet.

Fin was still getting his mind around what they were proposing.

"The head of the snake." Gert spoke in a growl.

Maru listened, showing no visible reaction. Hua nodded so slightly Fin wondered if it was an unconscious gesture.

"Are you sure?" Maru finally said.

Willem held his palms out. "What else can we do? We have to wait until he is away or everyone will know it was us." He seemed lost in thought. "Unless we could claim it was an accident…"

Gert stood. "You've lived here too long. I see the outside and have to deal with these people. You think Gagnon won't be prepared? We have to get to him when he thinks he's safe. When he thinks he's won."

Fin's mind began racing. All the way to his mouth. "Gert is right."

Everyone stared at Fin.

Hua shook his head. "You just said…"

"Hear me out. Please. I've met thugs all over the world in my travels. Gagnon is cut from the same cloth."

"What changed your mind?" Saskia looked at him with a curious expression.

"I'm just a dude with a camera. But I've seen how these guys work. Gagnon will be ready for a double-cross, so you'll have to get him later."

Gert nodded. "Not so stupid after all."

Fin smiled. "But you don't need to kill him, either. I've got an idea."

# Chapter 12

*New Cape, Hoku*

"Are you sure you can make it?" Julien stood in the doorway of the small hut and looked down at Henri's pale, shivering form while the man pulled on clothes. The straps on the pack containing the satellite phone and the rest of his gear dug into his shoulders.

A small price to pay. Julien had slept on top of the pack, if sleep was the right word. After the metal detector got trashed he knew he wouldn't rest until they found their proof and told Gagnon. The sooner the better.

"It's just the shits, I told you." Henri took a long drink from his canteen. Julien took it and refilled it. Wouldn't do to have the guy fall out on him. He glanced over his shoulder and saw Johannes, the little bastard assigned to follow them everywhere, waiting outside.

"Stay hydrated. We'll work fast and get back here so you can rest."

"Can we lose the kid? I want to check the waterfalls on the other side of that crest."

Julien spoke just above a whisper. "Not if we play nice, but perhaps he can show us. I can find a way through in any case."

"I'll try not to slow you down," Henri said.

"You'll be fine." Julien hoped it was true.

"Had my share of bugs, but this is worse than anything from those damned pits in the Congo." As if on cue, Henri signaled for the chamber pot and Julien decided to wait outside.

"Ready?" Johannes stepped to Julien with a fake smile plastered on his face.

He stood the same as Julien's six feet, but he had to have seventy five pounds of muscle on the kid. Julien hooked a thumb toward the hut and pointed to his gut.

"Ah. He will stay then?" Johannes seemed amused at the ailment.

"No, he's still coming." Now why did the boy look so surprised?

"Are you certain? We will need to do some climbing and it will be hot today."

"It's always hot. He's worked in every sweltering mine in the world." Julien wondered what that would even mean to one of these sheltered throwbacks. All the people here seemed off to him. He was a soldier, not a sociologist, but living disconnected from the rest of civilization couldn't be good.

"As you wish, but we should get moving."

A moment later Henri appeared and his lean frame already looked wrung out. "Okay. Let's go."

Julien took some comfort from the strength in the man's voice. But he looked as dried out as a week old baguette. Julien already steeled himself to conserve water so he could share later.

"You'll leave that here?" Johannes pointed at the sat phone backpack.

"No." Julien stared at the kid, wondering if he'd tampered with the detector. Didn't matter, someone sure had.

"But it is heavy."

"How would you know?" Julien saw that scored and the kid's face flushed red.

"Suit yourself."

Julien intended to.

* * *

Another fucking hill. Julien saw the sweat stains join in the middle of the back of Henri's shirt. He had to give the man credit, he'd kept up like he'd promised, squat breaks notwithstanding, but they'd burned through three quarters of their water already.

At least Johannes was sweating too, Julien was pleased to see, but he didn't seem bothered by the heat or exercise.

The chafing from the backpack straps grew worse. He'd carried heavier loads in greater heat but he was nearly thirty and starting to feel the difference from when he was a young man. The phone itself was nothing but he kept spare equipment and he was glad he'd decided to carry his own food and water. He wasn't about to leave that back at camp, not after he saw Henri. If they both got sick they'd never find what they needed.

No matter, the gear would remain welded to his person until he could make his report.

Julien gripped the machete. He'd half a mind to hack a direct route through the foliage and burrow through the rock and soil crests to save time. He couldn't be sure that Johannes was leading them on an extended trip to wear them out, but he might as well have been. This damn island made direct routes almost impossible.

"Not far now. You can make it?" Johannes spoke over his shoulder while they trudged along a narrow lane through the thick growth.

"Of course." Julien said, and looked to Henri to confirm. The man waved to say he was all right but the fact that he didn't waste breath on speaking told Julien to watch the man carefully.

The first mine had been as Henri described. It looked like a set for visitors and he took Henri's word that it would take serious machinery to extract the fine gold that remained in the soil.

Johannes reached the top of another narrow crest and waited for them. Julien squeezed past Henri who signaled the need to visit the bushes again.

"Don't pass out, monsieur. You'll fall down the hill." Julien kept his tone light but wasn't joking. He left his canteen on the trail. "Take this. I'll meet you on the crest."

"All right. Sorry."

Julien just shook his head to dismiss the idea and marched to the crest.

"Such a view. I never tire of it." Johannes sat on the rocky edge.

Julien wasn't there to sightsee but the kid was right. From their vantage he could see the waterfall cascade into the next valley. The turquoise ocean fanned out beyond the bright green valley sections.

A thin path threaded down the side of the steep slope and Julien wondered if he should tie a rope to Henri in case he stumbled. No. That would only mean they'd both fall.

"Are you certain you want to continue? Your friend doesn't look well. The way down is not easy." Johannes said.

"We'll be fine. We didn't come here for our health."

"Your choice. I had to ask." Johannes squinted and pointed at a spot in the distance. "See down there?"

Not far from the waterfall Julien could see a rectangular clearing. "What's that, some sort of farm?"

Johannes bowed his head. "That is where our ancestors are buried."

"A cemetery?"

"Brave men and women. We stand on their shoulders. It is the least we could do to honor them." He pulled out a small mirror and flashed sunlight. "One for the past. One for the present, and one for the future."

Julien frowned and scanned the area for any sort of return flash.

*Did this fool think he didn't know what a signaling mirror was?*

91

He pretended to listen while he kept an eye out for Henri. No screams, which was a good sign. He hoped. He peeked over the edge to where the approaching path speared into the foliage. A moment later he saw a pasty face break through and Henri, paler than ever, emerged.

Julien stepped to help and slipped on a loose stone. In an instant he fell onto his side and slid toward Henri. Rocks and sand ground under his shirt and burned along his ribcage. He came to a stop near Henri, who looked like he was going to try to grab him. Fortunately, once he reached the grass and vegetation area his boots gained purchase.

"Are you all right?" Henri gasped for breath.

"It's nothing," Julien hoped that was true. It felt like someone had rubbed rock salt into his flesh and he was bleeding but he could feel it was superficial. "My body protected the backpack."

Julien looked back at the crest and saw Johannes watching with one hand over his mouth to stifle laughter.

* * *

"Better?" Johannes shouted over the roar of the falls and Julien wanted to knock out the kid's front teeth. The trip down the hill had sapped all their energy more than he wanted to admit. But the water seemed pure and tasted sweet to his parched throat. Henri looked like a different person with a belly full of water and Julien didn't want to think how close the man had come to severe dehydration.

"Yes, much." Julien winced at the cool water on his shredded side, but if he avoided infection he'd be good as new. Henri stood with his boots off and pant legs rolled up in the water downstream and panned samples of the sand.

If the look on Henri's face was any indication, Julien would be able to recuperate in style soon.

"We think of the waterfalls as a magical gift." Johannes said.

"Excuse me." Julien slung his wet shirt over one shoulder and carried the backpack on the other hand and walked over to where Henri worked. Johannes didn't follow and seemed content as long as they were in sight.

"How does it look?"

Henri jumped. He glanced over to confirm Johannes was out of earshot. "Like you were dragged behind a truck."

"Not that. Is it like the other mine?"

Henri shifted his body so Julien blocked Johannes's view. "I've mined on every continent on the planet. Some legal and most not. Mon Dieu, I have never seen anything like it." He reached into his shirt pocket and dropped half a dozen grape sized nuggets into Julien's palm.

"So Gagnon was right."

"Gagnon wasn't even close." Henri's eyes danced and whatever illness he'd been feeling was swept away by gold fever. Julien had seen it before.

"If this is what is downstream, then what lies at the bottom of that waterfall…"

"Is a natural Fort Knox." Henri finished for him.

"No wonder they didn't want us here."

Julien waited for Henri to stash the nuggets. "I think I'm ready to make that call."

He waved to Johannes, who wasn't smiling, and now stared at the two of them with open hostility.

"Henri, pay attention. Something is not right."

Henri seemed unable to tear himself from staring at the stream and patting his shirt pocket.

Julien walked to the side of the stream and set the backpack on a dry rock. He unzipped the back and reached inside to power up the unit.

Johannes rushed forward. "No! No calls from here, only back at New Cape."

In French, Julien told him to screw himself. He kept an eye on the man and checked on the signal strength. One bar flickered. Maybe this close to the mountain the signal was blocked. Trees weren't much help, either. He looked around and saw a flat sandy beach of sorts downstream. And were those tracks? Two ruts leading toward a path...

"Henri can you move?"

"Move, yes. Fast? I don't think so."

"All right. See where the bank flattens?"

"Yes."

Julien rechecked where they'd stood at the top of the last crest. It seemed a mile away straight up. "I think that's where they move the gold off the site. And isn't that the same direction as that clearing? Their sacred cemetery?"

"It might be." Henri smiled. "Fort Knox part two?" He rubbed his shirt pocket like a talisman.

Julien glanced back to Johannes expecting trouble and wasn't disappointed.

"Merde!"

Johannes stood on a tall boulder and had found his own version of signal strength. He stood bathed in a patch of sun and worked the mirror in rapid flashes.

"This can't be good." Henri said.

"Their mask is dropping, n'est pas?" Julien looked at the phone again and was pleased to see one bar and a second flickering. "I'm going to try now. Make your way to the path and follow it to that cemetery or the nearest clearing." Henri was familiar with sat phones.

"And you?"

"I will meet you there. We should have brought two phones." That gave him an idea. He reached into the pack and took out a rectangular phone. "Here. My regular cell."

"It won't…"

"Of course not, but these savages don't know it isn't another satellite. Hurry, and let him see that you have it. After I reach Gagnon, I'll make sure we get out of this."

"All right."

Julien was glad Henri wasn't in the mood for questions. He may not have been a soldier like Julien, but he was a survivor.

"Wait!" Johannes stopped flashing with the mirror and called out to Henri who looked like a marathon runner in the last leg of the race. But he was moving and that's what counted.

Julien saw the signal eroding again and hit the speed dial.

He heard the phone ring amid bursts of static.

"Hey, you can't…" Johannes stood about thirty feet from Julien. Apparently, he'd just noticed what he was doing.

"Oui?" Julien heard Gagnon's deep voice like it was at the end of a tunnel.

"Sir, if you can hear me, no time to talk. Confirming…"

Pain exploded on his left elbow and he nearly dropped the phone into the stream. Julien thought he'd been shot but he hadn't heard anything.

He leapt off the rock and saw Johannes reach into his pocket with one hand and in the other he held a modified slingshot known as a wrist rocket. Nasty at close range.

He ducked down and tested his arm. Not broken but painful and it would probably swell. He put the phone to his ear and heard only static.

Now Johannes let loose with an ear-piercing whistle.

Enough. Julien snatched the pack off the rock and put away the phone. He then drew the pistol he'd stashed inside the pack before he took off his shirt. When he popped up he saw Johannes draw back the sling shot and he raised the gun. "Non!" He wouldn't ask twice.

Johannes eased the tension on the elastic bands and tossed the slingshot onto the grass bank. "Where does Henri think he is going?"

Julien splashed across the stream to reach the boy. The current was strong but it was shallow here. "Turn around." He pointed the muzzle at the kid's face.

"You are not the law here." But he turned as ordered.

Julien decided to skip the civics and clubbed the kid at the base of the neck. Johannes's knees buckled and Julien gave him three more sharp blows with the butt of the gun. He thought about finding some twine in his pack to secure him but decided it wasn't worth it. He seemed to be alive, but he'd hit people before who never regained consciousness.

Julien flung the slingshot into the jungle and scrambled to get his shirt back on, then the pack over his shoulders while he moved toward the path. One last glance at the stream bank confirmed Johannes was down for the count, if not longer. Better that he hadn't needed to alert someone with a shot.

\* \* \*

Down the path Julien saw it was wider than the ones they'd taken to reach the second mine. Wide enough for a Land Rover, or, of course, an ox cart. He'd seen a pen with several oxen. Sure enough, before long he saw a pile of scat in the middle of the road. He also noticed fresh footprints that he thought were Henri's.

He held the pistol ready and wished for a proper rifle. And a trained squad, while he was at it, but he only needed to make contact and then he and Henri could hide out and live off his rations for a while. Of course, they'd need to stay near water with Henri leaking out of his ass.

Many times Julien tried to get off the path and slip through the jungle, but even near the road the vegetation grew thick enough to halt his progress to a standstill in spots.

Finally he saw the road open up. It had to be the clearing. He wanted to approach from cover if possible and near to the end of the road. Henri must have thought the same thing because he saw the footprints head toward an opening.

It was low and barely more than a hole in the vegetation, but Julien managed to crawl into it. The tracks washed out and maybe Henri did the same thing. It looked like he'd struggled a bit to get in there and Julien supposed that was why some of the leaves and small branches were broken.

It opened up further in. Now he saw animal tracks and …drag marks. His heart sped up and he gripped the pistol in two hands and crouched low, ignoring the stiffness in his elbow.

He heard something up ahead and saw a bush start to shake. Julien took aim.

*Wait for a target, don't shoot Henri by mistake.*

Five yards ahead, a form burst onto the path and sprinted toward him. Dark fur, beady eyes and two tusks at near face level were all he needed to see. He got off one round that only seemed to make the boar squeal and it rammed into him while he tried to stand and dodge. The dense foliage interfered and the boar knocked him right off the path and into a snarl of vines.

One tusk nicked his leg but it wasn't bad. He saw the bristles on its tail as it bolted onto the road and Julien realized he'd dropped his gun somewhere.

That *was* bad. At least the squealing sounded further away, and even though it was wounded, it might come back.

He looked around but the leaves were so thick he couldn't see much. It couldn't be far. He sat up and heard a low groan. "Julien."

He scrambled around a tree where the trail widened and then he saw all the blood. Henri lay with his back against the trunk.

The lower half of Henri's clothes were soaked like he'd waded through a tub of blood. The man's face looked like wet chalk and his head lolled over as he looked at Julien. "Thirsty."

Julien knew better than to waste water on a dead man, but he opened his canteen anyway and leaned in, his ear out for the return of the animal. Up close he could see Henri was hugging his belly and tried not to think about what he was holding in. "The boar did this?"

Henri took a sip and closed his eyes in a long blink. He gave a tiny shake of his head. "Bayonet."

Julien went cold and he reached for the gun that was no longer there. He grabbed his machete. He had to find that pistol.

"Which way?"

Henri tried to lift an arm and might have been pointing the way he'd just come but his arm drooped down and his eyes stared into space.

*Finis.*

Julien heard motion coming from the direction he'd last seen the boar. He raised the blade and now he had more room to dodge and slash.

Then a man stepped into the clearing.

He looked familiar. Julien couldn't remember his name but had noted this big rugged Dutchman was one of the boat crew of the *Verdragen*. He carried a rifle, an old WWII style M1 Garand, complete with fixed bayonet. The front of the blade was smeared with blood.

Then Julien saw his HK pistol tucked into the man's waistband.

"You spooked my quarry, Frenchman." The guy smiled.

Julien shouted and flung the machete at the man like he was some sort of circus performer. He made the man duck and used the moment to turn and run down the path. The pack bounced around but he didn't dare drop it. The speed wouldn't help. Without his gear he'd be a sitting duck. Now he was all about escape and evade.

He raced toward the light at the end of the path and saw that the cleared cemetery was just ahead. The path had wound through the jungle and he hoped he was far enough ahead so the crazy guy couldn't get off a clear shot.

If he did, Julien hoped the round might hit something solid, like his entrenching tool.

Better to sprint hard and give the man the slip. He'd be happy to seat the tool in the man's brainpan. Then he could hide at his leisure and keep the rifle as a souvenir.

He let adrenaline carry him. Just before he reached the grassy field it felt like he'd been struck in the back by a rugby tackler. He tumbled forward and heard a single thunderous boom. He saw red splatter on his shirt and thought the guy must have gotten the spaghetti MRE in the pack. He wanted to get up but for some reason he couldn't feel his legs.

The last thing he heard was the faint trill of the sat phone.

# Chapter 13

*Papeete, Tahiti-- Safe House*

Stephon checked his watch again.

"He'll be here," Gagnon said, and leaned back on the kitchen chair. The legs creaked under his weight.

"You're sure it is safe?" Stephon stared into his coffee cup.

"No, of course I'm not sure." Gagnon let that hang for a moment. "But Jean-Paul is confident. You need to learn to trust the people you work with, n'est pas?"

"But to be wrong…"

"Then we'll have to be right, oui?"

They both jumped at the sound of a key in the lock. Gagnon let the chair down with a thump. He hoped Stephon hadn't noticed that he was also jumpy.

"It's me." They heard from the hallway and recognized the medic's voice.

"In here."

Jean-Paul walked in and Stephon stood up. He eyed the medical bag in Jean Paul's hand.

"No problems?"

Jean-Paul shook his head. "We are a go?"

Gagnon nodded. "As I told Stephon, the only word I received said 'confirmed' and nothing ever since. No radio contact either from the Dwazen."

"Then we proceed?"

"It's there. I am certain. Besides they owe us something."

"And you're sure you don't want me along?" Jean-Paul unpacked a set of syringes and a small vial.

"In good time, mon ami. We stick with the plan."

Jean-Paul held up an alcohol swab. "Who is first?"

Stephon glanced at Gagnon, then rolled up his sleeve.

*  *  *

*New Cape, three days later.*

Fin rode with Gert, Willem and Saskia back to their side of the island. They approached the dock.

"I feel bad leaving them with all the work." Fin said.

Saskia looked at him like he was crazy. "They've prepared for Feasts for many years without your help. We need you here."

"Oh, so I can help you make food for two hundred?" Fin smiled. She was a strange character. One minute she'd flirt with him like a co-ed, the next she'd snap orders like she was Joan of Arc.

She laughed. "I'm not sure I trust you to cook for one or two."

"I make the best Ramen noodles you ever tasted."

"I don't know those. Maybe you can show me sometime."

There were a few people standing at the dock. Fin found it odd that he saw no children at all here. Not that there were many at the village. He already missed chasing them around, especially Ruru. Maybe it was because the language barrier was easier to breach with kids or maybe he felt like he'd never grown up.

Willem ignored their banter. "What's this?" he frowned.

"I don't know," Gert said. Fin thought he looked worried as he turned his focus towards bringing the boat to the dock.

Two Dwazen stood from the group and Fin didn't need a translator to read the stress on their faces, even at this distance.

"Who are those guys?" Fin whispered to Saskia.

She didn't answer and stared as well. When the boat was tied up the three of them climbed onto the dock and rushed to the pair.

Willem waved away the other people, and they took the hint and walked away muttering.

Fin stayed near the boat. He saw the two men talk and the younger looking one pointed to the back of his head. Willem's face turned crimson and he grabbed the bigger guy by his shirt and Fin saw buttons burst and clatter on the dock. Saskia raised a fist to her mouth and bit down on a finger and Gert nodded.

Willem broke away from the group and approached Fin. "Come on. This concerns you, too."

\* \* \*

"*Both* Frenchmen dead?" Fin said.

In the mess hall of the *Verdragen* Willem, Saskia, and Fin sat while the two men, Johannes and Pieter, recounted what happened at Gert's urging.

Fin gathered that both of them were crew on the ship.

"We had no choice." The two men assigned to shadow the French kept looking at Fin and halting their explanation. Gert urged them to continue. "Fin knows about the gold. We trust him."

By the tone of Gert's voice, Fin wouldn't take any bets on that, but the men did continue.

Johannes rubbed the egg-sized lump on his head. "I tried. I was sure the sick one would back down. I didn't think he would come out at all. That one knows mining."

"Not anymore." Pieter said.

Fin saw a predatory glint in the man's eye.

Willem glared. His thick fingers drummed on the mess table. "And the second man?"

"He had the phone."

Willem continued. "What did he see?"

"He and the miner were right in the goudstream. He found nuggets."

"Wasn't that expected?" Fin said. Two men were dead, it was past time for good manners.

"The gold is pouring out of the mountain." Saskia said. She spoke to Johannes. "What did he tell Gagnon?"

Johannes looked proud. "Nothing. He tried but I could tell the signal was poor. I used my slingshot for preventing any more talk."

"*More* talk?" Willem asked and Fin saw the kid blanch.

"Just a few words, I don't think he got through. I nailed him in the arm. That was when he pulled out that pistol."

"You were brave." Gert said. He turned to Pieter. "You got his signal?"

Now the other man spoke and Fin saw more defiance than fear. "Of course. They separated. The first one, the miner, was headed right to the cemetery," he looked over at Fin.

Willem shook his head. "The sick one, by himself, you couldn't subdue him? Keep him quiet?"

"He's quiet now, Willem. You weren't there. We aren't playing a game."

"Neither is Gagnon!" Willem roared. "What do you think he'll do now?"

Pieter sat in silence. Gert faced Willem. "That's enough. We don't think word got out. So far Gagnon doesn't know what happened and since he sent spies we know he doesn't trust us."

"So what are you saying? We take out Gagnon after all?" Willem said.

Gert appeared to give the matter some thought.

"You'll start a war," Fin spoke out loud.

Gert fixed him with a stare. "Aren't we already in one? Perhaps we can take advantage before he expects."

Fin shook his head. "You said it yourself. He doesn't trust you. You're right. Look, I saw his kind all over hot spots in Africa."

"Hot spots?" Saskia said.

"War torn countries. I used to make all my money as a war photographer. I saw the very worst of mankind and took pictures. I thought maybe I could make a difference if I documented enough horror. Maybe others would learn."

"And did they?" Willem asked, and Fin was surprised to see on the man's face that it was a serious question.

"I don't know about others, but I learned a great deal. One of those things was that guys like Gagnon were always there to keep the wars going for their own gain." Fin paused. He rarely went on a tear like this unless he was plastered. "I also learned guys like him don't change. He will be ready for an attack, or will make sure you'll regret trying anything."

Gert ground his teeth. "After all this, you still want to go with your plan?"

Fin's mind raced. "What if it was an accident?"

Gert laughed. Pieter didn't and Johannes looked grim. Willem and Saskia still listened.

"I'm not saying Gagnon would necessarily believe you, but if he can't prove otherwise at least it interferes with any official investigation or pulling in more outsiders in some sort of murder case."

"Self-defense," Pieter growled. "Anyway, one look at the bodies would give us away."

Fin frowned. "Wait. You have them?"

"Cold storage. This ship has a refrigerator. We weren't sure what to do."

* * *

The room was bigger than Fin expected. He'd gotten so used to the limited technology that it hadn't occurred to him. The two sailors had created a makeshift morgue on the refrigerator floor and padlocked the heavy metal door.

Sheets covered the two bodies and despite the near freezing temperature, Fin could smell the death stench. That mixture of fear, sweat, and shit swam under the crude disinfecting efforts.

"This won't be pretty." Pieter said.

"I've seen worse." Fin tried to breathe through his mouth.

Pieter drew back the sheets on first one, then the other, body.

Saskia sucked air in through her teeth but never looked away. Gert just nodded and Willem's face seethed with frustration and revulsion.

Post-battle shots flashed through Fin's memory. Dead kids with AK-47s in their hands staring up from a wastewater ditch. Killers before their damn voices even changed, taken for one pointless power clash or another.

Boiled down, it was always the same. One strongman butting heads with another over ego or ideology, but underneath it always about money and power. And lots of innocent bastards were crushed in between.

Nobody won, not for long, but his lens captured plenty of losers.

And here were two more.

Fin's hands itched for a camera out of reflex. He didn't really want to document this. The men, nude, left no doubt about the causes of death. The smaller man, Henri, Fin recalled, looked to have bled out from several deep penetration wounds to the abdomen.

No coroner, Fin found it easier to detach himself from the fact these used to be people by thinking in the most clinical terms possible.

The bigger guy, who looked like a mercenary straight off the hottest zones Fin ever worked, had clearly been shot in the back. Julien showed a ragged exit wound from his stomach. Fin rolled the now-rigid corpse and saw the neat small entry point, right at the man's spine.

"Well?" Willem spoke first.

"See for yourself." Fin pointed at the corpses. "One dropped a rifle that went off behind him and the other guy was so upset he decided to knife himself? Several times?" Fin ran his hands through his hair. "And did you save their clothes?"

"We burned them." Johannes said. "Just the ruined ones."

It took Fin a moment, "You mean there's more from their luggage?"

"Right."

"How will you hide the wounds? Gagnon will have seen more battle casualties than I have." Fin turned away from the corpses. "Maybe just explain they went missing." That didn't feel right either.

Willem shook his head. "A perfect excuse to comb the island with search parties."

*Damn. Of course he would.*

Johannes looked at Fin with a cold smile. "I think I know how we can give Gagnon his spies back."

\* \* \*

*Two days later, Papeete Tahiti*

Gagnon ran down his mental checklists for the upcoming trip while he munched on a cold chicken sandwich. Two days to go. The office was quiet, not too much going on this late in the day and he'd already let his secretary head home.

He glanced at the list from the caterer. It looked straightforward enough. Bouillabaisse for two hundred fifty, but the portions would be small as this Hokutian Feast was a grand communal event. He hoped they'd send out enough strong backs to carry the insulated food carriers.

The satellite phone trilled. He glanced at the screen and read "Explorateur 1."

*Impossible.*

His heart pounded as he hit the button. "Oui?"

"Monsieur Gagnon?"

It wasn't Julien. "Who is this?"

"Willem DeBruin. I have terrible news."

Gagnon knew the phones were secure, at least they had been when Julien left. Now he couldn't be sure. He doodled an ear on a pad of paper and circled the picture while he spoke. "What is wrong?"

"There's been an awful accident."

*Of course there has.* "Are my men all right?"

"We're not certain how it happened but we found them both at the bottom of one of the steep crests, and at the top one of my men located the backpack and this phone."

"Are they hurt?" Gagnon poured the concern into his voice.

"I'm sorry, they are both deceased."

"Dead? How could you let this happen?" Gagnon slammed his open palm down on the desktop. He hoped it resonated on the other end of the call.

"The footing can be treacherous. We sent them out with a guide, but he seems to have hit his head somehow, and can't remember anything. He says he was with them one moment and then when he woke up they were gone."

"*Some*how? Are you suggesting my people attacked him?"

"We don't know. Perhaps they didn't care for our wishes for privacy." Willem's tone took on an edge that started Gagnon's ears ringing in fury.

*Patience.*

Gagnon let the pause drag out. "Monsieur DeBruin, I shall speak plainly. We do not trust each other, but I believe we can still work to our mutual benefit."

"Of course…"

*Off balance now, good.* Gagnon leaned back in his chair. "My men would never behave in so barbaric a manner, however if you can show me what happened when I arrive I shall accept your account and consider the matter closed."

"I am afraid there is not much left of the remains."

"What's that?"

"We have preserved what's left, but the Monitor lizards found them first…"

"Their next of kin will appreciate your efforts." Gagnon recalled what vultures could do to a ripe battlefield. He popped the last of his sandwich into his mouth.

"If it helps, we think they were gone before the lizards arrived." Willem said.

"We'll never know, will we?" Gagnon let that sink in. He wished he could see Willem's face. The man sounded repulsed. "Now, on to the future. I think it would be appropriate before the celebration that I get to say a few words and the gathering can proceed to show its respect."

"I don't see why." Willem sounded confused.

"Thousands of men and women work to preserve your privacy around the clock in several countries. You, your people, and the natives never see them or understand their sacrifice. Now that two are in their midst, I want them to show respect and appreciation. It is a small thing to ask."

"I…"

"Monsieur, I insist."

"…all right."

"Excellent. Mind you, leave the remains in safe keeping. We will take them away along with any… personal effects."

"I understand completely."

Gagnon savored the capitulation in the bearish-looking miner's voice.

# Chapter 14

*Hoku, Day of the Feast*

"This is the strangest cruise I've ever taken!" Fin yelled to Hua over the throb of the diesels on the *Verdragen*.

Hua grinned. "Everyone loves the ride over. Ruru has waited two years to get back on this ship."

Across the deck, Hokutians swarmed. Fin had tried to count them but they never seemed to stop moving. The children, led by Ruru, made Fin tired just looking at them. Hua and Chief Maru sat nearby, taking in the scene.

Stacks of baskets piled with food sat in the middle of the freighter. Fin watched an errant apple roll along the deck with the pitch of the ship.

Several Dwazen sailors played with the kids and placed caps on their heads. The kids saluted and whooped and chased each other. Fin worried with all the activity that nobody would notice if someone fell overboard.

Gert stood in the wheelhouse and Fin did see several other crewmen scanning the rails.

The boarding process had been just as unusual. A crane loaded supplies from rafts lashed together and towed out to the vessel by outrigger canoes.

Sailors tossed a dozen tied ropes overboard and the men and all but the youngest children swam to the ship and climbed up the sides. There were quite a few women as well, and Fin tried not to stare at the ones who chose to swim topless.

\* \* \*

*New Cape, Hoku*

Before the *Verdragen* reached the dock, the Hokutian men lined up and dove off the side of the ship into the water like some sort of cruise ship cliff divers. Fin looked up at Gert, who was busy concentrating on guiding the large ship to the dock. None of the other sailors seemed concerned.

"Is this usual?" Fin asked Hua, who was already removing his shirt.

"Yes. The men show their courage." Fin saw Ruru try to line up and look to Hua, who shook his head.

Maru wore his headdress and remained seated. Fin took it to mean he'd no intention of arriving soaking wet. Hua joined the dwindling line of men. The rest of the kids lined the rail and cheered.

Fin took the camera off of his neck and handed it to Maru. "If you don't mind."

Maru took the camera without comment but Fin thought he detected approval. Fin stripped off his shirt. He reached the rail and leapt to the top then launched himself far out over the water.

He heard the kids yell during the thirty foot drop before he knifed into the water. When he reached the surface and confirmed he was nowhere near the swirling propellers he felt hands clap him on the shoulder. He was surrounded by the other men who grinned at him and demonstrated their approval in a musical chant similar to those he'd heard when one of their own returned from a successful hunt.

He joined the group while they swam the remaining hundred yards to the shore. On this side of the island the waters were much calmer than the wild breakwater at the village.

The men and women of New Cape, dressed in white cotton pants and those handspun shirts waved and whistled. Fin had learned the clothing was one of a number of cottage industries as well as crafts that they exported to Tahiti. All part of the cover for what the Dwazen did with their time on the island.

At the shore the men dried off in the sun. Fin saw Saskia walk down and she spoke briefly to a few of the men in what sounded like fluent Hokutian.

She held out a homemade shirt to him.

"For me? Is this one of yours?"

"I hope it fits. You left before I could take measurements." She looked him up and down and he prayed his blush didn't show.

"It looks great. Thanks." He slipped into it and the cotton felt soft. He noticed the buttons were hand polished cone snail shells. "It's perfect."

"I didn't know you could dive," she said.

"You should see me surf. I've had to bail on some gnarly rides back in the day." He exaggerated the surfer dude accent and she just gave him a look that let him know she got the joke. Or at least that he *was* joking, which was close enough.

He turned serious and lowered his voice. "When's the guest of dishonor arrive?"

All the humor left her face and Fin felt like an ass to spoil the moment. "Soon. You heard the 'orders'?" She spat out the last word.

Fin nodded. "Once Johannes explained, I thought Hua was going to explode. He first said there was no way his people would pay tribute to shipwrecks, I think he called them."

"That's what they call uninvited visitors who defy the laws and sneak onto the island. Usually they get sent to us and kicked off the island when Gert can take them away. I'm not sure they always make it to us. Luckily it rarely happens." She looked worried. "He did agree to go with the plan?"

Fin made sure they were alone. "Yes. I tried to help him keep perspective and that paying our dues now would get rid of them later."

"Render under Caesar." Saskia said.

Fin looked at her.

Her dark blue eyes twinkled. "We do have books here."

* * *

While helping the islanders and Dwazen set up the tables in the cleared out common area in New Cape, Fin noticed a moment when he wasn't being stared at or whispered about. He was just another person setting up for the big feast. He felt a bittersweet wave of emotions starting with a sense of belonging he hadn't felt since his parents died.

Fin marveled at the way the islanders and Dwazen worked together. They looked so different, between the shirtless dark skin replete with body scarring and tattoos to the Dwazen's home spun clothing and tan skin. Yet they chatted with each other in familiar tones and all the adults seemed to be fluent in each other's language.

Hua strode up to Fin. He'd been speaking with the chief and Dwazen including Willem, Gert and Saskia. "You look like you've done this before."

"I'm just trying not to slow you down. These guys seem like they know each other well. You sure you all live apart?"

Hua shrugged. "It is a small island. The Feast lets us all remember we share a special place."

"I was just thinking they all look like actors in costume."

Hua gave him a puzzled look. "You have a strange perspective, my friend."

The whistle on the *Verdragen* sounded three times. The sound rolled up the hills to be absorbed by the jungle.

"They are here." Hua put one hand on Fin's shoulder. "You know what to do?"

# DARWIN'S PAUSE

"It's my plan, remember? Just get me in place."

# Chapter 15

The first thing Fin noticed while standing in the processional line was the size of the two wooden boxes. While he hadn't expected the two men to be in full caskets, if for no other reason than they wouldn't fit on the seaplane, he was still shocked at what the Dwazen had constructed. The ornate containers were hand polished and finished in only a few days.

But so small!

They were barely bigger than the portable food containers that had rolled down the dock earlier. Maybe the size of a two-drawer filing cabinet.

He'd skipped the second "autopsy" and shuddered to think what those stone-gray lizards must have left of the two corpses.

He'd seen monitor lizards pull apart an ox one time and it had looked like a grisly tug of war.

Now, next to the two boxes, Gagnon and his man Stephon stood at attention and saluted while Willem placed folded French flags atop the boxes. Fin would have loved to take shots of the moment but Gagnon had been quite clear. This was to be a private affair.

The funeral line looked even more surreal than setting up for the Feast. The islanders, still in their traditional attire of loincloths or grass skirts, stood in the queue like extras in an old Tarzan movie, waiting for lunch.

Fin noticed as he got closer that the two men made a point of shaking hands with every Dwazen and islander. All seemed familiar with the custom, and the islanders offered their hands and shook, then turned away and walked calmly back.

Many wiped their hands on their skirts or cloths, and Fin saw why when he got near the head of the line. After every few people shook the Frenchmen's hands, Gagnon would squeeze a thick liquid onto his and Stephon's palm.

*Hand sanitizer.*

Both men rubbed the gel with a poorly concealed look of disgust then resumed pressing the flesh.

By the time Fin had reached the front almost all of the population of the island had gone through this bizarre ritual.

"Ah, Monsieur Finn. I am glad you were not among the fallen." Fin wanted to keep his arms at his side but Gagnon seized his hand in both paws and threw in a kiss on both cheeks.

Bleh. Fin's hand felt clammy with that crap on it. "Sorry for your loss, sir." Fin said, instead of saying at least he'd been where he was supposed to be.

Stephon didn't kiss him but wrung his hand hard enough that he thought it'd slide right out of his grip with all that goop. If he wasn't standing next to the remains of two men he might have made some wise crack, but instead he just wanted to get somewhere so he could wipe off his hand.

\* \* \*

With the pseudo-funeral over, everyone seemed ready to get into the spirit of the festivities. Maru and Willem stood next to each other. Gagnon and Stephon sat at the front of one table and listened. The rest of the crowd, roughly three hundred total, stood around the common area.

"Thank you honored guests and friends from the other side," Willem said. "I know you have all heard it before but let's celebrate another year that would never have been possible if our peoples hadn't learned to work together so long ago."

The islanders cheered and the Dwazen clapped. Amid the cheering Fin noticed openly hostile glances toward the Frenchmen. Though he was also a stranger, the worst Fin received was curious looks.

Fin wondered what it must be like to grow up on this isolated scoop of land, cut off in so many ways from the rest of the globe, for good or for ill.

Maru rose and the chants and shouts got louder as did the applause. "Thank you. I speak to our young people when I say we come here not to point out our differences but to celebrate what we have in common." He raised his fists into the air. "Hoku!"

Both islanders and Dwazen went wild. When they began to quiet Gagnon stood and stepped in front of Maru. He cleared his throat. "Now that you have paid respect to my fallen comrades…"

Fin saw from Willem's and Maru's tense body language that they hadn't expected Gagnon to speak at all. Fin noticed a tiny shake of the head from Maru, and Hua, inside the crowd, raised his fist and shouted "Hoku!"

Instantly he was joined by the rest of the islanders and then a moment later all of the Dwazen roared the proud island name, drowning out Gagnon in mid-sentence.

Gagnon held his hand up as if to ask for quiet but it spurred ever louder chants.

After an awkward half-minute, Gagnon gave up and sat back down amidst cheers and, Fin could hear, some laughter.

Fin tried not to stare, but the blocky Frenchman's face turned pink.

Now the women separated out and began to chat and exchange small gifts with the Dwazen women. There were only about a dozen women living in the colony, not including Saskia. They'd made small wooden toys and brightly colored cloths, while the islanders presented carved figures and seashell necklaces.

The boys and men formed up into teams and they played a free-form version of soccer where rules were seemingly an afterthought. The Dwazen took out a regulation soccer ball and kicked it back and forth with great skill. The islanders took out a homemade inflated ball made from pigskin that Fin thought looked like an about-to-burst football, only rounder.

Apparently both balls would be in play, and there were no such thing as substitutions. Sides formed up, and the field had no defined borders. Fin watched Hua join in along with nearly all the men from New Cape.

Saskia wandered over to where Fin stood watching. "You should play."

"What are the rules?"

Saskia smiled. "You know football and rugby?"

Fin assumed she meant soccer and nodded.

"Long ago when the Dwazen and the locals first met and agreed to live in peace, they wanted to teach the islanders to play our games."

"Looks like something got lost in translation."

She laughed. Great smile when she allowed it.

"They tried to teach the regular way but after each lesson the islanders just kept adding the rules together and brought their own. Eventually we all accepted it as a sign of how we act when we're together."

"Does the game have a name?"

"We just call it Mash."

"How do I play?" Fin said. The two sides more or less squared off and the balls sat next to each other in between the groups.

Saskia shook her head. "That would take a week to explain. Over time the list has grown long."

Fin saw a mischievous smirk on her face. Mona Lisa with an agenda. "Run and kick one of the balls."

"Which way?"

She climbed up onto a rock for a better view. "It won't matter."

The groups all stood like they were ready to pounce and the tension grew.

*What the hell.*

Fin found a thin part of the mob of islanders and saw Hua, who looked as keyed up as the rest.

"Hey, buddy," Fin whispered as he raced past and out into the open. He had no idea which ball to choose so in the spirit of cluelessness he ran up to give the pigskin a boot.

Just before he reached the ball the entire crowd let out a shriek and all of them charged straight for him. He got to the ball and kicked it.

Good thing he didn't know where to aim because the irregular shape made it veer sharply left. People leapt into the air with outstretched arms and blocked it wherever it was going.

The crowd, players and spectators alike cheered, though Fin hadn't any idea if he'd done something good or bad.

He didn't get a chance to kick anything else just then because one of the burly Dwazen tackled him. Fin hit the sand, and while the guy had brought him down with force, the landing didn't hurt.

Fin was about to try wrestling when the guy got off him and yanked him back to his feet before racing in the direction of one of the balls.

Fin saw what looked like controlled chaos. Both balls got kicked back and forth like beach balls at a rock concert. When they hit the ground, someone would pick it up and try to run but would get tackled instantly. Then the tackler would sort of punt the ball and the action resumed.

Fin couldn't tell when there was a score except by the volume of celebrations from one side or another. He noticed Gert on the far side scribbling on a handheld chalkboard and every so often he'd hold it up with some markings to indicate score.

It appeared some points could get deducted while other plays generated offensive scores.

Fin gave up trying to keep track and raced around hitting or kicking the ball whenever he got close to one. One thing he did notice was that the experienced players were able to control the direction of the odd-shaped ball. Fin never got the hang of it, and he held off tackling anyone unless they actually had the ball.

The Dwazen didn't hesitate to knock him to the ground but the sand, exhausting to run in, did cushion the blow. Nobody wore padding, but Fin could tell they weren't trying to hurt him.

After what felt like an hour of wild fun scrambling around, Maru hollered out "Loto." Willem nodded and clapped Maru on the shoulder. He yelled to the Dwazen. "Pieter."

The crowd parted, forming a rough circle leaving only Loto, the muscular hunter and the solid Dutchman, Pieter. Pieter and Loto faced each other and looked like they were about to duel to the death.

Instead they held the balls to their chest and charged toward each other. They collided and the makeshift football and soccer balls sprung off each other. The two men ricocheted off one another. Loto landed on his feet like a cat and Pieter staggered but managed to stay upright.

The crowd reacted like they'd seen a barely missed goal. The men backed up and tried again, this time even faster, and they hit glancing blows that threw both off balance but still neither man fell.

Once more and this time they met square on. To Fin it looked like two men playing chicken. Neither flinched. They slammed into each other and the pigskin burst with a report like a starter's-pistol. The soccer ball squirted to one side and Fin saw the men crash skulls.

Both men went down, dazed from the impact. The crowd fell silent until Loto gained his knees and managed to take a few wobbly steps while Pieter only reached his knees and shook his head in an effort to clear the cobwebs.

The islanders went wild.

*Game, Set and Match.*

Loto walked over to Pieter and helped him up. Pieter looked more coherent despite a bruise and cut on his forehead. He gave Loto a quick hug and the two proceeded to the table and shared some water out of a gourd.

Gagnon leaned over and whispered something to Stephon who laughed.

# Chapter 16

*Hoku, The Feast*

The late afternoon sun hung low in the sky. Fin marveled at how fast the Dwazen had turned the playing field into an open air dining hall. Hua stood next to him while he shot pictures of the work, careful not to include the Frenchmen who hauled the food containers and plastic bowls to one of the tables.

"Hua, you guys should do weddings. They put caterers to shame."

"Practice makes perfect." His smile looked forced.

"What is it?"

"What else?" Hua spoke in a soft voice and flicked his gaze toward the Frenchmen who now worked fast to place a bowl and a ladle full of whatever was in the container by each place where they joined a plate of assorted meat and fruits.

"The food?"

"Bully something, he called it."

"Bully...? " Fin took a few steps closer and saw the head table where the bowls contained a broth filled with mussels and carrots and other chunky ingredients. "Oh, bouillabaisse. Very good when it's done right."

"Consider the source." Hua said.

"Damn. Good point." Fin thought fast. He didn't see anyone eating yet though several of the young ones had already been scolded for reaching over and trying to nibble something. "Can your dad or Willem make everyone wait until Gagnon eats it first?"

Hua dashed over to Maru and spoke to him and Willem. Maru gave him a pat on the arm.

When everyone was seated Maru stood with Willem and they held hands. Everyone around all the tables did likewise. Fin and Hua sat near the Frenchmen and Stephon was closest. Fin took his hand and though they were about to say the Hokutian version of Grace, the bastard gave him a crusher grip, reminding Fin of when he met Gagnon.

Maru spoke in Hokutian. It sounded melodic, like a poem or a song. Everyone hung their heads in respect. Fin did likewise but noticed Gagnon and Stephon rolled their eyes.

When Maru finished the crowd murmured and it looked like all were about to dig into the food. Maru remained standing. He pointed to Gagnon.

"Wait. The visitors from the government have brought us a dish from their homeland."

Gagnon stood and waved "You are welcome."

"We are grateful and wish to try it, so we ask of him to honor our ancient customs."

Hua tapped Fin's leg under the table and Fin realized Maru was inventing tradition on the spot.

Gagnon looked caught off guard. "Of course. What is the tradition?"

"Our peoples are unused to strangers, especially during our Feast. Long ago when outsiders were invited they always tasted the food first as a show of faith."

Gagnon smiled and gave a little half bow toward Maru. "Ca va." He hoisted his bowl for all to see and gulped down the broth then dug the meat out of the mussels with his fingers. "Bon!" He smacked his lips and rubbed his stomach.

Three hundred faces stared at him. Fin waited. Maru remained at his feet and then motioned over to Hua. They spoke in rapid Hokutian. Hua spoke next and Fin could swear his friend was trying hard not to laugh.

"The chief wishes to apologize for the misunderstanding. The tradition is that you taste from each guest's bowl."

Gagnon and Stephon exchanged a look and Gagnon shook his head. "A sip from several hundred bowls?"

Maru nodded and held his own bowl out. Hua picked up Willem's and carried it over to Stephon and held it under his chin. "You can help, Monsieur."

Stephon knocked the bowl out of Hua's hand and the mixture soaked into the sand.

The crowd watched in silence. Hua picked up the bowl, grabbed the vegetables and mussels (along with a fair amount of sand,) put it all into the container and carried it back to Willem's place.

Gagnon shook his head again. Maru gave a very western-looking shrug, bent at the knees and scooped a handful of sand into his own bowl.

In unison, the entire group of islanders matched the gesture and the Dwazen followed suit. Now the entire gathering had fragrant sand castles in place of bouillabaisse.

"Savages." Gagnon stared, and both Frenchmen balled their fists.

Maru turned to the crowd with a big grin and shouted a single word that Fin guessed meant "Eat."

Fin marveled at the sight of the islanders, most still shirtless and decorated in scars and tattoos proceed to pick up their knives and forks and commence eating like they were etiquette school graduates.

\* \* \*

Fin stuffed himself on everything except the now grit-filled bouillabaisse. Part of him enjoyed watching the Frenchmen pout. Neither Gagnon nor Stephon ate anything besides their own concoction. They also appeared more than ready to leave. Fin kept an eye on them as well as Maru and Willem.

True to the plan, Maru made them wait until all had eaten. The sun settled into the distant sea and when Willem and Maru stood the meal part of the celebration appeared over. Everyone rose and people scrambled to clear tables.

Hua tapped Fin and leaned toward Gagnon. "I believe they are almost ready for your meeting."

"At last. We aren't used to being kept waiting." Gagnon looked at Fin. "You will be ready to go when we're done?"

Fin stepped away from the table. "Nobody told you?"

"Told me what?" Gagnon sat up like his spine had turned to rebar.

"I'll be staying on a bit longer."

"Your ride leaves tonight." Stephon said.

"It's cool. I got permission from Willem, and Gert said I can catch a ride on the *Verdragen* next time they take it to Papeete."

"You can't have that many pictures to take."

"I disagree, sir. I feel like I have a chance to really get to know these two cultures." Fin lowered his voice to a conspiratorial whisper. "Dude, I met a girl…"

Stephon and Gagnon stepped away from the table and conferred.

"As you wish, but we had an understanding." Stephon held his hand out for Fin's camera.

"Right, I was careful. You aren't anywhere on this." Fin switched on the digital camera and set the screen to review the contents of the memory.

Stephon took the camera and while he and Gagnon scrolled through the pictures, Fin glanced up and saw that Gert and Willem had left. Hua stood by. In the distance, beyond where the kids were chasing each other around, Johannes waited at the edge of the jungle.

"Ca va." Gagnon spoke to Fin. Stephon held on to the camera.

"Satisfied?" Fin held out his hand.

"Oui, and since your extended stay is of a more personal nature, we'll take this back to make sure it is safe and you can retrieve it when you return to Papeete." Gagnon didn't try to disguise his smug attitude.

"I'm here as a photographer. I'd look foolish without a camera. You saw the pictures. What more do you want?" Fin could still see the silvery wrapping paper he'd torn off the box when his parent's gave it to him.

Stephon spoke French too quickly for Fin to catch it all. Gagnon nodded. "Surely there is more than one way to impress a girl..."

"It's my property and that particular camera has sentimental value."

Gagnon smiled. "Then I can feel confident we will see each other again soon."

"You can't keep it." Fin felt his anger begin to overtake his mission.

"I left my property receipts back at my office."

"No, listen..."

Hua stepped forward. "Sirs, if you'll come with me while there's still light. That special tour is about to begin."

Gagnon checked his watch. "We'll take this up again in Papeete. Stephon will keep it safe." Stephon jammed the camera into his pocket and took a step back before turning away from Fin. He moved slowly enough for Fin to nearly take the bait and try to grab the big man.

*Just what he wants, dumbass.*

Hua shot Fin a split second but withering glance.

"I'm still staying." Fin yelled at their backs.

When he was sure they weren't going to turn around or further acknowledge him Fin walked fast toward where he last saw Johannes.

"Ready?" The guy looked nervous as a cat.

"Not quite." Fin gave a low whistle. Ruru dashed around the corner carrying the small pack that Fin had left on the ship before his plunge into the water. He handed it to Fin.

"He's coming with. You know him?" Fin said.

"We all know each other." He said something to Ruru in Hokutian. Ruru grinned and bolted into the jungle.

"Wait, where's he going?"

"Same place we are but he'll make sure it is safe. Besides you'll slow us down. We have to hurry. You need that?" He pointed to the pack.

"Yeah, and I'm not as old as I look. I can hang."

Johannes was already down the narrow path and Fin dashed after him.

# Chapter 17

*The Dwazen Cemetery*

Fin's lungs still burned, but he'd hovered on the fringes of the entrance long enough to stop gasping.

"You're sure you don't want me or even Ruru to do this?" Johannes stared at the scabbed abrasions that lined Fin's arms from his attempt to climb the tree.

"We don't have time to argue. When Ruru gets back here we have two minutes, tops. This does us no good if we don't get the shot. Just get me up there, I know how to be quiet."

"Suit yourself." Johannes hefted the rope that was in the pack. He tossed it up and over a large palm tree that canted near the entrance to the burial sites.

The black iron gates crafted from construction rebar was an interesting touch, but then again the whole site was odd given the setting.

In the growing moonlight, the rope looked like a hangman's noose. He glanced up the wide path for a sign of Ruru. Not yet. Fin took out the compact digital camera and checked the battery and power. He took tape and covered the screen. Its light would be a dead giveaway.

"Ready?" Johannes looked like he was ready to dive into the bushes.

"Yep."

"That little thing will work?"

"A little late to worry about that now, dude. It may not be as good as the other one but it'll do."

*The bastards insulted him. What pro brought only one camera?*

"Going up." Fin tucked the camera away and stepped his foot into the rope loop.

*Damn, these wiry Dwazen were strong!*

Fin rose in a series of long yanks as Johannes hoisted him to the top of the tree. When he got up there he was able to scramble onto the trunk and make his way to the cluster of foliage. He wasn't sure how he'd get comfortable, but at least he was in cover. He tossed the rope down and decided to worry about getting down later.

He felt flushed with excitement and exercise. He found he could lie down among the thick fronds and realized someone had been up here and had cut just enough space to give him an un-obstructed view of the entrance.

Movement caught his eye, and Fin spotted two figures approaching from inside the cemetery.

When they stepped into the moonlit entrance Fin saw it was Gert and Willem. They carried four heavy canvas satchels. They placed the bags in perfect view of Fin's line of sight. The camera angle was ideal and Fin heard muffled clinking sounds when the bags hit the ground.

Neither man acknowledged Fin in any way but they lit a pair of torches and spoke to each other in normal conversational tones.

"When do you think they will get here, Gert?"

"It shouldn't be long now."

Fin used the stilted, faux-chatter as a sound check. He had the compact camera set to record video and even in the lower light conditions, he was sure he'd get what he needed. He double-checked that the camera's playback sound function was muted.

Ruru zipped into sight. Fin hadn't heard him coming though the little guy was sprinting down the path.

The boy whispered in Hokutian but Fin didn't need a translation for the little Paul Revere's "The Frenchmen are coming!"

Just then, Fin heard a soft bird call and Ruru slipped off into the foliage, no doubt to join Johannes, out of sight.

Now he heard Hua. "Won't be much further, gentlemen."

*They must be around the last bend in the path by now.*

"About time." Gagnon stepped into view flanked by Stephon.

"I'll be down the path if you need me." Hua said.

"Stay." Gagnon ordered.

Willem spoke up. "Hua and the islanders do not get involved with this part of our affairs."

"I'd say he's involved now, wouldn't you?" Gagnon sounded irritable.

"These are extraordinary circumstances." Willem said.

"Caused by you." Gert pointed at the two Frenchmen.

Fin controlled his breathing, both to remain silent and to steady the camera.

"Let him stay. He knows we aren't here to sample the evening air." Gagnon said.

"Why couldn't you meet us at the dock?" Stephon asked.

"We prefer to conduct business in private. You force our hand by intruding on our celebration and refusing to trust us to deliver your tribute in the customary fashion." Willem said.

Stephon smirked. "They don't even trust the very people who get their hands dirty."

Willem's back stiffened. "We already told you that how we obtain your extortion is our problem."

"It is difficult to feel the sting of your barbs out here sneaking about a graveyard while you keep your people in the dark." Gagnon said. "However, as you say, it is your concern." He pointed to the bags. "That's all of it?"

"Twenty five hundred ounces." Willem sounded like the words stuck in his throat. "We can get a scale if you'd like to wait."

Gagnon held up his hand. "Not necessary. We have one but I think it is time to show a little faith."

Stephon took off his backpack and pulled out a small case. Fin was relieved it wasn't a weapon. He opened the case and removed an electronic device the size of a tablet with a thick pen-like device attached.

Gagnon walked up to one of the bags. "May I?"

"They're yours." Willem said, and Fin thought the words could have drawn blood on their way out of the miner's mouth.

"Just so." Gagnon unzipped one bag and Fin took advantage of the perfect angle to capture the glittering array of roughhewn bars. He almost gasped at the sight of more gold than he'd seen in his life.

*And this was just one bag.*

Gagnon let out a low whistle. Willem looked like the man had just hit on his daughter, but remained silent. Gert looked away in disgust. "Thibaux never asked to work this way before."

Gagnon reached inside the canvas satchel, and Fin could hear the bars clank together. "I am not Thibaux." He removed a single bar and passed it to Stephon. "Your secrets and safety flow through me. You would do well to remember that, especially on days you think the price is too high."

While Gagnon spoke, Stephon took the bar, hefted it, and Fin was sure the camera would capture the raw greed gleaming in his eyes.

Stephon placed the bar on the pad and applied the pen-device. After a few seconds the unit beeped. Fin couldn't see the display.

"Twenty-four carat." He retested. Gagnon grabbed another satchel and repeated the process.

Stephon reconfirmed the gold's purity.

Fin did some fast math and realized that there was well over two and a half million dollars of gold in those bags.

"Now who wants to talk about trust?" Gert said.

Gagnon waved him off. He picked up the first satchel, and Fin could see the weight from the way the strap dug into the man's shoulder. Stephon packed up and picked up a second satchel. He pointed at Hua. "Get those."

Hua didn't budge but Fin knew the body language well enough. His friend was getting seriously pissed. Hua held his hands behind his back and his jaw muscles bunched. He said nothing.

Gagnon sighed. "Why do you think we wanted you to stay? For your translation skills? We can find our way back. Go on, make yourself useful."

Gert and Willem looked like they took some satisfaction in the exchange, or lack of one.

"I am in line to be the next chief of the Hokutians. As such, I shall pay my respects in the burial place of my neighbors."

"What?"

"This may take a while. Our people go way back and each one deserves the appropriate tribute."

"And you?" Gagnon spoke to the others through clenched teeth. "I was supposed to have two more men to help, but they became lizard food."

"I'm afraid our custom dictates we join Hua while he's on our hallowed ground."

"Both of you?" Stephon said.

Gert smirked at Stephon. "Willem's memory isn't what it was. I'll stay to make sure he remembers." Gert stepped up to Gagnon and towered over the Frenchman. "Perhaps you bit off more than you could chew."

"Au contraire." Gagnon looked about to close the remaining distance when Stephon grabbed his boss. "Sir, the hour is late. We can manage."

"Oui. We can." Gagnon spoke up so that Hua and Willem who now stood by the cemetery gate could hear him. "You would all do well to reconsider your attitude. Pray, if you do that sort of thing, that the arrangement doesn't change. I am not a good person to make into an enemy."

With that, Stephon and Gagnon hauled up the satchels, two apiece and labored down the path. Fin guessed each man carried about eighty pounds of extra weight.

"Merci pour la bouillabaisse." Hua called out after them.

Fin nearly blew his cover.

* * *

When they were certain the coast was clear, Johannes and Ruru emerged from their hiding places. Fin confirmed the camera captured the entire meeting. Now the men looked at him and he flashed a grin and thumbs up.

Johannes threw the rope over the tree and Fin reversed the trip up with Johannes and Gert helping to slow his descent.

"Thought you and Gagnon were going to tangle."

"We may yet if your idea doesn't work."

"You heard him. He was mad about the long walk, but he won't want any part of Thibaux learning about this little side trip."

"I hope you are right."

Fin felt a wave of fatigue sweep through his body. "If you're going to fight, you'll have to count on me in the morning. That took more out of me than I realized."

Hua called him over. Willem stood next to him and Fin saw they were by a grave marker. Lichen speckled the old stone. The moonlight shone enough for him to read: *Willem DeBruin, 1864-1930*.

"Your ancestor?"

"The first Willem."

Fin noticed a stone next to it. *Saskia DeBruin 1901-1930*.

"Are all of you named after your ancestors?" Fin said.

Willem nodded.

"And this Saskia was also Willem's daughter?" Fin looked again at the dates. "Both died 1930."

Willem nodded again. "A boating accident. They never recovered the bodies, but we think it is important to give them their due here."

Ruru came over to where they were standing. He seemed subdued and spoke to Hua in quiet tones.

"A first. He wants to go back because he's tired." Hua translated.

Fin smiled at the boy. "Tell him he's a hero and I'm proud of him tonight."

Hua did and Ruru beamed.

"This cloak and dagger stuff *is* exhausting. Willem, thanks for supporting my idea. I'm sorry about the…" Strangely, Fin hesitated to mention the gold directly. In all the years he'd been a photographer he'd only recorded similar expressions on faces of those who'd lost loved ones. Willem looked the same way when he turned over those satchels.

"Thank you. And understand Gert is one of our fiercest protectors and he has been the one to deal with this disgusting tribute exercise. Again, say nothing to our people or the islanders. If you have expenses of your own…"

Fin held up his hands. "No, thanks. I make enough to get by, that's all I need. We're not all like the Thibauxs or the Gagnons of the world."

"Many are, those in power most of all."

"I can't argue with that. But I'm just a shutterbug with a couple scruples left intact."

"Shutterbug?"

Fin held up his camera. "A humble photographer."

"Your continued silence means life or death to us."

Fin wanted to tell Willem he was being over dramatic. Instead, Gagnon's face loomed in his mind's eye. "You have my word of honor. That's *my* gold."

Willem looked him in the eye and shook his hand. "Ya. We work hard and risk our lives. When these outsiders take gold away they carry off part of the Dwazen soul."

"I understand." Fin didn't really, but he got the life and death part. So did Gagnon and his crew, who exploited their weakness to the hilt.

\* \* \*

Fin had sat with the others and waited until they saw the seaplane climb into the night sky. He hadn't wanted to take any chance that Stephon or Gagnon might see him.

He could have slept right there in the warm breezes and soft lapping of the waves in the distance. Then again, it was a graveyard and it seemed disrespectful and creepy.

Saskia arrived to let them know that both men had boarded the plane with their gear and satchels. Willem, Gert and Johannes left to go ahead.

Hua picked up Ruru and carried him on his shoulders. "We'll go ahead as well. Ruru may fall asleep on the way."

"My father said you got pictures?" Saskia looked shy in the moonlight.

"Better. Video." He pulled out the little camera.

He showed her a clip and while dark, that could be enhanced easily. More important, the sound came through so identifying the players would be a snap.

"Where is the other camera?"

He told her how Stephon confiscated it. "Says I can have it back later."

"After this..."

"Stephon will want to cram the camera down my throat or somewhere else when I get the video all the places I have in mind."

"I'm sorry. All those pictures, you were going to publish."

Fin smiled. "Don't let the blonde hair fool you. I've learned a few tricks over the years." He fiddled with a small slit he'd made in the collar of his shirt. He pulled out a memory card.

"The whole time I swapped these out so I'd have something to give the goons. I thought they'd leave me the camera. It was special."

"Why?"

They began walking and at some point he took her hand without breaking stride. It felt like the thing to do and she didn't object. "It was from my parents. Their last present before they were killed in a small-plane crash."

"I'm sorry."

"It's been a while, but I miss them."

"It has been a long time since I saw my mother as well."

"How'd she die?"

Saskia looked away and continued speaking. "She never wanted the island life. For my father it was everything and I was practically raised here. I suppose I favor him. Eventually she got sick and died back at home in South Africa."

Fin knew two things at once. He wasn't getting the whole story and if he wanted to keep holding the pretty girl's hand on the tropical island in the moonlight he better change the subject.

"It was a great party, outside of the uninvited guests."

"As you saw, we take our celebrations seriously."

"And the islanders go back in the morning?"

"Yes. But some won't quit until the dawn breaks." They neared the little town. "And you? Are you interested in a swim?" She stopped and faced him, taking his other hand in hers.

This was usually where an interesting night turned *really* interesting. Fin shocked himself when he heard himself say "Could I get a rain check?" He realized that might not translate. "I mean, I'd like nothing more, but I feel like I might fall asleep in the water."

She looked like that was the first time she'd been turned down. She reached a hand up to caress his cheek and frowned.

"What?"

She touched the other side of his face then the side of his neck. "You feel warm."

"Well the exercise and the company..." Fin wanted to reassure her and wasn't trying to push her away but just felt thrashed right now. "I'm fine. I think the whole week and tonight may be catching up with me. Could we...swim, tomorrow? I hear the moon will be back."

"I'd like that." They walked into New Cape and he could hear the festivities continuing at a more subdued pace.

"How long will the party last?"

"Hard to say. Things picked up right after the French departed."

"Makes sense," Fin said. "I'll have to pick a sleep spot away from the noise."

"You'll stay at my place."

"You sure?"

"I insist." She gave her little Mona Lisa smile. "No expectations. I want you well rested." She pointed to one of the huts. It was decorated with wind chimes on the outside.

"Anyone ever tell you that you're very direct?"

"Is there any other way? Why waste time?"

Fin stepped inside and she lit several lanterns, providing a soft glow inside the hut. It was roomier than he thought with a living room area, and a doorway leading to what had to be a bedroom. Fin supposed he could find a little extra energy, but even the bamboo couch with cushions looked perfect.

She must have seen him eye it. "Yes, tonight that's for you. We'll see about tomorrow."

"But no pressure," he was glad she got the joke.

He sat on the couch and looked around. There were small detailed paintings of beach scenes. He also noticed a single black and white picture of a woman in a simple skirt and blouse. Fin looked closer. "This could be you! What year is this?"

"1900."

"Your great-grandmother?" It was eerie.

She glanced at the floor. "The first Saskia."

"Like in the cemetery?" She didn't answer. "Well she's beautiful and you look just like her."

"Thank you."

She took a pitcher of fresh water and poured a couple glasses. "Thank you for all your help. I hope the rest of your idea goes as smoothly."

"Me too. You people live an interesting life but you deserve your privacy." Fin gulped the water and his throat felt scratchy. Still, the water while not cold, tasted fresh. "But don't you get curious about what other people your age are doing?"

"Not really. I wonder, but the outside moves so quickly and where are they all in such a hurry to reach anyway? We don't live as simply as the Hokutians but there's much they have taught us."

"They don't care about gold."

Her expression hardened and Fin could swear Willem possessed her at that moment. "That's what brought us here in the first place and to what we owe our life and very survival. As do the Hokutians who like to pretend they are above such concerns."

"I didn't mean to hit a nerve." Of course he had, he just didn't realize how touchy they all were.

"You'd understand it if you lived it."

Fin took the out she offered. "I bet you're right."

"Why don't you get some sleep?" She tossed a pillow from the other room.

He lay down and rested his head on it. He wanted to say goodnight but sleep overtook him before the words formed on his lips.

# Chapter 18

*New Cape, Island of Hoku*

*Fin swam, his lungs calling for air. Beneath him he could see the glow of the undersea lava. The underwater smoke billowed out like an ink cloud from a giant squid, and the fire beneath peeked out like an angry eye. He had to reach the surface before the heat overwhelmed him.*

*His head broke the surface and he sucked in sweet air. He couldn't see where the shore lay but he was glad for a moment of cool relief. Then he heard the drone of a plane and he looked up to see his parents waving out the window of a tiny single-engine Piper. His mother's blue eyes riveted him while he treaded water. Then her face was a silent scream while the plane plummeted and Fin could see it would never make it. He tried to shout a warning and coughed on a mouthful of water. The plane plunged into the sea, shattering like a child's toy, and then the wreckage burst into flame.*

*Now he could hear both her and his father screaming for help and the fire spread across the water. He didn't care and swam for them, all the while the heat grew more and more intense…*

"Fin, wake up!"

For an instant the hand that shook him had been his mother's, then as the fog of sleep lifted he saw Saskia's face. She looked terrified.

"What?" His voice croaked out and his throat felt raked with flame. For an instant he expected to smell smoke and wondered if the hut was on fire. No, it was dark, he was on the couch in Saskia's place.

"You're burning up, too." Her fear seemed to redouble.

Fin noticed his clothes were soaked. He sat up and his muscles ached, but her panic was contagious and the adrenaline kicked in.

Now he could hear shouting. His heart slammed against his chest. "An attack? Gagnon?"

"The children." He tried to focus on her face.

"Where?" He reached for his clothes and remembered he was already dressed.

"They're sick. Other's too, but they're bad. We need help."

"Sick?"

"Can you help? Will you make it?" She looked desperate.

"Yeah, of course." He fought a wave of dizziness when he stood too quickly. Where was the doc? At that moment he realized he never remembered seeing anyone claiming to have any sort of medical skills.

"We're putting everyone on the *Verdragen*. We have to reach the other side."

He followed her and half stumbled down the steps. The stars had faded and the sky was just beginning to lighten. A dozen questions stormed through his mind but it hurt to talk and made him cough.

Pandemonium reigned outside. A low horn sounded like a wounded beast and the entire village was awake. Fin saw islanders carrying whimpering children at a run toward the dock. Men staggered, propping each other up like drunks.

Fin ran as best he could to the sleeping area where he saw several small figures still prone near the makeshift fire pits. They were wrapped tight in blankets, though how anyone could sleep through the din was hard to imagine.

Everyone else seemed to be either running to the ship or coming to this common area to carry someone. Fin stopped at the nearest pair of sleepers. He saw a little girl with some bright red feathers still in her hair.

"C'mon sweetheart. Time to go. I won't hurt you." She couldn't have been more than five and he hefted her up, blanket and all.

Her head lolled and he saw a smear of blood on the blanket. He wasn't going to hurt her. She was dead.

The little one next to her was gone as well. Fin felt himself filing the images away for later processing. Right now he wanted to help anyone still able to receive it. Mentally he'd just zipped halfway around the world to Angola where he'd spent some time with a field hospital. They'd done their part to patch up the innocent victims of fighting, but he hadn't needed his camera to remember the crushing sense of futility.

He fought that sensation now even as his own head swam and he had to admit he wasn't just wiped out, he was sick.

But not dead. Neither was the next girl he saw. She was a little older, a shy islander he'd seen hanging with the other women in the village. She was probably in her early teens and just getting some height in that awkward adolescent way. Still, he had no trouble hoisting her up over his shoulder in a fireman's carry. He trotted toward the dock, and her body was so warm she felt like she'd fallen asleep next to a roaring fire.

Fin felt like he was running through a sauna with quicksand for floors. Sweat poured down his face and he felt exhausted after only a hundred yards. He slowed his pace so he wouldn't drop the poor whimpering girl.

At the dock, the crowd noise competed with a growing ringing in his ears.

Dwazen ran around shouting orders in what sounded like Dutch. Fin could see Gert racing in and out of the pilothouse barking orders and yelling to other sailors tending lines. The diesel engines far below deck rumbled like they weren't happy to be awakened so suddenly.

Saskia stood next to Willem with tears streaming down her face. She held a pair of black cases that looked like old fashioned doctor's bags.

Finally the queue up the gangplank thinned and he got close. "She needs help," he croaked to no one in particular.

Gray dots swam in his vision and he felt his body sway. Someone caught him before he dropped the girl.

It was Johannes.

"Thanks. You look like shit." It felt like a long speech but it was true. The kid's face was closer to purple than red and might as well have been dunked in the sea, his shirt was so drenched. His eyes held steady but Fin saw a smudge of blood in the corner of his mouth.

"Feel worse. Let's take her together, there are blankets on deck." Johannes sounded like he'd gone to the same singing coach Fin had overnight.

They half-carried, half-dragged the girl, who'd stopped whimpering, but when they lay her down she was breathing. With the help of a couple Dwazen ladies, Anna and someone…Fin was having trouble thinking. They checked the girl's pulse while they settled her and wiped her down with a wet cloth.

Gert blew the whistle again and the lines cast off. The ship pulled away from the dock and for an instant during the turn if felt like they weren't moving and Fin realized the rotation was countering the spinning from his own head.

And then it wasn't. Now he felt like the big vessel was one of those extreme rides for kids that made adults lose their overpriced hot dogs at amusement parks.

Fin heard and felt the engines rev, and across the deck dozens of people, more islanders than Dwazen, lay moaning or not making noise at all. Some clutched the blankets and shivered and others cast them off.

Fin wanted to go help others but now it felt like the deck had turned into quicksand, too. The emerging dawn seemed a great explosion of light and color in slow motion. He was sure if he wanted to he could speed it up and it would resemble a huge nuclear blast.

He noticed Maru and Saskia rummaging through her bags and counting something. They didn't appear to like the answers they were getting.

They seemed to get further away the more he tried to walk to them. The throb of the diesel running flat out vibrated through the soles of his feet.

Someone shoved a cup of water into his hand and he drank half of it before he staggered and spilled the rest on his arm. He expected steam to rise where it hit his scorching flesh. Now Hua appeared, yelling something about sitting down.

Fin sat. Or the deck rose to hit him in the ass, he wasn't sure. "Donfeelsogood."

Movement caught Fin's eye and he saw several young islanders shaking hard on the deck. A distant part of his brain summoned the word "convulsions."

Now Saskia and Maru yelled out commands, and several crew members slashed blankets into strips. Another crew member ran up with a hose and doused the cloth. Saskia, Maru and others began to wrap the sodden strips around the ankles and heads of the victims on deck. Saskia reached him.

"Fin, keep your eyes open. We can help you but you need to stay awake."

"That's freezing." He croaked out. It felt like strips of dry ice wound around his head and ankles.

"For the fever." She moved to the next row of people.

Hua came by a few minutes later. Fin was shivering but seemed like he could think again.

"Better?"

"Some." Fin didn't recognize his own voice but he was able to form coherent words. When he wasn't coughing. Others on deck shrieked at the cold shock and the ship drove on.

"Ruru. Is he sick?"

"We're doing everything we can. Why can't this tub go faster?"

"Let me help." Fin tried to sit up despite the invisible bags of cement on his chest and managed to get up on an elbow. The scene on deck exploded into a kaleidoscope of images and he closed his eyes. When he opened them again his vision was stable. Now he saw Johannes rolling from side to side on deck moaning.

Willem zipped into Fin's line of sight and he was giving water to everyone able to drink. Hua ran off when Willem reached Fin.

"Good. Go be with your son. Fin, are you awake?"

"Is this a nightmare?" Fin could see sick people strewn across the deck. He saw blisters breaking out on his arms. His nose was running and there was as much blood as mucous.

"Don't try to get up. We are almost there."

Fin saw several people now covered with the blankets. All the way over their faces.

"You're tough. I can see. Hang in there."

"I never would have told. Never." For some reason Fin felt it urgent that Willem understand.

147

Willem stopped and met Fin's gaze. "I know." He hurried across the deck, yelling for more water.

\* \* \*

Fin heard "Brace for impact!" over the ship's PA. It lurched, and then bodies slid across the deck as if Gert had a giant brake pedal in the wheelhouse and the ship decelerated.

Now shouts seemed to come from everywhere. He snatched sounds out of the air, the most frequent being "rope" and "hurry."

Fin summoned every last bit of strength he could muster and climb-crawled up until he could see over the rail.

The morning light illuminated the beach of the Hokutain village. He looked at the distance down to waterline where the surf washed up and realized that Gert had just grounded the *Verdragen* on the beach.

The Dwazen and the islanders who weren't sick all scrambled to cast ropes down. Then, they helped lower the sick to others who'd jumped off the bow ahead.

Soon litters appeared on deck and some of the little ones were loaded on like refugees on a Coast Guard stretcher.

The anguish on the faces of the healthy parents was almost worse to see than the sick ones themselves, many of whom seemed beyond caring.

Fin spotted Hua running toward the village with Ruru in his arms. Saskia was nowhere to be seen.

He tried to stand, and only the ache in his legs told him that he still had any feeling in them. Still, he was able to get them under himself by hanging onto the side of the ship.

Gert left the wheelhouse and ran to him. "Can you walk?"

Fin tried to respond but all that came out was a wracking cough. He wiped his mouth off with his sleeve. He followed Gert's wide-eyed gaze and saw a line of blood along the sleeve. He touched a finger to his lips.

A crimson dot perched on his finger like the red spot on a gull's bill.

# Chapter 19

*Nowhere…*

*Fin dreamt that he was a bird, soaring in an enamel blue sky. The sun and wind held him aloft.*

*Unseen forces drove him higher toward a cave. It looked cool, dark and safe.*

*Inside.*

*Soothingly cool. Almost cold.*

*He tried to fly again but his wing caught on something. No, it was held. TRAPPED! He thrashed with all his strength but now monsters held his wings with terrible claws and no matter how he struggled he couldn't move.*

*Now they brought water? No, something awful. One monster jammed a stick into his beak forcing it open and another poured in liquid that appeared clear but ran thick down his throat.*

Waking, Fin lifted his head expecting to see feathers but instead found only his arms and they remained pinned to the ground while the awful liquid crawled down his throat and into his stomach like a living thing. He expected to gag but his throat seemed paralyzed. The stench and taste of mothballs and eucalyptus coated his tongue.

An icy-hot feeling spread through his body and Fin was keenly aware of the advancing edge of the sensation as it crept to his organs and radiated out.

When it passed through his limbs Fin felt strength return, but strangely he didn't want to move or resist.

# Chapter 20

*Somewhere…*

Fin heard one clear word. "Breathe."

Sharp, pungent fumes spiked into his nostrils and didn't slow until they exploded in his head.

Like some primeval smelling salts, the vapor snapped his mind back into his body and he drew in the smoke out of reflex. Waves of mothball and eucalyptus surged into his lungs yet he didn't cough. It felt cleansing. He realized that he couldn't see because a basket had been placed over his head and was filled with these fumes. With each breath he felt more grounded and present.

"One more," A familiar voice said.

"Maru?"

"Shh. One more."

Fin did as instructed then held his breath. The basket came off his head. He still held the last vapor in and it felt fine, like he never needed to breathe again if he didn't want to.

Hands rolled him to his side and he saw he was lying on a cave floor. It all looked familiar.

"Exhale. Let it out." Maru said.

Part of him didn't want to. The sensation was so soothing. He'd felt horrible, like he was dying. He opened his mouth to exhale and he had to push, like the air had thickened. It looked like he was exhaling coal dust, it was so black. He coughed and more came out. He touched his hand to his mouth and squinted in the dim light at his fingers. A dark sooty smear, but no blood. He coughed until the soot was gone, and when he drew in clean air the urge to cough was gone as well.

His skin was clammy but he knew the fever had broken. The nearest sensation was like when he'd had a horrible bout of the flu along with a scorching 104 temperature. When that fever had broken he'd soaked the sheets. He remembered how amazing he'd felt after.

"What was that?" Fin noticed the rasp was gone from his voice.

Maru patted his chest and someone adjusted a cushion under his head.

"Stay here. Let your body adjust." Saskia's voice. She sounded exhausted. She leaned over and he could see exhaustion in her eyes and dirt smeared her face. "He's the last one."

Maru stood up and moved away.

"Are you sick too?" The question blurted out.

"Tired, but not sick. Neither are you, anymore." Her smile barely touched the corners of her mouth.

Fin wanted to sit up but decided to let everything slide into focus first. He looked at his arm. No sign of blisters.

"Are we in that same cave…"

"Yes. Just take a minute."

Fin decided not to argue. He took deep breaths and the camphor odor lingered.

There were other smells. Crap for sure, and vomit. He could hear coughing and shrill cries. It took a moment to realize they were human.

"Who's screaming?" He started to sit up. Saskia pushed on his shoulders. He noticed she didn't look alarmed but any trace of a smile was long gone.

"It's all right. It's all okay." She put no inflection into her voice.

Besides knowing that was a crock, Fin figured the immediate danger was past. He felt hungry and thirsty, but his legs seemed like they'd work for him.

Fin propped himself up on one elbow. He turned his body and this time Saskia made no effort to stop him. Fin sat up and his head felt clear. No dizziness. He scanned the cave floor and indeed it was the same place where he'd met with the island leaders.

The floor was covered with people. Some were draped in blankets, victims of whatever hit them. Fin noted with growing horror that they'd run out of blankets, sheets or other covering and had, at the end, resorted to fern branches.

Not all the branches stayed in place and Fin saw corpses crying dried blood tears. His gorge rose and almost choked him. He shut his eyes and fought for control. He'd seen worse, hadn't he?

He looked again and saw that some nearer corpses appeared to have vomited a thick, clear liquid the consistency of cold honey. Then he realized it had to be the same stuff forced down his throat.

His stomach clenched again and like magic there was Saskia with a wood bowl for him.

He retched and through his watering eyes saw that what came out wasn't last night's food at all. It looked more like runny tar. He heaved again and spat. He expected fresh vomit stench but all this smelled like was camphor and dirt.

 He gulped the water she offered him and immediately felt fine, and terrified.

"What the fuck was that?"

"The poisons in your body. They're purged. It looks frightening but it's a good sign. We couldn't save them all. We tried. We tried so hard." At the end her voice got a faraway sound Fin used to see in battle fatigue victims at the tent hospital in Angola.

"The others. That's the medicine you gave me?" Fin pointed to one of the dead he didn't know.

She stared at the bodies. "The purge can be strenuous, but some never got that far. They were gone before they reached the cave. We all moved as fast as we could but no one expected…"

Fin sat up and hugged her. She sank into his arms, but her voice retained that blank tone. "The children."

Fin looked again at the bodies and saw the covered ones nearer the back of the cave were indeed smaller. Now that he was more awake, the reminders of earlier horrors had triggered his protective mental walls. He'd survived Africa by being able to detach from the scenes even as he sought to capture the raw savagery and horror on film.

Until he saw Ruru.

His little head was uncovered and the excess medicinal concoction ran out of his mouth. His eyes had been closed but the crusted blood on his cheeks told Fin he must have looked like the others.

His walls crumbled and fell. He crawled over to the boy and instinctively felt for a pulse but the cool flesh told him awful truth. "Sorry, little man. Sorry." He wiped tears off his face and turned to Saskia.

"Not all the children?"

She just looked at him.

# Chapter 21

"How many total?" Fin saw more than a dozen ropes leading out of the mouth of the cave like fibrous drool.

Saskia leaned against the trunk of one of the crossed trees that marked the entrance. "Not sure yet. Many islanders. Perhaps fifty in all. All the young ones."

"I carried a young girl to the ship…"

"Gone." Saskia cut him off.

"And the Dwazen?"

"Fewer, about five. But there were less of us to start. And no children. We'd been hoping to change that." She glanced around like she'd spoken out of turn.

Images from the night before flickered through his consciousness. "Where's Hua?"

"He wants to be alone."

"What about Johannes? I know he was sick."

Fin saw a bit of life creep back into her eyes. "You and he were the last two we saved."

"Where is he?"

"He stepped out." Her eyes filled with tears. "He'd brought his girlfriend to live here. They were going to be part of a new generation and Martina wanted to raise their children on the island."

"Was she up there?" Part of Fin didn't want to see anything more than nameless bodies, but of course Ruru made that impossible.

A voice behind him spoke. "She never made it." Fin turned and saw Johannes and despite the disheveled appearance he looked infinitely better than the last time Fin had seen him.

"I didn't know. I'm sorry." Fin knew he'd be at a loss for words for so many here. "I'm glad you made it."

"It wasn't my time yet." Cold fury seemed to tighten Johannes's voice. "We were going to have children first. Purge together."

"Johannes." Saskia spoke in a sharp tone.

He just looked at her with a blank expression.

"Does it matter now? He came through it. You'll have to tell him sometime."

"That's enough." Saskia said.

Johannes seemed not to hear her. "I thought she'd made it there."

Fin's curiosity clashed with his sympathy. "Tell me what?"

* * *

With a simple "Not here," Saskia had dragged Fin down the path. They passed a few Dwazen Fin recognized but they were all struggling with the impact of the epidemic. Fin's mind raced and he forced himself to try to deal with one thing at a time.

"First off, what was it that you and Maru gave me?"

"Over time we've developed a treatment using local herbs that rival western medicine." She traced a finger along the edge of a frond while she spoke.

Fin took her by the shoulders and turned to make her face him. "Don't try to bullshit me. I've heard it all. As sick as we were, we should be strapped to IVs in a hospital, and you expect me to believe you rubbed some aloe leaves and tea on us and presto, we're good as new?"

"Better than new."

"What's that supposed to mean?"

Saskia met his gaze and he saw a spark in her eyes that looked like the one he first met. "It *was* a plant, but nothing as common as you say. We call it Silverstar and it grows in a patch of sparse soil inside the volcano rim."

"No shit?"

"The rarest plant in the world and it can't be cultivated outside that narrow band where it grows."

"Who figured that out?"

"Long ago the islanders experimented with it, suspecting it could heal."

"And I guess it did." Fin said.

"No, it killed the first to try it. It is extremely poisonous. The plant uses toxins leeched into the soil from the active volcano. It thrives in the heat and gases and concentrates them in the thick leaves."

"Go on."

"When our people first came to the island we didn't understand that we carried disease. But soon after we arrived the locals became sick. Many died."

"Like the way small pox clobbered the native American populations?" Fin said.

"Perhaps. Here the islanders were struck down and their chief and medicine man, Maru's family, was desperate to create a cure."

"Sounds familiar."

"Yes." Saskia's voice grew distant. "And they weren't alone. My people were horrified when we realized what was happening and one man, a doctor, brought along on the expedition vowed to find a cure. We lived apart from the islanders, but that did little other than to slow the spread of the disease."

"How'd they figure it out?" Fin said.

"Dr. Marius Vorster met with the medicine man who showed him the plant and explained what he'd tried. They didn't learn enough to stop the first wave of deaths but the quarantine bought them time. Marius was as brilliant as the medicine man and combined they were genius. Marius was able to add compounds that turned the toxins into a potent chemical 'magnet' that pulls poisons and disease from people."

"How?" Fin was no chemist or doctor but he also began to think about the ravages of disease he'd seen across the African continent that made war deaths pale by comparison.

Saskia shook her head. "We don't know. Marius changed when he got here. Some think he went mad. He spent more and more time with the medicine man and they must have improved the formula."

"It sounds like it worked fine."

"That effect was only temporary."

Fin's heart raced. "We're going to get sick again?"

"No. Your disease is gone. So are any other diseases you may have been harboring. They're all cured now."

"You're sure about that?"

"I told you. They perfected it. At least improved it."

"In what way?"

She sighed. "For all we owe Marius for saving everyone, he and the medicine man cursed us as well."

"I don't understand."

"It's a long story but as far as we know Marius and the chief's youngest son went into the cave and to the place where the Silverstar grows to harvest it. It is treacherous there and the fumes from the volcano swirl and sting, the plant grows upside down and only the bravest can reach it to collect it."

"What happened?"

Saskia paused and lowered her voice. "According to the chief, they both fell from the patch and tumbled into the volcano. Only the chief had the knowledge to process the medicine safely and he decided to hold the secret."

"Why?"

"Some say to keep a balance of power. We had the gold and influence with the outside world but he had the medicine."

"And others say what?"

Now she whispered. "That only the son was trying to collect the plant and he wasn't ready. That he fell alone and the chief blamed him and killed Marius himself. After he vowed not to trust us with the knowledge."

"And what do you think all this time later?"

"Both. They still won't tell us how to refine the plant. Not even last night. Maru prepared the medicine and I helped after. I'll never know if we could have worked faster, if I knew."

Fin could hear the bitterness in her voice. "You said yourself many never reached the cave alive, right?"

She nodded without looking at him.

"Try not to beat yourself up too much. Those of us you both saved are grateful. How could you expect this anyway?"

"I still don't understand what happened." Saskia still looked stunned.

"History was repeating itself, to a point." Fin began to compartmentalize the wave of emotions save one. Anger.

"How do you mean?"

"Outsiders brought in disease, only this time it was no accident."

* * *

Back at the Hokutian village Fin was again struck with the similarity between the distraught survivors and villages in Africa just after a fierce battle.

And wasn't that what he *was* seeing? Minus the fires and explosions, hadn't they been savagely attacked?

Islander women huddled together and wailed. The rhythmic chanting did nothing to dampen the raw emotion and Fin wiped his eyes as he passed them.

Fin stared at the tilted hulk of the *Verdragen*, now buried bow first in the sand. He barely remembered the chaotic arrival at the village and wondered how much of it he'd dreamt. Now, he noticed the vessel had run aground during high tide. With the water out, the ship looked like it had dropped from the sky. The stern barely sat in the water and the top part of the propellers showed.

He saw Gert and Pieter and some of the other men he recognized. They appeared to be discussing how to get the ship back in the water. When he saw Fin, Pieter ran over.

"You're all right?" He looked Fin up and down.

"Yes. I still don't know how exactly, but yes." Something was gnawing at Fin. The more his head cleared the more it bothered him.

"You were in the cave?" Pieter barely made it a question, telling Fin he was the last to be in the dark. "Yes."

"Others?"

"Many didn't get there in time. It hit so fast."

"We saw." Pieter seemed to struggle with the next question. "Was Johannes…?"

Saskia interjected. "He and Fin were the last. He made it. He purged."

Pieter looked relieved and sad at the same time. He spoke to Saskia. "Martina?"

Saskia shook her head.

Pieter walked off cursing in Dutch.

"Come on." Saskia led Fin to Maru's hut. They could hear animated conversation before they reached the door.

Fin stepped inside the hut and the reek of smoke buffeted him. Maru sat in his chair while Willem paced the floor.

The men looked exhausted.

"We're glad you survived." Willem said.

"Thanks to what you gave me. I'm grateful. I'm so sorry about your people, both of you. Especially for Ruru."

Maru's red-rimmed eyes blazed with anger, but he raised one hand in acknowledgement.

Saskia spoke in Dutch to Willem and Fin heard her mention Johannes and Martina. She continued, and judging by both Willem's and Maru's reaction she mentioned what she'd told him about the Silverstar concoction.

Willem took a deep breath and let it out. "So you know about the purge." He looked Fin over. "It seems to have agreed with you."

"It's like a miracle." Fin took a seat. "Another secret?"

Maru spoke. "More than their gold. The plant is unique and we can only use enough for the people here. Do you think the world would leave us in peace if it knew about such a find?"

Fin thought about that. "You're saying this cures *any* disease?"

All three nodded. Fin thought about the cave again. Packed with people but still just a fraction of everyone on Hoku. "And you used up your supply and had to scramble to make a new batch?"

The three exchanged glances. More secrets. Always more secrets with these people. Fin felt his temper creep up. "Do you know what that was that hit us?"

"We were hoping you'd know," Saskia said.

"I've had food poisoning take longer to kick in, and this hit faster and harder than that. I'm no doctor but I saw the bad end of wars and disease that follows it. This was worse than anything I ever heard of but one thing sounds close."

"What?" Willem said.

"The blood from the eyes, and coughing up blood makes me think of a hemorrhagic fever, like Ebola." Fin tried to think with a detached mind. "This hit faster than that. I once got a chance to shoot the aftermath of a small village hit with it. If anything, it reminded me of that." Fin recalled ruining a camera trying to disinfect it afterward while wearing the anti-virus space suit the UN doctors made him wear.

Maru just shook his head. "I don't know these. This was worse than the plagues of the early colony days."

Fin stared at his arms again and recalled the blisters. "I should be dead. I think we all should be dead."

"Why?" Willem asked.

"You all felt it. You think without your medicine you'd still be alive?"

More furtive gazes. "Tell us what you think happened." Willem said.

"Gagnon happened, that's what I think. Somehow he and his buddy avoided it. Think they grabbed some of your medicine?"

All shook their heads without looking at each other. "Impossible," Saskia said.

Fin thought back to last night before everything dissolved into a fever dream. "If he poisoned the bouillabaisse he was the only one I saw actually eat it, though some of the kids could have sneaked a bite." The little bodies flashed though his mind before he could push the images away.

"No, that's still wrong. I *know* I didn't eat it," Fin continued. "And it wasn't poison, it was infection."

Fin could still taste lingering camphor on the back of his tongue.

Willem resumed pacing. "We gave him his gold. Why would he do this? He couldn't know about you in the tree and even if he did, this took planning."

Maru sat and chewed the end of his unlit wood pipe. Saskia twisted a strand of hair around her finger.

*If they had all the answers they didn't act like it.*

Maru drew in a breath of air like it was smoke. "When did they have a chance to infect everyone?"

More memories lined up in Fin's head. He tried to work events backwards. He rewound until he got to when Gagnon arrived. "Their funeral ceremony?"

"Not all poisons or sicknesses have to be eaten," Maru held up his palm.

Fin remembered the slick goop. "That stuff they kept putting on their hands? No, that was hand sanitizer, they used that to *prevent* infection. I guess they thought they might catch something from your people."

Maru held his gaze.

"Wait. What if that stuff wasn't sanitizer? What if it had the disease in it instead?" Fin smacked himself in the head.

Maru smiled gently. "Then you are in good company. We all touched them, didn't we?"

Now Fin stood and moved as best he could while avoiding Willem's pacing bulk. "But if they didn't steal your medicine, they must have already been immune. That takes time to build up. If that's true, then you're right, Willem. This was planned in advance."

Something didn't make sense. "You're certain Gagnon or Stephon didn't swipe any of the drug? Do they even know it exists?"

A voice at the hut doorway answered. "It wasn't the drug. Even if they knew about it, it has to be made fresh." Hua stepped inside and held up his hands. The palms and fingertips were bloody and raw.

# Chapter 22

*Maru's Hut*

Fin tried to say he was sorry but Hua cut him off. "I almost fell a few times last night harvesting the Silverstar. We nearly exhausted our supply and it will be months before enough grows back for everyone."

"You were climbing on those rocks, sick as you were?" Fin tried to envision performing anything like that in the out of body state he'd been in.

Hua gave him a quizzical look. "Of course not."

"How'd you avoid getting sick like the rest?" Fin gestured to the others.

Hua glanced past Fin at his father, who shrugged.

"You purged." Hua pointed at Fin.

"So I'm told. And it cured me. I got that."

"No, you only got part. Once you purge you don't get sick again. Ever."

"Ever?" Fin's mind began to race. "None of you got sick at all? Even after they slathered that shit all over everyone?"

Saskia stared at the floor. "No. Only those who hadn't purged got sick."

"So none of the children…"

"Right."

Too many thoughts swarmed him. "And you're positive Gagnon had no way of knowing about the immunity or whatever the right word is for it."

Willem spoke. "We're sure."

"Then we've got a bigger problem."

"What's that?" Hua said.

"That means Gagnon isn't just a psycho, but that he was attempting to exterminate the entire island population."

"But he has his gold." Willem said.

"No. He has some of it. He wants it all. Which means he and his friends will be back to take it. Then they'll plan to disappear after pulling this mass murder. Does this sound like something Thibaux would try?"

Willem shook his head. "Never. We've known him for many years. He's corrupt but timid."

"Gagnon's coming back?" Hua glowered.

"I'd bet my just saved life on it." Fin said.

\* \* \*

An hour later Gert joined them inside Maru's hut.

"How's the *Verdragen*?" Willem asked.

Gert scratched his beard. He was sweaty and filthy but like the others, showed no sign of illness. "She's intact but the bow is buried. We might have a chance at high tide if we have enough people to dig out the sides to get water around the bow. I think once the props are clear I may be able to back it out."

"As soon as we're done here we'll put every able body on freeing the ship." Willem looked at Maru.

"Yes. We can make some shovels."

"Even boards will do." Gert said. "We have plenty on the ship."

Fin ran his fingers through his hair and tried to remember the last time he'd bathed. "That's good news. Now tell him about Gagnon."

They filled Gert in on what they figured out about the attack.

166

Gert remained still but his face flushed deep red. "So, what do the rest of you want to do?" He spoke with an eerie calm.

Hua answered immediately. "We kill him."

"How, exactly?" Fin tried to keep his own voice level.

"He thinks we're all dead. I'll break the news to him." Hua smacked his hands together and winced at the pain.

"Hua, he's a killer…"

"Don't you think we all know that? My son is dead in that cave, not yours!" Spit flew from Hua's mouth.

"I *do* know. And I'm with you but we have to plan this out. We only get one shot at this." Fin said.

Gert stepped over to stand with Hua. He looked at Fin. "Boy, have you ever killed anyone?"

"No." Fin said.

"Or you?" Gert jabbed Hua in the shoulder.

"That won't stop me. You think I'll hesitate to get that bastard?" Hua refused to step back.

"Neither will Gagnon. How's your trigger finger?" Gert grabbed Hua's hands. "And when was it you learned to shoot a rifle? At that fancy school?"

Hua pressed his lips together.

"You think Gagnon will just let you walk up to him and club him over the head?"

"There are other ways. We kill boar. He's another kind of pig." Hua said.

Fin raised his shirt and poked at his own belly. "I don't think the purge makes us bulletproof. Am I right?"

Willem rubbed his face. "But, we have guns, too."

Gert nodded. "We do this my way. I can form a welcome party from my crew. We all know how to shoot."

Fin saw Maru watching him and wondered why the chief was so quiet. The stakes couldn't be higher.

Willem jumped on the idea. "Okay, that's good."

Fin thought of a man grasping for a lifeline.

Gert pointed at Maru. "You and your people can fade back into the jungle and wait. This can be over quickly."

Maru said nothing. The silence grew and the tension squeezed down on Fin's chest.

Hua looked ready to explode. "Not me. You teach me to shoot. I want Gagnon."

"Stay out of it. You aren't trained."

"You're absolutely right, Gert." Fin said. "Do it your way and it will be over quickly."

"Ya."

"You'll all be dead two minutes after contact."

"You think Gagnon's the one who is bulletproof then?" Gert gave Fin a dismissive wave that caused the tension inside Fin's chest to squeeze the breath out of him.

"Look, damn it! I've seen these people at work up close. I've even gone into battle as a tag-along."

Hua and Saskia stared at him. Hua had heard some war stories from him, but he'd always given the tame versions, never the one he was about to share.

"You know Gagnon that well?" Gert's eyes narrowed.

"Not Gagnon specifically. I mean ruthless commandos in an outlaw war zone." Fin wanted a drink or ten about now. "Saskia, remember I told you I hoped to make a difference with my pictures?"

"Yes."

"That was true, as far as it went. I also wanted a Pulitzer." He considered his audience's background. "That's one of the most respected awards in my field. I was ready to do almost anything."

"Like running into battle without a weapon?" Willem said.

"Kind of. I was allowed to tag along with a group of rebels on the condition I didn't show their faces. I covered mine too since I didn't want to be associated with them in case I was recognized by their enemy."

"You weren't taking sides?" Saskia said.

"No. Both sides of this warlord clash were vicious. Unfortunately, being in the middle means getting shot at by everyone. So I thought I'd be safer if went in deep with this group."

"So they taught you to fight?" Gert folded his arms and Fin understood the man's impatience. But if he didn't establish his credibility Gert was going to get them all killed.

"Not as a soldier, but as a survivor. We were on a long recon mission to investigate reports of a small squad of killers brought from the outside."

"How many were you?" Hua asked.

"Ten. And I got to know them enough that they trusted me. They shared some tricks to stay alive in the jungle. I'm not that bad in the wild. I learned the difference between just surviving and living through being hunted."

"Did you ever find this other group?" Gert sounded skeptical.

"No."

"We're wasting time." He turned toward the door. "I have a ship to free."

"*They* found us. I was toward the back of our column." Fin noticed out of the corner of his eye that Gert stopped, but mostly he stared through the walls of the hut and found himself back in the Angolan jungle.

"Classic ambush. One of their guys must have scouted us and they set a trap." Fin felt his hands start to shake and pressed them against his legs. "I heard our first guy yell out and there was an explosion." He could see the fan of blood reach back to the line of men.

"I remember thinking 'Get down!', but my legs wouldn't move. The man behind me, Kenny, shoved me down. Then I thought he dove onto my back." Fin's mouth felt parched and he took a sip from a water skin.

"Gunfire blasted away from the front and sides. Very little return fire from our guys. Kenny wouldn't get off me and when I rolled out from under him I saw the top of his head was gone."

"Jezus mina!" Saskia shook her head.

"Just as the last of my group got cut down, a grenade landed among the bodies and rolled right under my nose."

"A dud?" Gert didn't look smug anymore.

"Dud, my ass. All I remember is grabbing it and flinging it back where it came from. I felt as much as heard the thing explode."

"Then what?" Willem said.

"I ran like hell deep into the jungle."

Saskia wiped her hand on her pants. "What about the others?"

"Nobody else lived through that barrage. It was a miracle I didn't get hit."

"Kenny saved your life." Gert said.

Fin nodded. "They chased me for two days. I pulled every trick I learned and made a few up on my own, but several times they got close enough for me to catch a glimpse or hear them, talking. White men, speaking French."

"Gagnon?" Doubt crept into Gert's voice again.

"I don't think so but if he knew some of the men chasing me it wouldn't surprise me. There's not an endless supply of ice-cold mercenaries."

"How did you get away for good?"

"I got lucky."

"It doesn't sound like it was luck," Saskia said.

"Well, I knew I couldn't lead them straight back to the rebel camp. I took a winding route but they still followed my trail. In the end I had to lay booby traps to slow them and reach a river where I ditched them for good."

Saskia reached over to him and gripped his hand. Fin returned the squeeze.

"Maybe you do know a thing or two." Fin could tell this was a huge concession for Gert. "But we'll be the ones doing the ambushing."

"I agree, but you have to let me help you."

"How? I told you we know how to shoot. You might be surprised how long we've been using our rifles."

Fin forced himself to be patient. Gert was the key and he wore stubbornness like a badge of pride.

"I'm sure you do. But do you think Gagnon knows what you have?"

"All our rifles are proven in battle. They can still kill a Frenchman."

Fin thought about the bullet hole in Julien.

"Gagnon and his men are hardened commandos. They live and breathe ambushes. I learned to avoid them but that's not always possible. The key is to do the unexpected. He knows the capabilities of, what do you have, the M1 Garand and Enfield?"

"Also some Krag's and a couple '03 Springfields."

Fin held his hand up. "I get the picture. Those are vintage weapons. Deadly, sure, but can you hit a man at a thousand yards? Maybe further? I promise they can."

Gert scratched his beard. "You have a better idea?"

Fin took a seat and leaned his elbows on the table. "Maybe. Gagnon got his hands on a bioweapon. I don't know how, but that means he can probably bring any weapon imaginable to the fight."

"Is that the good news?" Willem said.

"No. But we can use it." Fin leaned back in the chair. "I'm no expert on them, but even the worst diseases don't kill off everyone exposed. We can assume he intended to knock out most but not all resistance for when he comes back. Also, he'll want to wait long enough to let the disease eat through the population."

"How long?" Hua said. Maru had found some gel and bandages and was tending to Hua's damaged hands. Hua didn't even react to the tugging and pulling.

"I'm not sure. A few days at least, I'd think. Plus, I bet he'll come by boat. That might buy us time."

"Why by boat?" Gert said.

"Two reasons. First, if he's coming to loot the island in a one-shot deal he'll need more capacity than the seaplane. Second, if he's worried about survivors, then he may want to bring more friends than just the handful that will fit on the plane."

Willem jumped in. "If he thinks his plague is so strong why would he want to bring so many people?"

"Good point." Something bothered Fin. "But more workers help to load gold as well as hunt down stragglers."

"What does he care if we can't stop him from taking what he wants?" Saskia asked.

Fin remembered how isolated these people lived. "Witnesses. What Gagnon's done even with the immunity for many of you, is a crime against humanity. If he is caught and the world discovers what he and his people did, he'll rot in jail the rest of his life."

"He deserves worse." Hua said.

Fin thought of all the bodies and Ruru's laugh in his head. "Yeah. He does."

The thought nagging Fin broke to the surface. "I just thought of another possibility."

"What?" Gert said.

"What if he comes by seaplane expecting light resistance and intends to load the gold onto the *Verdragen*?"

"I'll sink it first." Gert said instantly.

"It is already sunk." Maru finished Hua's bandage.

Fin nodded. "I think we should leave it that way."

"What?" Gert said. "The tide is coming in."

"You said yourself you'll need help to get it out. It'll wait for you."

"It could be further damaged…"

"We have to take the chance." Fin spoke as fast as the thoughts entered his mind. "Gagnon expects a devastated population but there are many more of us left. That's our edge."

"And?" Gert said.

"And we need him in close. What do you think will happen if he gets here and sees life going on more or less as before? He'll either back off or change his attack."

"Snipers again?"

"Or worse. Helicopters? Bombs? Who knows? He's all in here."

"All in?" Saskia asked.

"Totally committed. After what happened, he has to finish what he started. And the other advantage we have is that he can't call in the French Navy and Air Force."

"I thought he could do whatever he wanted." Willem said.

"Within limits. He'll want to bring just enough force to get the job done and steal the gold. Any more increases his risk and dilutes his profit." Something else nagged Fin.

"Now what?"

"We have to keep most people away from the shore. I don't know how long before he'll watch the island. Maybe he's already started."

Gert spoke. "What is the point if they use satellites and other things?"

Fin nodded. "We can't defeat a modern military in a straight-on fight. But that's the good news. The people in charge of those things are not in the business of launching weapons of mass destruction. Gagnon is a rogue operation even inside the corrupt fiefdom this Thibaux dude has been running." Fin felt disbelief well up, as if to protect his mind, and recalled the stench from the cave. He couldn't have dreamed up those smells if he'd tried.

"So we have a chance?" Willem said.

# Chapter 23

"No luck on the surveillance drones." Gagnon deleted the encrypted message off his laptop.

"Any good news?" Stephon said.

Gagnon took a deep breath and forced his voice to sound calm. "Yes. There won't be any satellite coverage either."

"That means we'll have to go in blind." Stephon said.

"And there won't be any prying eyes watching us work," Gagnon said. "It shouldn't take long if the virus did its job." He glanced over to Jean-Paul who sat at the kitchen table deep in thought.

Stephon seemed to get the point. "Oui. Of course. But we only have twenty men to work with. If the germs failed..."

"You are alive because the vaccine worked." Jean-Paul snapped. "If you need further assurance that the virus is potent you should ask Dr. LaRaue."

"Is that supposed to be funny?" Stephon glared at Jean-Paul.

"Stop it, both of you. The doctor was our biggest loose end and Stephon was careful to make it appear accidental," Gagnon said.

"What about Thibaux?" Stephon asked.

"Non. That fool will be confused at first and then frightened. The longer we are missing, the better he will feel and he will do nothing to aid any investigation for fear of what would happen to him. He is exactly where we need him." Gagnon tamped down the frustration he felt at all the questions.

Jean-Paul checked his watch. "I have to go to the ship now. Everything is in place?"

Gagnon pointed to the refrigerator in the kitchen. "All but the vaccine. Three days will be enough?"

Jean Paul nodded. "It should. I'll have long enough to spot any adverse reactions."

"Keep your official paperwork close by. I don't expect any interference by the navy, but use my name if they interdict. Whatever you do, *don't* let them board," Gagnon said.

"Monsieur, we've all worked operations before, n'est pas?" Jean-Paul walked to the refrigerator.

"Not like this."

Jean-Paul took the satchel out of the refrigerator and let himself out. Gagnon and Stephon waited in silence until they heard the car start and pull away.

"How long did you give the serum in the microwave?" Stephon asked.

"Each dose got ninety seconds."

Stephon sucked in air. "I thought we said two minutes."

"It will be enough. The serum changed color at two minutes. Jean-Paul is loyal but he is no actor. If he doesn't believe in the stuff you know those men won't."

"I hope you're right. Are you sure the island will still be hot?"

"It should be." Gagnon shrugged off the concern. "It's all variables. That's what we train for. My question is, are *you* truly prepared?"

"For what?"

"To be rich the rest of your life."

# Chapter 24

*Hoku, three days later*

Green tunnels. That's what Fin kept thinking about while the survivors carved a maze of paths through the jungles leading to the interior of the island. They wouldn't be visible from the air, as no trees were downed to make the inroads.

"Come on." Saskia led the way. Fin and she had supervised moving vital supplies through the network of paths. He had to admit the islanders were amazing at disguising the entrances.

They exited one new path and moved along an old route with a dirt path. "Slow down. Hua said the surprises are nearly done."

"I understand his code. We all do." Saskia didn't break her stride.

The entrances to the paths were brilliant, but Fin knew the best operators wouldn't be fooled. In fact, they were counting on it. But despite the old lessons that had come back to him, Fin still would have difficulty seeing some of the openings in the dense growth if not for the dead tree snails fixed to the trunks. One fist-sized snail marked a "safe" path, two meant it was rigged. If the snail was moving, it was no path at all.

Saskia picked another established path, not part of the new network.

"Where are we going?"

"I told you. You need to see something." She smiled at him and he shrugged. One more mystery.

Eventually they reached a clearing by a secluded pool under a small waterfall emanating from the side of the mountain. Lush greenery surrounded the area, save for a patch of blue sky. The stones around the pool were covered in a soft spongy moss.

"This is incredible."

"Another gift from the island. Look in the water."

Fin stepped onto the flat rock. The moss covered the surface in a thick firm carpet. He peered at the water but the dark rock made it appear black. He took off his boots and socks and let his feet rest in the soft moss. He touched a toe to the surface and found the water cool but not cold. The surface rippled steadily from the falls.

"I can't see anything."

"Look closer. You have to stare at it."

"Ookay." He sat and rolled his pant legs up and stuck his feet in. Bliss. "Am I going to see my future?" The idyllic scene made it easy to forget the coming battle, if only for a moment.

"Keep looking." Saskia said.

Fin started to turn around to say something but all he saw was a white blur and he felt a foot plant on his back and shove him into the water.

It was deeper than he expected, and he started to try to kick to the surface when he heard a splash and felt his wrist get seized and he was tugged further under. All he could see was a light colored figure and he realized it was Saskia, and she'd taken off all her clothes.

He followed her under a low bridge of stone and they popped up behind the waterfall. She was laughing like a little girl.

She guided him to the rock behind the falls and it, too, was covered with a blanket of the same soft, spongy moss.

He held onto the side and looked at her sparking blue eyes, her body luminous under the water. "Are you sure about this?"

She wrapped her arms around his neck, pulled him close and kissed him hard.

\* \* \*

*Seaplane, 20 miles west of Hoku*

"Not too late to land further away." Stephon's nervousness was a persistent irritant Gagnon fought to ignore. The guy would always get keyed up before operations but came up cool when the bullets started to fly.

"So what if they see us? If they show themselves, so much the better. I don't remember seeing any Stinger missiles when we were there, do you?"

"Non." Stephon stared out the window. "Shall I radio the *Fanfaron?*"

The steel-hulled converted tugboat should have been close by now. "Maintain silence. We'll see it soon enough."

"I doubt they have scanners on Hoku."

"They are a bunch of treacherous bastards. Don't let the glint of gold blind you, mon ami." Gagnon could see the outline of the island in the distance now.

\* \* \*

"Merde." Stephon whispered. "Where's their rust bucket, the *Verdragen?*"

Gagnon banked the plane to get a better view of the New Cape compound. The dock was plain to see from several miles out but no sign of their container ship.

"The survivors panicked?" Gagnon frowned. "Where would they go? Would they not try the radio? If they'd reached any navy vessels at sea I'd know by now."

"Another island?" Stephon suggested.

There were dozens. "Where else but Tahiti has medical facilities that could handle their needs?"

"If the germs worked as intended, there's no such place."

180

Gagnon's stomach clenched. "And if they are contagious, they could wipe another island out."

"We have to find them first."

Sweat erupted on Gagnon's forehead. His mind raced.

Stephon reached for the microphone. "Looks like we're breaking radio silence."

Gagnon covered Stephon's hand with his own. "Let's circle the island first, perhaps we'll see more survivors. Then call in and take care what you say over the air."

Stephon shot Gagnon a withering look. Gagnon didn't care. They hadn't even landed and their plans spun out of control.

*If this bug got out…*

They got closer to the island. The volcanic mountain loomed and he could see more details on the beach. Stephon swept the shoreline with binoculars.

"What's that?" Gagnon straightened the plane out and pointed. "Mon Dieu, is that a bunker?"

Near the dock Gagnon saw a pile of sandbags and a makeshift window built into the wall.

A single rile barrel poked out of the opening.

"Exactement." Stephon said.

Gagnon banked the aircraft away. He wasn't overly concerned about a single rifle this far away but there could be others and they had enough to worry about. "See anything else?"

"I see signs of old fires in the common area where they had that dinner, but no smoke or other movement."

"If they expected rescuers would they come out and wave?" Gagnon asked.

"Not if they couldn't."

"Or if they *were* expecting invaders." Gagnon took a heading along the shore. "Let's see how the monkeys on the other side are faring."

Minutes later, the plane rounded the island and the village beach and Gagnon erupted in laughter. "You were right, Stephon! They landed on an island."

Gagnon feathered the throttle to bring the craft just above stall speed so they could get a lingering look at the beached ship.

"They must have been running at flank, look at how buried that bow is." Stephon whistled. "Wait, I see a body on the deck. It's a mess. Probably birds got at it."

The relief flooded through Gagnon with an intensity he'd never admit.

Stephon continued. "There's an even bigger fire pit. I can't be sure, but I bet there are remains in there."

"Any movement?" Gagnon throttled up and increased airspeed to come around again.

"No. But we know those corpses didn't burn themselves."

"Oui, there are survivors."

"And they seem to be expecting us." Stephon added.

"Yes, but most important, whoever they are, they are still on Hoku." The radio crackled with static. Three bursts, a pause then three bursts.

"The *Fanfaron* is on station." Stephon keyed their mike in reply to let their friends know they were in range.

# Chapter 25

*New Cape*

Fin and Saskia held hands while they walked down the path toward town and her hut. His wet shirt and pants still clung to his body and despite the warm temperatures he was more than happy to take her up on her offer of a dry set of homespun clothes.

He wondered if she'd try to jump his bones again. She wasn't shy about what she wanted, that was for sure. Not that he minded.

"Saskia, I should have said something but we kind of got caught up in things and…"

"Is that what we did?"

"No, that was amazing. I'm just, well, I'm usually more careful."

She cocked her head at him and he had no idea if she was teasing him or really didn't understand. "I mean there's no pharmacy around."

"But you aren't sick." She pulled him in close and kissed him. "Not anymore."

Was she messing with him?

He gently stepped back. "No, I mean you don't have any," he came up empty for the Dutch word. "Any, condoms. You know?" He pantomimed rolling one down a finger.

He expected a laugh or at least more confusion but her gaze dropped and a cloud passed over her features. When she looked at him he saw deep sadness in her eyes.

"That's not a concern. I'm unable to…"

He felt an inch tall.

"I'm sorry. I didn't mean to upset you." He was glad she let him hug her. He could feel her heart race through his shirt.

"I should be used to it by now. Sometimes the reminders can be cruel."

They walked in silence until they neared the deserted New Cape outskirts. "I should have checked with your father if they needed anything from town."

Now she smiled for real.

"What?"

"And what would you say if he asked why your clothes are wet?"

"The truth, that you pushed me in the water. And what if he asks why your clothes are still dry?"

She laughed and he pulled her in for another kiss.

When they separated she looked serious again. "What?"

"At my place. I need to show you something."

* * *

It was strange to hear the little town so quiet. Even with relatively few people in total, the place usually buzzed with activity. Now all he heard were birds and the lap of the water against the nearby dock wall.

Fin half-hoped this was Saskia's way of getting him alone at her place. She walked right back to the bedroom on the other side of the tin wall. She returned with a set of dry clothes for Fin and held the picture of her ancestor.

Saskia turned her back and stared at the picture while Fin took the cue to change into them. He was confused. "Thanks."

She turned back and held out the photo to him.

"Funny, that's one of the last things I can remember clearly before the sickness kicked in hard." He took the picture and glanced at. "The first Saskia, that's what you said, isn't it?"

She nodded and her eyes filled with tears. "And that is true."

"What's wrong?" He let the picture in his hand rest at his side and he stepped closer to her. He grasped her hand in his free one. "You're shaking."

"I didn't think this would be so difficult."

"What?"

"Look again. And wait here." She pulled her hand back and went back into the bedroom.

She closed the sheet so he knew not to follow. He could hear clothes rustle.

He felt a tinge of irritation. He looked at the photo again to humor her. "Spitting image. But that still doesn't..."

Saskia pulled the sheet back and emerged wearing the same skirt and white blouse, the match was so close she could have stepped out of the picture.

"Wow." Fin looked at the material and saw a few moth holes and fading in the skirt fabric. "Is that the original outfit?"

She nodded. "And the original owner."

"What do you mean?"

"I told you she was the first Saskia. She is also the only Saskia."

*Was she nuts?*

"So your name is something else and you go by Saskia to honor her memory?"

Now she laughed, but the tears came back. "I know this will be difficult to accept. I should have told you earlier."

"Told me what?"

"It's the purge. It changed us. And left us the same."

"What does you playing dress up have to do with the purge?"

185

She duplicated the pose from the picture.

"You're saying you *are* her? Like reincarnation?"

"You have to die to be reincarnated. I haven't done that yet. Maybe, never. I said the purge changed us. The first ones had a hard time believing it. Some couldn't cope with it."

Fin smiled. "So you said that this photo is from 1900, right?" Judging by the shot and the condition of the antique paper, that was plausible.

"Yes."

"And if I'm following you, you're telling me that that's you in 1900?"

She nodded.

"I was never very strong in math, but the young lady in that picture was what, twenty at the most?"

"Fifteen."

"Right. That would make you," Fin lost count wondering what the punchline was.

"One hundred twenty-eight." She looked dead serious. "Next month."

He could almost feel the number bounce off his skull. "And the rest of the people, your father, Gert, and so on. All past the century mark?"

Part of him waited for the hidden camera crew to pop out of the woodwork thanking him for being a good sport.

"Most, but not all. Everyone who didn't get sick had purged earlier. But not all of them were originals."

"Originals? As in original colonists?"

"Yes."

Fin could see in her eyes how desperate she was to have him believe.

"Hang on. I've seen their graves." He held up the photo. "Including hers."

He began to wonder if she'd cracked under the stress of the situation. Gagnon's threat was real enough.

But so was that bioweapon. Whatever the purge was or wasn't, the crazy shit cured him. He'd never felt better.

"Father's idea. The rest of us didn't think it would work but nobody ever figured it out." She smiled. "You saw graves but no bodies."

"Digging up corpses is considered rude in some cultures."

She ignored his quip. "The graves contain our future, not our past."

"Riddles now?"

She shook her head. "Sorry. We shroud ourselves in secrecy. It's almost second nature in the presence of outsiders." She took a deep breath. "We keep each person's share of the gold we mine in the gravesites. The cemetery is expected over time by the United Nations staff. We complete the narrative and play the role of quaint descendants."

"And you keep the same names to honor the past?"

"That was my idea. I like my name," she said.

"Don't take this personally, but this is a little hard to swallow."

"We argued about how much to reveal to you. None of us planned for any of these things to happen."

*That* certainly seemed true. "But if you had this ability to prevent death why did so many get sick? And the children? Why wouldn't you protect them, of all people?"

She stared at the wood floor. "We couldn't. Once you purge, you don't get older. Would you want to be a young child forever?"

"You're saying it stops growth and maturation?"

"Yes."

"How?"

"We don't know how it does these things. Only Maru knows the recipe for transforming the Silverstar, and even he doesn't know how it works, just what it does."

"But there were adults who got sick. What about Johannes and his wife or fiancée?"

Saskia stared at the floor and spoke in a soft voice. "They were waiting."

"Waiting for what?"

"To have children first."

Fin thought about Saskia's reaction when he'd brought up condoms. "The purge makes you infertile?"

She lifted her head. "And sterile. I'm sorry."

He was about to ask for what when he remembered that even if she *was* out of her mind, whatever the situation, he was now part of it. "You mean me too?"

"We never knew until later. All of a sudden there were no more children. Same for the Hokutian villagers."

"So where did the children I saw come from?"

188

"Sometimes we allow carefully chosen outsiders to join our group. If they wish after they have had their children and want to purge, they become part of us."

"What if they change their mind?"

"That is…rare. We're highly selective."

He noticed she hadn't quite answered the question. But so many new ones filled his head he was having trouble picking through them.

"So this Fountain of Youth you've discovered…"

She cut him off. "It's not that. It doesn't make you younger. You just won't get older."

"Or reproduce. So it's more like some sort of evolutionary pause?"

She thought about that. "Darwin's Pause. That sounds right."

Fin still didn't know what to believe. "You really think you're immortal?"

He saw terror on her face. "No! You must never say that. It's the most dangerous thought of all."

"Why?"

"You won't age or get sick but you can die in any other way. You can drown or fall to your death. You'll get cut and bleed as always. If you're shot you can be killed like anyone else."

"I see." What she said either made more sense or gave a plausible cover to her delusion.

Another thought flashed in his mind. "Wait. If Ruru wasn't purged, and he was Hua's natural child, how did Hua get his wife pregnant? Ruru was only ten. If Maru is so old how is that possible?"

"You'll have to ask him. I made him a promise."

"I sure will." Fin was going to ask as many people as he could. Was Saskia out of her mind or was there some sort of mass hysteria?

He fought the third possibility. *What if it was true?*

Then they heard the airplane.

They dashed out of the hut. Fin took Saskia by the hand and they crouched behind a tree. He could see only part of the sky but the sound of the engine was unmistakable.

The sound rose and fell and Fin could picture the aircraft banking and turning to scan the village and area.

"They won't see us here."

"I thought we'd have more time." Saskia said.

After a few minutes they heard the plane sounds fade away.

"He's leaving?" she said.

"Scoping out the rest of the island, gotta be. We need to get the word to the others." Before Fin could think about where the nearest scout sat hidden he heard a whooping bird call, soon answered and ringing out in several directions.

"They know."

Fin didn't want to say how relieved he felt. Part of him had worried late into the nights that they wouldn't take enough precautions in their thirst for vengeance.

* * *

Back in her hut Saskia dug through a trunk in her bedroom. She took out a large bowie knife and held it out to Fin.

"But I didn't bring you anything." He couldn't wait to get out of there. "Sorry, I say stupid crap when I'm nervous."

Fin heard the whooping calls again in the distance.

190

"I wish they wouldn't over do that. These guys are…" Then he heard an engine again. But it was different. He ran to the entrance and peered out from the blanket-door.

If the wind had been blowing the other way he might have missed the sound of the little outboard. "A boat. Someone's coming ashore."

"Let's get to the jungle."

Fin nodded but then he heard a second motor. "Wait. There's more. They're going to be keyed on this town." Even inside the hut he felt exposed.

Saskia had other ideas. She vanished back to her bedroom. A moment later she reappeared and took a low position on the floor with a huge revolver in her hands. It looked like a cowboy pistol on steroids. Fin shook his head and put his finger to his lips but saw she was playing it cool.

Fin peeked out the door and scanned the dock and bay for signs of craft. He hadn't heard the plane in a while.

From his spot by the door he could just make out the far edge of the common and the wide path leading to the dock. So far, no movement. He could see the second of the decoy bunkers. They'd made up scarecrow figures complete with old defunct rifles to hide in the bunker. Saskia and another lady painted carved wooden heads that looked real from a distance.

Fin had dubbed the two "Bert and Ernie." Seemed funnier when invasion was still just a theory.

"You don't have another pistol, do you?" He spoke in a whisper.

"No. Do you want this one?"

Fin knew how to use a gun but it never was his thing. "If you can handle it you keep it, but last resort, okay? They'll have rifles."

191

She nodded. "I don't hear any motors."

She was right. He strained his ears for anything outside of the gentle surf. Even the real birds had piped down.

He saw a puff of dust drift out of the second bunker and heard a distant crack. "Rifle." Another from a different spot rang out. "A second one. Not too close."

"The decoys?" Saskia said.

"I think so. I bet Bert and Ernie have holes in them now. We need to scoot. The goons'll probably come in now."

"Okay."

Fin didn't think the snipers would have a sightline this far into town but that wouldn't last. He started out the door and heard the outboard motors again.

Saskia climbed down to the sand and Fin debated which path to take. The wide lane that led to the cemetery was faster but was likely where the invaders would go. It also led to the mine.

Saskia headed for it and Fin had to call out. "Wait, not that way." She spun with the gun in her hand. Fin ducked and pointed toward the slender path. That way led to the jungle but first past the town and the dock.

Frying pan or fire? It wouldn't matter if they didn't hustle.

They crouch-ran along the path. It wound along the back of the development but forced them to cross some open spaces.

They paused. Fin noticed the small motors had stopped. Except one. Now he could see a Zodiac raft on the rocks to one side of the sea wall on the dock.

The bow pointed at the sky and the stern wriggled among the rocks like some sort of animal with an itchy ass. The engine screamed when the propeller popped out of the water and then dropped to grind on the stones.

"They crashed?" Saskia whispered.

Where were the people? The boat was empty and the throttle stuck open. "Whoever was on it got off first." Fin tore his gaze from the distraction of the lone Zodiac dancing itself to death on the rocks and scanned the areas near the dock. "By the dock." He saw a figure in a wetsuit creep up the ladder. He looked farther to the left and... damn! "Two more on the left edge of town." He saw the black glint of a submachine gun. No sniper weapon, it still had all the range it needed for where they crouched.

Saskia raised her revolver.

"Stop," Fin hissed. "We'll draw fire from the others. They haven't seen us yet."

"We can't cross to the jungle without being seen."

"I know." Fin was tempted to take his chances. No, those rafts looked like they'd hold six people and there was at least one more Zodiac out there.

Now Fin heard the whooping bird calls again and they were nearby. Up in the trees. "Why'd they send scouts so close?"

Saskia shrugged. "Gert's men."

"Don't they see what's out there?" Fin thought he heard some new distant engine sounds. "Can you tell them to shut up?"

Saskia shook her head. "They won't listen to me."

Now he saw the guy on the dock sprawled out prone on the boards like a beached sea lion but this one had a long gun with a scope. He propped up the weapon and tracked the muzzle left and right.

Men in green camouflage uniforms climbed over the dock wall and scrambled in pairs down the length of the dock. They appeared to be carrying assault rifles.

A couple more frogmen joined the first two Fin had spotted on the edge of town. They stood back to back and covered the entrance to town and the jungle on one side and the rest of New Cape from the other direction.

Fin and Saskia would be in the line of fire.

Shitty odds at seventy five yards. Fin reconsidered. These were pros. No odds at all.

"What do we do?" Saskia looked terrified. Fin felt the same way but fought to control his emotion. Panic was death.

Now men on the dock moved back and began hauling on ropes. Fin guessed another raft must be out of sight against the dock wall.

He saw a wood box about the size of a foot locker plop onto the dock. The soldiers pried it open and pulled out a metal tube with a base plate and legs to form a tripod.

"Crap."

"What?"

"A mortar." He pantomimed a lobbing motion. "They can level the town with a few of those."

Fin wasn't the only one to recognize what they were setting up. He heard the bird calls go out and from the tree line to his left he heard a couple shots ring out.

"Fools." Fin watched as one of the mortar men fall with a dark stain on his chest. The sniper got hit as well with one shot raking his shoulder and another taking off a chunk of his calf when he rolled to the side.

The frogmen started yelling in French and after a tiny pause began returning fire.

Fin heard more shots snap out from the left and then the chatter of automatic fire made it look like one treetop was being hit with an invisible weed whacker. Fin heard a short, all-too-human scream and a body fell from a hidden perch in one of the palms.

Sporadic fire now walked toward where a second Dwazen shooter had opened fire. Another shot rang came from the treetop and Fin heard an enemy Frenchman scream.

The men had scrambled into new positions and for an instant he saw a chance.

"Saskia, give me the gun." She handed it to him without hesitation. Fin looked and confirmed the old thing was loaded. It was an antique single-action piece and he cocked it.

*Careful, hair trigger.*

Instead of using it as intended, he gripped the barrel, keenly aware a loaded gun was aimed at him and reared back to fling the weapon like a tomahawk, deep into the huts of New Cape.

He felt an instant's gratification when the pistol discharged and the mercenaries pivoted in response to a new threat.

"Now!"

Fin and Saskia dashed across the thirty foot gap between the last structures and the entrance to the path leading to the jungle. Sand kicked up around them and bullets ventilated the nearby structures which offered concealment but scant cover.

Once they reached the path they kept low. Fin knew they needed to reach the thicker trees for any real protection. They scurried up the trail when a figure popped out. Fin saw feet and a rifle and nearly collided with Saskia, who let out a scream.

"Shhh!" Fin now saw it was Pieter, one of Gert's people and he was barefoot, carrying an old M1 Garand rifle.

He was also wounded.

"Come on. They're coming!" Fin said.

Pieter shook his head. He had a wild look in his eyes.

"You're hurt." Saskia said.

Pieter pointed at the blood patters visible on the white sand. "They'll find you if we stay together." He pulled out a rectangular en bloc clip of ammo and stuffed it into the rifle, letting the bolt slam home. "They'll find me no matter what."

Fin felt sick but the man was right. Those men would know all about following a blood trail.

"No, not without you." Saskia said.

Pieter glanced at Fin. "Trip wire around the first bend. Careful."

Fin nodded and whispered "Crazy bastard." Then he mouthed "Thank you."

Pieter blew a kiss at Saskia and winked at Fin. Then, holding his bleeding side with one hand and the heavy rifle in the other, raced off into the jungle.

"No!" Saskia tried to chase him and Fin grabbed her arm and forced her to duck with him. Several shots snapped at the nearby branches.

"We have to reach the others. He's gone. That was *his* decision."

The renewed gunfire broke through her determination and she wiped tears off her face. They scrambled toward the first bend.

After about ten seconds they heard a wild yell and a rifle shot. Now he heard voices near the entrance to the path.

He sprinted toward the turn nearly hit the vine barely visible in the sand, despite Pieter's warning. They hopped over it.

Fin heard another shout from Pieter and marveled at how much ground the man had covered through thick jungle, especially while wounded.

He wished he could hear if the others were chasing on the path but the sand muffled the soldiers' steps as it did their own. "C'mon. That may slow them down."

Saskia still looked like she wanted to double back and pick up Pieter.

"You'll only get yourself killed." Fin could see she understood but her emotion wasn't giving up easily.

"They'll pay."

"Damn right." Fin sprinted with her down the path. Soon they'd reach another new interior route where he knew the layout of the traps.

About a minute later they heard a cry of pain and Fin guessed that was the vine he'd almost stepped on.

Now he heard distant shots. Staccato bursts and then a string of booming shots that had to be the Garand. A pause then one long burst and silence.

*Thanks, man.*

# Chapter 26

*Seaplane, just outside of Hoku*

"Yes, damn it, break radio silence!" Gagnon snapped at Stephon. "This plane is making me seasick."

Gagnon wished that was the reason. The low powered radios the men used were deliberately short-ranged so they would have fewer concerns about their messages getting intercepted.

Even so, the dearth of communication was making the acid churn in his gut.

"Unit one. Wings six, to unit one." Stephon spoke into the portable unit.

After a long pause that Gagnon's imagination filled with all manner of calamities, they heard their first report since all the shooting started.

The facts were worse.

Ansel, the leader on the ground for the New Cape operation, came on.

"Oui, Six. Go ahead."

"Status?"

"Situation fluid. Four down and two being evacuated to the ship." The man yelled back.

Stephon blanched. Gagnon white-knuckled the steering yolk on the seaplane, then he snatched the microphone from Stephon. "Say again. Four of theirs down and two injured for us?"

Ansel replied, "No, sir. We got two of theirs but they opened up at the tree line. They got lucky and hit one of the long gunners."

Gagnon didn't believe in luck. "The ones in the bunkers?"

"Decoys, sir. We took out the targets but they were realistic dummies. We moved in closer and their snipers in the trees initiated contact."

"Numbers?" If that was the worst, maybe it wouldn't be so bad.

"Like I said, two enemy KIA. Sniper nests in the trees. We'll watch out for those."

"And?"

"Some light resistance in the town but we think they fell back. Not sure of numbers but we recovered an old handgun. Nothing else there but we spotted a man and woman running away. We decided to pull back from the main village to preserve our numbers. We still need to secure the village."

"Do it quickly."

"We pursued one of the snipers but my man reports the shooter led them into the jungle where he ambushed them. We lost one and the other was shot through the arm. He's out of the fight but expected to survive. Another pair tried to follow the couple."

"Tried?" Gagnon didn't like the sound of that.

"My fault sir. I spread the men too thin. One man triggered a booby trap."

"What kind?"

"Primitive…but effective. A simple whip trap. Poisoned spikes caught D'Arcy across the upper legs." A pause. "He didn't make it."

Damn. "The heavies?"

"Two units established on the dock. We're building a target and range list now."

"Ca va. Some good news."

"Yes, sir. Permission to secure the village?"

Gagnon ran through the options. "You said Bissette was down?"

"Yes sir."

"And the other long shooter?"

"Allard is fine. He's ashore now covering the mortars."

"Wait one." Gagnon made sure the mike was off. "What do you think?" He looked at Stephon. Now that the game was on he'd responded like the pro he was.

"We lost over half our combat strength."

"Oui. But we have the beachhead." Gagnon pointed out.

"If they were burning bodies, we hurt them with the preparatory strike last week. They can't cover the whole island. We can call back some of Delacroix's men when they're done mopping up the savages."

Gagnon rubbed his chin. "Or even before. We have to accept some stragglers may elude us. We just need to make sure we secure the town and the route to the mine or where they are hiding their bulk gold."

"We hauled those mortars all this way." Stephon said.

Gagnon nodded. "I would hate to have to dump them into the sea unfired."

\* \* \*

*Hoku, the* Islander *Village*

Thomas Delacroix lay prone along the rubber bow of the large Zodiak. He peered through the binoculars at the beach beyond the pounding surf. They'd planned on coming in fast but his group of ten commandos would need to be careful not to capsize one or both rafts. Each carried close to the raft's weight limit for gear but what he really needed were more decent men.

Damned Gagnon. He'd foisted thugs on him despite his misgivings. Delacroix should have insisted on bringing all of his own people.

"Anything?" Delacroix barked over his shoulder to the radioman, Perrin.

"Non. We'll have to backtrack to get a line of sight. That mountain blocks everything."

"Maybe it is full of gold." Delacroix half-joked. He'd keep that reward in mind and try to forget the task ahead. It was always this way until the first contact with the enemy. Incoming fire was a wonderful clarifier.

Would the other side have guns? Regardless, they'd killed Gagnon's men in cold blood, so it might not matter. They were bloodthirsty mongrels.

And his team? The men in the other boat looked drawn from the worst tribal conflicts and carried older AK-47s. Effective in hands willing to pull the trigger.

Gagnon's orders didn't require finesse. Take control of the grounded vessel. Clear out any opposition and ensure the locals didn't interfere with operations on the other side of the island.

He was the "B" team, in other words, and the personnel reflected the priority.

*Never mind.* "The tide will come in soon."

The second boat signaled and the short range radio hissed. "Go ahead." Delacroix heard Perrin say.

Perrin listened for a moment. "Sir, on the ship, movement."

Delacroix shifted his binoculars to the beached freighter. The stern moved slightly but the bow seemed truly stuck and the entire vessel canted to one side. Between wave breaks Delacroix could see the top of the ship's propellers.

He scanned the tilted deck and sure enough he could see a figure racing along the railing. A native. The dark-skinned savage ran to the stern deck and waved what looked like some sort of club in their direction.

The man wasn't wearing a shirt and appeared to have what amounted to a short grass skirt.

"I see him. Any others?"

"Cloutier says no. He's checking the tree line again."

Cloutier was a good man, with younger and sharper eyes than Delacroix's. If anyone could command the pirates in the other raft, it was him. "We can rule out body armor on this one." The scarring and decorations on the dark skin stood out even at this distance.

It gave him an idea. He turned and called to Lambert, an experienced hand at the helm. "Is the tide low enough to access the stern? They might not expect an approach from the sea."

The rest of the men grinned. Most had served in the worst hellholes Africa could conjure but they'd done some time snapping up ships off the coast of Somalia and pinning the subsequent murders on Islamic pirates.

Lambert used his own binoculars to scope their prospects. "Oui. If we approach the lee side the swells are less intense. If the men are quick that is." The crew in the cramped boat murmured their assent.

"And the welcoming party?" Delacroix got the laughter he expected, but had another thought. He turned to the men after signaling Lambert to make the approach.

Perrin spoke into the radio to the second raft and instructed them to provide cover for signs of resistance from the shore.

"Ca va. There could be others. This one doesn't appear armed other than that club, but that could be a trick. Don't put the boarding at risk, but if you can subdue him we can squeeze him for intel."

Delacroix didn't hold much hope. The native looked enraged hopping around on deck and he wasn't about to lose a man to a glorified cricket bat. He'd put the bastard down himself if he posed a threat.

A few minutes later they were all hunkered down while Lambert opened the throttle and the Zodiac bounced along the water. They gripped taut ropes that ran the length of the craft. Delacroix glanced up and down the port and starboard sides to make sure everyone was holding on but didn't have their arms wrapped under the rope. If they capsized, the twist would snap the bones like twigs and the careless troop would drown in agony.

He needn't have worried about his guys. The men were pros. The others looked like they'd been lashed to the raft. Too late to warn them if anything went wrong.

Delacroix knew he was getting too old to be out in the world playing mercenary but one last mission would put paid to a life of adventure.

Lambert hit the surf at full speed and the wave dropped faster than they expected. For an instant the entire zodiac was airborne and he heard the whine of props in the air. At the same time, the bow rose, pushed by the onrushing wind until all anyone could see was sky. For a split second Delacroix was sure they would topple backwards right into the worst of the breaking waves.

No. The bow dropped again and smacked the sea with a drenching splash.

The ship, *Verdragen*, came up fast. Once the raft settled, the two lead men were already preparing the tactical line throwers.

The devices always reminded Delacroix of a short-barreled shotgun with a large three-pronged hook protruding from the muzzle. A line on a spindle gave it a weaponized fishing rod look.

When the Zodiac pulled alongside, the men fired and dual blasts sent the hooks into the air. After seeing these two board tankers he wasn't surprised they hit the mark and the hooks held fast on the railings.

From this angle Delacroix couldn't see the deck but he held his carbine to his shoulder ready to fire at anyone trying to unhook the pair of metal claws.

Nobody popped into view and soon the two men scrambled up the side with submachine guns on slings ready for action as soon as they reached the top.

This was always the tough part. They knew the guy topside must have seen or heard the hooks. The question was what he'd do next.

When the pair had hauled themselves just below the deck, they pulled out flashbang grenades, flung them onto the deck and covered their ears. At the concussive sounds they both seized the bottom rung of the rail while using their legs on the line to prevent falling. One flopped onto the deck with his weapon in hand, and the other vaulted the rail and disappeared from Delacroix's sight.

He knew the drill. Even as the next two men began to ascend, the first set covered the deck with their compact sub-machine guns. He strained his ears for the muffled sound of suppressed 9mm fire but soon one of the men called out, then peeked over the side to signal that the area was secure.

When Delacroix reached the top along with Perrin, Lambert gunned the engine toward shore. One of the second group on deck was armed with an AK and he covered the raft while it landed.

Delacroix said a quick prayer to gods he'd long ago forsaken, that there wouldn't be a need for the coverage. The guy on the gun looked as likely to hit the raft as anything.

Topside, Delacroix saw that the first two men had taken positions forward and one watched the hatches on either side of the super structure.

So far no signs of the angry savage. He peered over the lee side and saw that Lambert was already on the beach and now aiming his own rifle, (a proper scoped weapon), toward the tree line.

With the other Zodiac just offshore and fighting the surf, Delacroix knew he needed to order them to the beach or risk capsizing half his strike force. He gave the okay to Perrin, who radioed word and they heard the little engine rev up.

Delacroix made his way up to the men nearest the wheelhouse. "Nothing?"

"All quiet, sir." A black mercenary named Alain whispered. Delacroix met him years ago in Angola on a messy job and he'd been with him ever since. The other two looked like washouts from the Foreign Legion.

Delacroix caught a whiff of decay and saw the dismantled corpse strewn on the deck. Dead sailor, not their man with the club, for sure.

"Let's grab the bridge first. Think they have any video cameras?"

"This bucket is older than you, sir." Alain and the other one, Hugo, gripped their Steyr AUG subguns. The short barrels gave them great mobility in tight spaces.

The men moved in tandem, one covering the other, and Delacroix scanned along the deck. Some boxes had slid until tether lines held them. Up here the tilt was noticeable but nothing that impaired movement. With a decent tugboat the whole ship could be back on the sea in no time.

Both men disappeared around the corner and Delacroix heard them pad up the exterior steps to the bridge. Just as he wondered if they'd need a breaching charge he heard another flashbang echo through the super structure and the pair burst into the bridge.

"Bridge clear." came over the radio in his ear. Delacroix ran up the canted steps and stepped through the lingering haze onto the empty bridge.

The bridge had a radio, and some basic navigation but lacked a sophisticated electronics package. Delacroix saw little else of use.

"You were right, Alain."

The man shrugged. "We should clear below decks. He's around here somewhere."

A deafening noise filled the bridge. It sounded like a howler monkey, but the rage was unmistakable. All three men jumped and Delacroix saw where it came from. A copper pipe topped with a brass mouthpiece.

"Speaking tube. Do you know where it leads?"

"Hard to say," Alain said. "But probably the engine room is a good place to start."

Now a voice screamed at them from the tube. Delacroix guessed it was Hokutian but the only word he understood was in French, "Salopards!"

"You heard the man. You bastards are the ones he's waiting for." Delacroix wished he could hook up a hose with some CS gas right down the tube to flush the bugger out.

# Chapter 27

Hua left Kai to the cramped storage locker in the mess hall just beyond the narrow passage connecting to the engine room hatch. He hoped the compartment masked some of the smell that smothered the makeshift hospital. The area still reeked of sickness and death from that horrific night. The memory of Ruru's face burned in Hua's mind. He'd carved his boy's likeness onto his chest. The pain added to the reminders that he and Amira would never have another child.

He knew that Kai waited not far from where his friend had lost his own little girl to the plague brought by these demons and their greed.

Hua checked everything in the engine room and confirmed the rear hatch was unlocked. The oil and grit conjured a much more pleasant memory of himself as a child running free on the *Verdragen* and getting screamed at by Gert and the other Dwazen sailors all the while listening to their stories and absorbing their lessons.

He'd always prefer the sky and trees, but the labyrinth of pipes and ducts formed an iron jungle in its own right. And he knew them both intimately.

Now he crept back toward the way he was certain they'd come for him. He held the war club and made sure the knife in his belt was tight, ignoring the pain in his still-raw fingers. Hua listened for the sounds of approaching footsteps.

For now, all he heard was the shift and creak of the vessel trapped in the sand.

He didn't hear a sound from Kai. A moment later footsteps told him someone was coming. Two people taking turns and moving in slow, deliberate steps.

\* \* \*

Hua hid on the other side of the open hatch at the end of the mess hall. He heard the whispers and imagined the hand signals to accentuate their stealth. He held his anger at a boil, just shy of exploding. Let them think he was a mindless primitive. He knew what their guns could do.

They sounded like they were about a third of the way into the fetid atmosphere of the mess hall.

They shuffled ahead and Hua heard the sigh of fabric being pulled off tables. The sheets would be stained with blood and other fluids. Gert had made the grisly decision to leave one of his dead sailors on deck to maintain the appearance of devastation. Maru refused to allow any Hokutian dead in place.

Hua waited as long as he could then drew in a deep breath. He gripped the club and flung it through the door while letting out his loudest war cry.

He started running as muffled shots followed. He kept his body to the right side of the door while he raced down the twenty-plus feet of the passage, knowing he'd be an easy mark as soon as they spotted him.

Their jumpy nerves gave him the moment he needed.

Just when he reached the turn in the passage that led to the engine room hatch he saw sparks and paint fly in front of him and felt a tug at his right shoulder and cheek. He realized one of the rounds had shattered on the steel wall behind him and he'd been grazed by bullet fragments.

Momentum carried him to the opening and he let out another war cry and leapt through the hatch sailing past the few metal steps into the large engine room. Hua landed on his feet and sprinted behind the huge generator where he found his gifts.

The men following him must have been near the hatch by now. He heard the footsteps echo, a strange sound as this room was near deafening when the engine was running.

But even now the room wasn't silent. Two frail baskets gave off a low hum. Hua picked up a small mirror he'd left here and used it to peek around the side of the generator which gave him a limited view of the metal steps and hatch. He saw one white face peer from the outside for an instant, then duck back. Hua didn't think they'd seen him.

He waited for them to charge, but first he heard a metallic rattle and glimpsed a pair of small cylinders roll through the open door. Hua dropped the mirror and clapped his hand over his ears and squeezed his eyes shut.

The twin blasts shook the air and he felt the shockwave through the metal side of the generator. If they'd seen him and been more accurate with their tosses they might have stunned him.

The pair zipped through the hatch and down the metal steps.

If they split up and one came around the corner they'd fill him with holes before he had a chance.

"Over here." Hua heard one man whisper.

The baskets vibrated with crazed buzzing. The concussion grenades hadn't stunned the trapped creatures inside. It had enraged them.

Hua saw the tip of one of the soldier's muzzles. Any moment he'd pop around the corner and Hua would be finished.

*Where was Kai?*

Hua saw a gloved hand signaling a count and realized the man didn't know he was partially visible.

Hua didn't let the count reach three. He stepped behind one basket and used his foot to loft it, soccer-style, through the air toward the man.

The basket remained intact and arced through the air just as the soldier pivoted low around the corner. He reacted on instinct to the object coming at him and tried to halt his momentum. The basket fell short and burst open right in front of him.

And the berserk Giant Tree Hornets erupted from the shattered nest taking their fury out on the nearest person.

The soldier seemed to forget his weapon and clawed at his face while the thumb-sized hornets swarmed it.

His scream was music to Hua's ears, so much so he almost didn't hear the other man yell out, "Hugo?" Then he cried out as well.

Hua saw another hand, gloveless and dark skinned, try to drag his partner back toward the hatch. He picked up the second basket and crept around the generator so he could peek and see the still open hatch.

The hornets remained focused on the first soldier who flailed at his face and Hua could see from his vantage point that it was swelling up. The dark soldier began to get stung as well, but Hua gave him credit, he managed to help his buddy to his feet. They scrambled toward the metal steps.

Hua hefted the remaining basket and lobbed it with all his strength. While it flew through the air he saw the hatch door swing shut in the soldier's faces and Hua heard Kai's war cry just before the hatch cut the sound off. The second basket shattered on the bottom metal step and a fresh wave of hornets exploded onto the soldiers.

Hua felt the burning stings of a few straggler hornets and sprinted toward the rear of the engine room.

When he reached the door he couldn't help but turn for a last look. The guy named Hugo was on his knees and trying to cover his head with his arms. Hua saw the hornets attack every piece of exposed flesh and he knew from experience that the insects would swarm up sleeves and down open shirts or pant legs to sting until they'd depleted every bit of their excruciating venom.

The other one was trying to open the door and Hua knew Kai already had jammed it from the other side. The man's effort looked to be waning.

Hua wanted to watch them both until they expired but he knew the hornets, once roused, would spend the rest of the day attacking anything nearby.

Besides, these two soldiers weren't alone.

Hua reached over and pulled the ship's fire alarm. A hornet landed on his arm and Hua felt the stinger jab more fire into the muscle. He slapped it off and knew the resulting pheromone would bring thousands more soon.

The alarm bells rang and stirred the two swarms anew and Hua could hear the ship's horn blast topside. He popped through the rear hatch, slammed the door shut behind him and took the metal pry bar he'd left there to wedge into the opening mechanism.

Now all exits were locked.

\* \* \*

*Topside, the Verdragen*

"Turn that fucking thing off!" Delacroix shouted over the blast of the ship's horn and continuous array of buzzers and bells that rang throughout the ship.

"The controls are disabled up here." Perrin said.

"Where is it coming from?" Delacroix couldn't see the board from his perch outside the bridge.

"Engine room."

"Where are Hugo and Alain?" Delacroix saw the men on the beach stare back at the ship and he couldn't tell if they were trying to get him on the radio. The din overpowered the small speaker. He raised his arms to indicate he wasn't sure what was going on.

As if they didn't know that already.

Now one of the forward hatches began to spew smoke.

"Merde! Check on that." Delacroix ordered the commandos with the rifles. The men raced past the door leading below deck to the loose hatch where smoke poured out. Delacroix drew a pistol and covered the door. He wanted to ask Perrin again to try to radio the two men below deck, but it would be a waste of time in this racket.

*Maybe a waste of time regardless.*

The thick black smoke continued to stream out of the hatch. Perrin raced around the bridge in a frantic search for another way to shut off the alarm.

The riflemen reached the smoking hatch. One used a pole he'd found on deck to push the cover off. Smoke billowed more freely but a breeze carried a whiff to Delacroix. He sniffed.

"Look inside. Quickly." Delacroix screamed to be heard. One man covered with his weapon and the other peeked over the side. Delacroix shifted his gaze between the hatch and the open door he guarded.

He sniffed again and noticed the air coming from below where he stood was clean. Also, the place where the smoke came out was near the bow and the engine room would be center or closer to the stern.

The man peering down jolted backward and for an instant Delcroix was sure he'd been hit.

No, he stood and jogged toward Delacroix with his weapon raised and aimed toward the stern.

Delacroix resisted the urge to duck out of the way. When the man put his fingers to his lips Delacroix understood that the guy didn't want to risk being overheard. The back of his own neck tingled. It was too exposed out here. He looked back and saw another hatch askew.

"Pitch," The Arab man whispered, and Delacroix drew a blank on the guy's name.

"What?"

"Burning pitch. In a barrel."

The alarms continued to shriek into Delacroix's skull. Now the smell of the smoke made sense. He kept expecting to smell diesel or plastic. The pitch smoke made him think of burnt newspapers. "A diversion."

Delacroix didn't wait for the guy to follow. He ran with his pistol outstretched toward the stern hatch.

When he reached it he kicked the cover aside and aimed into the compartment below. Nothing but a short ladder. And a few strands of dried grass.

He saw the merc with the bronze colored skin racing behind him. Mahmoud? That was it. He pointed at the hatch so the guy could cover the exit and then Delacroix peered over the railing.

He spotted not one, but two men swimming hard and ducking the incoming surf, like they were born to it. Already a hundred yards away.

"Hey, over here!" He shouted at the Arab.

Mahmoud looked up and joined Delacroix. The man raised the weapon to his shoulder and let fly with a long burst of automatic fire, wasting an entire magazine by spraying every shot well beyond the target.

Delacroix shook his head and rested his arm on the rail and aimed down the sights of his CZ 75 pistol. The 9mm might not have been the rifle he wished, but these were soft targets. He fought to control his panting while he squeezed off shots and saw one or two splash near the pair of swimmers.

They started to dive more frequently and it was difficult to adjust his fire with the foaming surf. Mahmoud burned through another thirty round mag and when Delacroix reached the end of his own magazine he holstered it and grabbed the rifle from the cannon fodder Gagnon picked out for him.

"Let go!" He took the AK and snatched a fresh magazine from the man's bandolier.

Never his favorite for distance work, Delacroix cursed the weapon's iron sights and his aging eyes. The two figures stuck together and merged in his blurring vision. Delacroix blinked to keep his eyes moist and flicked the selector lever to take the gun off full auto. He hoped for the best and squeezed off aimed, single shots until the two looked no bigger than dark grains of rice amid the sea foam.

*They swam like fish!*

By the time the others had reacted to the shooting and reached the railing they were gone around the side of the island.

# Chapter 28

"Not that way," Saskia yanked on Fin's arm. He stopped fast. The barely disturbed sand indicated another trap, he'd lost count of how many they'd stepped over or around. This was the third time Saskia had prevented him from getting skewered or worse, and he was supposed to know where he was going!

"Thanks again. How can you spot those?"

"I must think like the designers." She barely sounded winded. "We're almost there."

He'd guessed they must be close because the island wasn't that big and the last hour had been a meandering zig-zag course leading upward.

The markers at the entrance of the labyrinth of tunnels through the dense vegetation helped but once on a path it was too easy to drift onto a connecting booby-trapped trail. At least it seemed that way to him. Saskia never even hesitated. Soon they ducked through a wall of leaves and onto what looked to Fin to be a more established route. He followed her lead and began to hear rushing water. The mountain towered close by.

"The waterfall?"

She nodded. And pointed past where they were walking. "It's up there. We're going to another pool not far away."

After a quick detour through a patch of jungle and a rope swing over a narrow, but a fast-flowing stream, they came to a wider, well-worn path.

Fin sensed they weren't alone.

Bird calls sliced the air and he thought of Pieter and the other guy. Fin decided not to make any sudden moves and hoped whoever was out there could see them approach.

"You hear that?" he whispered to Saskia.

She cupped her hand to her mouth and began whistling in rapid notes. Just like another bird. Fin glanced up and noted subtle movement in the tops of the largest of the palm trees.

Unlike the snipers on the beach, these guards listened to Saskia.

More bird calls and he thought he saw the glint of sunlight on a muzzle. It had been years since he'd trained his eyes to search for clues, but the habits came back fast.

He was still embarrassed at how he'd missed those trip wires.

More bird calls, and then they rippled back into the jungle in a dwindling relay. Fin realized that was exactly what they were, a simple signal system to pass messages back and forth.

A single leaf dropped from a large palm tree to the ground and Fin saw there were two paths in front of them.

Saskia whistled a quick tune that Fin could swear sounded like "Thanks" and she walked to the route marked by the leaf. Fin picked it up and shoved it out of sight into the bushes and followed with a wave of his hand.

* * *

In the clearing Fin saw the rugged Dwazen camp. Sleeping spots were hewn under bushes to avoid observation from the air. The camping spots encircled a spring-fed pond about half the size of an Olympic swimming pool. Volcanic rocks walled in the water opposite the mountain and just beyond the pond the vegetation gave way to a flat expanse of cooled lava and a narrow fissure billowing steam and smoke.

Gert and Willem were waiting for them.

"I guess the whistle-gram worked."

Saskia gave him that "What are you talking about?" look he was getting used to and hugged her father.

216

"We thought the worst. We could hear some shooting, hard to get a clear fix up here."

"We're fine." She stopped.

Fin spoke up. He looked right at Gert. "Did you order Pieter and the other one to take up sniper positions?"

From Willem's expression it was clear they hadn't made that decision together.

"Ya."

About twenty of the other Dwazen came in close. Fin shared what happened. He didn't want to rip into Gert with everyone listening.

"Pieter was brave. He led them away after the counterattack even though he was wounded. I heard more shots and I don't know if he took any with him. But we have to assume he's gone."

"Damn." Willem shook his head.

"We have to stick together. If we try to go head-to-head with them we'll lose more, probably everyone." Fin described the mortars he saw. "I think Gagnon means to kill everyone he sees."

Willem had simmered quietly while Fin explained what he knew about mortars, which wasn't much. "Let's just say none of us want to be under those shells when they fall," he'd concluded.

"We had a plan." Willem said to Gert.

"We still do. I just made it better." Gert snapped.

"How's that?" Fin asked.

"When they look for the gold and find what they find we have some surprises."

"Your first surprise got two of your men killed," Fin spoke softly.

Gert looked like he wanted to grab Fin the way his hands clenched and unclenched. "You said it yourself over and over. Gagnon is coming for his prize and won't leave anyone alive."

"You got me there. But even if we have the numbers, *they* have the muscle." Fin looked around the camp. He pointed at the pond. "That water is fresh, drinkable?"

Willem let a little smile slip. "It is precious. Look closer."

A cloud moved out from in front of the sun and the light shone on the pond. The inky black of the pond he and Saskia had romped in was nothing like this water. There seemed to be lighter sand at the bottom of this one and the water almost glowed with the reflection.

*Wait.*

Fin stepped closer and the bottom of the shallow pond flared a brilliant gold. "Bars?"

Willem grinned. "Not bad for a bunch of backward, broken-down miners who sailed half way around the world to become a laughingstock." His face flushed red and looked orange in the golden light when he stepped closer.

"Papa," Saskia said.

Fin tried to imagine how much gold it would take to cover the bottom of a huge swimming pool and broke his mental calculator.

"While you were helping with other preparations, we moved the gold here."

"All this in a week?" Fin shook his head.

"Not quite, but most of it. Army ants have nothing on us. We live to work." Willem seemed about to burst with pride.

"But won't that lead Gagnon right to it?"

Gert broke in. "We left enough. If he's still too greedy, it will be his death."

Fin thought for a moment. "He'd have to relocate the mortars but that's not difficult if his people find this place."

Willem shrugged. "We had to put it somewhere. It will take him even longer to bring it all down even if he gets past us."

"I got lost coming up here but I wouldn't count on him having the same trouble." Fin thought about the numbers they were up against. They had some weapons here, true, but they were nothing more than old rifles.

"The traps will slow them and if they have wounded among them, that makes them even less efficient, doesn't it?" Saskia asked.

Gert nodded. "I'd love to see Gagnon dangling from a snare."

"Have you heard from Maru and Hua?"

Willem shook his head. "We have runners who should be back soon. There's a mix of our people and islanders stretched across the jungle and out towards the crest leading to the Hokutian village. We can get an emergency signal relayed in a matter of minutes. More complex messages require a note run across the distance."

"Like a relay race?" Fin wasn't sure the reference would translate but they all nodded.

Gert added, "And if Gagnon orders search parties into the interior, chances are one of ours will see him and send signals to let us know."

"Those bird calls?"

Saskia spoke. "Right, and we know by the tone of the call or the type of bird who sent the message."

"You guys get any better and you'll replace texting." Only Gert seemed to get the reference.

"Now what?" Gert challenged.

"I thought I heard that you're going to sit tight? At least until you know more or one of your men signals that Gagnon is on the way."

Gert shrugged.

"Please tell me you haven't told your people to act alone against these men."

"When you have men breaking into your home and promising death to you and your family will you hide in a closet and hope they leave?"

"No, but…" Fin started.

"We've all lost family. Everyone here is family, blood or not. And Maru and Hua have lost more than any. Perhaps you can't understand."

"No," Fin felt his face flush. "I think I do." They were right. But so was he. "I just don't want to see any more die for no reason."

"Ya. We all have reasons."

At that moment, they heard the first distant boom echo off the rocky sides of the volcano.

Fin knew that sound. "Mortar! Take cover!" Fin had no idea where the shell might land and it was only in the movies that they gave any warning whistle. He belatedly realized the niches cut into the thick jungle would be ineffective against shrapnel.

With the distance involved the sound would reach them a second after the shell was in the air so the warning was almost worthless anyway. He pulled Saskia to the ground.

They heard the second blast not long after, also in the distance.

"They aren't targeting here. Somewhere lower." Fin called out.

Dwazen peered around. Not all of them spoke English but given the situation and the body language Fin saw they understood the alert.

Willem spoke in English, then switched to Dutch. "The explosions are in New Cape."

Fin looked to Gert. "I hope you got everyone else out."

# Chapter 29

*Hoku Island, New Cape*

"Fire for effect." Gagnon instructed the gunner on the mortar. The loader scrambled to adjust the propellant in the rounds for the short lob into New Cape.

He covered his ears for the next round and peeked at the destruction already under way in the pitiful shack cluster.

One round shattered a shack's roof, but they weren't intended to level the place. They were white phosphorus smoke rounds. Billowing clouds of dense, white smoke blanketed New Town.

Four men with assault rifles moved into the outer edges of the town and donned gas masks. The smoke drifted slowly away from them but Gagnon could smell the distinctive garlic odor, even from here.

From his visit earlier, he'd noted most structures used screens or curtains for doors. He got on the low-powered radio and addressed the men advancing to clear the town. "Listen for coughing or panicked running. The smoke should penetrate the buildings but they might have breathing gear."

He heard quick-keyed acknowledgements from the men who'd vanished into the fog. The rifleman, Allard, looked through his scope but he'd have a hard time seeing through the smoke. Even their thermal gear would be blocked by this type of smoke initially.

But that didn't matter. By the time the smoke dissipated, they'd own the town. The concrete structure he'd most worried about was empty, perhaps the survivors thought it would be too obvious.

The thermals would be a godsend if this ran into the night and they needed counter sniper action. A man in a treetop then would do as well as if he waved a flashlight at them. Damn Bissette! If that arrogant sniper had used his thermal scope in the first place, he might still be in the game. Instead the man was back on the *Fanfaron* riding a morphine cocktail.

He forced himself to calm down. They had the initiative again, that was what mattered.

The wind picked up and tugged at the blanket of smoke which began to rise in a huge white column.

Gagnon caught glimpses of the men moving and covering each other as they advanced on the town, and with the breeze at their backs they began to deploy smoke and CS teargas grenades to continue their push.

Gagnon saw Stephon climb up the ladder to the dock and he brought lightweight gas masks for the two of them. Gagnon carried an MP-5 9mm sub-machine gun and Stephon held his preferred folding stock AKM rifle. The big man favored the added firepower it provided.

"Ready?" Stephon looked keyed up, all signs of trepidation gone. Gagnon relaxed a little.

"Oui." He spoke to the mortar men. "Keep the smoke handy and listen up. If we run into an ambush I want the smoke rapidement, n'est pas?" While they nodded, he unfolded a map with grids for fire missions laid out for them. "Most likely spots are here," he jabbed a finger, "and here." Wood boxes with assorted mortar rounds sat stacked behind a wall of sandbags.

Gagnon double checked his own copy of the map to confirm the match. Smoke wasn't the only fog generated by combat, and he'd seen entire platoons wiped out by friendly fire thanks to a miscommunication.

Which reminded him. "Stephon, you have some repeaters?"

"Of course. Three."

"That should do." The portable signal boosters would extend the radio range and circumvent interference that might be caused by the hills or structures. Delacroix had several on him, as well, and part of his job was to install a couple on the high ground so they could stay in touch.

"Ca va. Let's go." He and Stephon trotted to the first set of buildings. The garlic stench lingered but not enough to concern him. If the wind shifted back toward them, the CS teargas was a much bigger concern and the gas masks would have to go on.

Gagnon's radio hissed in his ear. "Six, Squad one."

It was Letang, in charge of the team ahead of them. "Oui?"

"One structure burning, the way the tin roof is smashed I think it was the WP."

"Probably so." The stuff burned ferociously and was a fire risk, among other things, whenever it was used. "Will it spread to the other buildings?" Gagnon had thought about torching the whole place but didn't need the distraction and definitely didn't want the fuel tank near the dock to go up.

"I don't think so."

"Let it go then. Press on, and we will clear the buildings. No signs of resistance or traps?"

"No people. Be careful of trip wires. A couple whip traps and a body you'll smell when you get close."

"Merci."

Gagnon and Stephon took turns clearing huts and small buildings. He kept a sharp eye out for tripwires and neither saw a single person. When they reached the hut with the dead body inside, he put on his mask to take a look and immediately wished he hadn't. Judging by the clothes and length of hair it appeared to have been a woman, evidently too sick to leave her hut and overlooked in the evacuation.

*Why hadn't they burned the body with the others?*

He wasn't going to touch her. The flies were doing their part and no doubt some horrid creatures would do the rest.

The rest of the huts contained personal effects but each appeared to have closets or crude armoires with some items removed, judging by the number of hangers.

Dead men didn't pack.

So where were they? He made a mental note to recheck the fire pit where they had seen the torched corpses. Maybe later he'd check to see if there appeared to be clothing burned as well.

Fear of contamination? Could be. If they thought along those lines.

Even so, where were the others?

Gagnon followed Stephon into one of the larger huts and saw wood carvings and paintings inside. This hut had two rooms and they made sure it was empty. The second room, the bedroom, held a framed photo.

Saskia. Dressed in old-style clothing but the girl was still stunning. Gagnon wondered where she might be now. If she'd survived....

Madness. That bitch would cut his throat in his sleep.

Of course she would, and yet the fact she would try intensified his lust. He removed that back of the picture frame. One edge of the photograph crumbled and he realized it didn't just appear old, it actually *was* old. Ancient even, and yet the resemblance was uncanny.

He tossed the photo aside and dropped the frame on the floor. "If you find her…"

Stephon heard him and said nothing while he left.

They understood each other.

\* \* \*

*Outside the Dwazen Graveyard*

After Stephon attached the radio repeater high up on the palm trunk they heard from the advance four-man group.

"Go ahead." Gagnon said. The mortar team had reported all quiet. Good, in terms of trouble from the Dwazen. But they'd still heard nothing from the team on the native side of the island who should have gotten their own repeater up and running by now.

"Sir, we're outside that cemetery." Letang sounded excited.

"And?"

"I glassed the yard and didn't see anyone but when I swept with the thermal scope I spotted two figures burrowed into the turf like ticks on a dog's fur."

"Did they see you?"

"Not sure. When we got within sight of the entrance we heard bird calls, then more answered in the jungle."

"A signal?"

"They sound authentic but you taught me about coincidences."

Letang's instincts were second to none. Gagnon pushed aside a pang of regret that this was their last job together. "Can you still see the man in cover?"

"He moved and was so cautious I suspect the signal. I sent one man to probe the jungle but all he heard was movement in the distance, hard to say what it was, could have been a spooked animal."

"Or a scout."

"Yes, sir. The man on the ground shifted position and had a rifle. Iron sights."

They'd still be in easy range hemmed in by this dense foliage. "You don't see any others?"

"Not in range of the scope, which means the graveyard itself is likely clear after we get rid of this one," Letang said.

"Try to wait for us but if you get a clear shot, take it."

"Yes sir."

Gagnon briefed Stephon.

"We need to hurry, Monsieur." It will be dark soon enough and we cannot assume we'll have much time after that."

Frustration flared anew in Gagnon's chest. "I wish there'd been a better way."

Stephon nodded. "Also, I don't like the sound of those bird calls. How many of those mongrels survived?"

"We did our part. But we know if they are guarding the gravesite it must be worth protecting. I think we can secure it and keep the locals away long enough."

Stephon had already shouldered his pack and held his rifle.

Fifteen minutes down the path Gagnon saw the first of his men. They blended well along the side of the road. He crept up to Letang, crawling the last twenty yards.

"Sniper still there. He knows something is going on. He keeps looking at the road and the gate."

"Head shot?"

"No," Letang said. "He has a rock to hide behind. He's using a mirror to peek at the gate. If he is careful, he can hit a man just inside the gate and I don't have the angle from here."

Gagnon looked and the dense foliage near the opening formed a natural barrier. Once they got inside the gates the graveyard opened up. Could they use headstones for cover? They might have to, depending on how many Dwazen were left and if this was going to be their last stand.

"CS?" Gagnon asked.

"Only a couple left and some smoke. Enough for one rush but after that, I'm out."

"Hopefully they are out of men. Give me what you have. Stephon, your best bowling form, s'il vous plait." Stephon had been a hell of a cricket player a decade ago and had the best arm for grenade tosses this side of a launcher.

They formed a quick plan and Gagnon made sure that the three men with Letang got the message.

"At my signal." Gagnon said. "Now!"

With Letang on the thermal-scoped rifle, Stephon stood and yanked the pin on the first smoke grenade. He heaved it deep past the gate and into the yard. By the time the third and final one landed, a thick cloud had billowed into the space.

"Vite!" Gagnon snapped.

The three commandos scrambled into the yard and dove behind the nearest set of headstones. They wore gasmasks and Stephon dashed in and popped the last two CS cans. He flung one into the nearest jungle and tossed the other as close as possible to the sniper.

"Out of your warren, rabbit." Letang whispered.

228

A shot rang out from the sniper and it burrowed into the sand not far from the entrance. A second later, two more shots, one of them pinging off the metal gate.

The delay between shots indicated he was likely was firing blind. Decent guesses, Gagnon gave the shooter credit.

"Bastard. Just a bit more. Here comes the gas."

They heard another shot and Gagnon had no idea where that went but immediately after he heard coughing in the distance.

"Ah, now you move!" Letang smiled and tracked his weapon left. He squeezed off a single round. "Sniper down."

Gagnon heard a single loud grunt from the target.

"I have cured his cough, Monsieur."

"Move up and scope the area. While we have the advantage. That smoke won't last."

Letang was already on his feet and moving into the space. He squatted at a grave and used the top of the headstone as a rest for the rifle. Already the smoke was beginning to dissipate, but it had done its job. The CS would soon follow and the offshore breeze worked in their favor and drove the remnants into the jungle.

The other three men fanned out and formed a loose perimeter in the graveyard. Letang turned in a slow semicircle to allow the resolution in the scope's image to keep pace. Stephon and Gagnon stood near the grave marker.

Gagnon took off the mask and sniffed the air. No worse on eyes than chopping raw onions. He hoped the gas that blew into the jungle drove away any other Dwazen. He needed the time.

"Stephon." Gagnon toed the soil at the grave. It was soft and spongy, unlike the terrain closer to the beach not covered with fine white sand.

Stephon stifled a cough when he removed his own mask. "Freshly dug?"

"Like the others." Gagnon pointed at one for Saskia and others nearby. Recently turned soil lay in front of each headstone.

Gagnon unfolded a field entrenching spade. He then used his bare hands to probe the topsoil looking for wires or other signs of a mine or trap. Stephon dropped his pack. "Letang?"

"Still clear." Letang never looked up from the scope. "I think the man I dropped was running for a path entrance."

Gagnon stepped back to let Stephon work. The tall man held a portable metal detector. Gagnon spoke to Letang. "Send one man to check it out. Also make sure that sniper isn't playing possum."

"Even possums need hearts and lungs," Letang relayed the message and one of the commandos worked his way toward the downed man. Letang covered the advance with the rifle.

Gagnon heard the squeak in Stephon's earpiece while the man fiddled with the volume control.

"Big?"

Stephon nodded and swept the sensor to find the edges. He used a twig to draw a rough rectangular outline for Gagnon.

Gagnon still worked with his hands. He cleared the dirt away a little at a time, feeling for any sign of wires. He'd seen men before, too frightened to place their dainty fingers in jeopardy only to poke a rifle butt or bayonet into a thin bit of near invisible fishing line and lose a leg or worse.

No wires so far. He scooped more soil away. Still nothing. Once he got below where a typical antipersonnel mine would be hidden he took larger amounts of material. Periodically he'd step back and let Stephon recheck.

Letang's man had confirmed the sniper was dead, a young white man. Probably one of the fellows he or Stephon had touched about a week ago. But he seemed healthy enough, at least right until Letang put a round through his back. Maybe a pocket of Dwazen were busy at the mines that day? They still should have caught it from the others.

The screech from the metal detector grew louder. Getting closer. Gagnon wanted to rush, but knew better.

He began to take turns with Stephon and Letang, rotating between the radio, the rifle, and the shovel. While they unearthed the recently dug up grave, Gagnon learned that the other two men now guarded a second path and reported what looked like wheel ruts leading in the direction of the base of the volcano.

Damn, they were just too thin here.

"Mon Dieu!" Letang blurted. Gagnon put down the radio and rushed to the gravesite.

Letang hoisted a gold bar. He grinned "And there are more. Many more. I feel like an Egyptian tomb raider." The man hopped into the open grave.

# Chapter 30

*Hoku,* Islander *side*

Delacroix stomped back and forth on the deck of the *Verdragen.* He couldn't remember the last time he was this furious. "Find out who has it and get back here."

"Aren't we wasting time…sir? Those men are already dead and the savages are getting away."

Delacroix checked his temper. The other goons looked up to this one, a nomad originally from Mexico that the rest nicknamed Pancho. Delacroix questioned this namesake's leadership skills compared with the real Pancho Villa but also knew it would be a problem to alienate him.

"We can't afford to lose their gear. We need those radios." He didn't add that they couldn't bear to lose the men, either. "I'd do the same for you if you were found dead under a cloud of bugs," he lied.

"We can get them later and we're not afraid of those pigs in the jungle."

Under other conditions he might have the man shot for insubordination. Out here, he knew he'd have to make the most of every gun available. Especially with his two best shooters dead.

"You'll get your chance. That's a promise."

The merc huffed off and climbed back down the rope ladder.

"Thank you, sir." Perrin had seen the exchange.

At least they'd found a working control panel for those damned fire klaxons. They'd broken the loudest ones on deck but others pounded all over the ship until Perrin was finally able to shut them off.

"They want payback. So do I, but something isn't right. We were told to secure and search the ship for survivors and gold," Delacroix said.

"Yes sir. Once we clear the bees, we'll be able to tackle that mission."

"That's not what I mean. You'll agree we're up against more than just a bunch of mindless primitives?" Delacroix touched the welt above his eye from the bug that attacked him when he went to see for himself what had taken out his best two men. "We must make sure Hugo and Alain didn't die in vain."

"Sir?"

"Don't you get it, Perrin?" Delacroix said. "These 'monkeys', as Gagnon called them, turned insect nests into IEDs. They disabled the electronics on the bridge so those alarms sounded for a long time. Think someone ashore might have been listening?"

"Good point."

"They may not have our weaponry but if we aren't careful they'll prove they can outsmart us anyway."

The lump throbbed over his eye. Delacroix didn't want to imagine what hundreds or thousands of stings must feel like. For a while, he'd even wondered if he was having an allergic reaction to the venom. He felt warm and his nose was running. He shrugged it off. Some of the men were starting to sneeze. Maybe a strain of pollen on this rarely visited oasis.

"You may have hit one of them. We'll get them sir."

Pancho returned a minute later. He held a pair of smoke grenades and a single gas mask.

"Lauder told me Gagnon took the last thermal scope."

"We haven't got one at all?"

"Right, and this is the only gas mask. The boss kept the CS all for himself, too." The contempt dripped from his voice. "Don't worry, sir. My guys can do their job with what we brought." He patted the AK-47 slung over his shoulder.

233

"Knock it off. Gagnon's our commander and makes the call on equipment. He has his reasons." Even though he was thinking the same thing, Delacroix refused to tolerate criticism of a superior, least of all from these dregs.

"Let's go. I see in the schematics there's a back way into the engine room. The bugs won't be as thick there."

Down by the hatch for the engine room, Delacroix could see a dozen huge insects crawling on the window. It was a small mercy that he couldn't see the bodies of his friends.

He used the fury to tamp down the fear he felt but didn't dare show. He'd volunteered and quietly told Lambert to take over if Delacroix joined the dead men in the engine room.

"Use some of that pitch in here 'cause even one sting feels like a cigar burn." Delacroix felt like a mummy. He'd wrapped himself head-to-toe in an improvised bee keeper's outfit. The gas mask would double as a protective shield against the nasty buggers. The thought of a sting in the eye made him shudder.

Their footsteps echoed in the metal passageways. The heat below decks combined with the stifling clothing made Delacroix sweat profusely. He reminded himself to drink his fill of water and hoped he didn't pass out from the exertion.

"Smoke on the door." He squashed the gas mask tight against his head. He carried the two smoke grenades in his gloved hands.

He wished he had fireproof mittens so he could set off the grenades and hang onto them but they used an incendiary device to generate the smoke and would become too hot to handle in moments. Just time enough to throw.

Perrin and one of the mercs sent by Pancho waved burning rags dipped in pitch. They caught quickly as the men waved the flaming rags all around the doorway and Delacroix concentrated on his task.

"Going in. Watch that rag!" Delacroix tried not to get ignited himself. He saw several of the bugs zip out and heard one guy yelp in pain.

He knew it wasn't professional to take pleasure in the sound and focused on the tasks.

The steel door slammed behind him and shoved him into the room. The thick cloth, wrapped over his head, muffled his hearing. He fired up one smoke grenade and rolled it down by the bodies of his men.

*Chew on that, my winged friends.*

He didn't know much about bugs other than they were a constant nuisance in the jungles. He was going to retire somewhere in the desert. Or in the cold. He waited to make sure it worked and for a moment was confused when he saw not one cloud but two.

No. Only one was smoke. The other made noise and gathered in a corner of the ceiling. Then it moved toward him.

He popped the second canister and dropped it at his feet. The mask seemed to work but so did the smoke and he needed to hurry or he risked being blind down here. He kicked it in the same direction as the first, knowing he'd have to search the bodies by touch.

Maybe that would make it easier to not have to see their swollen faces.

Every time he stepped out of the smokescreen he heard a faint hum and it felt like someone was throwing handfuls of pebbles at his back. Even through the padding, the vicious little bastards smacked into him relentlessly.

The smoke only seemed to piss them off. They avoided contact but hadn't he read bees got sleepy?

He felt an agonizing sting on his face *under* the clothing. They were landing on his head and crawling around looking for openings.

He smashed himself in the face in an effort to crush the thing and the padding worked against him as the gloves and face wrap cushioned the blow. It also made the insect angrier and he felt two more stings near the first. He stopped and hovered over one canister so he was bathed in smoke and began to punch himself in the face with a closed fist.

For a second he wondered if he'd knock himself out before he hurt this fucking bug. He stopped when the stinging ceased and he shook his head to clear the cobwebs.

He shuffled forward, dribbling the canister like a smoking soccer ball and made sure he never let his body get out of the cloud for long.

It was getting hard to see, but the deck space was narrow and straight so he had no trouble finding the bodies. He knew they were next to each other, so that helped.

He used his hands to locate the heads and worked down from there. He wasn't sure which one he found first but the head felt like a large pumpkin.

Using the head as a reference point Delacroix was able to find the radios. He managed to unhook them and stuff them into a pouch they made in his makeshift beekeeper suit. It felt more like a giant dog-bite suit with about as much mobility.

"Sorry, mes amis. We will have to get you later." Delacroix had to abandon his thought of bringing the bodies out. With the partial failure of the smoke there was just no way. When they were finished, he'd come back to get them.

The smoke canisters began to sputter. They'd done the job and filled the engine room. Now he could barely see more than a few feet through the haze. The filter on the gas mask was holding up and for an instant he hoped the smoke's permeation would keep the buzzing bastards occupied.

Not so.

With nowhere to escape they turned the full force of their fury on him and they hit the thick layers like pellets from an air rifle. He put his hands over his face and felt the two radios inside the loose pouch with his elbows.

He moved as fast as he could, cursing nonstop in every language he knew. One bug found a gap that must have opened between his boot and pant leg and needles of fire stitched along his shin. He slammed a hand onto his leg while trying to run.

He got the insect but one of the radios bounced out and skittered to the floor. Delacroix could see the light peek through the door at the other end and realized his suit was past it's hastily constructed life expectancy.

One radio would have to do.

He fought the urge to sprint as the suit began to unravel. He must look like a mummy on amphetamines.

After what felt like an eternity he began to hear the men on the other side of the door cheer him on. The heat was becoming unbearable and his legs felt like they were turning into lead with each step. He staggered to the steps and the bugs smacked against his back like a cloudburst on a tin roof.

Delacroix tried to tug on the wheel to open the hatch. His gloved hands slipped on the metal rim. He began to feel lightheaded and sank to his knees to catch his breath.

# Chapter 31

Fin crept forward near the entrance to the hidden Dwazen camp. He took Johannes' lead and tried to keep track of all the traps they stepped over and around. Many appeared to be modifications of various hunter traps like snares and whips that could be used to catch animals.

Johannes had even said, "Good enough to catch a pig."

Fin worried about the kid. He realized they had more in common than might appear. Both had purged at the same time. Fin hadn't had time to absorb what had happened and events overtook his growing mountain of questions.

Right now he just wanted to make it to the observation point without getting skewered.

Johannes kept slowing to allow Fin to catch up. He looked annoyed but didn't say so. Finally he ducked straight into the brush and Fin saw it was a cover for another path.

Fin noticed not all of the mazes of paths were new. This one showed signs of wear and also fresh cuts in the plants but at the rate everything grew any path not maintained would soon be swallowed by the jungle.

"Hurry!"

Fin did his best. He caught up with Johannes who was halfway up a tree. "Wait for the rope." Johannes whispered. Fin felt like the fat kid who couldn't climb the same fences as his friends.

A knotted rope dropped down once Johannes had reached the tree nest observation spot. Fin climbed it and tried to use his legs as much as possible. Even so, his arms burned as he hauled himself onto the well concealed planks.

"You can see the edge of the graveyard from here." Johannes hauled up the rope.

Fin spotted it in the distance. He took out his spare camera and the weak zoom didn't help much. He snapped a couple shots any way.

The wind shifted and he caught an acrid whiff.

Johannes did too. "What's that?"

Fin knew the smell. He'd known it up close and personal. "Teargas. They use it to..."

"I know what teargas is."

"I forgot you haven't been here all that long." Fin felt like an ass.

"It's the only real home I've ever known, but I grew up in Pretoria. On the streets, mostly."

"That's why you came here?"

"You can't emigrate."

"Of course not." Something was eating at Fin, distracting his thoughts.

"I worked in the mines, then I started at the docks in Port Elizabeth and one day my boss introduced me to a man who needed some grunt work done on his boat."

"The *Verdragen?*"

"Yah. I got to know Gert and Pieter. When they offered to let me work on the crew I jumped at it. I didn't know at the time what it would mean, but when they were ready to invite me to be part of the community I never thought twice."

Fin's concerns grew by the minute but since he had a Dwazen right here, he had to ask. "You really believe all that stuff about not aging?"

"I've lived here ten years almost. The kids aged, I got bigger. Everyone not purged grew and got older. But everyone else looked exactly the same as the day I set foot on the *Verdragen*."

Fin wasn't so sure but he'd seen plenty of liars and this guy believed what he was saying.

Johannes shaded his eyes and scanned the distance. I can see a few of the bastards." He grinned. "Two of them are digging."

"Digging at the graves?" Fin asked.

"Yes." Johannes spoke to himself. "Just like Gert said they would."

Fin's eyes adjusted to the lighting and the edge of the place became a little clearer. Already he knew his eyes weren't what they had been when he was twenty.

"I think I see a third man."

"Where?"

"Behind that headstone. See? Moving side to side, what's he doing?" Fin couldn't spot details from here. They had to be more than 500 yards away. Maybe more.

"Duck." Johannes whispered. Fin scrunched down but with three boards nestled up in the tree there wasn't much space. "Rifle scope. We should be okay if we keep our heads down."

Earlier at the camp they'd heard distant booming shots but they hadn't heard any for a while. Whatever had happened was over. Fin didn't think it was a good sign but saying so wouldn't change anything so he kept the thought to himself.

The precarious perch brought back his unease. At first he thought it was an issue with heights, but that wasn't it. Airplanes yes, but not trees. "Johannes, do you guys always use palm trees for the observation posts?"

"Usually. They're the ones that are tall and strong enough."

That was it. "We should get down."

"Why? I can see what they are doing, and as long as we keep our heads down they can't see us. Besides I'll know if they start up the path."

"You don't understand. Pieter and another guy already opened up on them from trees."

"I hope he killed everyone he fired at."

"He might have." Fin felt frustration even as he understood the fury all the people felt at the attack and invasion. "The point is, we're in easy range and they know this trick."

"We're not going to be shooting at them."

Fin found himself glad this young man wasn't armed or the guy might try. Fin recognized Gagnon among the figures working in the cemetery. There was no mistaking that boxy build. "They're smart. They will learn to look for the tops of palm trees. Shooting or no shooting. Get it?"

Fin had the awful thought that if the sniper fired at them the first indication might be one of their heads bursting apart. At this distance the sound of the report would lag behind the bullet itself.

Johannes cupped his hands to his mouth and let a Kingfisher call fly.

Nothing. He called again and now, maybe halfway between them and the graveyard Fin heard a response.

As if to contradict Fin, they then heard the crack of a rifle.

A moment later a scream of pain rose from the jungle not far away from where the response had come.

"That's Roy!" Johannes tossed the rope and barely touched it before dropping to the soft earth below. Fin reached for the rope and something tore through the branches and dug a furrow along the board next to Fin's head.

Splinters stung his cheek and Fin decided to take his chances with gravity and bailed over the side as a second bullet zipped through the fronds.

The loose soil absorbed the fall better than he'd imagined, as severed leaves fell around him. Fin didn't hear any more shots but kept low, following the path and hoping like hell that Johannes would let him know if there were traps along the way.

About a hundred yards ahead, Fin thought he'd run into one of Gagnon's men. He didn't see Pieter and wasn't about to test his rusty tracking skills. He wished he could whistle like those guys but he might as well scream "Over here!"

He crept closer, ready to dive into the bushes if he saw anyone coming around the corner.

"Get down, stupid." Johannes hissed and Fin felt his heart nearly leap out of his chest. A hand reached out and yanked him into cover.

Fin saw another man about Johannes' age. Roy, he assumed. He was wincing in pain but being quiet. Johannes pressed a torn piece of shirt against what looked to be a minor wound. It was plenty bloody and Fin knew blood trails led killers to their quarry.

"Are they chasing you?" Fin whispered. He had a knife on him, a small comfort against a sniper or soldier with a rifle.

Roy spoke through clenched teeth. His eyes were bloodshot. "I don't know. I got hit as soon as I whistled."

"What happened?"

"Calvin had the rifle. He said he'd be careful, but I think they got him."

Fin could see the fear and strain, not to mention the pain, taking a toll.

Roy continued. "They bombed the graveyard then Calvin signaled for me to move out and report. That's when they used the gas and he told me to run. They shot him. I wanted to check on him but the gas stung and then… I'm sorry."

Johannes shook his head. "You'd be dead, too. You want to help, pull it together and get yourself back to the camp."

Roy gritted his teeth. "What about you?"

"Just move it." Johannes said.

# Chapter 32

Delacroix felt a jolt on his arm and he snapped awake. He was floating down a passage. No. He was being carried. He tried to sit up and he could now see Perrin held his legs. He assumed the other one was the guy right outside the engine room.

"Almost there, sir," Perrin glanced over his shoulder while he walked backwards.

Up one more flight of stairs and they laid him on the deck.

"I passed out?" The air felt blessedly cool as they unwrapped his body from the layers of protective clothing. Another man, the Arab fellow, poured cool canteen water into his mouth.

"I think you overheated. Do you feel better?"

He still felt hot but the air, water and shedding of his makeshift bee armor gave him major relief. "We should have brought an exterminator. Those bastards hurt." He felt the throbbing on his face. "Still do."

But his head felt clearer, so he tried sitting up. The ship didn't seem to whirl. "I think I'm all right, thanks."

"Sir, your face…"

"Still looks better than yours on a good day, Perrin." The communications expert laughed, but the Arab looked serious and shot a look at the other man.

Delacroix stood and allowed Perrin to steady him. He still didn't feel right. He guzzled the remainder of the canteen and poured the dregs over his head. "What?"

The Arab, Mahmoud, spoke rapidly and the other one listened.

Perrin seemed to catch more of the conversation, and he grabbed his portable radio and reached their man on the rifle guarding his Zodiac.

Delacroix snatched the microphone and earpiece from Perrin. "Delacroix here. Repeat last."

"They went around the point after those two that escaped."

"Who? I told Cloutier to sit tight." Delacroix said.

A new, deeper voice came on. Cloutier, the man that was supposed to keep those thugs in line. "Sir, I was over talking to Lambert when that fool Pancho and one of the other clowns took the second Zodiac."

"What?" It came out as a screech. "Why did you let them?" Delacroix felt like he must have been out for hours, not minutes.

"I tried to stop them but unless you wanted me to shoot both, they weren't going to come back."

Delacroix leaned against the wall of the wheelhouse. "Let's hear the rest."

Cloutier finished. "The only radio response I got was that Pancho said he was following Gagnon's orders and they were going to nail the guys who killed our men."

"Can you reach him now?"

"Gone silent, sir or he's out of range."

The next thought dropped like a brick in his gut. Delacroix keyed the mic. "Is that the raft with our signal repeater?"

The pause told him all he needed to know.

* * *

The breakwater wasn't so fierce once they got around the stony tip of the island. The calmer water also contained a viper's nest of sharp volcanic rocks that jutted out of the water. Many obstacles would be covered at high tide.

The rubber skin and inflatable pontoons of the Zodiac would make a tasty snack for these volcano-forged teeth.

"Steady as she goes, Lambert."

Delacroix leaned against the bow of the zodiac, clutching the ropes and scanning the water beyond the modest bow wave. Inside the boat, Mahmoud and the other guy who carried him on deck, who simply went by "Jean" gripped their AK-47s.

Perrin and Cloutier stayed behind with the two mercs and the rescued radio. Only two other mercs remained. He'd deal with Cloutier's incompetence later. Right now they had to get that repeater and call for help.

As much as he wanted to keep the group a coherent whole, he couldn't afford to allow the *Verdragen* to be re-invaded. If that happened, he'd need to be rescued *from* Gagnon.

The breeze felt wonderful against his skin. His pulse raced with all the screw-ups and his face felt flushed with anger.

Up ahead, away from the rocky shoreline, Delacroix saw a figure floundering in the water. A white man. About a hundred yards over he saw the mangled zodiac in the light surf. One side was collapsed and the whole craft was upside down.

"One survivor. Slow. They hit something, I bet." Delacroix was perched over the bow like a figurehead and their Zodiac moved forward at a crawl.

Now he could see who it was. Pancho. Part of him wanted to pump an entire magazine from his pistol into the man's chest. Of course, he'd have to take out all the mercs Gagnon had saddled him with.

*Just survive this op and you'll never have to see any of these fools again.*

He called out course corrections, determined not to repeat Pancho's headstrong mistake. This close to shore, the rocks hid just beneath the surface. He saw Pancho wasn't a strong swimmer and was standing atop a rocky spire that allowed him to just keep his head above water as long as he maintained balance. As a result he kept losing his footing on the underwater rock and then flailed and sputtered until his feet regained purchase.

Under other conditions Delacroix could have watched this spectacle with a cold glass of beer and never grow bored.

"Easy now."

"Socorrow!" Pancho cried out in Spanish.

Delacroix tossed a life vest, which the dolt should have been wearing already and then they hauled him aboard.

"What happened? Where's the other one?"

"We saw them." All signs of bluster had now gone from the Mexican.

"The natives?"

"Yes."

"And?"

"They were on the beach. One was wounded, at least we thought so."

"But?"

"When we started toward the beach they jumped up and ran. I made for the shore but we hit a rock. It wasn't our fault."

"I blame the rock as well." Delacroix saw the sarcasm was lost on this waterlogged thug. "That's how the raft was destroyed?"

"I almost drowned."

"And the other man?" Delacroix felt his fist curling.

"He couldn't get his gear off. He's down there somewhere." Pancho pointed at the bottom.

"So you lost the raft, the equipment, another man and your weapon?"

"The rock…"

Delacroix spit and turned away. "Lambert, on my mark, let's see if there's anything worth salvaging from the wreck." He turned to Mahmoud and pointed at his own eyes. "You two watch the shore, I'll watch for rocks."

Several agonizing minutes later Delacroix's nerves felt shot. There was a damn good reason boats didn't land on this part of the island. Anything less buoyant than this raft wouldn't stand a chance, and even now he'd bet Lambert had burned through a quarter of their gas just back-throttling trying to find a clear passage.

"It's like an underwater maze. Almost there." Delacroix's voice sounded hoarse. He kept an ear out for warnings from the two mercs.

"Mahmoud, ready on the rope. Can you swim?" Lambert said.

Delacroix kept his gaze trained on the approach so he never saw the response. He'd already ordered everyone into life vests.

"Slight starboard," Delacroix said. That's it. Now straight, good. Ready to hit the shore."

"Go on!" Lambert barked. Delacroix heard a splash and wriggled further up to fend off the rock which was as close as they could get. At least it was shallow and the current was mild. Delacroix looked over and saw Mahmoud had made it and was now hauling the rope and their raft to a more stable position.

The trashed Zodiac lolled nearby like an animal beaten half to death.

Lambert cut the engine and hopped out after he grabbed his shotgun. Then Jean and Pancho waded to shore. Delacroix shook his head in disbelief at Pancho. Of course that idiot didn't have his rifle. Come to think of it, where was that stupid stainless steel revolver he was always showing off?

Delacroix checked the raft for any spare weapons. All he saw was a set of paddles and he was tempted to give one of those to that worthless prick.

Once ashore, the trees hemmed in and crowded the "beach." What they were left with was a vulnerable strip of rocks that gave way to dense jungle.

Delacroix's whole body felt itchy and he couldn't shake the sensation of being watched. Lambert caught his eye and he looked like he shared the same feeling.

"Pancho, what do you have on you?"

The man looked at Delacroix like he'd lost his mind. "Wet clothes, gringo."

"Cut the bullshit! Any weapons? Any ammo?"

"Yeah, I got all that shit. Right over there." He pointed in the general direction of where they rescued him. He sneezed twice and ran a soggy sleeve across his nose.

"You take point and check the wrecked Zodiac."

Pancho and the two mercs marched toward the crumpled raft.

Lambert whispered in French to Delacroix. "Sir, if you don't take out that piece of crap, I will."

# Chapter 33

*Hoku, Outside the Dwazen Graveyard*

"Follow me!" Johannes said while he inched forward. They wanted to make sure they presented little, if any, target for the sniper.

Fin had given up trying to convince Johannes to watch the path further up in order to provide warning.

"Our scout is wounded. We're it. If they find our camp you know what they will do." Johannes had pointed out.

*Maybe he was right.*

The approach to the graveyard from this path led downhill and curved around part of the mountain. Fin had never seen this way to the graveyard but the path seemed to level off and then curl around the wall of the mountain to the open area of the graveyard.

So far they hadn't seen any sign of another soldier. Fin had been sure that the shot had come from the rifleman they spotted but he didn't understand how the sniper could have seen Roy. The guy had been down in the jungle, heading up an incline but shielded by vegetation. The observation platform in the tree made more sense, but even if the sniper had zeroed in on the sound of the signal whistling, at that distance it was a hell of a shot firing blind into the bushes.

Fin felt his senses ratchet up and could almost smell Africa again. Nostalgia blended in with raw fear.

*Weird.*

"Stay low. I have an idea." Johannes' voice was barely a breath of air. "See that fallen tree across the path?" Johannes pointed.

"Yeah?"

"Notice the way those leaves are stacked? Hog nest."

Reaching the nest would take them across the path entrance to the compound albeit about fifty feet back.

"So?"

"We can crawl over and I might get a view of the field from there. Gert wants a count if we can get it."

"We're going to get shot, is what." Fin had to try.

"They can't see us this low. Come on."

Fin knew the nest would likely give them a chance to be in a shallow depression and he liked the idea of the cover. They belly-crawled across the actual path.

Shivers ran up Fin's back while they were exposed but they made it across without incident. Johannes rooted like a hog himself until he saw the entrance and crawled in without hesitation. Fin heard muffled squealing. He wriggled in with his knife drawn.

The dark nest stunk of rotten vegetation and pig shit, which became part of their camouflage as he and Johannes were now slimed with the mixture.

Fin relaxed for a moment when he realized that the noise was several piglets, too young to pose any threat. They writhed in a fuzzy black and tan pile and Fin noticed that their tails were short and straight. The nest was just large enough for the two of them to leave the piglets alone and when they gave them some space, they seemed to calm down.

"Where's mom?" Fin whispered. He clutched the knife.

"Out looking for food. We'll be long gone before she gets back." Johannes crept forward and Fin saw over the guy's shoulder that they had a well-protected view of the entrance. "Hey, what's that?"

Fin wriggled alongside and gazed where Johannes pointed. "What?"

"Right across the path. Wait. There, see it?"

It took a moment but then he saw it too. While a breeze stirred some of the foliage above the last trees before the clearing Fin saw a tiny white light winking a few inches above the ground.

After a moment his brain processed the image. It was intermittent sunlight glinting off a thin silver line. "Tripwire." Fin followed its length until it reached a thin tree just off the edge of the path. Another gust of air gave him a glimpse of the green, curved rectangular object strapped to the tree. "That's a Claymore mine. Very strong, throws ball bearings out in a fan. It would take us both out in an instant."

Johannes nodded. He certainly understood traps but likely had spent no time in a war zone where ignorance wasn't bliss, it was death.

The young man appeared lost in thought. Then he grinned. "That goes off when the wire's pulled?"

Fin thought back to the crash course on mines that the mercs in Angola had given him. "Yeah. Wait. They also are good for ambushes. They can be remote detonated," he mimed a thumb depressing a button.

"That's what I have in mind. Stay here. You move like an elephant."

Fin couldn't raise his voice this close to the entrance, especially since there could be a guard nearby, though maybe not with a claymore in place. Besides, the sniper was doing a fine job so far.

*Aw, crap.*

Fin watched while Johannes reached into a pocket and pulled out thin twine, the same he had used to set the many traps guarding the other paths. Fin saw what he had planned. He was going to slither up to that line and tie his own trigger on the mine.

*Too damn risky.*

There was no way to recall him and Johannes hadn't shown any inclination to listen anyway.

Then Fin heard the grunting behind him. He turned in the confined space and saw a flash of bristles. He tried to crawl away but as soon as he raised his body, the enraged sow barreled into his ass and sent him flying out of the nest. Fin jumped up out of reflex and Johannes shook his head and waved for him to get down.

Fin ran for the bushes with the sow on his heels. She caught one leg and his feet tangled up and sent him to the ground. Just as he fell, the sound of a rifle shot cracked and he heard a tearing noise pass by where he'd been standing not one second earlier.

The pig also whipped around to face the sound and Fin realized he still had his knife in his hand. He lashed out and caught her in the rump. No more than a shallow jab but the sow squealed and sprinted away from Fin, right toward the opening in the path. The piglets squealed, burst from the nest and raced after the sow.

Just before she reached the opening, Fin realized what was about to happen.

So did Johannes, and both he and Fin dove to the side, away from the mine and rolled.

The pig hit the tripwire and let out one final terrified shriek when the mine tore her apart. A couple of piglets survived and scattered and Fin saw the one running on the path get cut down by a rifle bullet.

*How the hell can the shooter see his targets?*

He and Johannes flew as deep into the jungle as possible and hid at the base of a tree while they caught their breath and listened for signs of pursuit.

\* \* \*

*The Dwazen Graveyard*

"Are you done hunting pigs?" Gagnon yelled at Letang. "At least you could leave some behind so we'd have something to eat." He wasn't intending to be funny.

The hours of grunt work digging had left the small group exhausted and hungry. They carried field rations and he'd eaten his second, (or was it his third?) lunch. He'd left strict orders for his men to leave any food they found in the villages in place. With all the traps and tricks these bastards had left in them, he wouldn't doubt the food supplies were full of toxins.

The thought of fresh pork set his stomach rumbling but he wasn't about to eat pig meat contaminated with the animal's guts and marinated in C4 and steel.

"Pigs don't climb trees. And I could swear I saw one of those just now stand up. Would you like a turn on the rifle? The scope is giving me a headache."

Gagnon bit his tongue. He knew this leadership was going to be brief and the last thing he needed was to provoke a rebellion when they were already so short-handed.

"Just be careful. We need enough rounds to fight our way back to town if necessary."

Letang wiped his forehead. Gagnon didn't like the look of the man's flushed skin.

True, he and Stephon were also florid-faced but that was from the exertion of digging. His hands were covered with first-aid tape that gave scant relief to his blistered palms. He needed to make sure he could handle his pistol.

Stephon took a break and tore into a packet of rations. Their shirts stuck to their skin. Gagnon switched on the radio and raised the mortar team who reported no enemy contact.

"Any word from the *Fanfaron*?" He wondered how the wounded were faring but really he needed to reach the team he'd sent to the *Verdragen*. The handful of scopes they had wouldn't work in the dark.

"Yes sir. Doc Jean-Paul has been calling in and insists on speaking only to you."

"Did you explain we haven't got a direct line yet?"

"Every time, sir."

Gagnon could hear the man's voice rise in exasperation.

"Wait one." He switched off the microphone and stepped away from the latest open grave he and Stephon were digging. They'd unearthed a considerable sum of gold and so far none of the recently dug graves had failed to contain gold bars. Still, each time they didn't find so much as a skeleton inside the graves Gagnon grew convinced this place had been some sort of major repository.

He stepped outside of earshot for Letang. The others continued to take turns and watch the second entrance to the graveyard.

"We still have more than a half dozen graves to open." He said to Stephon.

"Can we rig lights?"

"Torchlight, and maybe even defend ourselves, but we can't keep up this pace."

Stephon spoke in a whisper. "Onset a lot faster than we thought." He looked over at the stash on the ground.

"Maybe it will level off."

"We have to be ready if they go down. I think we should bring back the cart." Stephon said.

One small bit of good news. The guard at the second entrance had spotted wheel tracks and Gagnon had decided to risk a quick scout down the path where they found the wood cart rigged to be pulled by oxen or cows. They were able to roll it back and could use it to transport the gold.

"The mother lode is still out there."

"We've got over a hundred pounds already. At this rate we should pull that much again, at least."

"The cart can carry twenty times that. This was a tempting distraction, but how far could a handful of them carry the real stash?" He could almost smell the stuff. "Once we get the ATV rolled off the ship we can rig it to tow a lot more than we can push."

"Docking the ship at this point is dangerous," the big man warned.

Gagnon was about to disagree when a new idea flashed into his mind.

"You may be right. Let's dig up a few more, as fast as we can and roll what we find back to town. I'll tell the mortar crew to relay to the *Fanfaron* they need to get around to the other side of the island and see what's going with Delacroix's men. He keyed the mic. "Base team?"

"Go ahead." The man by the mortar said.

He passed along the instructions and didn't care for the delay.

"*Fanfaron* wants to talk to you."

"Tell them the feeling is fucking mutual."

# Chapter 34

*Hoku, Islander side*

"It's still here!" Pancho yelled out while he pawed through the wrecked Zodiac.

Delacroix didn't dare trust his luck. Saltwater would prove merciless on the repeater's internals. One miracle at a time. "Is it dry?"

"I can't tell."

Delacroix's heart sank until his saw the grinning Mexican hold up a package over his head. "It's wrapped too tight!"

"This clown will get us all killed." Lambert said, but Delacroix heard the hope in his voice.

Bad luck and incompetence aside, this entire operation appeared to be draining for his team. Delacroix blamed his own strain on age but knew he had enough left in the tank to see them through.

Pancho and the other mercs returned. Mahmoud and the second man, Jean, set up a crude perimeter where they faced the trees and watched for threats.

"Anything else from the raft?"

Pancho held up two loose bottles of water and a soggy candy bar. He also had a pair of cylindrical speed loaders. Cartridges bristled from them in a ring.

"What's that?" Delacroix held out his hand.

Pancho dumped them into his palm. "Spare ammo for my revolver."

Which was nestled somewhere on underwater rocks.

"Keep them. You can throw the bullets at the enemy."

Pancho shrugged, took a bite of the candy bar, made a face and chucked all but the water into the sea.

Sticks and seaweed collected and floated in thick clumps between some of the rocks. The white candy wrapper stood out among the debris before sinking.

"Good news, sir" Lambert called out.

Delacroix almost said something sarcastic and checked his tongue. Morale might be hanging by a thread.

They went over to Lambert who'd unpacked the repeater. Such a small, simple looking device but if it had been damaged their survival chances would shrink.

"Good battery strength, test, test?" Lambert said.

Delacroix heard the man loud over the radio earpiece. "Okay. We just need to reach high ground. We'll be able to contact our men on the *Verdragen* and then get some help from Gagnon."

They heard a whooping sound joined quickly by more. Many more. They sounded like howler monkeys caught in a drainpipe. The thought created a weird mental picture, but that hollow quality sounded like nothing he'd ever heard in a jungle.

"Phalanx!" Delacroix ordered the men to a defensive crouch, guns pointed outward toward the jungle. Though he hadn't trained with the mercs, the two followed Lambert's lead. Pancho squatted near the rest of them, looking out of place without a weapon.

Delacroix almost felt sorry for him. He raised his pistol and wished for a nice FN rifle or at least another 12-gauge pump like Lambert carried. He carried two spare mags and the one in the pistol gave him more than thirty rounds to work with, and he knew how to make them count. Gagnon had told him to expect no more than a handful of survivors.

So far the handful they had run into had been enough and what he now heard sounded like more than that.

The mercs carried AKs and between them probably more than two hundred rounds, but that was deceptive. Full auto burned through ammo at a frightening rate.

The howling, still deep in the jungle, seemed to move closer. First to their left, then to their right.

"They're trying to trap us against the sea." Lambert said.

Delacroix thought quickly. He glanced at the water. The wind had picked up and some of the sluggish debris floating on the water began to catch the current.

He didn't know how fast storms could pop up around here. He could operate small boats as needed, but he wasn't a true sailor. Also they were bunched up and vulnerable on that patch of rubber.

Gagnon had told him his own group needed more of the hardware since the natives lived like primitives and didn't use rifles but the Dwazen did. At this moment Delacroix didn't know what to believe.

One "savage" with a bolt action deer rifle could nail his group and swamp the raft, leaving them helpless in the water.

The hollow moaning, whooping and screeching drew ever closer. To their right the sharp crested ridge beckoned.

Decision time.

"Lambert, we need off this beach. One way or another."

"Agreed, sir. We'll be in range of anything including spears if we stay put."

"Let's take the boat!" Pancho acted like this was a democracy. He was sweating despite the cooling temperatures. The sun would dip down over the horizon in less than an hour.

Delacroix shook his head. "Negative. We stay together and make for high ground. The jungle gives way and we'll have a clear field of fire and a better chance to reach Gagnon."

The mercs looked relieved that someone was in charge. That they'd imagined Pancho a leader made Delacroix question where in the hell Gagnon found these mutts.

"I'll take point," Lambert said. "Watch your feet and your fields of fire. Anyone hits me in the back and you better kill me."

They nodded and prepared to move to the right.

Except Pancho. "The raft! Hey, puta!"

Delacroix glanced over his shoulder.

*Merde!*

He saw two figures, both natives, had swum up behind them and one was fully in the raft and a second was over by the engine.

Pancho ran toward the raft, slowed by the rocky footing. The one in the raft looked like he was going to cut the rope with a knife he held. The man paused to gesture and scream something at Pancho then bent to sever the mooring line.

"Wait." Delacroix spoke in a calm voice and forced his heart to slow down. He knelt and braced one elbow on his knee, concentrated on the front sight of his pistol, then took the shot.

He saw a wet puff from the man's back and a surprised expression on the native's face. He reached forward as if to continue his task then simply pitched forward into the raft.

"Great shot." Lambert said.

The one by the engine didn't climb all the way into the raft. Instead, he tossed something and slid backward, splashing into the water.

Delacroix saw the sequence in slow motion and he was able to note that the second man paddled away underneath a thick stick that jutted out of the water like a…snorkel.

*You fool.*

The thought danced across his mind just as the first of the smoky orange flames erupted at the rear of the raft and spread across the bottom.

"Hold fire. I have this." Delacroix trained the pistol at the receding stick he now realized must be hollow. He took deliberate shots, but when the raft wasn't in the way, the smoke and heat distortion spoiled his aim. Sweat dripped into his eyes and the slide on the pistol locked back before he was sure he had a hit.

"He went behind the pair of rocks." Lambert shouted.

Now the chorus from the jungle started up again closer, shrill with mocking.

"Screw it." He rammed another magazine home and dropped the slide release to chamber a round. "That's it then. High ground or die, gentlemen. Simple as that. Leave the pyromaniac. Let's go."

The famed Chinese General, Sun Tzu, wrote about placing soldiers in a desperate situation he called "Killing Ground" in order to force his men to fight hard and win, or die. Delacroix always thought he'd understood what that meant.

Up until now he hadn't been close.

They moved quickly to the right and the voices in the jungle went silent. Delacroix could hear the hiss of the raft pontoons expelling their air when the flames ate through the rubber and fabric walls.

"There's the path." Lambert whispered.

Delacroix knew better than to warn him to look out for traps.

Lambert crept into the jungle and before the whole group had made it under the canopy he held up a fist to signal a halt. Delacroix watched the two mercs closely. They stopped right away and were paying attention to direction. There might be hope for them. Forget Pancho. He'd heard the guy was an ambitious peasant's kid who'd been kicked out of the cartels before he freelanced all over the world, a far better bullshitter than a soldier.

Delacroix kept him in the back, figuring if he got ambushed he'd at least scream before he died.

After a long minute with the jungle's silence magnifying the tension, Lambert crept back to Delacroix.

"What have you got?" he asked the point man.

Lambert held up a whip-like sapling with a series of barbs tied to the business end. There was a dark paste stuck to the long thorns. "Simple spring trap. Not that tough to spot if you know where to look.

"Keep looking and don't underestimate them. Show the others and make sure they don't touch that crap."

Lambert nodded. "I'd love a chance to put this where it belongs."

Right about now Delacroix could think of a few candidates outside of their purported enemy. "Stay on task. We have to get up that hill."

The group moved into the jungle and the canopy enveloped them. The waning daylight added urgency. He didn't want to hold this group together in the dark without established perimeters and fields of fire.

Even the birds were quiet.

The path wound along the edge of the mountain where the rocks were nearly sheer and then deeper into the jungle. When it was close enough to the stone-face, Delacroix was able to see a series of switchbacks. He'd committed to the idea that as soon as they spotted an accessible place to reach the path, they'd bushwhack to it, if necessary.

Right now the thick jungle crowded them on both sides.

They found two more similar traps without incident. Lambert walked back to Delacroix. They spoke in hushed tones, not just to avoid the enemy overhearing but to try for privacy from the mercs.

"Sir, the path bends right up ahead and I think it's where we will get a chance to get out of the trees and start climbing."

"Okay. The locals will also know this. It's probably their best chance to make a move."

"Agreed."

"Bastards hide well, don't they?" Delacroix said.

"It's their home."

"If it jumps off in here, hit the deck. Don't bet your life on their fire discipline. I won't." Delacroix watched Pancho, who was sweating like a pig and pawing at his shirt, looking for cigarettes that weren't there.

Just as well, Delacroix didn't have to waste time arguing with the asshole about not smoking in the field.

"Right. I'll pass the word. We move as a unit and not to bolt for the hill when they see daylight."

Just when the group started forward Delacroix got the pins and needles feeling all up and down his back.

He heard a single bird call.

Time got that sticky, slow quality and before he could pass a warning up the line, the left side of the jungle exploded with sound. Fierce native battle cries sounded just beyond his line of sight.

The words made no difference, this was a full throated charge in any language and the horror it conjured felt primal. Delacroix and Lambert both called out "Ambush left!"

He pivoted and dropped to the ground. He'd kept his pistol in hand all along and now his finger was on the trigger.

He saw several branches in the foliage ahead begin to shake and that did it. The two mercs knelt and opened fire, raking the jungle with a withering hail of bullets.

The cordite stench permeated the air and Delacroix held off until whatever shook the branches directly in front of him gave him a proper target.

Over the din of the gunfire, he heard the distinctive blast of Lambert's shotgun. Delacroix noted with satisfaction there were screams of pain and fewer voices.

The only lull in the rate of fire came when the mercs had to change magazines.

Delacroix still didn't see any enemy in front of him. All he saw was that damn branch shake back and forth. He sat up and looked at the line. None of the men appeared to be hit or under any sort fire. No arrows or spears or bullets that he could see. He looked behind.

Where was Pancho?

That branch stopped moving and all they heard were moans of pain.

"Cease fire!" Delacroix called out. He gave the mercs credit for listening right away. They were spooked. Delacroix could see it all over their faces. Lambert, at the end of the line, stuffed fresh shotgun shells into his weapon and kept his head on a swivel. He'd dropped to the ground, Delacroix was glad to see.

An instant later, they heard Pancho scream from their right side. Just after that, another barrage of war cries, too close. Then projectiles started raining down on the group.

A couple spears flew over their heads and one crude arrow grazed Mahmoud's cheek.

The man cried out in pain and Delacroix was certain the arrow must have been tipped with poison or something.

But the Arab was tough. He got mad and hosed the foliage ahead with his AK-47. More shrieks followed the gunfire bursts and Delacroix felt pride in how this barely trained ragtag force was performing under a nasty ambush.

Several round objects rolled onto the path. Coconuts.

No, smoking coconut *shells.*

*Something burning inside, like a fuse…*

"Grenades! Take cover!" Delacroix took his own advice and dove to the left, firing blind at the direction the phantom attackers had tossed them.

He covered up and hoped the other's had done the same. He heard a scream and one burst of an AK.

Lambert cried out followed by two shotgun blasts and more native screams. "Sir, if you're alive, up the path, run!" Delacroix almost tripped over something. He glanced down and saw a narrow, man-sized depression in the jungle floor and what looked like a bamboo periscope. His mind didn't grasp the significance but unconsciously filed the detail for later.

*If there was going to be a later.*

Once he got moving he decided against firing behind him to discourage pursuit as it would give away his position.

Delacroix fell flat on his face after stumbling over a body. It was Jean. The man still clutched his rifle but he'd been stabbed and his throat was slashed. Delacroix grabbed the weapon and saw the magazine was out and sticks had been jammed in the barrel and broken off inside the chamber.

He tossed the rifle, scrambled to his feet and broke through to the path. He stood alone and the smoldering coconuts sat there. A pair of legs stuck out of the brush and he recognized the camo pants as Mahmoud's.

"Boom!" Several voices yelled from the jungle behind him. More voices mocked and laughed.

Delacroix bolted up the path. The cries chased after him.

Out in the open, Delacroix jogged the switchbacks and knew Lambert must not be far ahead. There were fresh boot tracks on the path. Even better, he had a good view of the jungle below.

As the taunting faded behind him, he felt his lungs burn with the effort to keep up his pace. His skin felt warm even while the scorching sun yielded to the coming sunset. Sweat poured off of him and he remembered intensity training at altitudes where the thin air starved his body of oxygen. Here the air should be rich. He was barely a hundred feet above sea level.

The next turn was marked by a rock large enough to use as cover. He knew he had to rest. Something wasn't right, he wasn't a kid anymore but he worked hard to stay in shape.

He'd shoot the first figure he saw in pursuit but he had to get a breather.

When he rounded the rock someone grabbed him by the lapel and slammed him against the rock hard enough to blur his vision. One hand gripped his wrist so he couldn't aim his pistol. The other held a combat knife to his throat.

Lambert. He was also a mass of sweat and despite the fierce expression, seemed to have something wrong with his eyes. Lambert blinked a bunch of times and squinted. "Sir?" He answered his own question and used his knife arm to wipe a sleeve across his eyes. Delacroix noticed a thin smear of blood.

Now that the cobwebs had cleared, Delacroix could see Lambert's eyes looked pink and he saw a red drop well at the tear duct.

"Lambert? What happened?"

"Hard to see. They nicked me but I'll be all right. Who else made it out?"

"I'm it. Got my pistol and a mag and a half. Twenty rounds tops." Delacroix saw the bloodstain along Lambert's ribs.

"Hit by a spear. Believe that?" Lambert shouldered his pack where they'd put the radio repeater.

"Want me to take that?"

"I can manage. Take my shotgun. Can't see far for some reason. Up close is not too bad," Lambert took his canteen and poured water over his upturned face and rinsed his eyes. "That helps."

Delacroix noticed the canteen was nearly empty but decided not to mention it. Water wouldn't matter if they couldn't get to the crest and rig the repeater.

The sun was a huge orange fireball sliding toward the water. He wished he could jump in the sea himself to quench his fever.

*No sense lying to yourself. You're sick. You both are.*

"Can you see to set up the unit?" Lambert let Delacroix take the lead and stayed close behind. In different circumstances, he'd have advised against bunching up. Right now it didn't seem to matter.

"I think so. Wish we had a flashlight. Don't know what they put on that spear but my whole body feels like it got dipped in hot mustard."

Delacroix knew exactly how he felt but didn't want to say so. "Let's just get help."

"We made them pay for that ambush, didn't we?" Lambert coughed and spit. It looked black in the fading light. The good news was Delacroix could see they were almost at the top.

"A little bit further." The bamboo contraption reappeared in his mind's eye.

"I got two. Saw them go down." Lambert coughed again.

They reached the top of the crest. Lambert sank to his knees and dug into the pack. "Still clear?"

"We're alone." *For now.*

Up here Delacroix could see the *Verdragen* in the distance. This side had less open space before the tree line reappeared. More disturbing was that the spine of this crest vanished up the mountain and trees grew closer to the edge in some places that might provide cover if there were paths up there.

He decided not to mention it. Lambert was focused on setting up the radio transmitter. While the location might not be optimal for defense, it was perfect for boosting the range of their communications.

He just hoped they'd hurt the attackers enough to make them hesitate.

# Chapter 35

Gagnon wiped his brow and shared a glance with Stephon, who leaned over the shovel. He could see some red stains had bled through under the white medical tape that wrapped his fingers. Same for his own hands and those of the men.

Gagnon noticed that the men were looking run down so he and Stephon had begun doing more of the heavy work, allowing Letang and the others to watch out for Dwazen.

"Any more water?" asked one of the men who'd been tasked with setting up torches. "Think they used these to work at night?"

"They were certainly busy. Take those bars over to the cart," Gagnon said and refilled a canteen from their last water skin. He wasn't about to ration water at a time like this.

The shadows grew longer off the trees and the tombstones. They wouldn't be done by dark but that was all right.

"Not as many in this one." Stephon stood in the dugout grave. He probed the dirt with his shoe.

"Wait for the metal detector." Gagnon scolded. "There could be tripwires."

"I think this *is* the trap." Stephon spoke in a soft voice. Gagnon saw one man was busy with the torches after gulping down the water.

Letang continued his vigilance, especially focusing on the path where the claymore blew up the pig. They could still get a whiff of singed raw pork when the breeze came from that direction.

"I can't hear you over the clank of gold bars," Gagnon said.

"Didn't you say we should move what we have to the dock?"

Sometimes Stephon's ability to recall everything he said was inconvenient. "I also said we'd have nearly two hundred pounds by now."

"I bet we have closer to two fifty. Not worth a damn if we don't get it out."

The idea of leaving blocks of pure gold in the ground caused an itch in Gagnon's mind that near blinded him to the treasure they'd unearthed. He walked over to the cart and placed his hands on the cool glittering bars.

The first of the torches were lit and the flames played along the yellow surface in a warm, reassuring way. He pictured losing the pile under his fingertips and the siren cry of the unearthed metal faded.

"Perhaps you are right. If we had more people…"

"Sir! The radio." Lambert called over. He had one of the portable rigs on his belt.

"See, Stephon! Our luck is turning."

Stephon climbed out of the hole and the men gathered around except for the one guarding the rear entrance to the graveyard.

"Say again." Letang pulled the earpiece out and let the sound come out of the speaker. He turned up the volume.

"Team Two to Team Lead."

Gagnon took the microphone. "This is Team Lead, go ahead."

"Yes sir. We need…" It was Delacroix.

Gagnon cut him off. "Override. Prepare to evacuate. Expedite."

Now the buried gold found its own voice again. With a few more strong backs maybe they could get it after all.

A new voice chimed in. "Break. I say again, Break. *Fanfaron* to Team Lead." Jean-Paul interrupted.

*Not now.*

"Team Two, this is Lead, confirm receipt prior instructions."

"Sir, urgent request for you return to *Fanfaron*," Jean-Paul insisted.

"What is your location?" Gagnon felt the frustration rise.

"*Fanfaron* remains on station. We have a, uh, technical situation…"

Delacroix cut in. The signal was loud and clear so Gagnon knew the repeater had to be in place. "Break. Team Two to Lead. Request fire support or immediate exfil assistance."

A loud moaning and shrieking cut off Delacroix's words.

Gagnon keyed the mike. "Repeat, Team Two."

The noise continued to rise, and they could barely hear Delacroix. "Enemy contact."

"Where, Team Two?" Gagnon shouted.

"Everywhere."

\* \* \*

*Hoku, Ridge Crest*

"Are they coming?" Lambert held Delacroix's pistol and was trying to aim it toward the sound of the natives.

But there was one problem. As he'd just tried to tell Gagnon and anyone who'd listen, the sounds bombarded them from every direction. And he'd twice ducked under the wavering muzzle when Lambert aimed at each new noise.

The sky grew dark now that the sun had slid beneath the sea and the last vestiges of light were fading. Delacroix no longer felt hot, now he began to shiver and a part of his mind registered that the temperature couldn't have fallen that much.

But Lambert seemed in worse shape. In the deep dusk, he seemed to be completely blind. Delacroix clutched the shotgun.

"Should I shoot? I can hear them."

"Don't waste ammo."

"When is Gagnon coming?"

*Not soon enough.*

Now he could see shapes darting and skittering between the rocks and just over the crest he could hear movement. Along the ridge, near where the jungle grew closer to the top, the sounds boomed out low and high.

"Sir," Lambert gave a wet-sounding cough. "I hear them. Lean me against a rock and tell me when to fire. I'll scare them. I'll…"

Delacroix wasn't sure if Lambert had passed out or was simply out of breath. He saw a target in the gathering dark. A human shape a shade darker than the rock he moved over. Delacroix raised his shotgun and his peripheral vision caught more shapes.

These moved like shadows, flowing over the landscape and his fogged brain gave up trying to count them. Dozens and dozens. His target vanished behind a rock. The shotgun held eight shells. He doubted there'd be time to reload. He put the gun down in front of his feet.

He saw the muzzle of his pistol touch the ground as it dropped out of Lambert's hand.

"Team Two, come in." Gagnon's voice crackled over the tiny speaker.

Delacroix was a few feet from the radio. He couldn't see much at all now. The moon would help when it rose, but like a great many things, he feared that wouldn't be soon enough.

The rustling from the natives ceased, like a switch had been flipped.

The radio repeated the call, and in the silence it sounded like a bullhorn to Delacroix.

Now a voice called out from atop the nearby rock. In French. "We can reach you."

"Who are you?" Delacroix considered the shotgun but he figured he'd be skewered. That one of them spoke a civilized language gave him a shred of hope.

"I speak for the tribe," the French was flawless but the voice had a hollow sound.

Delacroix remembered the bamboo periscope and realized what it was. It was like a modified speaking tube. Now he envisioned natives hiding in those dug out positions, taunting the foolish soldiers into wasting their ammunition by shooting too high.

No wonder there were so many out there. They hadn't inflicted more than a scratch on their numbers.

*Fool. You've been outsmarted by savages with sticks and coconut shells.*

"What are your terms for surrender?"

There was a pause and Delacroix considered whether or not this man was really fluent or just a skilled mimic.

"We are trying to decide."

"Decide the terms?" Delacroix asked. At his feet Lambert groaned and slumped over.

"Whether or not to eat you."

Several matches flared and torches ignited in a circle. Delacroix cried out.

They'd crept up almost close enough to touch him. Dark faces, white eyes and bared teeth.

# Chapter 36

*Dwazen Camp*

Fin and Johannes finished recounting their scouting mission. Gert and Willem sat in the front of the loose circle. Fin would have liked a warm fire but that was out of the question. At least the moon had risen enough to allow them see each other.

Saskia put one of her homemade blankets over his shoulders.

The trip back was nerve wracking when Johannes almost put them on the wrong path. Fin relied completely on the young guy's skills.

"We know where they are and how they are covering the approach. We should creep in and hit them before they find all the crumbs we left for them." Gert said. Several of the Dwazen sailors sat and nodded while they leaned on their old rifles.

Fin looked out into the jungle beyond the moonlit clearing. He couldn't see anything but the darkness drew him. He could feel an idea bubbling up in his mind.

He'd learned to go with these feelings and not try to rush them. He took a few deep breaths and imagined how far he could see even in daylight in this thick jungle. Not far at all, so how did the sniper…

"Wait. Don't try that. That sniper wasn't just tracking noise, he could see us."

Johannes looked at him. "Didn't *you* hear those pigs squeal and run? And I said, you move like an elephant."

Fin ignored him. "Son of a bitch! I know how they did it. I should have realized it right away. We're lucky to be here."

Johannes shook his head. "I already know that, Fin."

"Not how lucky. They've got thermal imaging scopes. That's got to be it."

"What's that?" Saskia said.

Fin gave a quick explanation about how the thermals didn't amplify light but detected heat and that was how they saw through dense foliage.

"Never saw one on a gun but you can get camera lenses that can detect heat." Fin nodded to himself. "That's why they spotted me on the platform. I was like a beacon."

"Then why shoot at pigs?" Johannes said.

"I'm not sure but now that I think of it the guy took a shot at me when I stood up." Fin rubbed his bruised backside and lifted his pant leg to show dark contusions on his lower leg. "If that sow hadn't knocked me down, I would have been hit for sure."

Willem spoke. "So we can't use cover of dark?"

"If they are using thermal tech we might look like blobs of heat at that range, easy to see the rough size and certainly the position but probably not close detail. Out in the open, I don't know."

"So you're not sure?" Saskia said.

"No. It could be they saw us when we were crawling and thought we were pigs. I blew it when I stood up." Fin saw Gert lean in at this last comment.

Gert frowned in thought. "So they only shot the one pig, that you know about?"

"I think so. Things happened fast and after the explosion it was hard to hear." Fin said.

"Many pigs on the island."

"Yeah?" Fin didn't like the sound of this.

"If they get used to pigs running around then maybe it won't surprise them to see a few more."

Saskia spoke. "What if they decide they want to shoot all the pigs as well?"

276

Gert scratched at his beard. "Were they shooting before you got close, say at the platform in the tree?"

"No," Johannes said. "After the platform the first shot was at Fin when he stood up. And it was loud."

"We should wait." Willem said.

"For what? Your idea about leaving some gold behind worked well, my friend," Gert said.

"It should be enough for him. At least for now." Willem said.

Gert pointed to Fin. "You said before you know how this man thinks. Will that satisfy Gagnon?"

The pressure knotted the muscles in Fin's shoulders. "I can't read his mind." Fin felt the gaze of Dwazen drill into him all over their makeshift refugee camp.

Saskia touched his shoulder and spoke softly. "Will it?"

Fin took a deep breath. "If Gagnon thinks there's so much as an ounce lying around, he'll want it. When they finish looting the graveyard they'll come for the rest and kill every witness they find."

Gert looked almost smug. "You won't have to send anyone, Willem. I'll take volunteers."

Fin wasn't surprised that sailors stepped forward. He saw half a dozen rifles.

*Maybe it would be enough. With surprise and a little luck.*

Fin joined the men. "I don't know if it's a good idea. But I'm in." He ran his fingers through his hair and looked over at Willem. "If they come looking and beat the traps, that scope will see everyone here. They could call in a fire mission and those mortars would wipe you out in minutes."

"I'm coming too." Saskia said.

"No, I forbid it." Willem said.

Saskia smiled. "You haven't tried that in over a hundred years."

A few people laughed but nobody looked at her like she was insane.

Nocturnal Kingbirds began to chatter in a rapid *ki, ki, ki* sound. One of the Dwazen darted to the entrance path and imitated the call to perfection.

*The sentries.*

* * *

A group of islanders rushed into the camp. The moon had risen and Fin could see everyone well enough to know Maru and Hua led a group who carried two men over their shoulders. The men had cloth sacks over their heads and were silent.

All the islanders were covered in sweat and from their breathing Fin guessed they'd run the entire way from their village.

Hua looked ragged and Fin noticed some swelling on his arm. He stepped toward his friend. Gert and Willem approached and Saskia walked with Fin.

Maru looked every bit the chief, even without his headdress. He recovered his breath and appeared calm but there was a wild light in his eyes.

Hua had a similar look.

"You okay?" Fin said to Hua.

"Not yet, but soon." Hua clapped Fin on the shoulder and pointed to Maru.

"We aren't too late. I'm pleased." Maru said. "We heard some shooting in the distance."

"We know where they are." Gert spoke to Maru. "We have a plan. But maybe you can help."

Maru smiled. "Leave them there. Enough blood has been shed."

"Give me one good reason why. He won't stop." Gert said.

"He will." Maru dropped into a cross legged seated position. His body language projected calm even as his eyes continued to dance with excitement. He gestured to invite the others to gather around. The other Dwazen pressed in from all sides.

"The other day I watched a swamp hawk being attacked by a group of reed warblers. They knew he wanted their eggs. At first, I thought they would drive him off. They were fierce and flew hard at him, but he kept on soaring." Maru paced his speech and despite what Fin thought was an urgent situation, nobody rushed the man.

"I noticed while the hawk rode on the wind, the other birds had to thrash the air to reach him," he continued. Maru pointed to the islanders tending the captive men and motioned that they be dragged forward. "One by one, the small birds tired out, while the hawk needed only to turn his body this way and that." He stood up.

"Soon the hawk was alone and the others had quit." He pulled off the hood and Fin saw a man who looked like he'd been slow roasted over a fire. His face was brick-red and shiny. He blinked at the moonlight. His body began to shiver and a thread of blood ran out of one nostril.

"They have the sickness." Saskia said.

For an instant Fin wanted to explain that they'd worked the man over and had maybe given him something but he saw she was right. That was what he must have looked like barely a week ago.

"This one led the attack team on our village," Hua's voice came out low and hateful. Hua lifted the man's head and forced him to gaze at the raw scarring on his chest. "You like it? My boy went through it."

"Enough." Maru said and Hua turned away. Fin saw the recently carved image on his friend's chest was a likeness of Ruru's face.

Hua pulled the hood off the other man, whose head lolled back, and dried blood streaked down his face. He was dead. "He was alive when we started here. They were using this." Another islander unrolled a blanket to reveal a radio booster and communications gear.

Willem came forward and looked at the still-breathing prisoner. "It looks like the same disease."

"It is." Maru said. He turned to Gert. "All we have to do is ride out the invasions and the intruders will drop away." He opened his fingers and blew on them.

"I hope you can still feel it, pig." Hua poked the man in the belly and elicited a cry of pain.

The man was sick, no doubt about that. Fin felt sympathy, at least at a visceral level, but something wasn't right. "Can he talk?"

Maru gazed at Fin like he trying to read him. "He could earlier. The trip has taken a toll."

Fin glanced at the equipment. "Can he again?"

Maru followed his gaze, and dug into a pouch he carried.

\* \* \*

*Dwazen Graveyard*

"That's the last of it," Gagnon said. It wasn't. There were two more sites that showed promise when he'd waved the metal detector over them, but he knew more digging would invite open mutiny.

"Lambert, keep that muzzle elevated. You won't see anything on the ground." Stephon snapped at their best rifleman.

*A relative term.*

"Arm's cramping."

"Do your best." Gagnon forced a supportive tone into his voice. He waved Stephon over.

The other two men rested by the cart that now held over two hundred fifty pounds of solid gold. Not the bonanza he'd wanted but in time, perhaps, they could amend the total.

"He doesn't look good," Stephon whispered.

"None of them do. We don't have a choice but to press on. Delacroix fucked up, that much is clear, and I have a good guess Jean-Paul is doing some thinking of his own."

"You have the card for the ship's sat phone?" Stephon looked worried.

"Of course. Best he could do is reach a passing ship on the maritime. How likely is that?"

Stephon knew the size of the restriction zone as well as he did. "Bon." He paused. "How did so many natives survive?"

"We don't know that they did. Delacroix might have been delusional," Gagnon didn't want to voice that he'd had the same concerns. Not at this critical point. He just needed to get that plane loaded.

"Pass around the last of these." Gagnon dumped out a handful of pills, a Jean–Paul special mix of codeine and amphetamine. "None for us. I need you straight to fly the plane."

Gagnon stepped behind the wagon and pushed. The soft terrain made the task even more difficult but the cart was far from full and it creaked forward.

He watched Stephon dispense the pills and gave the men a couple minutes rest to let the meds take effect. He'd tried them before and they were a great asset when used sparingly. Pain vanished and so did the fatigue opiates usually brought.

He didn't need these men clear-headed as much as upright. He and Stephon could fight, if it came to that. He hoped the Dwazen were content to hide. He wouldn't blame them. They wouldn't even miss this pittance, considering what they must be sitting on.

*Why* were *there so many left?* The thought tugged at his consciousness.

He saw the impact of remnant virus on his own men. He suppressed a shiver and looked over at the three who were left. One man who had looked like he was about to fall over was actually smiling! Amazing.

"Let's go. Lambert, can you man that scope?"

"I got it, sir." The man's eyes were turning glassy from the meds.

"Saddle up. You stay on the cart and sweep the area. Sound off if you see anything." Gagnon saw the man nod and knew the drugs were taking hold.

All Gagnon needed was some warning of an ambush or pursuit. He could handle the rifle fine and Stephon was lethal with just about any weapon. Or none at all.

He let Stephon take point and joined the giddy men at the back of the cart. Lambert sat atop the gold bricks. The whole sight must have looked like a joke, but at least the men seemed lively and could help push.

The cart began rolling. Gagnon felt like he was being watched.

They rolled through the gate and reached what passed for a road. The cart maintained momentum as long as the men kept their legs churning.

He was grateful for the moonlight. They'd left the torches burning, hoping at a distance that it might appear they were still in place, laboring into the night. It didn't take long to adjust to the moon-washed night.

The drugs had apparently kicked in hard for Lambert. He called out, "Four birdies in the tree, if I shoot one then there'll be three."

Gagnon glanced up in fear that Lambert was about to blast away into the jungle but the sniper's finger was nowhere near the trigger. He was just enjoying the high.

When they cleared the graveyard Gagnon began to pace himself. The other men were panting and Gagnon figured they must be overheating.

They just needed to hold up until they made it to the dock. Stephon rotated back to give him a break.

At least the other men didn't complain. They reminded Gagnon of the dray horses that would literally work themselves to death. The man on his right was drenched in sweat, like the rest, but Gagnon noticed a dark trickle of blood crawling from the man's ear. It looked like wet, black paint in this light.

"Give me the radio." They were near where their small repeater hung in the tree. Still too weak to reach the *Fanfaron*, it would provide a strong signal to the mortar team.

Stephon let him have the microphone and adjusted the speaker volume.

"Team Lead to Mortars."

Nothing.

He repeated.

Static.

And again.

The static dropped and the signal sounded clean but the person on the other end was far less robust. "Lead? Mortars here."

"Lead here. Over." He and Stephon shared a look.

"Lead, request permission to report to Doc. He won't come to us."

"Negative. Hold in place. We are coming to you."

"We're sick."

Radio discipline was fraying. "Understood. We will be there in thirty. How is the weather?"

"Weather?"

*Loopy idiot forgot the code words already. Fuck it.*

"Any sign of the enemy? Are you under fire?"

"So cold but can't stop sweating…"

Gagnon shook his head. He whispered to Stephon. "Mortars are down. Hope we don't need them." The other men, still pushing, weren't paying attention.

"Sit tight, Mortars."

Now the static cut in and out like someone keying the handset. It was stronger than the mortar team's signal.

"Break, Break, Break."

"Who the hell is this?" Gagnon couldn't help himself.

"Delacroix. You all know me. Everyone on this net. I know you are sick. I am too. Gagnon betrayed us. Anyone not infected is part of this."

"Shut up. Are you compromised?" Gagnon yelled.

"I'm speaking the truth. The vaccine we received was a fraud. Get Jean-Paul and make him help us."

Now the radios erupted in crosstalk. Gagnon glanced at the men pushing the cart. They were watching the radio and slowing their pace. Lambert, still the rifle, looked even more alert.

*Damn!*

"All units. This is Jean-Paul. I've also been tricked. I didn't know. It was Gagnon! He is betraying us all."

*Double-damn!* He'd give anything to override Delacroix's signal booster.

"Help us. We're on the beach," the voice sounded like Perrin, Delacroix's radio man. "Cloutier is down. He's vomiting blood and I hear voices in the trees. Bullets don't hurt them."

"Clear the net!" Gagnon shouted and the cart came to a halt. They were close to town now. "Delacroix is confused. Jean-Paul prepared the vaccine. I don't feel well, either. He's the one. We must all reach the ship. We'll get treatment there."

"Don't trust him." Delacroix cut in.

"Gagnon and Stephon will kill all of you. They want it all for themselves. Stop them and I can cure you," said Jean-Paul.

"Capture all three and we'll see who is lying. Take them, my friends." Delacroix urged.

Lambert's good humor had vanished and Gagnon didn't like the way the other two men looked at each other, then at him. Stephon stepped back and gave Gagnon a quick nod of his head.

Gagnon switched off the radio. The men frowned. "Nothing will get solved this way. Delacroix is out of his head."

"But why *are* we all sick?" Lambert said.

*Hadn't loosened the grip on that rifle, either.*

Gagnon felt nervous sweat creep down his ribcage.

"I was fine before we left," one of the men spoke slowly, awakening from a stupor.

"Me too," said the other.

"Could be a coincidence," Gagnon said. Now he was mindful of Lambert's rifle barrel. If it swung in his direction…

"And why aren't you and Stephon ill?" Lambert's eyes narrowed in a suspicious gaze. He rose and now the muzzle came up.

The other two saw the body language and turned to pick up their own rifles from the cart where they'd placed them.

Gagnon drew his pistol and fired one round in the back of the first man's skull, then pivoted to the second guy, who moved faster than Gagnon expected. He saw out of the corner of his eye that Lambert was trying to aim at him as well.

Stephon had moved when he saw Gagnon draw the pistol and Gagnon spotted the flash of his blade when the big man leapt onto the cart and took Lambert down.

At the same time, Gagnon used his left hand to grab the last man's rifle while it was close to the his body and with his right fired three quick pistol rounds into Lambert's belly.

Any fight left in the man ran out between his fingers as he clutched his gut, which gushed like a punctured wineskin.

*Must be the bug breaking down his organs.*

"You could have gone out easy but you chose the wrong side, mon frère." Gagnon stared at the man's stunned expression. He let the man fall in the path and held onto the rifle.

"Merci." Gagnon said to Stephon, who was already wiping off the blade of his knife on Lambert's pant leg. When he was done he picked up the rifle with the thermal scope and kicked the corpse off to the side.

# Chapter 37

*Dwazen Camp*

Fin sat by Delacroix. The man swayed in his seated position on the rock.

Hua paced in the background and Maru continued to grind herbs and add water and drops of liquid from a small bottle he kept tied to his belt.

"Was that okay?" He asked in French. Fin understood enough to pick up that much. Hua and Maru had supplied the prompts, and whatever Maru had given him made the soldier quite suggestible.

"You spoke from the heart," Fin said.

Delacroix looked up in mild surprise at hearing a different language. He'd forgotten their talk not thirty minutes earlier. Maru's potion propped the man up but it wasn't doing anything else to cure him.

"Too much." Hua said to Maru and reached toward the wood mixing bowl the chief used. Maru slapped his hand away, hard.

Fin stepped back and Delacroix stared straight ahead. Saskia watched the soldier while winding a strand of hair around her finger. The hard expression combined with the youthful gesture somehow suited her.

Fin felt mixed emotions churn through him. He knew exactly what this disease felt like and part of him wanted to believe that this man was a victim of Gagnon's lies. Even so, he wasn't here as a tourist. "What is Maru making?"

Fin took out his camera and took several shots of Delacroix, careful to exclude any islanders or Dwazen.

"He will get the only suitable punishment but at least he will not suffer. It is more than he deserves." Saskia said.

Maru approached. He'd overheard their conversation. "The island will be cleansed of these toxins." Maru swept his arm to encompass all the invaders. "This one, at the end, will have clarity before he is spread to the sky."

Maru used two fingers to scoop a small amount of the pungent, pale green paste onto his fingers and dabbed it onto the soldier's mouth. Delacroix started as if Maru had been invisible before his fingers made contact.

Delacroix licked his lips and reacted to a second jolt. He clutched his chest. "My heart."

"You are with us?" Maru said.

"Yes, better now. Did, did you cure me?" Delacroix began weeping blood.

"You are between two worlds. Stand up. Do you have truth you wish to share?"

Maru led Delacroix across the camp. The Dwazen and islanders followed. Fin walked alongside and saw Hua shadow them on the other side. His friend looked impatient but kept his distance.

"Truth?"

Maru dabbed the lips again. "What would you leave behind in this world, to begin anew?"

"I …Everything. But I own what I did. I deserve to take it with me."

"Are you sure?"

"I'm glad we failed. You aren't what Gagnon said. I bought his lie for a payoff."

"You're saying you sold your soul?" Fin asked and Maru translated.

They reached the side of the mountain where the crevasse opened up. Straddling a narrow section of the gap was a winch and steel bucket where the Dwazen molded the gold into bars over the heat of the underground lava flow.

Delacroix patted his pockets. He pulled out a worn, dirty envelope. "Not sold. I gave it away for nothing."

They reached the edge. Smoke and steam curled out and from deep inside the lava glowed.

Fin opened the envelope and unfolded a single piece of stationery. The handwriting was childlike and he couldn't make out all the words but got the gist it was from his daughter, Chloe.

At the bottom he saw a notation in an adult's hand. It looked like a bank name and account number.

Delacroix sniffed the air and turned to look into the pit. "Enfer." He muttered.

*Hell.*

"I deserve this, she does not. Can you find her and give her this? She's the only good I leave behind."

Hua rushed forward to grab him but Delacroix shrugged once and batted Maru's hands aside and tumbled backwards into the fiery maw.

Hua roared his frustration and Maru restrained him. A momentary cloud of steam marked the man's passing.

* * *

*Hoku, New Cape*

"Keep pushing." The gold bars were all that kept Gagnon going. No, that and what he was going to do to Jean-Paul for interfering.

"Still clear." Stephon said when they stopped to rest at the edge of the little shanty town. He peered through the scope.

Gagnon turned on the radio again. "Nothing. That son of a bitch Delacroix must have turned off the repeater or one of those monkeys is kicking the unit about like a ball."

"It'll be light soon. I didn't realize how much those men were pushing. I'm amazed their hearts didn't explode."

"Maybe they did and they were too stupid to realize it. Shall I try the mortar team?"

"Why spoil the surprise?" Stephon said. He hefted the rifle. "Give me twenty minutes, I'll be in position, then you can approach on foot."

"Be careful where you aim monsieur, there is a great deal of ordnance in place."

Gagnon ate an energy bar while he waited and saw the moonlight fade along with the stars. He listened for any signs of natives and heard nothing. His tactical radio hissed twice in his ear. Stephon's "go" signal.

The sky was beginning to lighten and he could see well enough to make his way. He held a short-barreled carbine at the ready and tried to get as close as possible without a line of sight to the dock area. He walked past the one hut that got set ablaze earlier, and the stench of burned wood and cloth lingered. Those that somehow survived the plague were lucky the whole place didn't burn up.

Gagnon reached the other end of the little town and saw the edge of the dock where the makeshift bunker shielded the mortar team.

He knew the mortar tube was behind the sand bags and he expected to see a rifle barrel or their sentry. He moved in closer. Not a sound outside of the small waves lapping at the rocky shore.

Now he crouched at the edge of the dock. An alert sentry should have detected him by now. He had no idea how impaired they might be but the radio man had sounded fairly incoherent and that was hours ago. Gagnon scooped up some stones and lobbed them.

They made a satisfying thud on the wood and he waited for a reaction.

Nothing.

He assumed Stephon had him covered. He gathered pebbles in his left hand and walked down the dock with the carbine one-handed and his finger on the trigger. He flung the pebbles so they showered the mortar area.

No response. He waited a minute and then looked back and raised his arms in an exaggerated shrug for Stephon.

He raised the gun and peered over the wall of sandbags.

Nobody.

Traces of blood striped the sandbags on the other side like finger paint. He saw no sign of combat or struggle. The makeshift bunker would have reeked if it had included a roof to house the stench.

A sniper rifle and two assault rifles leaned against one side of the bunker.

One or more of them must've lost control of their bowels. Gagnon left the mortar tube and walked slowly around the sandbags to the other side.

When he could peek around the side where he stood on the end of the dock, he had an obstructed view of the deep-water channel to his left and the rocky approach to the shore. Panic choked him. If the men had taken the raft, he and Stephon would have an impossible task trying to paddle out to the seaplane with the gold. He peeked over the edge, braced for an ambush.

He let out a breath at the sight of the raft still tied to the pier. He saw movement in the village. One figure, moving cautiously. Gagnon raised his weapon, braced on a stack of sandbags.

The radio hissed in his ear. "C'est moi."

"Be more careful. I almost…"

"I see them."

"Who?"

"Look to your left. Along the shore."

Gagnon looked down at the water against the dock wall. He let his gaze linger along the dark rocks. The ambient light was growing, but the sunrise wasn't here just yet. He saw white foam and black rock and was about to ask for clarification when he saw the first body.

The second and third ones were close by. All three men near glowed in the dim light against their pale, and he could now see, naked bodies.

As the light increased he could see the uniforms washed up on another rock.

Stephon approached.

"No sign of struggle other than with the virus. I don't think their position was overrun."

"Fever and madness. I would have spared them that." Stephon said.

"You would have preferred a fair fight?" Gagnon said.

Stephon gave him a twisted smile. "I didn't say that."

"I thought we'd have them longer. We are proof the vaccine can work."

"As is Jean-Paul. What is your play for him?"

"Help me get the gold to the dock and I will explain."

\* \* \*

*Dwazen Camp*

"You think us cruel? Barbarians?" Fin could hear the challenging note in his friend's voice.

"Maybe he could have helped us more alive. As a hostage?" Fin wasn't sure what he meant by that, but despite all the horrors he'd seen across Africa, he'd never witnessed death by volcano.

"Hostage? The man felt no pain beyond what was in his soul," Maru added.

"I meant as a bluff." Fin said.

Hua shook his head to disagree but translated the term for Maru.

"These men do not 'bluff.'" Maru's pronunciation made the word sound like "bloof."

"And neither do we." Hua said.

"At least they will suffer the same fate they inflicted on some of us." Saskia said. "You weren't serious about saving that swine with the purge? We nearly exhausted the Silverstar as it is."

"I don't know what I meant." Fin still had that letter in his pocket. "But you are wrong about them all getting what they deserve."

"Why?" Saskia started but then she must have remembered.

Hua spoke up. "Gagnon. He's still down there."

"Maybe his own men killed him." Willem joined the conversation.

"Want to bet?" Fin looked to Gert. "He planned all this. I don't think he intended to get himself killed. But we have the numbers now."

# Chapter 38

*Hoku, New Cape*

"More than one alive, at least there was. Can't see shit through the steel hull with this thing." Stephon sat inside the seaplane and peered through the thermal scope. The *Fanfaron* was just in view.

"Anyone on deck?" Gagnon fiddled with the volume knob on the radio. No sign of traffic.

"Not since Jean-Paul dragged that man topside to wash him off. If not for the body heat I would've though he was going to dump a corpse."

"Almost done. Two more trips and we can leave this slice of hell." Gagnon stacked some more bars under the seats next to Stephon. The last loads would go into the hold.

Stephon looked at them. "Not a bad haul."

"We should have been able to get it all. How the hell did they avoid the virus?"

* * *

Fin ignored the burning in his legs. He, Hua, Johannes, Gert and several armed Dwazen sailors raced down the path to reach the shore. Johannes had bolted ahead of them and was disarming traps along the way. They weren't needed anymore.

Maru had left to rejoin the rest of the islanders. Already the bird calls were relaying across the jungle to rally his warriors.

Fin's group startled some pigs along the way but otherwise encountered nothing. Fin wasn't surprised. The virus worked quickly. He figured by now the invaders would be looking for places in which to curl up and die.

The ground levelled off and Fin welcomed the chance to exhaust a different set of muscles. The Dwazen and islanders shamed him with their fitness but he managed to keep pace.

Before he knew it, the group slowed and fanned out. Fin could see patches of blue water and the first of the tin roofs that dotted the outskirts of the village.

He'd already warned the riflemen to avoid the tree-top nests. They had that thermal scope out there. Fin crept up to Hua. "Remember their scope, stay low and maybe they'll think we're pigs."

"The only pigs are on the end of the dock." Hua glared out between the palm fronds. "I see them."

"Me too." Gert said. "Busy stealing our gold."

Now Fin could hear the outboard motor rev up and they saw the Zodiac head out to the seaplane. "They're going to fly out what they found."

"We can advance. I see more gold stacked up so they'll be back," Gert said. He was using an old pair of binoculars.

Fin snapped some pictures. Though they were distant shots perhaps someday they could be enhanced and used as evidence. "Guys, stay low."

Johannes spoke. "I'll try to work my way through the town. They can't see through layers of buildings, can they?"

"I don't think so, but I don't want to gamble with your life." Fin said.

Johannes winked at him, and with a nod from Gert, dashed away to the left to try to flank the sandbagged position.

"I only see one in the raft for sure." Gert panned back to the end of the dock. "Down!" He whispered and then louder with bird calls.

"A guard?"

"That bag of shit Stephon. He's on that scope you mentioned," Gert muttered.

Hua crawled up to Gert. "Wait for my people. You'll get your chance to shoot."

\* \* \*

Gagnon shoveled the bars into the back seats of the seaplane as fast as he could. He kept peeking up to see if he could make out any activity from the *Fanfaron*. Nothing so far.

He wished Stephon was here to scope the ship. On second thought, he was where he needed to be. Gagnon didn't trust those vermin in the jungle. They were bound to try something.

Any pity he felt for the mortar crew had vanished when they realized the thermal scope on the other rifle had been deliberately shattered. Maybe Jean-Paul's desperate plea got through their fevered minds before they broke down.

*So many accounts to balance, but first things first.*

Gagnon pulled the last bunch of bars from his satchel. His bruised and bloody fingers screamed in protest but he paid scant attention. One more load, and he and Stephon could ride out together.

He climbed back into the raft. If they worked fast they could be airborne in thirty minutes.

Just as he moved the throttles forward he heard the radio hiss in his ear. Without the earpiece he'd have never heard it over the engine noise. "Say again?"

"Movement in the jungle. Multiple targets. Use evasive pattern to approach the dock."

*Damn.*

"How many?"

"Looks like seven plus." Stephon sounded cool and Gagnon began to steer in a zig-zag while he kept an eye out for splashes that might tell him he was under fire. He couldn't rely on his ears with the distance and gas motor's rasp.

"Be there in five, take them out if you can." Gagnon sped up and was glad the raft wasn't loaded down for this approach. He'd need to be careful on the way out with the raft weighted down.

"Roger...Merde!"

"What?"

"Wait one."

It felt like ten, and Gagnon nearly capsized when he went full throttle into a sharp turn. He recovered and reached the shadow of the dock. "On the ladder." He used the radio even though he was a mere twenty feet below Stephon. Wouldn't do to have the man shoot him because he'd startled him.

"Get up here!" Stephon shouted.

Stephon didn't sound cool now.

Why wasn't he firing? Gagnon drew his pistol and climbed one handed.

He hauled up to the dock and made sure to keep below the sand bags. Stephon stood, bent over the rifle with his legs spread, and he tracked the weapon far right and left.

Gagnon re-holstered the sidearm and picked up one of the assault rifles. He lined up next to Stephon and made sure the man had enough room to maneuver.

"Where are they?"

"Bastards." Stephon's chest worked like a bellows. "One small group across the village square. Down low among the trees. Right after I told you about them, these showed up."

Now Gagnon heard howls and shouts. The jungle to their left was alive with sounds. Unmistakably man-made sounds.

"Let me see." Gagnon switched places with Stephon and peered into the thermal scope. The rubber eyepiece felt slick with sweat.

Now he could see why.

Away from the first group the thick jungle teemed with white blob shapes. They swayed and swarmed all among the trees. Some hopped up and down while others waved their arms as if doing calisthenics.

And there were more than a hundred of them. Easily.

Gagnon stepped away from the scope. Stephon took his place. "I can hit some of them but we don't have enough ammo here for each one."

Gagnon looked around the small open bunker. He took a fast inventory of the spare magazines and couple of boxes of sniper rifle ammunition. Then he nearly tripped over the heavy metal answer. "Of course we do."

\* \* \*

Fin felt a strange mix of emotions when the islanders appeared and began to berate the men in the sand box from the cover of the jungle. He was gratified to have the all-seeing eye atop the deadly rifle drawn away from them for a time, less so to know the weapon was now trained on islanders.

"Fire." Gert's voice startled Fin. Shots rang out from Gert's riflemen. Fin saw a couple of bags begin to bleed grains of sand. One shot made a puff of dust when it hit the top of the bag near Stephon's face.

Fin saw the two duck down.

"Cease. Now move." Gert barked out the orders.

The sailors ducked and rolled. Fin heard some return fire but the way the bullets snapped overhead, they didn't appear to be aiming.

"Up, left pair, and fire." Gert shouted.

The din from the nearby islanders grew and the entire jungle near their position seemed to shake. Two shots cracked and the men dropped and moved just as the ones on the right popped up and squeezed off two shots. Fin could see these men all carried M1 Garands that allowed for more rapid fire. Over the booming reports, he heard the distinctive metallic ping when a rifle ejected the clip.

It seemed to be working. The return fire from the dock diminished.

Even so, one rifleman went down with a head shot. He was crouched and Fin knew the sniper could see through the foliage. Gert swore and grabbed the dropped weapon. He fired the rest of the clip in the old M1 and dropped to a knee to scavenge another en-bloc clip from the fallen sailor.

Before he shot again, he called out "Hold fire."

Hua let out a war whoop Fin never would have thought possible from his friend. It was answered tenfold, and a group of warriors burst from the jungle. They screamed in fury with war clubs and spears and sprinted across the field.

Fin looked up. They were fast, but not nearly fast enough. Gert stepped out of cover and used a rock to perch his rifle. Fin glanced over to see where Stephon was aiming and then he saw Johannes.

The young man had made it deep into the town unnoticed. He stood atop the tin roofs of one of the shacks and with his back to the sea held a clear vantage point over the dock. But he had no gun. Instead he held his wrist-rocket slingshot.

Fin estimated the distance but it didn't matter. Anything other than extreme close range put the weapon in the non-lethal category.

Johannes pulled back far on the elastic and let fly. The sun winked off the ball bearing and streaked into the sand box.

To Fin's amazement, Stephon jumped like he'd been shot and even dropped the rifle so it fell between two sandbags.

A moment later Stephon was back up only to get yanked down by Gagnon. Gert and the remaining sailors opened fire again and the front wall of bags erupted sand from the impacts.

Johannes reloaded and launched his ball bearings into the box with a frantic energy Fin didn't understand. "Get out of there!" Fin yelled, but might as well have waved a paper sign. The guy couldn't hear him and appeared to be solely focused on his own rate of fire.

The islanders continued their charge but scattered and dove to the ground the moment two round balls arced out of the sand bunker. One grenade exploded harmlessly as it landed in one of the fire pits and scattered wood and ash along with the sand that absorbed its force. The second blew closer to several islanders and two screamed with flesh hanging in tatters from their legs. The third man never got off the ground.

Johannes pulled more ball bearings out of the pouch and tugged back again. This time his body jerked back and the shot clanged off the tin roof. Johannes dropped the slingshot to clutch his belly.

* * *

*Sand Bunker*

"Now throw the smoke. Last one." Gagnon didn't think the fool with the kid's toy would bother them anymore and hoped the belly wound would give him a painful death. He popped up and let half a magazine rip with swift bursts to keep the savages at bay. The remainder he turned to fire at the Dwazen sniping at them with antiques.

Stephon's eyes blazed with fury. Gagnon liked to see it. He was in full combat swing. After the ball bearing hit the man in the back Stephon had been sure he was mortally wounded. Once he realized he'd only have a deep bruise he turned into a berserker.

The smoker might help the charging natives as much as them, but only for an instant.

Now Gagnon grabbed the base of the mortar and pivoted it to fire on the jungle. He set it to land fairly close, and maybe they'd get lucky and nail the field.

But it was a guess. The sheet with the firing grid was long gone.

"Where are we targeting?" Stephon handed a round from the wood box.

"Over there." Gagnon grinned. "We just need to get these goddamned barbarians off our backs for a few minutes. Cover your ears." The first round boomed out of the tube and sailed over the wall of smoke and out of sight. They heard a muffled report after a few seconds but the smoke made adjustments impossible.

"As soon as this box is empty, we go."

In rapid succession they loosed half a dozen rounds, and when Gagnon adjusted the aim to spread the impacts around Stephon fired into the dissipating smoke to discourage attackers.

"Get in the boat."

Stephon pointed at the last load of gold. "Non?"

"Not funny. Vite!"

Stephon scrambled down the ladder and began to untie the boat. Gagnon turned back and grabbed the scoped rifle. Through it he could see a bunch of figures retreating and the numbers in the jungle were way down.

*Perfect.*

He aimed back towards the Dwazen. One on the left looked like he might be lifting a weapon and Gagnon took the shot. The man fell back.

*Bon.*

He took a frag grenade he'd kept in reserve and tied some cord to the pin. He ripped open a fresh box of mortar rounds and wedged the grenade inside.

Finally, he paid out the line as he climbed down the ladder. Shots began to smack into the sand bags again.

Gagnon reached for the pilings to steady himself and kept one hand on the string. "A going away present."

Stephon stared across the water. "Look!"

The *Fanfaron* was turning toward the island and now moved forward. "He can't operate a vessel that size." Gagnon realized the stupidity even as the words left his mouth.

"Could he have cured the captain?"

"There is no cure."

"Tell that to them." The natives were starting to get loud again.

"He won't get far." Gagnon switched on his radio.

"I was wondering how you were going to handle this detail." Stephon said. He kept his assault rifle nearby.

"Lead to *Fanfaron*. Monsieur, what do you think you are doing?" The ship appeared to drift.

Gagnon's hands began to sweat, making the string feel slick.

"*Fanfaron* to lead. Last chance. Surrender to the locals."

"Jean-Paul, you're not in the position to make demands. You may have managed to start the engines and get the boat moving. Do you really think you are capable of operating and navigating across open seas?"

"I'm a fast learner. Decide quickly."

"What are you talking about? We have business to discuss and we're the only ones left, am I right?"

"I know what you have planned for me. You sabotaged the vaccine didn't you?"

Gagnon knew better than to answer that question. For all he knew Jean–Paul had rigged a recorder onto the radio. "Monsieur, you are confused. I don't know what you are talking about."

"Last chance."

"We are leaving with or without you," Gagnon held a finger to ask for a moment. His friend grew agitated and Gagnon shared the feeling.

This would be worth the wait. Gagnon switched the radio to the highest frequency and pressed the transmitter for ten seconds. He released it and heard a faint beeping. He spun the dial to the lowest frequency and held for another ten seconds. "We shall see how fast he learns."

At the ten second mark Gagnon saw a plume of water rise in the distance and a couple of seconds later heard the explosion.

*No!*

He returned the setting to the communication channel and caught the laughter coming from Jean-Paul. "I know you too well, Gagnon! I found the bomb in the water cooler."

"You think you found them all?" Gagnon shook his head to tell Stephon he was bluffing. The one he'd planted had been more than enough to put the *Fanfaron* on the bottom. "Shut it down and let us aboard. We can go our separate ways as friends."

Now the *Fanfaron* accelerated and turned, directly toward the seaplane.

"Go!" Gagnon yanked the string tied to the pin and grabbed hold of the ropes on the sides. Stephon gunned the engine and the Zodiak roared ahead. Now small splashes told Gagnon the Dwazen had opened fire from the island. Stephon began to zig-zag, but the important thing was to get clear.

In a matter of seconds Gagnon knew two things. The Dwazen wouldn't be shooting at them for a little bit, and they weren't going to be able to do anything about Jean-Paul's desperate gambit.

The *Fanfaron* may not have been a big as the *Verdragen*, but the tug boat's rugged steel hull would snap the wings off the seaplane like a flimsy wood toy. Even if the raft weren't hopping over the water their rifle was useless to them.

Behind them the grenade touched off the loose mortar rounds and the rest of the stockpiled ammunition went up in grand fashion. He hoped the curious were caught in the blast. A huge pall of black smoke rose and would cover their exit.

*Exit to where?*

Stephon saw the same thing and rolled back on the throttle to slow the craft. The fires and secondary blasts made the Dwazen a remote threat for the moment.

Gagnon got on the radio and Stephon topped off the magazine on the assault rifle while muttering curses.

"Jean-Paul!"

The ship looked like it was also on a zig-zag course, but Gagnon realized it wasn't evasive. It was Jean-Paul over correcting.

*Maybe he'd miss...*

Whether it was the right adjustment or just luck, the *Fanfaron* looked like it might just miss before it turned hard to port and first brushed the tail section then caught the left wing at the root. The wing tore off and peeled back the fuselage like it was a can opener.

The *Fanfaron* batted the plane aside and wobbled away. The engines picked up tempo and it pointed out to sea at full throttle.

Gagnon saw the seaplane list to one side and he thought he caught a glint of gold before the whole craft capsized and slid underwater. The last to go was the right wing, which stood like a giant shark fin before sliding to the bottom.

* * *

*New Cape*

"Holy shit!" Fin saw the first blast at the dock bunker. "Everyone down!"

Any of the group of warriors caught crawling toward the bunker when the larger explosions began had dropped. Whether they'd get back up again was an open guess. Fin started to rise to run and help when the secondary blasts began. Small-arms ammo cooked off and he knew that wasn't so dangerous. Once, in Angola, one of the soldiers demonstrated by tossing a live AK round into the campfire. When it exploded it was loud, but the bullet and case popped apart harmlessly.

Mortar rounds were different. They exploded and threw shrapnel that shrieked through the air. Until those were done, it was crazy to stand in the open.

Which is exactly what he did right after he saw Hua bolt to the middle of the field.

He helped drag several badly wounded men toward the jungle edge. The pace of the explosions slowed.

Everything happened in a blur. The loud blast on top of all the gunfire made Fin's ears feel like they were stuffed with cotton.

After a few minutes, islanders swarmed out of the jungle, led by Maru. They removed the bodies. Four men were killed outright, two more looked in need of a miracle and six others suffered wounds they'd likely survive, barring infection.

Gert and the two remaining riflemen covered the dock and shore. The fire on the dock appeared to be burning itself out.

"Gert, can we get a detail to put out the remains of the fire?" Fin asked.

Gert set his weapon down. "We have hoses and gear on the *Verdragen*, but I never thought I'd be so glad she was beached on the other side of the island."

The smoke had dwindled. Fin could see that the sand bag bunker looked like a giant had kicked it apart.

Hua pointed toward the sea. "The plane went down. They'll have to come back now."

Maru joined them. "Perhaps not. I saw them go after the ship."

"I hope they both sink." Fin said. He ran to the shore and saw the tug weaving in the distance. The Zodiac looked like a gnat buzzing around it.

"I hope they return." Hua's eyes were rimmed red and he glared at the receding vessels.

"We could overhear some of their chatter on the radio. It sounded like there was only three left." Willem said. "Maybe now they know better than to try us."

"I wish that were true." Fin said.

# Chapter 39

*Hoku, New Cape, One week later*

"Don't go," Saskia said.

"What do you mean?" Fin held up his camera. "You have a photo printer and mail drop I haven't heard about yet?"

She shook her head. "Not the meeting with Thibaux. You know what I mean. After that."

He wondered if Hua had told her anything. "I haven't made any specific plans."

She wasn't buying it.

"That's the problem. You're going to go after Gagnon, right?"

"Maybe." Fine, might as well have it out now.

"You can't."

"Oh really? And why?" Fin felt color rise to his cheeks.

"I don't want you to die."

Fin relaxed. "I don't want to die either, but it isn't only about justice…"

"You mean revenge." She shot back.

"I meant *justice*." Fin paused. "And revenge. But mostly self-defense."

"We all want …justice," Saskia sat on the ladder steps in front of her hut. "But he's gone."

"Come on. I happen to know you weren't born yesterday," Fin's attempt at levity fell flat. "You can't believe that. Gagnon will be back and he won't make the same mistakes again."

"We won't make the same mistakes, either."

"We can't risk another attack. How many died this time, and how many are still recovering?" Fin asked.

"Too many."

"So what's wrong with trying to end it now?"

"Fin, you're a brave man, but…" She chewed on her lip. "Gagnon is a trained killer."

"Gagnon is an ongoing threat and he's got so much to answer for. Stephon as well."

"I know."

"I don't think I'm tougher than either of them. But I have two things on my side."

"What?"

"Surprise and time." Fin felt better talking it out. Being willing to take a life was one thing. A huge thing, but willing and able were not the same, were they? "They may not be together, which could make it harder to find them, but when I do I can wait to strike when they won't expect it."

Now she looked like she was going to cry. "You *don't* have time."

"Sure I do. I can be patient. They won't be guarded like the President. If anything, they'll be on the run."

"Then how do you expect to find them? Wait for them here, if you are so sure they will be back." She seemed happy to find an excuse for him to stay.

"Why? You worried you'll miss me too much?"

"Yes. That's right."

"Saskia, what the hell? That's *not* it."

"You can't leave. Even if you wanted."

Fin felt like he'd been kicked in the gut the way she said it. "Spit it out."

"The purge. You, me, all of us have to recharge with the Silverstar every three months."

"Or what?"

"You age."

Part of him wanted to think this was the way she'd wriggle out of what she said about never dying, like this was the punchline to a bad joke.

She wasn't laughing.

"That's it? I wasn't really expecting to live forever anyway."

"No. You'll age much more rapidly than normal. We don't know why, and it varies person to person."

"How do you know that? I thought everyone here was more than a hundred." He didn't mean his tone to come out so harsh.

"Some can't take it and stop with maintenance." She paused. "Or they leave the island for too long. That's how we learned."

"You're serious?"

"Remember when you were confused about how Hua could have a child only ten years ago if Maru was so old?"

"That's right." So much had happened he'd never had a chance to ask Hua.

Saskia whistled and Fin saw Hua approach. He'd been waiting for her signal.

"She told you?" Hua said.

Saskia recapped their conversation.

Hua nodded and took a deep breath. "You remember when we came out here we brought out Hunapo's ashes?"

"Seems like ages ago, but of course."

"Hunapo wasn't my grandfather, he was my father. Maru was *his* grandfather."

"I never actually saw Hunapo." Fin still wanted to think this was all some elaborate prank.

"He ran off the island when I was in my late teens. He couldn't take the idea of never seeing the world and after his father died in an accident, he knew he'd be the next chief after Maru."

"Why didn't he come back?"

Anger showed in Hua's clenched jaw. "Weakness? Some sort of breakdown? We don't know. He must have felt the pull to return home at the end, but before that he never reached out to anyone."

"I'm sorry. I don't understand."

"One of the biggest reasons I was allowed to attend college was to get a chance to see the outside and know what I'd be missing once I purged and took father's place as next in line." Hua said.

"And how long did you say Hunapo was gone?"

"He was about fifty when he purged. He looked much like Maru, and in just ten years he looked like he was a hundred. If not for the scarring, I wouldn't have recognized him when I had to identify the body."

"Again, I'm sorry but…" Fin scratched his head.

"Don't you see? If you go after Gagnon, it could take a long time. The longer you are away from the island and without the Silverstar infusions, you'll age too."

"But Gert and the crew leave the island all the time."

"But never for long," Hua said. "If I knew where to find Gagnon and that other vermin, I'd do it myself."

Saskia added, "Gert was younger than he looks when he purged. He stayed away too long once and learned."

"And he stays whatever age he appeared after the rapid aging?" Fin didn't believe them, but wanted to at least understand the ground rules.

"Yes. But I know what you are thinking."

He hoped not. He still thought they all might be insane. "You do?"

"You're thinking you can find Gagnon and Stephon and then if you get him, you'll return to the island."

"Are you saying I wouldn't be welcome?"

Saskia took his hand. "Never. But nobody knows how fast you'll age. For some, a year can be like five. For others, more like a decade."

"Everyone on the island goes through that whole process every three months?" Fin didn't remember everything he experienced in that cave but at the time it seemed extensive.

Hua shook his head. "Not like that. Maru prepares a mixture that we drink."

Fin thought about it for a moment. "So why not bring a supply? Say, six months' worth?" He figured he could play along.

"The mixture requires fresh Silverstar. Once made, it turns poisonous within hours."

"This is a lot to accept."

"We understand," Saskia said.

"I don't understand why nobody wants to catch Gagnon while the trail is warm," Fin said.

Hua grabbed Fin by the shirt so hard one of the buttons popped off. "You're not the one who lost his only son. Believe what you like but you'll find out."

"Let go of me." Fin spoke through his teeth. "What do you expect? I know Maru did something amazing, I've never been so sick."

Hua released Fin's shirt and smoothed the fabric.

"But the whole fountain of youth thing is a bit much."

"I know what I know," Hua said.

Saskia retrieved the fallen button and put it in a pocket. "We originals only learned over time when we didn't seem to get older," she said and then paused. "And when some of the children didn't either."

That caught Fin off guard. "You're saying some of those children were actually old?"

She wouldn't meet his gaze. "Even Maru and Marius, when they first developed the process, had no way of knowing all the effects. We thought we were helping those children."

"They aren't still here?"

"The older they got the more they learned, but their minds or brains really stopped growing and eventually each and every child who purged went mad and killed himself."

Hua listened. "Maru told me about them."

"We tried everything to reverse the madness. All of us were terrified that the same thing would also happen to us but eventually we failed to help the young ones and adults never had the same reaction."

"But didn't you say some couldn't take living so long?"

"Yes, but this was different. This was a compulsion to die. Before long all the children who'd purged were gone."

"We're getting ahead of ourselves. We still have to get to Thibaux first."

"If the *Verdragen* will hold together for the trip." Hua said.

Good point. Fin had half-expected it to snap in two after they'd spent four days digging it out.

"Let me go with you," Saskia said. "We need supplies. If it stayed afloat this long it should be all right."

Fin knew she didn't trust him. Smart lady. "They have enough sailors to help Gert with that. There are plenty of wounded here."

"Maru can't do it all by himself," Hua said.

Fin didn't react, but wanted to stare at his friend.

*A minute ago he wanted to punch me, now he's got my back on this?*

"Nobody is getting infected," she pointed out.

"I still can't believe it." It was true. Despite unsanitary conditions not a single Dwazen or islander caught any infection. Fin's cuts and bruises were mending well, with no sign of complication. "Good thing. We used every bottle of alcohol washing the ship down."

"You aren't expecting to be boarded, are you?" Saskia said.

"I understand that you never had to be concerned under the old terms, but that's another issue. Right now we don't know what to expect and there's a good chance we'll break down and require a rescue."

"You think it is safe?"

"As far as the virus, I'm no expert. Without fresh hosts and with the cleaning it should be gone by now, but to play it safe we'll each decontaminate before we go ashore." Fin prayed that was the case, otherwise they'd accidentally unleash a plague.

# Chapter 40

*Papeete, Tahiti*

"Tell him the delegation from Hoku is here. He'll see us." Gert spoke into the intercom at the gate to Assemblyman Thibaux's house. The servant spoke French with a local accent.

The city felt like Times Square compared to Hoku. Fin's mind wandered while Gert and Hua talked their way inside. He shifted the weighty envelope from one arm to another.

A moment later the door buzzed and they entered a small courtyard. Fin's pulse quickened.

They saw the dark-skinned servant inside the glass of the door to the house, a two story whitewashed building with terracotta tiles on the roof.

According to Gert's brief, Thibaux was a bachelor who lived here in semi-seclusion.

Their reception would tell them a great deal about what they'd face.

"Entrez." The friendly man at the door gave them a broad smile like they were old friends. "Monsieur Thibaux will be here in a moment." He gave a little bow and left them inside the foyer. Polished white marble tile floors gleamed and showed their reflections.

Thibaux emerged from a study door. He was a thin, timid-looking man with a pale bald head and steel-rimmed glasses.

He looked flummoxed at the sight of the three of them. "I had no idea you were in port, Gert, Monsieur Hua. And aren't you that photographer? You went to the island with my team, did you not?"

Fin couldn't believe the man was serious. "Yes, sir. We need a word with you in private."

"This is my home. And I don't understand…"

"Where is Gagnon?" Hua said. He looked less fierce in a button-down shirt but that blaze in his eyes never left.

Thibaux glanced at the floor and when he looked up Fin saw a tinge of fear in his gaze. He ushered them into a large study complete with a sofa covered in emerald-colored tooled leather. "I would ask the same question of you, since he just visited your island."

*Was that supposed to be a joke?* Fin felt an angry flush crawl up his face. "So you haven't seen him?"

"No. He said there were some complications and he was going to prepare a detailed report."

Gert stepped in to speak. "Complications? That's how he put it?" Gert lowered his voice and Fin felt the menace in his tone like waves of heat. "Are you going to tell me you aren't aware of him changing the terms of our arrangement?"

Thibaux began to sweat and he stared at Fin. "Arrangement?"

Many faces flashed through Fin's mind at that moment and he hoisted the file folder onto the desk. "Don't be shy on my account. You apparently you have no idea of the kind of trouble you are in."

"I don't…"

"What kind of monster are you to sic that maniac on these good people?"

"That's quite enough." The man could still do haughty. "For your information, Monsieur Gagnon announced his retirement." Beads of sweat covered his vast forehead.

"Did he? That must have been some report. And yet, I'm not surprised." Fin said. "Where would we find him?"

"I don't know. This was all so sudden." Thibaux said.

"No address to send his pension?"

"He wasn't eligible. I think he wished to be left alone." Thibaux squirmed in the leather swivel chair. The huge mahogany desk seemed to swallow him up. "I don't think he will be bothering you again. And we may resume the prior arrangement."

Hua shook like he had advanced palsy. "You'll give us his address, now!"

Thibaux flinched. "I don't have it."

Gert spoke in a low tone. "Then get it."

"And that goon Stephon's."

"I can't."

*Was he trembling?*

"Can't or won't?"

"He'll kill me." Thibaux whispered. "He sent a note to forget about him and get on with my life or he'd come back and take care of me."

"You really have no idea what he was doing?"

Thibaux looked confused and turned to Gert. "I swear I never heard about any new arrangement. I apologize."

"Not that." Gert snapped. "His operation on the island?"

"The ceremony? He said he would attend."

"Nothing else?" Gert and Hua stared at him as if their gaze could pin him to the chair like a bug.

Thibaux shook his head. He seemed to shrink further in the chair.

Fin believed him. He also had no trouble imagining that Gagnon would know he could run roughshod over this toad.

Fin was glad they'd agreed to play this his way. Hua wanted to roast him over an actual fire, but Gert understood that they needed this jellyfish.

Fin spoke slowly. "You will listen and then you will do what you are told. Don't try to call for security because after you see the pictures I've taken there won't be enough protection on the planet to keep you safe.

"This package is one of many duplicates set to go to all the major news agencies should anything happen to me." Fin pulled out the thick stack of prints. They'd about worn out his printer at home making copies.

* * *

An hour later, after just enough scotch to keep the pale worm upright, Fin replaced the photos in the envelope. They'd explained about the virus followed by the attack and betrayal of the mercenaries.

Hua had turned away when Fin showed the bodies in the cave and knew there was a close up of Ruru.

"It can't be." Thibaux reached out for the cut crystal tumbler.

Gert clapped his huge hand over the stopper and held it down. "Not until we have an understanding."

"Impossible. If this virus was so powerful how are you here?"

Fin deferred to Gert and Hua. This part was their play. "We thought you might not believe. We'll explain during your visit to the island."

"I'm not..."

"Oh, yes you are." Gert said.

Fin spoke. "You'll see for yourself. In the meantime, it's enough to believe we're serious." Fin pulled out some additional sheets of paper. "You're named all through here and when it hits the worldwide news, you're going to be famous. Gagnon will see it too, wherever he is, and how do you suppose he will react after he discovered you sold him out?"

"But your secret about the gold, that'll be exposed."

"Gagnon wanted to exterminate everyone on the island for the gold. We think he still does. Compared to that, selling to a South African mining company doesn't look too bad, does it?" Fin said.

Gert spoke. "We've already agreed, the Dwazen and the islanders will throw open our island to investigators and we'll tell them all about what you've done over the years and blame you for this attack."

"Then you'll have the world after you for crimes against humanity."

"But I didn't lie. I don't know where he is."

Fin pulled out the letter he'd saved from Delacroix. "One of his hired guns gave a sort of dying confession. He included a bank and account number on this old letter from his daughter."

Fin folded the letter. "Maybe this isn't the same bank you and Gagnon use to launder the gold you sell, but I know you have contacts. I think this might make a good starting point."

"If he closed the account..." Thibaux sounded weak.

"Then the person he dealt with knows where they wired the funds, don't they? Don't insult us." Fin said. "You've got leverage over the banker."

Hua leaned in close to Thibaux's face, his dark skin a sharp contrast to the pale, small man behind the desk. "Spare no expense. Everyone leaves a trail."

Thibaux nodded. "Give me a day or two, I should have something."

Fin stood and Hua leaned back. "It is better this way. If you run or try to send anyone after us…" Hua didn't need to finish.

Thibaux may have been a coward but he wasn't stupid.

# Chapter 41

*Island of Phuket, Thailand --Three Months later*

Fin nestled in the corner chair, tucked in the shadow of the room and trained the binoculars on the huge home perched atop the hills in the gated community in the Surin Hills neighborhood.

His own suite boasted breathtaking views of the aqua and emerald sea and the honeymooners who populated the adjoining rooms all seemed to appreciate the spectacular scenery.

He didn't. The only view he was interested in was as ugly as it was dangerous.

At 4:00 pm, a lone figure strolled out into the courtyard of the large house and walked the perimeter of the dramatic private swimming pool that jutted out seemingly right off the hill into the air. The guard was too far away to notice a man hiding in a hotel room two hundred yards away. Still, as he always did, the guard scrutinized the foliage all the way down to the winding road and swept his own pair of binoculars to look for suspicious activity.

Fin wondered what exactly the man looked for in a town that buzzed with activity and motion. How did he distinguish a threat from background action? More to the point, how could Fin appear to be part of the crowd to get close enough to make a try?

And what would he "try"? Despite his experiences in the bush, armed with a camera, he reminded himself daily that he was an amateur spy and no hit man of any stripe.

Not that he doubted he could pull a trigger on Gagnon or, Monsieur Grenadier as he was called here. The problem was, even if Thibaux could help him score a weapon, anything other than close range would more likely get him arrested or killed.

Best to stick to the plan.

Another guard appeared alongside the man himself. Gagnon. Now with a shaved head that looked like a pink eraser atop a squat brick of a body from this distance. A skilled sniper could make short work of the target.

The pool extended out from the hillside and the railing was seamless glass, giving Fin a good view of the vanishing edge of the deep end. The view must be amazing from the pool itself. This room was about as close as he could get safely. He'd learned eyes both electronic and human observed the approach to the villa.

Right now his job was watching and waiting, and the worst thing he could do would be to spook Gagnon, when they were so close.

Gagnon dove into the water for his daily laps. If he held true to form he would swim for forty-five minutes.

Fin passed the time fantasizing that Thibaux's newfound resources and co-operation extended to control of drones or airstrikes. He imagined a missile or even a well-placed explosive charge hitting the underside of the pool while Gagnon was swimming. The blast would blow a hole in the bottom and the water would pour out, draining the pool in a swirling flush like a giant toilet, taking that turd Gagnon with it.

*Couldn't have everything.*

Still, the fact that Gagnon maintained a predictable routine told Fin that the man's guard was down or at least as down as it could be for someone supposedly in hiding.

He wasn't sure if the second guard, a Thai man with a lean whip-like body, knew Fin was watching. In this case, it didn't matter.

He hoped.

\* \* \*

*One week later.*

Each morning Fin walked past the smiling ladies at the front desk and half-expected them to inform him the credit card was denied and he had to leave. Or worse, the police or even nameless goons would pick him up.

Gagnon had remained faithful to his routine, and lately Fin had taken advantage of the opportunity to get out and stretch his legs while he knew the man was occupied. He wore a loud print shirt, hat and sunglasses to affect tourist camouflage just in case, but so far he'd kept a low profile and followed the directions he'd been getting from the mail drop.

At 5:00 pm sharp he returned to the hotel. Nods and smiles from the ladies at the desk. He picked up several message slips, part of his own routine. Usually they were bland faux-business calls planted by Thibaux's connection. Meaningless chatter to give him cover, but he knew if he ever got one from the Flying Dutchman corporation it meant his cover was blown and to get out of there at once.

He thumbed through the remaining messages until he got to a note written on a slip of paper with a Tahitian grocery store on the top of the letterhead. The neat, simple lettering was brief. UPSTAIRS.

\* \* \*

"I hope you aren't getting used to living like this." Hua gave Fin a bear hug when he reached his room.

"I want it to be over. You didn't bring a sniper by any chance? He's up there every day, just about."

Hua was dressed like Fin remembered when he attended University, a simple white cotton shirt and tan slacks. His smile vanished. "Too easy, and no. But we're almost done here. Let's get down to business."

"How'd Thibaux find this place and what happened with Stephon?"

"Stephon is the reason we found Gagnon here."

"He turned on him? I don't believe it." Fin said.

325

"Other way around. Thibaux's connection tracked Stephon via the bank account but it was emptied. They followed the proceeds here."

"And where is Stephon?"

"Dead."

"Did you…"

"I wish. It looks like Gagnon severed the last connections and moved here to start a new life."

"A little late to be asking, but why's Thibaux being so helpful?"

"You know why. He wants Gagnon out of the picture."

Fin thought about it and it certainly made sense, but there was something else. "Why leave me here to watch him? Why not hire a real shooter to take him out? Thibaux could hire a dozen for what he's paid to keep me here."

"We don't want him to do that. Too easy." Hua repeated.

"Did you tell him *I'd* expose him if he didn't follow your instructions?" Fin felt irritation well up in his chest. "Because Gagnon dead, period, works for me. Exposing *him* exposes all of you." Fin stopped. Hua was grinning.

"He works for us now. He'll do things our way."

"How can you be so sure?"

"Remember when you left, we planned to show Thibaux what Gagnon did to us?"

"Yeah, a 'tour' of the island."

"He got more than a tour."

"What do you mean?"

Hua grinned. "We purged him."

326

"Why'd he agree to…?" Fin realized the answer. "You *forced* him?"

"We should have thought of this long ago." Hua said. "Now we own him. He will keep supporting the island and we ensure he lives in comfort as before, but now he must come back to Hoku on a regular basis."

"But I thought that the Silverstar had to grow back."

"It was worth it. We'll ration among ourselves for a while."

"Are you people insane?"

Hua looked genuinely hurt. "Why?"

"You think he buys the longevity and maintenance crap?"

Hua slammed his fist down on the coffee table. "He does! He better. And so should you. You're overdue as it is."

Fin thought about the way he'd wake up and felt a weird, dull ache in his bones. Like hunger, only all through his body. He wondered if that was the way drug addicts felt when they went through withdrawl.

*Bull.*

"Hua, are you sure that isn't some trick? You know I'd never reveal any of the island's secrets, least of all the Silverstar."

Hua stared at Fin. "This isn't about trust. You've proven yourself. You still doubt the effects of the purge?"

"Not the cure. But the rest? Come on, it's just us here. Maybe Saskia wanted to use it to keep me there."

"She can speak for herself. Fin, make your own decisions but the aging is real. Have you looked in the mirror?"

"Very funny." Fin saw he wasn't joking. He stepped away from the window and walked to the hall mirror. He saw what he expected. An ex-surfer with a few gray strands in his blonde hair. "I'm tired is all."

Hua rummaged through a desk drawer and came up with a room service menu. "Read from this."

"Don't need to. I think I have it memorized. Not senile yet, bro."

"Read." Hua pointed.

"They have books in the lobby...."

"Read!"

Fin picked up the menu. "Why do they make the print so small?" He stretched his arm out and the letters focused enough for him to make out the words. "Coconut shrimp with mango. Happy?"

"Another month or two and you'll need glasses to read that."

"Bullshit. You try staring through binoculars in the dark for weeks and see if your eyes don't get strained."

Hua shook his head. "We can talk again about this later." He pointed at Gagnon's place. "Tell me about the guard."

Fin pulled out a photo of the wiry man and pushed it across the table. "His name is Krit. I've met with him a couple of times. I thought I was dead meat the first time. I still half-expect it. I don't know who to trust anymore."

Hua looked it over. "All I know is Thibaux found him and spent plenty to buy him. Apparently his family owes a deep debt. If he gets us close enough to act, his debt will be paid."

"He told me that's what he's willing to do. He flat refused to take Gagnon out himself. But if we're successful isn't that almost the same thing?" Fin felt confusion wash over his body.

"We don't want *him* to hurt Gagnon." Hua said.

Fin understood the implication. "I'm in to the end, but Hua, this man is dangerous even when he isn't cornered. How are we supposed to beat him?"

# Chapter 42

*Phuket, One week later*

Years ago friends had tried to talk Fin into going to the vegetarian festival in Phuket. He'd been unable to attend but had a hard time believing the stories they told. Overall it was a nine-day extravaganza intended to honor the gods and renew and purify the spirit. Held in the ninth lunar month, this fall festival was far more than an abstinence from meat, alcohol and other temptations.

None of which had interested his friends. They were selling the freak show.

They said ceremonies peaked with masses of people inflicting gruesome self-mortification injuries, committed in a trance-like state where the participants claimed to be acting as mediums for the gods.

Fin didn't fully understand the spiritual nature of the bizarre facial piercing with objects as small as pins and as large as spears. From what he had heard, anything that could fit through a cheek was fair game. One pal told him to imagine a yard sale jammed through a bunch of people's faces.

This year he would see the festival for himself. He wondered if there would be much blood. He'd seen what shrapnel through a face could do. Nothing divine, he was sure about that.

Chaos was already swelling the streets. Hua had left a couple of days ago to work with Krit on the final phases of their plan. Fin wasn't sure if it would work but his part was simple enough, at least to start.

He was to wait, dressed in standard tourist garb, and bring his camera. Hua made it clear they wanted this recorded. Krit had showed him the corner he was to stake out and said when the time came, he'd know.

Uncertainty knotted Fin's stomach, but he couldn't get Krit to say another word. Maybe Hua had left the plan intentionally vague to protect Fin or prevent him from objecting. Likely both.

Fin acceded to the first part of the plan. He and Hua agreed they'd found a potential weakness, or sickness, to exploit.

In a meeting with the bodyguard Krit, Hua and Fin listened to the stories of the girls brought to the house to perform for Gagnon. In the short time he'd been there it was clear why Gagnon had picked this location to hide from the rest of the world. His compound was a sadist's playground.

The girls, some barely in their teens, arrived in dark SUVs. Sometimes days passed before they were carted off, not always under their own power, Krit had added.

It seemed Gagnon's money paid for the girl's screams as well as the authorities' deafness.

For the plan today, Krit had promised to show Gagnon a local perspective of the most depraved mortification ceremonies. Krit said he jumped at the chance.

Fin completed packing. He'd already lined up a hotel on the other side of the island. If things went bad, he'd need a place to hide, unknown to the bodyguard or anyone else. Come to think of it, he'd need that even more if things went right.

* * *

Two hours later Fin shouldered his way down the streets of Phuket amid a barrage of noise. Gunpowder and incense thickened the air while firecrackers exploded all around. Fin saw a cart selling all sorts of fireworks and handed over a few bills for several packets of firecrackers and a book of matches.

Along the streets, the procession of costumed Thais, made up almost entirely of locals dressed in white tunics or robes, marched down the street. Fin pushed his way to the front, near a corner, and felt a moment of panic when he couldn't find the street sign. If he was lost, he'd never make it through this mess in time. Blood red and saffron yellow banners waved and the crowd cheered the approaching throng. Fin mopped his brow with a maroon silk handkerchief.

A breeze made the banners flap like dancing flames and Fin finally managed to wriggle through the packed throng to glimpse the street sign where Krit had told him to wait.

The group around him was a mixed bag, racially. White tourists like him, some British, others speaking German, hovered nearby and Fin saw a western hotel sign down the cross street. Krit had chosen well. Fin blended in here just fine.

The tip of the procession began to pass and he could see the real show was about to begin. The first of the entranced monks arrived, their eyes shining. Fin glanced to the right to scan the crowd though it was hard to tear his gaze from someone who had over a dozen pencils through his cheeks and wandered straight ahead in a daze.

Drums pounded and small cymbals clanged. Some marchers cried out or moaned, as if accompanying music only they could hear.

Fin snapped pictures and used the camera lens as a spotting scope. Soon he saw the crowd jostle and part near a perfect vantage spot for the festivities. Fin saw it was Krit who was muscling his way through the mass of humanity with elbows and knees flailing. Gagnon, wearing a fedora with a large purple peacock feather in the brim took his place at the curb. He stood on tiptoe so often it looked like he was bouncing.

Fin hid behind the camera and snapped shots using the zoom to make sure it was him. As if there could be a doubt. The hat covered the man's shaved dome but the blocky build gave him away.

Gagnon's eyes lit up and Fin wondered if he were high or just getting off on the bizarre mortification.

Fin was only thirty feet away at the most, but between the noise, mobs of people and obvious distractions he was as good as invisible to Gagnon.

But not to Krit. Fin caught his eye for an instant before the guard continued his vigilance, keeping passersby from Gagnon.

For his part, Gagnon was fixated on the procession of ever more peculiar piercings. Wrenches, screwdrivers, bicycle chains and wheels were reassembled through the faces of these men. It seemed impossible, yet there they were wandering the streets with their eyes rolling and hands reaching toward heaven.

The crowd cheered, none louder than Gagnon, who hooted with delight at the more extreme mortifications. The throng on the streets became denser and Krit made sure to highlight the standouts.

When one man passed by with a pair of revolvers pushed through his face Gagnon looked like he might piss himself from laughter. Krit clapped him on the back and brushed the hat off Gagnon's head.

The signal.

Fin squirmed between people, and when he feared he wouldn't get through, he let his camera dangle from the strap and lit a pack of firecrackers to clear a path.

The noise added to the din, and the little explosions caused the people closest to him to move away. Fin rushed through the gap and raised his camera. Gagnon looked straight at him, waving a hand to say he didn't want his picture taken.

At the same time, one of the marchers broke from the pack and Fin noticed the white robed man was darker skinned than the rest of the Thais.

Hua.

Only Hua appeared to have bitten into a porcupine as quills emerged from all over his face like some sort of masochistic beard. He closed the distance to Gagnon.

Fin knew what to do. He lowered the camera and removed the hat and sunglasses and tossed them aside. "Say cheese, asshole!"

The color drained from Gagnon's face, and the laughter turned into a choked roar.

Before he could move forward, Krit stepped in the way and Fin realized the guard was actually running interference.

Hua ran up behind Gagnon and Fin aimed the camera, now set on burst mode.

Hua gripped Gagnon by the shoulders, and faster than Fin would have believed, the burly Frenchman pivoted and whipped his head around.

Gagnon intended to head-butt his attacker but Hua moved as well and the Frenchman's head swiped into the side of Hua's face.

Hua was knocked down, but not out, and he scrambled backwards like a crab into the marching crowd. Some of the parade-goers who were assisting the entranced helped him up.

Fin saw a number of quills now embedded in Gagnon's face. "Merde!" he bellowed while he tore them out of his skin. Gagnon drew a double-edged combat knife from his waist.

Krit made as if to chase Fin again, but Gagnon wouldn't be fooled twice. He smashed Krit in the back of the head with the handle of the knife, and the Thai collapsed. Several people nearby screamed but the surrounding cacophony masked the shouts.

Fin turned, remembering the escape route, which was a joke at the moment, unless he could leap and run atop people's heads.

Fin spun back around and Gagnon strode toward him, the knife held low. Fin almost fell trying to back away, but there were too many people. He let the camera drop back to his chest and pulled out the last pack of firecrackers. Gagnon squinted in pain and spit on the ground, pawing at his cheek.

When he glanced up again he looked like he'd lost sight of Fin for a second, then locked onto him. He bared his teeth in an animal snarl.

Fin touched the flaring book of matches to the firecrackers and flung them both toward Gagnon's head.

Gagnon batted them aside with his knife hand. The broad swipe caught a long-haired white guy wearing a backpack with the sharp edge of the knife. The blade raked across the guy's side and he screeched loud enough to scare the people closest to Fin, giving him a brief opening.

Like a herd of gazelle in the presence of a lion, they shrank away from Fin. He managed to wriggle through the mass of people and bolted around the corner. His head pounded and breath came short.

The side street, little more than an alley, stood empty. The crowds were concentrated on the main road, trying to get a look at the procession. Fin raced down the path, riding on pure adrenaline. Hua hadn't told him what to expect, just to take pictures and be ready to escape down this smelly, garbage strewn street.

Fin heard some shrieks behind him, but focused on weaving in and out of the junk piles.

Just down the block he spotted a space between two buildings, just wide enough to pass through.

Only it was blocked. A fireworks cart stood across the space and one of the wagon-style wheels was broken. A tiny old Thai man sat with the cart and barely took notice of Fin.

The end of the street was cut off by a fence. He could either crawl under the cart or climb the fence. Maybe Gagnon couldn't climb. He ran to the fence and began to clamber up the chain link. There was barbed wire at the top, but he'd already decided to take his chances.

Then the dogs came.

Three stocky, slate-gray Thai Ridgebacks slammed into the fence and began snarling and barking. From where he was on the fence, Fin didn't see an easy way out through the yard.

Behind him the old man screamed.

Fin glanced back and Gagnon was fifty feet away. The old man lay sprawled in the gutter, unmoving.

"You son of a bitch!" Fin dropped down and nearly turned his ankle on a shattered cinder block. He picked up the pieces and began to throw them as hard as he could.

He noticed something. As Gagnon walked deliberately toward him he would dodge the chunks of cinderblock aimed at the uninjured, left side of his face. When Fin threw at the right side, where Hua got him with the quills, he ignored the chunks.

*He can't see out of the right side.*

Fin took more careful aim and now Gagnon was close enough that the light pieces might hurt the guy if he connected. Fin whipped a jagged palm-sized piece that looked to be a perfect strike right at his forehead.

Gagnon must have seen something coming because he jerked his head at the last second. Still, the chunk caught him right where the swelling distorted Gagnon's cheek.

As the chunk drew blood from a small cut, Gagnon bellowed, his face contorted, and he broke into a sprint.

Fin scooped up the last of the block, a nice heavy chunk, but before he could raise it Gagnon wrapped him up in a tackle and slammed him against the fence. The two rebounded onto the filthy street. Gagnon regained his feet and kicked Fin in the side. He straddled him and put the cold blade of his knife against Fin's throat.

"How'd you find me?" Gagnon wheezed. The side of his head where the quills had stuck was swelling more and bleeding like mad.

Gagnon pushed his face close, just above the blade. Fin could smell garlic, lemon grass, and wine on his breath and noticed the man was squinting and shaking his head.

"Stephon," Fin gasped. Whatever Hua had done wasn't working.

Gagnon removed the knife and seized Fin by the throat. "Stephon is dead."

Fin felt the fingers squeeze on his windpipe and stop. Just enough so he could still speak. "We know. Tracked you when you stole his money."

"He didn't need it anymore."

"Greedy. How much is enough?"

"Spoiled cockroach. You never felt real hunger before, lived in a filthy shack. I'd fix that, if I had time. Make *you* eat rats," Gagnon growled.

"Everyone knows. They'll never stop looking for you." Fin said.

"They won't have to find me. I'll find them. One by one." Gagnon shook his head again. The fingers relaxed a bit then returned with crushing force. "Starting with you."

Now Fin couldn't speak, but there seemed nothing more to say. They had gambled and lost. He struggled to push the man off him, but he felt like a pile of rocks on his chest.

Fin's ears rang and gray curtains closed in on his field of vision. Now sounds seemed far away. His arms felt too heavy to lift and he let them drop to his side…

The gray turned to black and Gagnon's face swam before his eyes. Fin began to sink into the darkness. The last dot of light looked like the sun seen from deep water. He waited for it to wink out.

Instead, the light began to grow again. Sounds returned and he was aware the pressure on his chest was gone. A terrible headache bloomed at the base of his skull, but it meant he was alive.

The curtains receded and he saw the alley. Next to him Gagnon was on his hands and knees trying to stand and seeming to have poor control of his limbs. He brayed like a donkey. Gagnon looked around. Instead of rekindled rage Fin saw …was it fear? Strength flowed to Fin's limbs as oxygen returned and he felt soreness when he swallowed, but he could breathe freely.

Fin scrambled back away from Gagnon and regained his feet. He saw the knife on the ground and snatched it up. Gagnon looked like he was so drunk he couldn't move. He made a final attempt to stand and tipped over onto his back.

Fin glanced up the alley and while the sounds of the procession bounced off the walls he saw only the old man who hadn't moved at all.

Gagnon's breathing grew shallow. He pawed in clumsy swipes at his face and the deep scratches were angry and swollen. Gagnon's mouth opened and closed like a landed fish.

Fin jabbed him in the side with toe of his shoe. His own ribs ached and he remembered how hard the man had kicked him. Gagnon glanced at him but only the eyes moved. His arm barely twitched. His fingers splayed open and didn't move at all. Hua had done something to him after all.

*He's helpless.*

Could be a trap. Fin took the knife and poked gently at Gagnon's arm. The tip didn't break the skin. "You feel that?"

"He feels it." Fin jumped at the sound of Hua's voice. His friend had blood smeared down his cheeks, but he'd removed the quills and Fin saw them clutched in his fist.

Fin also noticed the wet black tips on the barbs. The knife he held was both sharp and long enough to reach Gagnon's heart. He'd never done anything remotely like it but knew one good thrust under the breast-bone could pierce the man's heart.

Hua knelt down and closed his fingers over Fin's hand. "Not like that. *You* don't need to do this."

Fin felt confusion and staggering relief. He gave the knife to his friend. He saw a trace of fear in Gagnon's eyes. The rest of his face remained ashen and still.

"Help me sit him up," Hua said. He set aside the knife and the black-tipped quills.

Fin saw no one else in the alley and the two of them dragged Gagnon's bulk behind a trash can. His body felt stiff, yet warm. They lifted him by the shoulders and he folded slowly, like a block of melting wax. He remained in an upright seated position propped against a wall.

His chest still moved so he was breathing but other than that, only the dancing fear and blinking of Gagnon's eyes said he was still alive.

"What about the bodyguard?" Fin kept his tone neutral.

"He ran off when he recovered."

"Now what?" Fin thought they should call the police but he couldn't bear to do it.

"You can go. I'll finish this."

Fin wanted to ask what Hua meant but he knew the answer.

"No. I own part of this and he bought every bit of his fate. I'll stay."

Hua gave him a long look. "If you're sure, then take pictures. The island deserves to see this."

Fin nodded. He'd seen executions in Africa. Even beheadings. Then there was the nightmare this monster unleashed on Hoku.

*Would it really be so hard to watch this?*

It would.

\* \* \*

Fin stood lookout and took pictures with a fresh data card he would hide well when leaving the country. He was close enough to see and hear everything.

Hua knelt in front of Gagnon and stared at his face. He held up a black-tipped quill. "I know you can hear me and I know you can feel everything."

Hua held the tip under Gagnon's nose. "This is the essence of Silverstar, a plant found nowhere else on earth. It's a spoiled form of Hoku's real treasure."

Fin saw Gagnon's gaze dart back and forth. His nostrils may have twitched, but otherwise he was paralyzed.

"It's why you failed. Why so many of us survived. But not everyone." Hua took the quill and removed one of Gagnon's shoes and socks. He jabbed the quill into the sole of Gagnon's foot.

340

Fin detached his mind the way he would when he recorded atrocities in Angola. The camera provided a buffer but he still heard a tiny hiss when the barb pierced the flesh.

"It hurts, doesn't it?"

The pain registered in Gagnon's eyes. First they went wide then squeezed shut. The shallow breathing picked up speed.

Hua reached inside the robe and removed a battered photograph. Fin recognized it as one of his pictures of Ruru. The boy was smiling and mugging for the camera on the beach.

Hua held it up with one hand right in front of Gagnon. "My son. The only child I ever had. Or ever will."

Fin saw Gagnon cut away his gaze.

Mistake.

Hua jammed another poison quill into Gagnon's inner thigh. "No! You watch him. You killed him and he's the last thing you'll see."

Gagnon began to sweat. He looked at the picture and Fin saw Hua was sweating himself. He thought about saying something but he'd never seen Hua this focused.

And the scary thing was part of him enjoyed seeing Gagnon in agony.

Hua continued to waggle the photo in front of Gagnon. With his free hand, he took out a small vial. "Enough quills and the pain will make you feel like your entire body is on fire from the inside out. Eventually the paralysis will touch your lungs, then chest muscles, then your heart. You'll suffocate in the open air, but more importantly the last thing you'll feel is pain so intense you will beg for death."

Gagnon glared at Hua now.

"Or you can beg me now while you stare at my Ruru. Beg him for forgiveness. If you do that I give you what's in here." Hua held up a small vial. "You'll slip away quietly."

Gagnon glanced at the picture, then back to Hua.

"Blink rapidly to beg. Do we have a deal?"

Fin caught the expression on camera. If Gagnon could have spit in Hua's face he was certain it would have already happened. It was amazing how much hate could come from two eyes. The rest of Gagnon's face remained placid, as if he'd overdosed on botox.

"This could take a while." Hua picked up another quill.

Hua was right. Fin kept his promise to stay, but the absence of screams made Gagnon's tormented gaze all the more expressive. Hua added quills up the body, and by the end Gagnon looked like a life-sized voodoo doll.

All the while Hua whispered stories about Ruru. In many ways it made the spectacle harder to watch.

Tears flowed from Gagnon's eyes, the red rage eventually dimmed and in the end, he begged.

# Chapter 43

*Papeete, Tahiti-- Three days later*

"You feel it too?" Hua packed the last of his things from the apartment they once shared.

"What?" Fin didn't want to guess, as they'd said little about Phuket after they'd left Gagnon in that alley. When they had closed his eyes, he'd looked like a festival participant who'd fallen asleep.

"That hollow sensation? It starts in the chest and spreads out when I get past three months without recharging at home."

He had. At first it felt like a cross between the end of a bad hangover and the beginning of a migraine. Then the feeling faded and he found himself sleeping longer than usual. "I'm okay."

"You feel like a new man when you do. Gert said the new rudder went in faster than they had expected. That was the worst of the damage, thank goodness. We'll be under way by lunchtime."

"Yeah." Fin said. He zipped up his own luggage.

\* \* \*

At the dock the *Verdragen* sat, dwarfed by a nearby cruise ship. Fin saw Gert speaking with some locals at the gangplank. A crane loaded supplies aboard. They'd already made one emergency run back to the island, apparently when they'd brought over Thibaux.

Fin walked with Hua to the gangplank and Gert broke away from the men he was chatting with to greet them.

"Congratulations."

Fin didn't know how to take that. He certainly didn't feel like some conquering hero. He felt like a survivor at best and a killer to boot. He wasn't sure how Hua felt exactly. They'd spoken little of that awful time in the alleyway. Part of him still felt sick, but a growing part knew it had to happen.

*Like that?*

Maybe, maybe not. Regardless, he had no interest in glad-handing about it.

"It's done." Fin passed a manila folder with photos in it. "Wait until you get underway. That's life in a Thai prison you have in your hands." A tad dramatic but Fin never wanted to see the pictures again. That Gagnon hadn't been able to make a sound made the photos that much more realistic.

"You won't change your mind? We'll be back here in six months." Gert said. "Maybe go then?"

"No time like the present." Fin saw Gert and Hua glance over his shoulder. He turned. Saskia stood there in a simple white shirt and skirt she'd made herself.

"It's true? You aren't coming back with us?"

Fin tried to give her a hug and she held out a hand to prevent it. Gert and Hua disappeared up the gangplank. "I can't."

"I thought the threat was past. You heard about Thibaux?" She seemed pleased with their solution as well.

"I did. And is that also intended for me? To control me?"

Anger crossed her features. "You were dying. As for the after-effects, they are what they are. How many in this crowded latrine would kill for such an opportunity?" She wrinkled her nose in distaste.

He'd never heard Tahiti referred to as a toilet before, but he did know Saskia had grown to despise cities and this must have felt like a bustling metropolis to her. "But it would be their choice."

"Why can't you accept it? Maybe even enjoy it?"

"I have to do something first." Saying it out loud confirmed in his gut that it was the right thing to do.

"But you have to come back. Please tell me you believe."

He took both her hands in his. This time she allowed it. "I feel fine." She began to protest. "Let me finish. I *do* believe you."

"What convinced you?"

"In Thailand, while I was waiting for Hua, I used some of the funds Thibaux transferred to see a doctor." Fin said. "A fertility specialist."

She nodded.

"He tested me and it was just like you said. No motility." Fin spat the word.

"Motility?"

"No chance of kids."

"I understand." Saskia said.

"I suppose you've had more time to get used to the idea." The flare of anger surprised him.

"That doesn't mean I like it," she shot back.

"I never thought about having children before but now…" He couldn't go a day without such thoughts crowding into his mind.

"I know." She squeezed his hands. "Come back with us. Help us rebuild and other than that, we can do anything."

He pulled her close and inhaled the fragrance of her hair. The scent took him right back to the grotto on Hoku. "I'm tempted," the word landed on the dock with a meek thud. "That's not what I mean. I could be happy with you. But trapped on Hoku for all time? I don't know."

"Why not try it? You could always leave."

"But I'd be leaving to die, right?"

She eased out of his embrace. "Your life is on Hoku. You can have your death anywhere you like."

"After everything that happened I want to do something good, make a difference first."

"But you *have*."

"You'll see in the pictures I left with Gert. Maybe what we did had to happen, but I can't call it good. I need a chance to balance the scales."

She looked confused. "What is so important you'd postpone your ... treatment?"

Fin took out the envelope from Delacroix. "Thibaux has found this soldier's daughter. He was part of the attack, but I believe he had a change of heart."

"I saw, but the fear of death can have that effect."

"Maybe so. But he included bank information Thibaux was able to crack and we can move the funds over to her."

"Why help her?"

"She had nothing to with Delacroix, and she grew up in the same Africa he was attacking. She barely knew him. Her mother was a nurse and this woman, Chloe, now works as a relief aid worker. The money he saved up by doing evil can now do some good."

"Let Thibaux handle it."

"I want to tell her in person, and Thibaux won't leave Papeete."

"He has more sense than you."

"Probably."

A moment of silence opened a gulf between them. Maybe it was better that way.

"Saskia, I will be back. I promise." Fin said.

Gert blew a pair of blasts on the ship's whistle.

She teared up but smiled as she said, "I wasn't born yesterday, Fin Campbell."

# Chapter 44

*Papeete, Tahiti--Four Years Later*

Fin squinted in the late morning sun and rose from his seat on the bench. He could still smell the gardenias, though he didn't think the scent was as powerful as before.

Perhaps it was just him.

His back crackled in protest with the movement and he walked slowly to give his joints a chance to loosen up. He pulled his luggage in a rolling bag behind him. It wasn't far to the pier and the buzz of activity was just as he remembered.

And why wouldn't it be? Four years wasn't long.

*Yes, it was.*

The walkway to the ship stretched before him but he didn't mind. Not at all. He savored the walk. The metal gangplank stretched to the dock from the *Verdragen.* Fin saw men down there and squinted to see if any looked familiar.

A minute later he realized they recognized him. Two of them broke away from the group with a whoop and ran toward him.

Now Fin remembered. Gert… who could forget him? And Thibaux.

Their expressions were all he needed to see.

"Fin?" Gert spoke first.

"Yes, it's me." Fin gave Gert credit. He'd recovered his wits faster than Thibaux, who looked like he might become ill.

"Monsieur Thibaux, you're looking well, if a bit green around the gills."

"I just…"

Nobody else was in earshot. "Now you know you were right to believe."

"You could have come back sooner," Gert said. He took Fin's suitcase and offered an arm, which Fin waved off. "Of course. My choice. What's done is done anyway."

"How do you feel?" Thibaux said, louder after Fin asked him to speak up.

"How do I look?"

"The truth?"

"No time left for bullshit." Fin winked at Gert. "That can be very liberating."

"All right. You look eighty years old. At least." Thibaux swallowed hard.

They reached the gangplank. The sun felt especially warm and Fin thought he'd like some water and to sit for a while. First he was determined to make it up the gangplank under his own power. "Thank you for all the support. Chloe said to thank you as well."

"We spoke over the phone."

"Yes, that's right. So many details jostling around in my head, I think I won't be able to lift it some mornings."

Aboard the ship Fin nodded at the sailors but he couldn't recall their names. "Is she there?"

Gert spoke up. "She's waiting for you."

* * *

*Hoku*

Standing on the dock with Hua, Saskia watched the gangplank settle onto the wood into well-worn groves. Her stomach knotted when the door to the bridge swung open and she saw Gert step out and offer an arm.

A crowd of Dwazen bunched up twenty feet back and she appreciated the space they gave to her and Hua.

Her heart pounded in her chest and she smoothed the fabric of the new dress she'd made. It had taken Gert three trips and a year of badgering to find the proper color blue dye that matched Fin's eyes.

For an instant she saw the Fin who stepped out of the bridge when they first met. Her mind's eye saw blond hair and knew tanned muscle was beneath the heavy shirt and long dark slacks.

Then Fin stumbled on the gangplank and Gert caught him just in time.

At once, she saw Fin as he was. The hair, much thinner now, was white, not blonde. The tan now a mosaic of liver spots. Taut skin now slack with age. He moved with deliberate stiffness that was a jarring contrast with the smooth graceful movements of a man who used to ride waves.

Saskia said nothing while he made his way to the dock. She tried to set her face in a stoic expression but braced herself on the railing when her legs went weak. She bit her lip and looked down at the water, her dreams of a life with Fin dying, the midnight swims, the long hikes, building a cabin together…gone.

When Fin stopped watching his footing and looked up at her, she saw his eyes were the same as ever. It was a relief and a horror at the same time. It really was him.

She noticed Hua's jaw clenched and looked like he was fighting to hold his tears in check. Maru and Willem stepped from the crowd, grinned, and both shook his hand.

Fin smiled and Saskia noticed he'd managed to keep his teeth. "You all look well, and you," Fin paused and she waited for him to come to her. "Breathtaking."

He spoke with the same voice, tired but the same, as if Fin were using this old figure like a ventriloquist's dummy.

The dam burst inside her chest and Saskia opened her arms for a hug. She wrapped her arms around him and eased up when she felt how thin he'd become. "Please don't be angry," he whispered to her.

The crowd of Dwazen parted to allow them to pass.

\* \* \*

They held a subdued "feast" where the Dwazen and a number of islanders gathered. The islanders stepped forward and lay flowers at Fin's feet so that it seemed he'd be buried in fragrant blossoms. They served traditional pork and vegetable dishes and Saskia noticed that Fin took care to taste every one.

Fin seemed to draw strength from the group but eventually he signaled that he was ready to chat in private. He gave a slow, stiff bow but never dropped the smile.

Saskia's heart ached watching him, sensing the effort it cost him. She held his hand, which trembled as it grew tired, but he returned her squeeze. She felt his swollen joints, the fingers twisting with arthritis, but he never let go during the walk to her place.

Inside her hut Maru, Gert, Willem and Hua joined them and sat in a circle like kids waiting for a bedtime story.

Fin cleared his throat. "What a wonderful party. But I owe all of you more than just a debt of gratitude."

"You don't owe us anything," Willem said.

"Of course I do. An explanation," Fin said. "After I caught up with Chloe, that soldier's daughter, it took some convincing to get her to accept the money from her father's account. She viewed it as blood money, which it probably was."

Fin sipped some water from a wooden cup that trembled in his grasp. "After I spent a few days helping her out and seeing how many of the refugees were children, I finally convinced her to let the money do some good."

"But that wasn't so long. You could have returned. While you were still…" Saskia trailed off.

"The years I spent following the mercenaries exposed me to horrors as they were inflicted, but I had never spent much time at the hospitals."

"Why now?" Hua said.

Saskia could sense she wasn't the only one feeling angry, deprived.

"Maybe it was a newfound perspective. All I know is that I wanted to create something that would last. Not this." He pointed to his chest. "Absence of dying isn't the same as living. My parents died young, but they lived every minute they were here." Fin said.

"We *live* right here." Willem sounded defensive.

"Not everyone is suited to last forever. Who knows, maybe I would have gotten eaten by a shark while out surfing off the village coast." He gave a tired laugh.

Maru looked away.

"When I felt the aging start to kick in hard, I had an overwhelming urge to finish what I started. Somehow I knew if came back first that I would never complete the project."

"What project?" Saskia said. "What could be so important?"

Fin lifted up a wrapped package Gert had carried for him. He tore off the brown paper to reveal a high-quality book of photography. He held it up.

On the cover there was a close-up of a child's face, a little girl with warm bronze skin and striking green eyes and a long scar down one cheek. The title was *Faces of War by Fin Campbell.*

"I travelled to every country on the continent that was torn up by rebels. I worked like I had a fatal disease, which I suppose is true. I certainly didn't fear getting killed. Got shot at a few times and even stepped on a live mine that had a faulty detonator."

"Fool's luck," Gert shook his head.

"I'm sure, but it told me I was meant to do this."

He flipped the book to show a picture of himself as they remembered him. Blonde locks to his tanned shoulders with him gazing out at a set of waves.

He opened the book and read the dedication page. "For Ruru and all the other little ones who never got a chance to grow up."

"Thanks to some help from Thibaux, it goes worldwide next month. The publisher is still upset I won't do interviews or book signings." Fin patted the tome. "It may not change the world, but it'll tell it I was here."

\* \* \*

*Islander Village*

"Not much further," Fin told Saskia, who held his arm and helped him up the beach. Nearby, Johannes waved and prepared to turn the motor boat around. Fin had complimented him on a smooth passage of the waves which were calm this evening.

The moon hung fat and yellow in the star-scattered sky. Maru had given strict orders to leave them alone so the beach was theirs.

Finally they reached a tree. "That's the one, by the big rock." They sat down at the base of the large palm.

"Ruru climbed this tree and dropped out of it the first day I was over here. He about gave me a heart attack. Thought my expression was the funniest thing he ever saw."

Saskia could picture it and thought about the sweet, lively little boy. She put a blanket that she'd brought around his shoulders.

"One of yours?"

"Of course."

They sat for a moment and listened to the waves. He spoke at last. "If I *had* stayed, I might have come to resent you, maybe even hate you." He paused. "I couldn't bear that thought."

The idea stung.

"That sounds foolish, doesn't it?" Fin asked.

Tears marked warm streaks down her face. "I guess not."

"I hope you don't hate me for leaving."

"Never. I was angry and confused, but I couldn't hate you." She tried to imagine what it must have been like for him to feel his strength fade and carry on. She stroked his arm. "We could have adopted."

"It wasn't just children. Maybe if I'd grown up here like you did, I wouldn't have felt like the island had become my prison."

"I wasn't born here. But I got used to it." She didn't know why she was arguing now, when it was too late, but she couldn't help herself.

"That was what frightened me the most. That I would, too. I'd just exist. Forever."

"But we could have *existed* together." It didn't sound right to her as she said it. Fin patted her arm. "Content. But never free."

Saskia felt the strangest pang of jealousy. "The longer I live, the more I fear death."

He looked at her in surprise at first. Then he nodded. "I thought that would go away when I knew my time was coming." He drew in a deep breath and exhaled in a thin wheeze. "I was wrong."

"I think I understand now." She put her arm around him and his body was trembling despite the warm air and blanket.

"Then it's okay." He reached out, "Take my hand?"

Her fingers laced inside his and the surf lulled in the distance.

The End

## Note from the Author:

Thanks so much for reading. If you enjoyed this book I'd greatly appreciate a review on the book's page at sites like Amazon or Goodreads. They don't take long and can help give the book important exposure to other readers. Even if you didn't care for the story, let me know why so I can learn from your feedback.

If you have any questions or would like to reach me directly, my e-mail is gregsmithbooks@yahoo.com

You can follow upcoming releases and author doings at my Facebook page here: https://www.facebook.com/pages/J-Gregory-Smith-Author/297074464674

You will also find my Thriller/Mystery novels published by Thomas & Mercer here at my author page on Amazon:

http://www.amazon.com/J.-Gregory-Smith/e/B002VW9IIU/ref=ntt_athr_dp_pel_1

# Other Titles by J. Gregory Smith

## Thrillers

*A Noble Cause* (Kindle Bestseller U.S., UK and Germany)

*The Flamekeepers*

## The Paul Chang Mystery Series

*Final Price*

*Legacy of the Dragon*

*Send in the Clowns*

## Young Adult

*The Crystal Mountain*

## Short Stories

"Heroic Measures" (Amazon StoryFront)

"Blenders" (*Insidious Assassins*, Smart Rhino Publishing)

"The Pepper Tyrant" (*Uncommon Assassins*, Smart Rhino Publishing)

"Something Borrowed" (*Zippered Flesh: Tales of Body Enhancements Gone Bad*, Smart Rhino Publishing)

"Street Smarts" (*Stories from the Ink Slingers*, *A Written Remains Anthology*, Gryphonwood Press)

# ACKNOWLEDGEMENTS

On top of the dedication, I want to give a special thank you to my wife, Julie, whose support makes all my books possible.

Once again, an enormous thank you to Connie Garcia-Barrio for her reading edits and insights.

Thanks to Malcolm McClinton for the fantastic cover art.

# About the Author

In addition to his first young adult title with *The Crystal Mountain*, Greg Smith is the bestselling author of the thrillers, *A Noble Cause* and *The Flamekeepers*, a doomsday cult thriller. He also writes the Paul Chang Mystery series including *Final Price*, *Legacy of the Dragon* and *Send in the Clowns*.

Prior to writing fiction full time, Greg worked in public relations in Washington, D.C., Philadelphia and Wilmington, Delaware. He has an MBA from the College of William & Mary and a BA in English from Skidmore College.

He lives in Wilmington, Delaware with his wife, son, and dog.

www.ingramcontent.com/pod-product-compliance
Lightning Source LLC
Chambersburg PA
CBHW051945240626
47153CB00005B/1633